THE HOPE OF HAPPINESS

CHAPTER ONE

I

Bruce Storrs stood up tall and straight on a prostrate sycamore, the sunlight gleaming upon his lithe, vigorous body, and with a quick, assured lifting of the arms plunged into the cool depths of the river. He rose and swam with long, confident strokes the length of a pool formed by the curving banks and returned to the log, climbing up with the same ease and grace that marked his swimming. He dashed the water from his eyes and pressed his deeply-tanned hands over his shapely head. It was evident that he was the fortunate inheritor of clean blood in a perfectly fashioned body; that he had used himself well in his twenty-eight years and that he found satisfaction and pride in his health and strength. He surveyed the narrow valley through which the river idled and eddied before rushing into the broader channel beyond—surveyed it with something of the air of a discoverer who has found and appropriated to his own uses a new corner of the world.

It was a good place to be at the end of a day that was typical of late August in the corn belt, a day of intense dry heat with faint intimations on the horizon of the approach of autumn. With a contented sigh he sat down on the log, his feet drawn up, his shoulders bent, and aimlessly tore bits of bark from the log and tossed them into the water. Lulled by the lazy ripple, he yielded himself to reverie and his eyes filled with dreams as he stared unseeingly across the stream. Suddenly he raised his head resolutely as if his thoughts had returned to the world of the actual and he had reached a conclusion of high importance. He plunged again and now his short, rapid strokes threshed the water into foam. One might have thought that in the assertion of his physical strength he was testing and reassuring himself of his complete self-mastery.

Refreshed and invigorated, he clambered up the bank and sought a great beech by whose pillar-like trunk he had left his belongings, and proceeded to dress. From a flat canvas bag he produced a towel and a variety of toilet articles. He combed his thick curly hair, donned a flannel shirt and knotted a blue scarf under its soft collar. His shoes of brogan type bore the imprint of a metropolitan maker and his gray knickerbockers and jacket indicated a capable tailor.

He took from the bag a package of letters addressed in a woman's hand to Bruce Storrs, and making himself comfortable with his back to the tree, he began to read. The letters had been subjected to many readings, as their worn appearance testified, but selecting the bulkiest, he perused it carefully, as though wishing to make sure that its phrases were firmly fixed in his memory.

"... Since my talk with you," he read, "I have had less pain, but the improvement is only temporary—the doctors do not deceive me as to that. I may go quickly—any day, any hour. You heard my story the other night—generously, with a fine tolerance, as I knew you would. If I had not been so satisfied of your sense of justice and so sure of your love, I could never have told you. But from the hour I knew that my life was nearing its end I felt more and more that you must know. One or two things I'm afraid I didn't make clear ... that I loved the man who is your father. Love alone could be my justification—without that I could never have lived through these years.

"The man you have called father never suspected the truth. He trusted me. It has been part of my punishment that through all these years I have had to endure the constant manifestations of his love and confidence. But for that one lapse in the second year of my marriage, I was absolutely faithful in all my obligations to him. And he was kind to you and proud of you. He did all for you that a father could, never dreaming that you were not his own. It was one of my sorrows that I couldn't give him a child of his own. Things went badly with him in his last years, as you know, and what I leave to you —it will be about fifty thousand dollars—I inherited from my father, and it will help you find your place in the world.

"Your father has no idea of your existence.... Ours was a midsummer madness, at a time when we were both young. I only knew him a little while, and I have never heard from him. My love for him never wholly died. Please, dear, don't think harshly of me, but there have been times when I would have given my life for a sight of him. After all you are his— his as much as mine. You came to me from him—strangely dear and beautiful. In my mind you have always been his, and I loved you the dearer. I loved him, but I could not bring myself to leave the man you have called father for him. He was not the kind of man women run away with....

"When I'm gone I want you to put yourself near him—learn to know him, if that should be possible. I am trusting you. You would never, I know, do him an injury. Some day he may need you. Remember, he does not know—it may be he need never know. But oh, be kind to him...."

He stared at the words. Had it been one of those unaccountable affairs—he had heard of such—where a gently reared woman falls prey to a coarse-fibered man in every way her inferior? The man might be common, low, ignorant and cruel. Bruce had been proud of his ancestry. The Storrs were of old American stock, and his mother's family, the Bruces, had been the foremost people in their county for nearly a century. He had taken a pardonable pride in his background.... That night when he had stumbled out of the house after hearing his mother's confession he had felt the old friendly world recede. The letters, sealed and entrusted to the family physician for delivery at her death, merely repeated what she had told him.

In his constant rereadings he had hoped that one day he would find that he had misinterpreted the message. He might dismiss his mother's story as the fabrication of a sick woman's mind. But today he knew the folly of this; the disclosure took its place in his mind among the unalterable facts of his life. At first he had thought of destroying himself; but he was too sane and the hope of life was too strong for such a solution of his problem. And there had been offers—flattering ones—to go to New York and Boston. He convinced himself that his mother could not seriously have meant to limit the range of his opportunities by sending him to the city where his unknown father lived. But he was resolved not to shirk; he would do her bidding. There was a strain of superstition in him: he might invite misfortune by disregarding her plea; and moreover he had the pride and courage of youth. No one knew, no one need ever know! He had escaped from the feeling, at first poignant, that shame attached to him; that he must slink through life under the eyes of a scornful world. No; he had mastered that; his pride rallied; he felt equal to any demand fate might make upon him; he was resolved to set his goal high....

Life had been very pleasant in Laconia, the Ohio town where John Storrs had been a lawyer of average attainments—in no way brilliant, but highly respected for his probity and enjoying for years a fair practice. Bruce had cousins of his own age, cheery, wholesome contemporaries with whom he had chummed from childhood. The Storrs, like the Bruces, his mother's people, were of a type familiar in Mid-western county seats, kindly, optimistic, well-to-do folk, not too contented or self-satisfied to be unaware of the stir and movement of the larger world.

The old house, built in the forties by John Storrs's grandfather, had become suddenly to Bruce a strange and alien place that denied his right of occupancy. The elms in the yard seemed to mock him, whispering, "You don't belong here!" and as quickly as possible he had closed the house, made excuses to his relatives, given a power of attorney to the president of the local bank, an old friend, to act for him in all matters, and announced that he'd look about a bit and take a vacation before settling down to his profession.

This was all past now and he had arrived, it seemed inevitably, at the threshold of the city where his father lived.

The beauty of the declining day stirred longings and aspirations, definite and clear, in his mind and heart. His debt to his mother was enormous. He remembered now her happiness at the first manifestation of his interest in form, color and harmony; her hand guiding his when he first began to draw; her delight in his first experiment with a box of colors, given him on one of his birthdays. Yes; he should be a painter; that came first; then his aptitude in modeling made it plain that sculpture was to be his true vocation. To be a creator of beautiful things!—here, she had urged, lay the surest hope of happiness.

Very precious were all these memories; they brought a wistful smile to his face. She had always seemed to him curiously innocent, with the innocence of light-hearted childhood. To think of her as carrying a stain through her life was abhorrent. Hers was the blithest, cheeriest spirit he had known. The things she had taught him to reverence were a testimony to her innate fineness; she had denied herself for him, jealously guarding her patrimony that it might pass to him intact. The manly part for him was to live in the light of the ideals she had set for him. Pity and love for one who had been so sensitive to beauty in all its forms touched him now; brought a sob to his throat. He found a comfort in the thought that her confession might be attributable to a hope that in his life her sin might be expiated....

He took up the letters and turned them over for the last time, his eyes caught and held now and then by some phrase. He held the sheets against his face for a moment, then slowly tore them into strips, added the worn envelopes and burned them. Not content with this, he trampled the charred fragments into the sandy turf.

II

The sun, a huge brazen ball, was low in the west when he set off along the river with confident, springy step. He stopped at a farmhouse and asked for supper. The evening meal was over, the farmer's wife explained; but when he assured her that his needs were few and that he expected to pay for his entertainment, she produced a pitcher of milk and a plate of corn bread. She brought a bowl of yellow glaze crockery and he made himself comfortable on a bench by the kitchen door. He crumbled the bread into the creamy milk and ate with satisfaction.

Her husband appeared, and instantly prejudiced by Bruce's knickerbockers, doggedly quizzed him as to the nature and direction of his journey. Bruce was a new species, not to be confused with the ordinary tramp who demands food at farmhouses, and suddenly contrite that the repast she was providing was so meager, the woman rose and disappeared into the kitchen, returning with a huge piece of spice cake and a dish of sliced peaches. She was taken aback when he rose deferentially to accept the offering, but her tired face relaxed in a smile at his cordial expressions of gratitude. She joined her husband on the stoop, finding the handsome pilgrim's visit a welcome break in the monotonous day. As he ate he answered their questions unhurriedly.

"I guess the war left a lot o' you boys restless," she suggested.

"Oh, it wasn't the war that made a rover of me!" he replied with a smile. "It was this way with me. When I got home I found I had something to think out—something I had to get used to"—he frowned and became silent for a moment—"so I decided I could do it better by tramping. But I've settled things in my own mind pretty well now," he ended, half to himself, and smiled, hardly aware of their presence.

"Yes?" The woman's tone was almost eager. She was curious as to the real reason for his wanderings and what it was that he had settled. In the luminous afterglow her dull imagination quickened to a sense of something romantic in this stranger, and she was disappointed when he told of an experience as a laborer in a great steel mill, just to see what it was like, he said—of loitering along the Susquehanna, and of a more recent tramp through the Valley of Virginia.

"I reckon you don't have to work?" the farmer asked, baffled in his attempts to account for a young man who strolled over the country so aimlessly, wearing what struck him as an outlandish garb.

"Oh, but I do! I've done considerable work as I've sauntered around. I'm an architect—or hope to be! I've earned my keep as I've traveled by getting jobs as a draughtsman."

"Going to stop in the city?" the woman inquired. "I guess there's lots of architects over there."

"Yes," Bruce replied, following the direction of her glance.

"You know folks there?" she persisted. "I guess it's hard getting started if you ain't got friends."

"There's a chap living there I knew in college; that's all. But when you strike a strange town where you don't know anyone the only thing to do is to buckle in and make them want to know you!"

"I guess you can do that," she remarked with shy admiration.

The farmer shuffled his feet on the brick walk. For all he knew the young stranger might be a burglar. He resented his wife's tone of friendliness and resolved to deny the request if the young man asked the privilege of sleeping in the barn; but the stranger not only failed to ask for lodging, but produced a dollar bill and insisted that the woman accept it. This transaction served instantly to dispel the farmer's suspicions. He answered with unnecessary detail Bruce's questions as to the shortest way to town, and walked with him to a lane that ran along the edge of a cornfield and afforded a short cut to the highway.

Bruce had expected to reach the city before nightfall, but already the twilight was deepening and the first stars glimmered in the pale sky. Now that he was near the end of his self-imposed wanderings, he experienced a sense of elation. The unhappy thoughts with which he had left his Ohio home a little more than a year earlier had gradually become dim in his memory. The letters he had burned at the riverside really marked in his consciousness a dispersion of doubts and questions that left his spirit free. His mother's revelation had greatly shaken him; but she need never have told him; and it spoke for her courage and her faith in him that she had confessed the truth. They had been companions in an unusual sense. From his earliest youth she had interested him in the things that had been her delight—books, music, pictures. She was herself an accomplished musician, and strains of old melodies she had taught him recurred to him now, and as he swung along the country road he whistled them, happy for the first time in the awakening of old memories.

With the cool breeze blowing upon him from fields of tall ripening corn, there was no bitterness in his soul. He had beaten down the bitter thoughts that had assailed him in the early days of his journeying—the sense that a stigma attached to him, not the less hateful because he alone had knowledge of it; and the feeling that there was something fantastic in the idea that he should put himself where, in any need, he could serve the father he had never known.

This had now all the sanctity of a commission from the dead. Again he speculated as to what manner of man this could be who had awakened so deep a love in the heart of the good woman he knew his mother to have been—a love which she had carried in her heart to her last hours. In his long ponderings he had, he felt, come to understand her better than he ever had in her lifetime—her imaginative and romantic side, her swiftly changing moods, her innumerable small talents that had now a charm and a pathos in the retrospect. Age had never, to his eyes, laid hands upon her. Even through the last long illness she had retained the look and the spirit of youth.

Rounding a bend in the river, the flare of an amusement park apprised him that he was close upon the city—a city he had heretofore never visited and knew of only from his newspaper reading as a prosperous industrial center. Here, for the strangest reason in the world, he was to make his home, perhaps spend the remainder of his days! He crossed a stone bridge with a sense that the act marked an important transition in his life, and quickly passing through the park, boarded a trolley car and rode into town.

He had formed a very clear idea of what he meant to do, and arriving at the business center he went directly to the Hotel Fordham, to which he had expressed his trunk from Cincinnati.

III

He spent an hour unpacking and overhauling his belongings, wrote notes to his banker friend in Laconia and to the cousin there with whom he had maintained a correspondence since he first went away to school.

The pencil with which he idly scribbled on a sheet of hotel paper traced his name unconsciously. *BruceStorrs.*

It was not his name; he had no honest right to it. He had speculated many times in his wanderings as to whether he shouldn't change it, but this would lead to endless embarrassments. Now, with his thoughts crystalized by the knowledge that this other man who had been his mother's lover was within reach, he experienced a strong sense of loyalty to the memory of the man he had called father. It would be a contemptible thing to abandon the name of one who had shown him so tender an affection and understood so perfectly his needs and aims.

Somewhere among the several hundred thousand people of the city about him was the man his mother had described. In the quiet room he experienced suddenly a feeling of loneliness. Usually in his wanderings he had stopped at cheap lodging houses, and the very comfort of his surroundings now added to his feeling of strangeness in having at last arrived at a goal which marked not merely the end of his physical wandering, but the termination of a struggle with his own spirit.

He sent down for the evening papers and found himself scanning carefully the local news, thinking that he might find some clue to the activities of Franklin Mills.

His attention was immediately caught by the caption, "Franklin Mills Sells Site of Old Homestead to Trust Company." The name fell like a blow upon his consciousness. He seized the telephone book and hurriedly turned the pages.

Mills Franklin—r 5800 Jefferson Ave...King 1322
Mills Franklin—1821 First Ntl Bnk....Main 2222

He stared at the two lines till they were a blur before his eyes. There was but one man of the name in the directory; there could be no mistake as to his identity.

It was a disconcerting thought that by calling these numbers he might at any time hear Franklin Mills's voice. The idea both fascinated and repelled him. What, after all, had he to do with Franklin Mills?

He turned to the newspaper and reread the report of the real estate transaction, then opened to the personal and society page, where he found this item:

> Miss Leila Mills of Jefferson Avenue gave a luncheon yesterday at the Faraway Country Club for her house guest, Miss Helene Ridgeway of Cincinnati. The decorations were purple asters and pink roses.

Helene Ridgeway he knew; she had been the college chum of one of his Laconia cousins. He had not realized the strain he had undergone in the past year till he saw the familiar name. The nightmare pictures of his year-long speculations faded; whatever else Mills might be he was at least a reputable citizen, and this was something to be thankful for; and obviously he was not poor and helpless.

The Leila referred to must be Mills's daughter, and the same blood ran in her veins as in his own. Bruce flung the paper away; touched his forehead, found it covered with perspiration. He paced the floor till he had quieted himself, paused at the window, finding relief in the lights and sounds of the street, the bells and whistles of trains at the railway station somewhere in the distance. The world surged round him, indifferent to his hopes and aims and fears. He must keep tight hold of himself....

His mother had urged him to think kindly of Franklin Mills; and yet, now that the man was within reach, a contempt that bordered upon hatred filled his heart. For his mother his love turned for the moment to pity. He recalled the look she had bent upon him at times when he and his putative father had talked happily together. John Storrs had lavished an unusual devotion upon his wife to the end of his life. The wrong done him seemed monstrous as Bruce thought of it, remembering Storrs's pride in him, the sympathetic interest he had taken in his education, the emotion with which they had parted when Bruce went away to war. There was a vast pathos in all this—in the very ignorance of his wife's infidelity that John Storrs had carried to his grave.

CHAPTER TWO

I

Awake early, Bruce donned a freshly-pressed gray suit and went down to breakfast. His immediate concern was to find employment, for in work, he knew, lay his hope of happiness and peace. He had thrust into his pocket letters from architects who had employed him in various cities commending him as an excellent draughtsman; and he bore a letter certifying to his good character and trustworthiness from the president of the bank in his native town. He was not pressed by immediate need. His travels had been inexpensive; in fact, he had a little more than earned his way; and he had not only the fifty thousand dollars his mother had left invested in securities, but he carried drafts for the accumulated income—something over a thousand dollars—to tide him over any possible difficulties in finding an opening that promised well for the future. He had finished his breakfast, and lingered at the table, deep in thought, when a young man who had just entered the dining-room paused beside him.

"Is it or is it not Bruce Storrs?" he demanded. "I spotted you from the door —didn't think there could be another such head and shoulders."

"Bud Henderson!"

Storrs was on his feet, wringing the hand of the young man, who was regarding him with a pleased grin.

"You good old Indian! I was just about to go out and ask the nearest cop where to find you! You're the only man in town I know!"

"Thanks for the compliment. You might have warned me of your approach. I'll sit right here and eat while you unfold yourself."

Henderson was short, lean and dark, with a curiously immobile face. His lips smiled oddly without any accompanying expression of humor in his rather small brown eyes. Without inquiring what had brought Storrs to town, he began talking of their years together at Boston, where they had been fellow students at the Tech. He had a dry, humorous way of saying things, particularly when he talked of himself, which puzzled strangers but delighted his friends. He was treating Storrs quite as though there had been no break in their intercourse.

"Met some of our old Boston pals during the recent unpleasantness and heard of you occasionally on the other side," he was saying. "Frankly, I'm not keen about war"—he was composedly eating a melon—"war is fatiguing. I hope the great nations will behave for the rest of my life, so I won't be annoyed by having to go out and settle the row."

"Here too, Bud; I got enough. I want to have a try at the arts of peace."

"So say we all. By the way, are you married yet?"

"No."

"That's bad. Marriage is an honorable estate; I'm rather keen about it. I took me a wife as soon as I got back from France. Oh, Lord, no! None of the girls we knew around Boston. Couldn't afford them, and besides it's a mistake not to marry in your home town, and it's also easier when you're a bloomin' pauper. I married into one of the strongest wholesale grocery houses in all these parts. I'll drive you by the warehouse, an impressive pile —one of the biggest concerns west of Pittsburgh. Maybelle is the name of the lucky girl, and Maybelle is the only child of the Conrad of Conrad, Buxton and Pettibone. A wonderful girl—one of the really strong, powerful women of this great nation. She's out of town at present, playing a golf tournament for the huckleberry association championship. That's why I'm chasing downtown for breakfast—cook's on a vacation. You'll meet Maybelle; she's a person, that girl! Married me out of pity; thinks I'm half-witted, and right, at that!"

"Of course you'd have to marry a girl who'd make allowance for your mental infirmities," Bruce replied. "Getting on in your profession, I suppose?"

"Hell, no! I chucked that. There are too many really capable electrical experts, and after Maybelle's father had tried me for six months in the grocery and I failed to show any talent for distributing the well-known Verbena Brand of canned stuff, he set me up in the automobile business. Shameful to relate, I really make money. I handle the Plantagenet—one of the worst cars on the market. You know it was a mistake—my feeling that I was called to be another Edison or Marconi. I was really cut out for the literary life—another sad case of mute, inglorious Milton. I exercise my talents now designing 'ads' and come-on letters as a lure to customers for the Plantagenet. Would you ride with kings? The Plantagenet is the car that takes you out and brings you back. That's my latest slogan; you'll find it glaring at you all over the landscape."

"Oh, what a fall, my countryman!"

"Not at all. You know I always had a knack of making phrases. It's a gift, my boy. I suppose you're here to figure on a new state-house or perhaps a hospital for lame cats. I know nearly everybody in town, so if I can be of use to you, just warble."

"My aim isn't so high," said Bruce, who remembered Henderson as somewhat eccentric but the kindest of souls. His manner of talking was no indication of his true character. Bruce's heart warmed to Henderson; already the town seemed less strange, and he at once disclosed his intention of establishing himself in the city, though without in the least surprising the imperturbable Bud.

"Welcome!" he exclaimed with his mouth full of toast. "You shall be our Michelangelo, our Sir Christopher Wren! I see, as in a dream," he went on as he thrust his fork into a poached egg, "I see our fair city adorned with the noble fruits of the genius of Bruce Storrs, the prince of architects. You will require a fleet of Plantagenets to whirl you from one rising edifice to another. I might make you a special price on six cars—but this must be confidential."

"I really want to get into a good office, and I'm not expecting to be taken right into the firm," said Bruce, laughing. "It will take me a year or two to get acquainted, and then I'd like to set up for myself."

"Certainly a worthy ambition, Bruce. It's a good thing I'm here on the ground to give you the true dope on the people who count in this teeming village. The old order changeth, yielding place to new, and there's danger of getting pinched between the old hard-boiled bunch and the birds of gayer plumage who flew in when no one was looking and insist on twittering sweetly on our tallest trees. Let me be your social booster; no one better fitted. I'm the only scion of one of our earliest and noblest families. My grandfather's bank busted in seventy-three with a loud bang and I had an uncle who was indicted for embezzling public funds. He hid in Patagonia and died there in sinful splendor at a ripe old age. Talk about the aristocracy —I'm it! I derive a certain prestige among what you might call the paralytic group from the fact that my ancestors were mixed up in all the financial calamities that ever befell this town. But it's the crowd that are the spenders —build the lordly palaces and treat the Eighteenth Amendment with the contempt it so richly deserves—that you want to train with. Your profession is cursed with specialization and I'd warn you against public work. Too much politics there for one of your fastidious nature. Our best man in domestic architecture is Freeman—he's a Tech man, about seven years ahead of our class. He has a weakness for sun parlors with antique Italian fountains that are made for him special by a pottery right here in town. You're sure to like Freeman; he's a whist fiend, but otherwise he's a decent chap. His wife and Maybelle are chums and we play around together a good deal."

While listening to Henderson's rambling talk Bruce had been turning over the pages of a memorandum book. He asked about several architects whose names he had noted. Henderson described them succinctly, praising or deriding them for reasons which struck Bruce as not necessarily final as to their merits.

"I don't expect to land a job the first day," said Bruce. "I may have to go through the list before I find what I want."

"Oh, Freeman will take you on," replied Henderson easily. "But he never does anything important without consulting his wife—one of his eccentricities. My own system is to go ahead and tell Maybelle afterward, being careful, of course, to conceal my mistakes."

"You haven't changed a bit," laughed Bruce. "I wish I could view the world as chipperly as you do."

"My dear Bruce"—with his forefinger Henderson swept Storrs's breakfast check to his own side of the table with a single gesture—"never try to view the whole world at one glance; it's too damned big. All I see at present on this suffering, sinning planet is a Plantagenet runabout with Maybelle and me rolling through fields of asphodel. Everything else is superfluous. My fellow creatures simply don't exist except as prospects for the Plantagenet."

"Oh, rot! You're the most unselfish biped I ever knew!"

"Superficially, yes; but it's all on the surface. Let's go out and plant our feet firmly upon the city."

He led the way to his car and drove to the Plantagenet salesroom and garage. A young woman whom he introduced as Miss Ordway apparently ran the whole establishment. Henderson said that she did. He sat down at his desk and signed, without reading, a pile of letters which she had written the day before, talking to her meantime, not of business, but of a novel he had given her to read. Her attempts to interest him in the fact that one of the salesmen wanted his assistance in rounding up a certain difficult customer were provocative only of scornful comments, but when she handed him a memorandum of an appointment with the prospect at ten o'clock the next morning, he meekly thrust the paper into his pocket and said all right; he'd see what he could do. Miss Ordway was already busy with other matters; she seemed to make due allowance for her employer's peculiarities.

"This girl's mighty firm with me," he said in a tone perfectly audible to Miss Ordway. "A cruel tyrant; but she really does get some work out of me."

He sat on the edge of his desk as he talked over the extension telephone. Bruce inferred that he was speaking to Mrs. Freeman, and it was evident from his tone that Bud had not exaggerated in speaking of his intimacy with the architect and his wife.

"Maybelle's pushing the pill somewhere and won't be back for a week. This being Friday, I'd like to be invited to your shanty for the week-end.... Ah! That's nice of you. And may I bring a little friend?... Oh, a man, of course! And list, Dale, he's an architect—a Tech grad and everything pretty, and I want Bill to take him on—see? Nice boy and perishing for a job. You fix it for me—that's the girl!... Oh! my friend isn't fussy; we'll both sleep on the grass.... What? Yes; I'll bring some poison; my pet bootlegger broke through the entanglements yesterday."

"All set," he remarked as he hung up the receiver. "Mighty nice girl, Dale."

Miss Ordway intercepted him on his way out to ask what she should do about a claim for damages to a car belonging to a man named Smythe, which had been scratched in the garage. The owner threatened to sue, and Miss Ordway expressed the belief that the valued patron was not bluffing.

"We took the stand it wasn't done in our shop and we can't weaken," said Henderson. "Also, we don't want a row. Were my eyes deceiving me or have I seen Smythe looking longingly at that blue touring car in our front window? Yes? Well, suppose we send Briggs to call on him, carrying the olive branch. Tell him to roll home in the blue car and we'll take his old junk and seven hundred berries cash on the counter."

"I think we could get eight hundred on the deal." Miss Ordway's tones were crisp and businesslike.

"Sold! I despise Smythe, but it's worth a thousand to have him riding in a Plantagenet. I'll look in again at five."

II

Henderson spent the morning exhibiting the city's industries and wound up at the University Club for luncheon.

"Now I'll show you where the big frogs of our little puddle live," he said as they started off again.

In his racy description of the owners of the houses they passed, their ancestry, the skeletons in their closets, their wealth and how it was attained, Henderson shone effulgently. Bruce, marveling that one head could carry so much local history, was almost equally astonished by the sins and foibles of the citizens as Henderson pictured them.

"Great Scott! Are there no perfectly normal people in this town?" he demanded.

"A few, maybe," Henderson replied, lifting his hand from the wheel to stroke his chin. "But they're not what you'd call conspicuous."

Pausing before a handsome colonial house, the presence of an elderly gentleman calmly perusing a newspaper on the veranda, inspired Henderson to a typical excursion in biography. The owner, thinking visitors impended, pattered down the steps and stared belligerently at the car.

"Note the carpet slippers," remarked Henderson as the gentleman, satisfied that his privacy was not to be invaded, returned to his chair. "Here we have Bill Fielding, one of the most delightful old scoundrels in town. Observe his pants—sleeps in 'em to avoid the fatigue of disrobing. To keep off evil spirits he wears the first nickel he ever earned on a string around his neck. He's the smoothest tax-dodger in America. His wife starved to death and his three children moved to California to get as far away from the old skunk as possible. Why does he live in a house like that? Bless your simple soul, he took it on a mortgage and camps in two rooms while he waits for a buyer."

"I don't believe I'd like him! If you've got many such birds I'd better try another town," laughed Bruce as Henderson started the car.

"Oh, don't worry! He's the last of his school. Now we're approaching a different proposition—one that baffles even my acute analytical powers."

He drew up before a handsome Georgian house that stood lengthwise to the street in a broad lot in which a dozen towering forest trees had been preserved when the land was subdivided. There were no frivolous lines in this residence, Bruce noted, surveying it with a professional eye; it was beyond criticism in its fidelity to type. The many windows were protected by awnings of deep orange and the ledges were adorned with boxes of flowers. The general effect was one of perfect order and uniformity. Bruce, with his interest in houses as an expression of the character of their owners whetted by Henderson's slangy lectures before other establishments, turned expectantly to his friend.

"Wind up the machine and put on the record! That's a sound piece of architecture, anyhow, and I can see that you are dying to turn out the skeletons."

"Painful as it is for me to confess it, the truth is that in this case I can only present a few bald facts and leave you to make your own deductions." Henderson lighted a fresh cigarette and drew a deep draught of smoke into his lungs. "Franklin Mills," he said, and crossed his legs. "Mills is around fifty, maybe a shade more. The first of the tribe settled here in 1820 and Frank is the fourth of the name. The family always had money and this bird's father never lost a cent in his life. Now Frank's rich—nothing spectacular, but recognized as a rich man. His pop left him well fixed and he's piled up considerable mazuma on his own hook. Does this interest you?"

"You always interest me, Bud; please proceed."

"Well, you might call Franklin Mills the original man who couldn't lose. No active business now, but he controls a couple of banks and a trust company without figuring in the picture at all, and he set his son up in a storage battery plant and is a silent factor in a dozen other flourishing contributors to the smoke nuisance. Nice chap, by the way, Shep Mills; pleasant little cuss. Franklin Mills isn't one of the up-from-the-office-boy type nor the familiar variety of feverish business man; velvet glove stuff. Do you follow me? Only human touch I've discovered in this house is the billiard room, and Mills is a shark at the sport. I've poked the ivories with him now and then just for the fun of watching him play. His style of playing is a sort of clue to his character—cool, deliberate, never misses. One thing, though, I've never been able to figure out: once in a while he makes a wild shot, unnecessarily and with malice aforethought, as though to spite himself. If you'd tell Franklin Mills he'd lost his last cent he wouldn't blink an eye, but before you got out of the room he'd have thought up a scheme for making it all back."

"A business genius," commented Bruce, who had missed no word of Henderson's sketch. "I can't say your snapshot's very alluring."

"Oh, I may be wrong! If you'd ask anybody else about him you'd hear that he's a leading citizen and a cultivated gentleman, which he is! While of our city's back-number or paralytic group, he's far from being ripe for the mortician. One sees him around socially now and then—on occasions when our real nobility shake the moth balls from their dress suits. And that's characteristic; he has the pride, you might say, of his long connection with the town. If it's necessary for somebody to bunk a distinguished visitor, Frank Mills opens his door—not that he's keen to get his name in the village sheet, but he likes for the town to make a good impression—sort of 'I am a citizen of no mean city,' like St. Paul or whoever the bird was that said it first. I doubt if the visitors enjoy his entertainments, but they're probably used to being bored by the gloomy rich."

"There are other children, perhaps? A house like that rather suggests a big family," Bruce remarked.

"The size only indicates Frank's pride. He's given only two hostages to fortune. There's Leila, the daughter. There must have been a naughty little devil in some of the Mills or Shepherd tribe away back yonder, for that girl certainly is a lively little filly. Shep, who is named for his mother's people, never browsed in the wild-oat fields, but Leila makes up for it. Bounced from seven boarding schools—holds the champeen record there. Her mother passed hence when Leila was about fourteen, and various aunts took a hand in bringing the kid up, but all they got for their trouble was nervous prostration. Frank's crazy about her—old stuff of doting father bullied by adorable daughter."

"I think I get the picture," said Bruce soberly as his thoughts caught up and played upon this summary of the history of Franklin Mills.

Glancing back at the house as Henderson drove away, Bruce was aware of the irony of his very presence in the town, sent there by the whim of a dying woman to be prepared to aid a man who in no imaginable circumstances could ever require any help it might be in his power to give. His mother had said that she had kept some track of Mills's life; she could never have realized that he was so secure from any possibility of need. As Bruce thought of it, Henderson had not limned an attractive portrait. Only Mills's devotion to the daughter, whom Henderson had described in terms that did not conceal his own admiration for the girl, brightened the picture.

"What can such a man do with his time in a town like this?" asked Bruce meditatively. "No active business, you say. Shooting billiards and cutting coupons hardly makes an exciting day."

"Well," Henderson replied, "I've seen him on the golf links—usually alone or with the club professional. Frank's not one of these ha-ha boys who get together after the game with a few good sports and sneak a bottle of unlawful Scotch from the locker. Travels a bit; several times a year he beats it somewhere with Leila. Shep's wife bores him, I think; and Shep's not exciting; too damned nice. From all I can see, Leila's her pop's single big bet. Some say he's diffident; others hold that he's merely a selfish proposition. He's missed a number of chances to marry again—some of the most dashing widows in our tall corn cities have made a play for him; but he follows G. Washington's advice and keeps clear of entangling alliances."

"Interesting personality," said Bruce carelessly. But Mills had fixed himself in his mind—he had even fashioned a physical embodiment for the traits Henderson had described. On the whole, Bruce's dominant feeling was one of relief and satisfaction. Franklin Mills was as remote from him as though they were creatures of different planets, separated by vast abysses of time and space.

<h2 style="text-align:center">III</h2>

In spite of Henderson's sweeping declaration that he needn't waste time calling on architects, that Freeman would take care of him, Bruce spent the next morning visiting the offices of the architects on his list. Several of these were out of town; the others received him amiably; one of them promised him some work a little later, but was rather vague about it. When he returned to the hotel at noon he found Henderson waiting for him. He had nothing to do, he declared, but to keep Bruce amused. Everything was a little incidental with Henderson, but he seemed to get what he wanted without effort, even buyers for the Plantagenet. Bruce related the results of his visits to the offices of the architects and Henderson pursed his lips and emitted a cluck of disapproval.

"Next time mind your Uncle Dudley. Bill Freeman's the bird for you. You just leave every little thing to me. Now what else is troubling you?"

"Well, I want a place to live; not too expensive, but a few of the minor comforts."

Two hours later Bruce was signing the lease for a small bachelor apartment that Henderson had found for him with, apparently, no effort. He had also persuaded some friends of his who lived across the street to give the young architect breakfast and provide a colored woman to keep his place in order.

Henderson's acquaintance with his fellow citizens appeared to be unlimited. He took Bruce to the State House to call on the Governor—brought that official from a conference from which he emerged good-naturedly to shake hands and hear a new story. From this interruption of affairs of state Henderson convoyed Bruce to a barber shop in the midst of an office building where there was a venerable negro workman who told a story about a mule which Henderson said was the funniest story in the world. The trimming of a prominent citizen's hair was somewhat delayed by the telling of the yarn, but he, like everyone else, seemed to be tolerant of Henderson's idiosyncrasies; and the aged barber's story was unquestionably a masterpiece. Henderson began telephoning acquaintances who had offices in the building to come forthwith to meet an old college friend. When two men actually appeared—one an investment broker and the other a middle-aged lawyer—Henderson organized a quartette and proceeded to "get harmony." Neighboring tenants assembled, attracted by the unwonted sounds, and Henderson introduced Bruce to them as a new man in town who was entitled to the highest consideration.

"This is a sociable sort of village," he said as they left the shop. "I could see you made a hit with those fellows. You're bound to get on, my son."

At noon on Saturday Henderson drove Bruce to the Freemans', where with the utmost serenity he exercised all the rights of proprietorship. The house, of the Dutch Colonial type, was on the river in a five-acre tract. A real estate operator had given Freeman the site with the stipulation that he build himself a home to establish a social and artistic standard for the neighborhood.

"Don't be afraid of these people," remarked Henderson reassuringly. "Take your cue from me and act as though you had a deed for the house in your pocket. Bill's a dreamy sort of cuss, but Dale's a human dynamo. She looks fierce, but responds to kind treatment."

Bruce never knew when Henderson was serious, and when a diminutive young lady ran downstairs whistling he assumed that he was about to be introduced to the daughter of the house.

"Dale, this is old Bruce Storrs, one of the meanest men out of jail. I know you'll hate each other; that's why I brought him. At the first sign of any flirtation between you two I'll run you both through the meat chopper and take a high dive into the adjacent stream."

Mrs. Freeman was absurdly small and slight, and the short skirt of her simple linen dress and her bobbed hair exaggerated her diminutive stature. Having gathered from Henderson an idea that Mrs. Freeman was an assertive masculine person, Bruce was taken aback as the little woman smiled up at him and shook hands.

"It really isn't my fault that I broke in," he protested. "It was this awful Henderson person who told me you'd be heart-broken if I didn't come."

"I should have been! He'd have come alone and bored me to death. How is every little thing, Bud?"

"Soaring!" mumbled Henderson, who had chosen a book from the rack on the table and, sprawling on a couch, became immediately absorbed in it.

"That's the way Bud shows his noble breeding," remarked Mrs. Freeman, "but he is an easy guest to entertain. I suppose you're used to him?"

"Oh, we lived together for a couple of years! Nothing he does astonishes me."

"Then I needn't apologize for him. Bud's an acquired taste, but once you know him, he's highly diverting."

"When I began rooming with him in Boston I thought he wasn't all there, but finally decided he was at least three-quarters sane."

"One thing's certain; he's mastered the art of not being bored, which is some accomplishment!" said Mrs. Freeman, as Henderson rose suddenly and disappeared in the direction of the kitchen, whence proceeded presently a sound as of cracking ice.

Mrs. Freeman had something of Henderson's air of taking things for granted, and she talked to Bruce quite as though he were an old friend. She spoke amusingly of the embarrassments of housekeeping in the new quarter; they were pioneers, she said, and as servants refused to bury themselves so far from the bright lights, she did most of her own housework, which was lots of fun when you had everything electric to play with. There was an old colored man who did chores and helped in the kitchen. She told several stories to illustrate his proneness to error and his ingenuity in excusing his mistakes.

"You've never lived here? Bud gave me that idea, but you never know when he's telling the truth."

"I never saw the town before, but I hope to stay."

"It's up to us to make you want to stay," she said graciously.

She had settled herself in the largest chair in the room, sitting on one foot like a child. She smoked a cigarette as she talked, one arm thrown back of her head. She tactfully led Bruce to talk of himself and when he spoke of his year-long tramp her eyes narrowed as she gave him a more careful inspection.

"That sounds like a jolly lark. I want to know more about it, but we must wait for Bill. It's the sort of thing he'd adore doing."

Freeman appeared a moment later. He had been cleaning up after a morning's work in the garden. He was thirty-five, short and burly, with a thick shock of unruly chestnut hair over which he passed his hand frequently, smoothing it only to ruffle it again. He greeted Bruce cordially and began talking of the Tech and men he assumed Bruce might have known there. He produced pipe and tobacco from the pockets of his white flannel trousers and smoked fitfully. Mrs. Freeman answered the telephone several times and reappeared to report the messages. One had to do with changes in a house already under construction. Freeman began explaining to his wife the impossibility of meeting the client's wishes; the matter had been definitely settled before the letting of the contract and it would be expensive to alter the plans now. He appealed to Bruce for support; people might be sane about everything else in the world, but they became maddeningly unreasonable when they began building houses.

"Oh, you'd better fix it for them, Bill," advised Mrs. Freeman quietly. "They pay the bills; and I'm not sure but you were wrong in holding out against them in the first place."

"Oh, well, if you say so, Dale!" and Freeman resumed his talk.

Henderson reappeared wearing an apron and bearing a tray with a cocktail-shaker and four glasses.

"Don't flinch, Bill," he said; "it's my gin. You pay for the oranges. I say, Dale, I told Tuck to peel some potatoes. And you wanted those chops for lunch, didn't you? There's nothing else in the icebox and I told Tuck to put 'em on."

"He'll probably ruin them," said Mrs. Freeman. "Excuse me, Mr. Storrs, while I get some work out of Bud."

It was some time before Bruce got accustomed to Freeman's oddities. He was constantly moving about with a quick, catlike step; or, if he sat down, his hands were never quiet. But he talked well, proved himself a good listener, and expressed approval by slapping his knee when Bruce made some remark that squared with his own views. He was pleased in a frank, boyish way when Bruce praised some of his houses which Henderson had pointed out.

"Yes; clients didn't bother me; I had my own way in those cases. I've got some plans under way now that I want to show you. Dale said you were thinking of starting in here. Well, I need some help right away. My assistant is leaving me—going to Seattle. Suppose you drop in Monday. We might be able to fix up something."

IV

There was tennis in the afternoon and in the evening visitors began to drop in—chiefly young married people of the Freemans' circle. Some of these were of well-to-do families and others, Henderson explained to Bruce, were not rich but "right." The talk was lively and pitched in that chaffing key which is possible only among people who are intimately acquainted. This was Dale Freeman's salon, Henderson explained. Any Saturday or Sunday evening you were likely to meet people who had something worth while to offer.

He drew Bruce from one group to another, praising or abusing him with equal extravagance. He assured everyone that it was a great honor to meet a man destined, as he declared Bruce to be, to cut a big figure in the future of the town. He never backed a dead one, he reminded them. Bruce was the dearest friend he had in the world, and, he would ruefully add, probably the only one. It was for this reason that he had urged the young architect to establish himself in the city—a city that sorely needed men of Bruce's splendid character and lofty ideals.

A number of the guests had gone when late in the evening the depleted company was reinforced by the arrival of Shepherd Mills and his wife.

"Shep and the Shepherdess!" Henderson cheerfully announced as he ushered them in.

Mrs. Mills extended her hand with a gracious smile as Bruce was presented. She was tall and fair and moved with a lazy sort of grace. She spoke in a low, murmurous tone little broken by inflections. Bruce noted that she was dressed rather more smartly than the other women present. It seemed to him that the atmosphere of the room changed perceptibly on her appearance; or it might have been merely that everyone paused a minute to inspect her or to hear what she had to say. Bruce surmised from the self-conscious look in her handsome gray eyes as she crossed the room that she enjoyed being the center of attention.

"Shep just would spend the day motoring to some queer place," she was saying, "where a lot of people were killed by the Indians ages ago. Most depressing! Ruined the day for me! He's going to set up a monument or something to mark the painful affair."

Shepherd Mills greeted Bruce in the quick, eager fashion of a diffident person anxious to appear cordial but not sure that his good intentions will be understood, and suggested that they sit down. He was not so tall as his wife; his face was long and rather delicate. His slight reddish mustache seemed out of place on his lip; it did not quite succeed in giving him a masculine air. His speech was marked by odd, abrupt pauses, as though he were trying to hide a stammer; or it might have been that he was merely waiting to note the effect of what he was saying upon the hearer. He drew out a case and offered Bruce a cigarette, lighted one himself, smoking as though it were part of a required social routine to which he conformed perforce but did not relish particularly.

There was to be a tennis tournament at the country club the coming week and he mentioned this tentatively and was embarrassed to find that Bruce knew nothing about it.

"Oh, I'm always forgetting that everyone doesn't live here!" he laughed apologetically. "A little weakness of the provincial mind! I suppose we're horribly provincial out here. Do we strike you that way, Mr. Storrs?"

One might have surmised from his tone that he was used to having his serious questions ignored or answered flippantly, but hoped that the stranger would meet him on his own ground.

"Oh, there isn't any such thing as provincialism any more, is there?" asked Bruce amiably. "I haven't sniffed anything of the sort in your city: you seem very metropolitan. The fact is, I'm a good deal of a hick myself!"

Mills laughed with more fervor than the remark justified. Evidently satisfied of the intelligence and good nature of the Freemans' guest, he began to discuss the effect upon industry of a pending coal strike.

His hand went frequently to his mustache as he talked and the leg that he swung over his knee waggled nervously. He plunged into a discussion of labor, mentioning foreign market conditions and citing figures from trade journals showing the losses to both capital and labor caused by the frequent disturbances in the industrial world. He expressed opinions tentatively, a little apologetically, and withdrew them quickly when they were questioned. Bruce, having tramped through one of the coal fields where a strike was in progress, described the conditions as he had observed them. Mills expressed the greatest interest; the frown deepened on his face as he listened.

"That's bad; things shouldn't be that way," he said. "The truth of the matter is that we haven't mastered the handling of business. It's stupendous; we've outgrown the old methods. We forget the vast territory we have to handle and the numbers of men it's necessary to keep in touch with. When my Grandfather Mills set up as a manufacturer here he had fifty men working for him, and he knew them all—knew their families, circumstances, everything. Now I have six hundred in my battery plant and don't know fifty of them! But I'd like to know them all; I feel that it's my duty to know them."

He shrugged his shoulders impatiently when Henderson's sharp little laugh at the other end of the room broke in discordantly upon Bruce's sympathetic reply to this.

"Bud, how silly you are!" they heard Mrs. Mills saying. "But I don't know what we'd do without you. You do cheer things up a bit now and then!"

Mrs. Freeman effected a redistribution of the guests that brought Mrs. Mills and Bruce together.

"Shep, you mustn't monopolize Mr. Storrs. Give Connie a chance. Mr. Storrs is an ideal subject for you, Connie. Take him out on the terrace and put him through all your degrees." And then to Bruce: "Mrs. Mills is not only our leading vamp but a terrible highbrow—reads all the queer stuff!"

Shepherd Mills was not wholly successful in concealing his displeasure in thus being deprived of Bruce's company. And noting this, Bruce put out his hand, saying:

"That's a deep subject; we shall have to tackle it again. Please don't forget that we've left it in the air and give me another chance."

"My husband really wants so much to save the human race," remarked Mrs. Mills as she stepped out on the tiled flooring of a broad terrace where there were rugs and comfortable places to sit. There was moonlight and the great phalanx of stars marched across the clear heavens; below flowed the river. She seated herself on a couch, suffered him to adjust a pillow at her back and indicated that he was to sit beside her.

"I'm really done up by our all-day motor trip, but my husband insisted on dropping in here. The Freemans are a great resource to all of us. You're always likely to find someone new and interesting here. Dale Freeman has a genius for picking up just the right sort of people and she's generous about letting her friends know them. Are you and the Freemans old friends?"

"Oh, not at all! Bud Henderson's my only friend here. He vouched for me to the Freemans."

"Oh, Bud! He's such a delightful rascal. You don't mind my calling him that? I shouldn't if I weren't so fond of him. He's absolutely necessary to our social existence. We'd stagnate without him."

"Bud was always a master hand at stirring things up. His methods are a little peculiar at times, but he does get results."

"There's no question but that he's a warm admirer of yours."

"That's because he's forgotten about me! He hadn't seen me for five years."

"I think possibly I can understand that one wouldn't exactly forget you, Mr. Storrs."

She let the words fall carelessly, as though to minimize their daring in case they were not wholly acceptable to her auditor. The point was not lost upon him. He was not without his experience in the gentle art of flirtation, and her technic was familiar. There was always, however, the possibility of variations in the ancient game, and he hoped that Mrs. Shepherd Mills was blessed with originality.

"There's a good deal of me to forget; I'm six feet two!"

"Well, of course I wasn't referring altogether to your size," she said with her murmurous little laugh. "I adore big men, and I suppose that's why I married a small one. Isn't' it deliciously funny how contrary we are when it comes to the important affairs of our lives! I suppose it's just because we're poor, weak humans. We haven't the courage of our prejudices."

"I'd never thought of that," Bruce replied. "But it is an interesting idea. I suppose we're none of us free agents. It's not in the great design of things that we shall walk a chalk line. If we all did, it would probably be a very stupid world."

"I'm glad you feel that way about it. For a long time half the world tried to make conformists of the other half; nowadays not more than a third are trying to keep the rest on the chalk line—and that third's skidding! People think me dreadfully heretical about everything. But—I'm not, really! Tell me you don't think me terribly wild and untamed."

"I think," said Bruce, feeling that here was a cue he mustn't miss, "I think you are very charming. If it's your ideas that make you so, I certainly refuse to quarrel with them."

"How beautifully you came up on that! Something tells me that I'm not going to be disappointed in you. I have a vague sort of idea that we're going to understand each other."

"You do me great honor! It will be a grief to me if we don't."

"It's odd how instantly we recognize the signals when someone really worth while swims into our ken," she said pensively. "Dear old Nature looks after that! Bud intimated that you're to be one of us; throw in your lot with those of us who struggle along in this rather nice, comfortable town. If you enjoy grandeur in social things, you'll not find much here to interest you; but if just nice little companies and a few friends are enough, you can probably keep amused."

"If the Freemans' friends are specimens and there's much of this sort of thing"—he waved his hand toward the company within—"I certainly shall have nothing to complain of."

"We must see you at our house. I haven't quite Dale's knack of attracting people"—she paused a moment upon this note of humility—"but I try to bring a few worth while people together. I've educated a few men to drop in for tea on Thursdays with usually a few of my pals among the young matrons and a girl or two. If you feel moved——"

"I hope you're not trifling with me," said Bruce, "for I shall certainly come."

"Then that's all settled. Don't pay any attention to what Bud says about me. To hear him talk you might think me a man-eater. My husband's the dearest thing! He doesn't mind at all my having men in for tea. He comes himself now and then when his business doesn't interfere. Dear Shep! He's a slave to business, and he's always at work on some philanthropic scheme. I just talk about helping the world; but he, poor dear, really tries to do something."

Henderson appeared presently with a dark hint that Shepherd was peeved by their long absence and that the company was breaking up.

"Connie never plays all her cards the first time, Bruce; you must give her another chance."

"Oh, Mr. Storrs has promised me a thousand chances!" said Mrs. Mills.

CHAPTER THREE

I

Sunday evening the Freemans were called unexpectedly into town and Bruce and Henderson were left to amuse themselves. Henderson immediately lost himself in a book and Bruce, a little homesick for the old freedom of the road, set out for a walk. A footpath that followed the river invited him and he lounged along, his spirit responding to the beauty of the night, his mind intent upon the future. The cordiality of the Freemans and their circle had impressed him with the friendliness of the community. It would take time to establish himself in his profession, but he had confidence in his power to achieve; the lust for work was already strong in him. He was satisfied that he had done wisely in obeying his mother's mandate; he would never have been happy if he had ignored it.

His meeting with Shepherd Mills had roused no resentment, revived no such morbid thoughts as had troubled him on the night of his arrival in town. Shepherd Mills was his half-brother; this, to be sure, was rather staggering; but his reaction to the meeting was void of bitterness. He speculated a good deal about young Mills. The gentleness and forbearance with which he suffered the raillery of his intimates, his anxiety to be accounted a good fellow, his serious interest in matters of real importance—in all these things there was something touching and appealing. It was difficult to correlate Shepherd with his wife, but perhaps their dissimilarities were only superficial. Bruce appraised Connie Mills as rather shallow, fond of admiration, given to harmless poses in which her friends evidently encouraged and indulged her. She practiced her little coquetries with an openness that was in itself a safeguard. As they left the Freemans, Shepherd and his wife had repeated their hope of seeing him again. It was bewildering, but it had come about so naturally that there seemed nothing extraordinary in the fact that he was already acquainted with members of Franklin Mills's family....

Bruce paused now and then where the path drew in close to the river to look down at the moonlit water through the fringe of trees and shrubbery. A boy and girl floated by in a canoe, the girl singing as she thrummed a ukulele, and his eyes followed them a little wistfully. Farther on the dull put-put-put of a motor-boat broke the silence. The sound ceased abruptly, followed instantly by a colloquy between the occupants.

"Damn this fool thing!" ejaculated a feminine voice. "We're stuck!"

"I had noticed it!" said another girl's voice good naturedly. "But such is the life of the sailor. I wouldn't just choose this for an all-night camp!"

"Don't be so sweet about it, Millicent! I'd like to sink this boat."

"It isn't Polly's fault. She's already half-buried in the sand," laughed the other.

Bruce scrambled down to the water's edge and peered out upon the river. A small power boat had grounded on a sandbar in the middle of the stream. Its occupants were two young women in bathing suits. But for their voices he would have taken them for boys. One was tinkering with the engine while the other was trying to push off the boat with an oar which sank ineffectually in the sand. In their attempts to float their craft the young women had not seen Bruce, who, satisfied that they were in no danger, was rather amused by their plight. They were presumably from one of the near-by villas and their bathing suits implied familiarity with the water. The girl at the engine talked excitedly with an occasional profane outburst; her companion was disposed to accept the situation philosophically.

"We can easily swim out, so don't get so excited, Leila," said the girl with the oar. "And do stop swearing; voices travel a long way over the water."

"I don't care who hears me," said the other, though in a lower tone.

She gave the engine a spin, starting the motor, but the power was unequal to the task of freeing the boat. With an exclamation of disgust she turned off the switch and the futile threshing of the propeller ceased.

"Let's swim ashore and send back for Polly," said the girl addressed as Millicent.

"I see myself swimming out!" the other retorted. "I'm not going to leave Polly here for some pirate to steal."

"Nobody's going to steal her. This isn't the ocean, you know."

"Well, no fool boat's going to get the best of me! Where's that flask? I'm freezing!"

"You don't need any more of that! Please give it to me!"

"I hope you are enjoying yourself," said the other petulantly. "I don't see any fun in this!"

"Hello, there!" called Bruce, waving his arms to attract their attention. "Can I be of help?"

Startled by his voice, they did not reply immediately, but he heard them conferring as to this unlooked-for hail from the bank.

"Oh, I'm perfectly harmless!" he cried reassuringly. "I was just passing and heard your engine. If there's a boat near by I can pull you off, or I'll swim out and lift your boat off if you say so."

"Better get a boat," said the voice he had identified with the name of Millicent. "There's a boathouse just a little farther up, on your side. You'll find a skiff and a canoe. We'll be awfully glad to have your help. Thank you ever so much!"

"Don't forget to come back," cried Leila.

"Certainly not!" laughed Bruce and sprang up the bank.

He found the boathouse without trouble, chose the skiff as easier to manage, and rowed back. In the moonlight he saw Millicent standing up in the launch watching him, and as he approached she flashed an electric torch along the side of the boat that he might see the nature of their difficulty.

"Do you need food or medical attention?" he asked cheerfully as he skillfully maneuvered the skiff and grounded it on the sand.

"I think we'd better get out," she said.

"No; stay right there till I see what I can do. I think I can push you off. All steady now!"

The launch moved a little at his first attempt to dislodge it and a second strong shove sent it into the channel.

"Now start your engine!" he commanded.

The girl in the middle of the boat muttered something he didn't catch.

"Leila, can you start the engine?" demanded Millicent. "I think—I think I'll have to row back," she said when Leila made no response. "My friend isn't feeling well."

"I'll tow you—that's easy," said Bruce, noting that her companion apparently was no longer interested in the proceedings. "Please throw me your rope!"

He caught the rope and fastened it to the stern of the skiff and called out that he was ready.

"Please land us where you found the boat," said Millicent. She settled herself in the stern of the launch and took the tiller. No word was spoken till they reached the boathouse.

"That's all you can do," said Millicent, who had drawn on a long bath wrapper and stepped out. "And thank you very, very much; I'm sorry to have caused you so much trouble."

This was clearly a dismissal, but he loosened the rope and tied up the skiff. He waited, holding the launch, while Millicent tried to persuade Leila to disembark.

"Perhaps——" began Bruce, and hesitated. It seemed unfair to leave the girl alone with the problem of getting her friend ashore. Not to put too fine a point on the matter, Leila was intoxicated.

"Now, Leila!" cried Millicent exasperatedly. "You're making yourself ridiculous, besides keeping this gentleman waiting. It's not a bit nice of you!"

"Jus' restin' lil bit," said Leila indifferently. "I'm jus' restin' and I'm not goin' to leave Polly. I should shay not!"

And in assertion of her independence she began to whistle. She seemed greatly amused that her attempts to whistle were unsuccessful.

Millicent turned to Bruce. "If I could get her out of the boat I could put her in our car and take her home."

"Surely!" he said and bent over quickly and lifted the girl from the launch, set her on her feet and steadied her. Millicent fumbled in the launch, found a bath wrapper and flung it about Leila's shoulders. She guided her friend toward the long, low boathouse and turned a switch.

"I can manage now," she said, gravely surveying Bruce in the glare of light. "I'm so sorry to have troubled you."

She was tall and fair with markedly handsome brown eyes and a great wealth of fine-spun golden hair that escaped from her bathing cap and tumbled down upon her shoulders. Her dignity was in nowise diminished by her garb. She betrayed no agitation. Bruce felt that she was paying him the compliment of assuming that she was dealing with a gentleman who, having performed a service, would go his way and forget the whole affair. She drew her arm about the now passive Leila, who was much shorter— quite small, indeed, in comparison.

"Our car's here and we'll get dressed and drive back into town. Thank you so much and—good-night!"

"I was glad to help you;—good-night!"

The door closed upon them. Bruce made the launch fast to the landing and resumed his walk.

II

When he returned to the Freemans, Henderson flung aside his book and complained of Bruce's prolonged absence. "I had begun to think you'd got yourself kidnapped. Go ahead and talk," he said, yawning and stretching himself.

"Well, I've had a mild adventure," said Bruce, lighting a cigarette; and he described his meeting with the two young women.

"Not so bad!" remarked Henderson placidly. "Such little adventures never happen to me. The incident would make good first page stuff for a newspaper; society girls shipwrecked. You ought to have taken the flask as a souvenir. Leila is an obstreperous little kid; she really ought to behave herself. Right the first time. Leila Mills, of course; I think I mentioned her the other day. Her friend is Millicent Harden. Guess I omitted Millicent in my review of our citizens. Quite a remarkable person. She plays the rôle of big sister to Leila; they're neighbors on Jefferson Avenue. That's just a boathouse on the Styx that Mills built for Leila's delectation. She pulls a cocktail tea there occasionally. Millicent's pop made a fortune out of an asthma cure—the joy of all cut-rate druggists. Not viewed with approval by medical societies. Socially the senior Hardens are outside the breastworks, but Millicent is asked to very large functions, where nobody knows who's there. They live in that whopping big house just north of the Mills place, and old Doc Harden gives Millicent everything she wants. Hence a grand organ, and the girl is a regular Cecelia at the keys. Really plays. Strong artistic bent. We can't account for people like the Hardens having such a daughter. There's a Celtic streak in the girl, I surmise—that odd sort of poetic strain that's so beguiling in the Irish. She models quite wonderfully, they tell me. Well, well! So you were our little hero on the spot!"

"But Leila?" said Bruce seriously. "You don't quite expect to find the daughter of a prominent citizen tipsy on a river, and rather profane at that."

"Oh, thunder!" exclaimed Henderson easily. "Leila's all right. You needn't worry about her. She's merely passing through a phase and will probably emerge safely. Leila's hardly up to your standard, but Millicent is a girl you'll like. I ought to have told Dale to ask Millicent here. Dale's a broad-minded woman and doesn't mind it at all that old Harden's rolled up a million by being smart enough to scamper just a nose length ahead of the Federal grand jury carrying his rotten dope in triumph."

"Miss Mills, I suppose, is an acceptable member of the Freemans' group?" Bruce inquired.

"Acceptable enough, but this is all too tame for Leila. Curious sort of friendship—Leila and Millicent. Socially Millicent is, in a manner of speaking, between the devil and the deep sea. She's just a little too superior to train with the girls of the Longview Country Club set and the asthma cure keeps her from being chummy with the Faraway gang. But I'll say that Leila's lucky to have a friend like Millicent."

"Um—yes," Bruce assented. "I'm beginning to see that your social life here has a real flavor."

"Well, it's not all just plain vanilla," Bud agreed with a yawn.

CHAPTER FOUR

I

Henderson made his wife's return an excuse for giving a party at the Faraway Country Club. Mrs. Henderson had brought home a trophy from the golf tournament and her prowess must be celebrated. She was a tall blonde with a hearty, off-hand manner, and given to plain, direct speech. She treated Bud as though he were a younger brother, to be humored to a certain point and then reminded a little tartly of the limitations of her tolerance.

When Bruce arrived at the club he found his hostess and Mrs. Freeman receiving the guests in the hall and directing them to a dark end of the veranda where Bud was holding forth with a cocktail-shaker. Obedient to their hint, he stumbled over the veranda chairs until he came upon a group of young people gathered about Bud, who was energetically compounding drinks as he told a story. Bruce knew the story; it was the oldest of Bud's yarns, and his interest wavered to become fixed immediately upon a girl beside him who was giving Bud her complete attention. Even in the dim light of the veranda there was no mistaking her: she was the Millicent Harden he had rescued from the sand bar. At the conclusion of the story she joined in the general laugh and turned round to find Bruce regarding her intently.

"I beg your pardon," he said and bowed gravely.

"Oh, you needn't!" she replied quickly.

He lifted his head to find her inspecting him with an amused smile.

"I might find someone to introduce us—Mr. Henderson, perhaps," he said. "My name—if the matter is important—is Bruce Storrs."

"Possibly we might complete the introduction unassisted—my name is Millicent Harden!"

"How delightful! Shall we dance?"

After the dance he suggested that they step out for a breath of air. They found seats and she said immediately:

"Of course I remember you; I'd be ashamed if I didn't. I'm glad of this chance to thank you. I know Leila—Miss Mills—will want to thank you, too. We must have seemed very silly that night on the river."

"Such a thing might happen to anyone; why not forget it?"

"Let me thank you again," she said seriously. "You were ever so kind."

"The incident is closed," he remarked with finality. "Am I keeping you from a partner? They're dancing again. We might sit this out if I'm not depriving you——"

"You're not. It's warm inside and this is a relief. We might even wander down the lawn and look for elves and dryads and nymphs. Those big trees and the stars set the stage for such encounters."

"It's rather nice to believe in fairies and such things. At times I'm a believer; then I lose my faith."

"We all forget our fairies sometimes," she answered gravely.

He had failed to note at their meeting on the river the loveliness of her voice. He found himself waiting for the recurrence of certain tones that had a curious musical resonance. He was struck by a certain gravity in her that was expressed for fleeting moments in both voice and eyes. Even with the newest dance music floating out to them and the light and laughter within, he was aware of an indefinable quality in the girl that seemed somehow to translate her to remote and shadowy times. Her profile—clean-cut without sharpness—and her manner of wearing her abundant hair—carried back loosely to a knot low on her head—strengthened his impression of her as being a little foreign to the place and hour. She spoke with quiet enthusiasm of the outdoor sports that interested her—riding she enjoyed most of all. Henderson had intimated that her social life was restricted, but she bore herself more like a young woman of the world than any other girl he remembered.

"Maybelle Henderson will scold me for hiding you away," she said. "But I just can't dance whenever the band plays. It's got to be an inspiration!"

"Then I thank you again for one perfect dance! I'm afraid I didn't appreciate what you were giving me."

"Oh, I danced with you to hide my embarrassment!" she laughed.

Half an hour passed and they had touched and dismissed many subjects when she rose and caught the hand of a girl who was passing.

"Miss Mills, Mr. Storrs. It's quite fitting that you should meet Mr. Storrs."

"Fitting?" asked the girl, breathless from her dance.

"We've all met before—on the river—most shockingly! You might just say thank you to Mr. Storrs."

"Oh, this is *not*——" Leila drew back and inspected Bruce with a direct, candid gaze.

"Miss Harden is mistaken; this is the first time we ever met," declared Bruce.

"Isn't he nice!" Leila exclaimed. "From what Millie said I knew you would be like this." And then: "Oh, lots of people are bragging about you and promising to introduce me! Here comes Tommy Barnes; he has this dance. Oh, Millie! if you get a chance you might say a kind word to papa. He's probably terribly bored by this time."

"Leila's a dear child! I'm sure you'll like her," said Millicent as the girl fluttered away. "Oh, I adore this piece! Will you dance with me?"

As they finished the dance Mrs. Henderson intercepted them.

"Aren't you the limit, you two? I've had Bud searching the whole place for you and here you are! Quite as though you hadn't been hiding for the last hour."

"I'm going to keep Mr. Storrs just a moment longer," said Millicent. "Leila said her father was perishing somewhere and I want Mr. Storrs to meet him."

"Yes; certainly," said Bruce.

He walked beside her into the big lounge, where many of the older guests were gathered.

"Poor Mr. Mills!" said Millicent after a quick survey of the room. "There he is, listening to one of Mr. Tasker's interminable yarns."

She led the way toward a group of men, one of whom was evidently nearing the end of a long story. One of his auditors, a dark man of medium height and rather stockily built, was listening with an air of forced attention. His grayish hair was brushed smoothly away from a broad forehead, his neatly trimmed mustache was a trifle grayer than his hair. Millicent and Bruce fell within the line of his vision, and his face brightened instantly as he nodded to the girl and waved his hand. The moment the story was ended he crossed to them, his eyes bright with pleasure and a smile on his face.

"I call it a base desertion!" he exclaimed. "Leila brings me here and coolly parks me. A father gets mighty little consideration these days!"

"Don't scold! Mr. Mills—let me present Mr. Storrs."

"I'm very glad to meet you, Mr. Storrs," said Mills with quiet cordiality. He swept Bruce with a quick, comprehensive scrutiny.

"Mr. Storrs has lately moved here," Millicent explained.

"I congratulate you, Mr. Storrs, on having fallen into good hands."

"Oh, Miss Harden is taking splendid care of me!" Bruce replied.

"She's quite capable of doing that!" Mills returned.

Bruce was studying Franklin Mills guardedly. A man of reserves and reticences, not a safe subject for quick judgments. His manner was somewhat listless now that the introduction had been accomplished; and perhaps aware of this, he addressed several remarks to Bruce, asking whether the music was all that the jazzy age demanded; confessed with mock chagrin that his dancing days were over.

"You only think they are! Mr. Mills really dances very well. You'd be surprised, Mr. Storrs, considering how venerable he is!"

"That's why I don't dance!" Mills retorted with a rueful grin. "'Considering his age' is the meanest phrase that can be applied to a man of fifty."

Bud Henderson here interrupted them, declaring that dozens of people were disconsolate because Bruce had concealed himself.

"Of course you must go!" said Millicent.

"I hope to meet you again," Mills remarked as Bruce bowed to him.

"Thank you, Mr. Mills," said Bruce.

He was conscious once more of Mills's intent scrutiny. It seemed to him as he walked away that Mills's eyes followed him.

"What's the matter, old top?" Bud demanded. "You're not tired?"

"No; I'm all right," Bruce replied, though his heart was pounding hard; and feeling a little giddy, he laid his hand on Henderson's arm.

CHAPTER FIVE

I

Franklin Mills stood by one of the broad windows in his private office gazing across the smoky industrial district of his native city. With his hands thrust into his trousers' pockets, he was a picture of negligent ease. His face was singularly free of the markings of time. His thick, neatly trimmed hair with its even intermixture of white added to his look of distinction. His business suit of dark blue with an obscure green stripe was evidently a recent creation of his tailor, and a wing collar with a neatly tied polka-dot cravat contributed further to the impression he gave of a man who had a care for his appearance. The gray eyes that looked out over the city narrowed occasionally as some object roused his attention—a freight train crawling on the outskirts or some disturbance in the street below. Then he would resume his reverie as though enjoying his sense of immunity from the fret and jar of the world about him.

Bruce Storrs. The name of the young man he had met at the Country Club lingered disturbingly in his memory. He had heard someone ask that night where Storrs came from, and Bud Henderson, his sponsor, had been ready with the answer, "Laconia, Ohio." Mills had been afraid to ask the question himself. Long-closed doors swung open slowly along the dim corridor of memory and phantom shapes emerged—among them a figure Franklin Mills recognized as himself. Swiftly he computed the number of years that had passed since, in his young manhood, he had spent a summer in the pleasant little town, sent there by his father to act as auditor of a manufacturing concern in which Franklin Mills III for a time owned an interest. Marian Storrs was a lovely young being—vivacious, daring, already indifferent to the man to whom she had been married two years.... He had been a beast to take advantage of her, to accept all that she had yielded to him with a completeness and passion that touched him poignantly now as she lived again in his memory.... Was this young man, Bruce Storrs, her son? He was a splendid specimen, distinctly handsome, with the air of breeding that Mills valued. He turned from the window and walked idly about the room, only to return to his contemplation of the hazy distances.

The respect of his fellow man, one could see, meant much to him. He was Franklin Mills, the fourth of the name in succession in the Mid-western city, enjoying an unassailable social position and able to command more cash at a given moment than any other man in the community. Nothing was so precious to Franklin Mills as his peace of mind, and here was a problem that might forever menace that peace. The hope that the young man himself knew nothing did not abate the hateful, hideous question ... was he John Storrs's son or his own? Surely Marian Storrs could not have told the boy of that old episode....

Nearly every piece of property in the city's original mile square had at some time belonged to a Mills. The earlier men of the name had been prominent in public affairs, but he had never been interested in politics and he never served on those bothersome committees that promote noble causes and pursue the public with subscription papers. When Franklin Mills gave he gave liberally, but he preferred to make his contributions unsolicited. It pleased him to be represented at the State Fair with cattle and saddle horses from Deer Trail Farm. Like his father and grandfather, he kept in touch with the soil, and his farm, fifteen miles from his office, was a show place; his Jersey herd enjoyed a wide reputation. The farm was as perfectly managed as his house and office. Its carefully tended fields, his flocks and herds and the dignified Southern Colonial house were but another advertisement of his substantial character and the century-long identification of his name with the State.

His private office was so furnished as to look as little as possible like a place for the transaction of business. There were easy lounging chairs, a long leathern couch, a bookcase, a taboret with cigars and cigarettes. The flat-top desk, placed between two windows, contained nothing but an immaculate blotter and a silver desk set that evidently enjoyed frequent burnishing. It was possible for him to come and go without traversing the other rooms of the suite. Visitors who passed the office boy's inspection and satisfied a prim stenographer that their errands were not frivolous found themselves in communication with Arthur Carroll, Mills's secretary, a young man of thirty-five, trained as a lawyer, who spoke for his employer in all matters not demanding decisions of first importance. Carroll was not only Mills's confidential man of business, but when necessary he performed the duties of social secretary. He was tactful, socially in demand as an eligible bachelor, and endowed with a genius for collecting information that greatly assisted Mills in keeping in touch with the affairs of the community.

Mills glanced at his watch and turned to press a button in a plate on the corner of his desk. Carroll appeared immediately.

"You said Shep was coming?" Mills inquired.

"Yes; he was to be here at five, but said he might be a little late."

Mills nodded, asked a question about the survey of some land adjoining Deer Trail Farm for which he was negotiating, and listened attentively while Carroll described a discrepancy in the boundary lines.

"Is that all that stands in the way?" Mills asked.

"Well," said Carroll, "Parsons shows signs of bucking. He's thought of reasons, sentimental ones, for not selling. He and his wife moved there when they were first married and their children were all born on the place."

"Of course we have nothing to do with that," remarked Mills, slipping an ivory paper knife slowly through his fingers. "The old man is a failure, and the whole place is badly run down. I really need it for pasture."

"Oh, he'll sell! We just have to be a little patient," Carroll replied.

"All right, but don't close till the title's cleared up. I don't buy law suits. Come in, Shep."

Shepherd Mills had appeared at the door during this talk. His father had merely glanced at him, and Shepherd waited, hat in hand, his topcoat on his arm, till the discussion was ended.

"What's that you've got there?" his father asked, seating himself in a comfortable chair a little way from the desk.

In drawing some papers from the pocket of his overcoat, Shepherd dropped his hat, picked it up and laid it on the desk. He was trying to appear at ease, and replied that it was a contract calling for a large order which the storage battery company had just made.

"We worked a good while to get that," said the young man with a ring of pride in his voice. "I thought you'd like to know it's all settled."

Mills put on his glasses, scanned the document with a practiced eye and handed it back.

"That's good. You're running full capacity now?"

"Yes; we've got orders enough to keep us going full handed for several months."

The young man's tone was eager; he was clearly anxious for his father's approval. He had expected a little more praise for his success in getting the contract, but was trying to adjust himself to his father's calm acceptance of the matter. He drummed the edge of the desk as he recited certain figures as to conditions at the plant. His father disconcertingly corrected one of his statements.

"Yes; you're right, father," Shepherd stammered. "I got the July figures mixed up with the June report."

Mills smiled indulgently; took a cigarette from a silver box on the taboret beside him and unhurriedly lighted it.

"You and Constance are coming over for dinner tonight?" he asked. "I think Leila said she'd asked you."

His senior's very calmness seemed to add to Shepherd's nervousness. He rose and laid his overcoat on the couch, drew out his handkerchief and wiped his forehead, remarking that it was warm for the season.

"I hadn't noticed it," his father remarked in the tone of one who is indifferent to changes of temperature.

"There's a little matter I've been wanting to speak to you about," Shepherd began. "I thought it would be better to mention it here—you never like talking business at the house. If it's going to be done it ought to be started now, before the bad weather sets in."

He paused, a little breathless, and Mills said, the least bit impatiently:

"Do you mean that new unit at the plant? I thought we'd settled that. I thought you were satisfied you could get along this winter with the plant as it is."

“Oh, no! It’s not that!” Shepherd hastily corrected. “Of course that’s all settled. This is quite a different matter. I only want to suggest it now so you can think it over. You see, our employees were all mightily pleased because you let them have the use of the Milton farm. There’s quite a settlement grown up around the plant and the Milton land is so near they can walk to it. I’ve kept tab this summer and about a hundred of the men go there Saturday afternoons and Sundays; mostly married men who take their families. I could see it made a big difference in the morale of the shop.”

He paused to watch the effect of his statements, but Mills made no sign. He merely recrossed his legs, knocked the ash from his cigarette and nodded for his son to go on.

“I want you to know I appreciate your letting me use the property that way,” Shepherd resumed. “I was out there a good deal myself, and those people certainly enjoyed themselves. Now what’s in my mind is this, father”—he paused an instant and bent forward with boyish eagerness—“I’ve heard you say you didn’t mean to sell any lots in the Milton addition for several years —not until the street car line’s extended—and I thought since the factory’s so close to the farm, we might build some kind of a clubhouse the people could use the year round. They can’t get any amusements without coming into town, and we could build the house near the south gate of the property, where our people could get to it easily. They could have dances and motion pictures, and maybe a few lectures and some concerts, during the winter. They’ll attend to all that themselves. Please understand that I don’t mean this as a permanent thing. The clubhouse needn’t cost much, so when you get ready to divide the farm the loss wouldn’t be great. It might even be used in some way. I just wanted to mention it; we can talk out the details after you’ve thought it over.”

In his anxiety to make himself clear Shepherd had stammered repeatedly. He waited, his face flushed, his eyelids quivering, for some encouraging word from his father. Mills dropped his cigarette into the tray before he spoke.

“What would such a house cost, Shep?”

“It can be built for twenty thousand dollars. I got a young fellow in Freeman’s office to make me some sketches—Storrs—you met him at the country club; a mighty nice chap. If you’ll just look at these——”

Mills took the two letter sheets his son extended, one showing a floor plan, the other a rough sketch of the proposed building, inspected them indifferently and gave them back.

"If you'd like to keep them——" Shepherd began.

"No; that isn't necessary. I think we can settle the matter now. It was all right for those people to use the farm as a playground during the summer, but this idea of building a house for them won't do. We've got to view these things practically, Shep. You're letting your sentimental feelings run away with you. If I let you go ahead with that scheme, it would be unfair to all the other employers in town. If you stop to think, you can see for yourself that for us to build such a clubhouse would cause dissatisfaction among other concerns I'm interested in. And there's another thing. Your people have done considerable damage—breaking down the shrubbery and young trees I'd planted where I'd laid out the roads. I hadn't spoken of this, for I knew how much fun you got out of it, but as for spending twenty thousand dollars for a clubhouse and turning the whole place over to those people, it can't be done!"

"Well, father, of course I can see your way of looking at it," Shepherd said with a crestfallen air. "I thought maybe, just for a few years——"

"That's another point," Mills interrupted. "You can't give it to them and then take it away. Such people are bound to be unreasonable. Give them an inch and they take a mile. You'll find as you grow older that they have precious little appreciation of such kindnesses. Your heart's been playing tricks with your head. I tell you, my dear boy, there's nothing in it; positively nothing!"

Mills rose, struck his hands together smartly and laid them on his son's shoulders, looking down at him with smiling tolerance. Shepherd was nervously fumbling Storrs's sketches, and as his father stepped back he hastily thrust them into his pocket.

"You may be right, father," he said slowly, and with no trace of resentment.

"Storrs, you said?" Mills inquired as he opened a cabinet door and took out his hat and light overcoat. "Is he the young man Millie introduced me to?"

"Yes; that tall, fine-looking chap; a Tech man; just moved here—friend of Bud Henderson's."

"I wasn't quite sure of the name. He's an architect, is he?" asked Mills as he slowly buttoned his coat.

"Yes; I met him at the Freemans' and had him for lunch at the club. Freeman is keen about him."

"He's rather an impressive-looking fellow," Mills replied. "Expects to live here, does he?"

"Yes. He has no relatives here; just thought the town offered a good opening. His home was somewhere in Ohio, I think."

"Yes; I believe I heard that," Mills replied carelessly. "You have your car with you?"

"Yes; the runabout. I'll skip home and dress and drive over with Connie. We're going to the Claytons' later."

When they reached the street Shepherd ordered up his father's limousine and saw him into it, and waved his hand as it rolled away. As he turned to seek his own car the smile faded from his face. It was not merely that his father had refused to permit the building of the clubhouse, but that the matter had been brushed aside quite as a parent rejects some absurd proposal of an unreasoning child. He strode along with the quick steps compelled by his short stature, smarting under what he believed to be an injustice, and ashamed of himself for not having combated the objections his father had raised. The loss of shrubs or trees was nothing when weighed against the happiness of the people who had enjoyed the use of the farm. He thought now of many things that he might have said in defence of his proposition; but he had never been able to hold his own in debate with his father. His face burned with humiliation. He regretted that within an hour he was to see his father again.

II

The interior of Franklin Mills's house was not so forbidding as Henderson had hinted in his talk with Bruce. It was really a very handsomely furnished, comfortable establishment that bore the marks of a sound if rather austere taste. The house had been built in the last years of Mrs. Mills's life, and if a distinctly feminine note was lacking in its appointments, this was due to changes made by Mills in keeping with the later tendency in interior decoration toward the elimination of nonessentials.

It was only a polite pretense that Leila kept house for her father. Her inclinations were decidedly not domestic, and Mills employed and directed the servants, ordered the meals, kept track of expenditures and household bills, and paid them through his office. He liked formality and chose well-trained servants capable of conforming to his wishes in this respect. The library on the second floor was Mills's favorite lounging place. Here were books indicative of the cultivated and catholic taste of the owner, and above the shelves were ranged the family portraits, a considerable array of them, preserving the countenances of his progenitors. Throughout the house there were pictures, chiefly representative work of contemporary French and American artists. When Mills got tired of a picture or saw a chance to buy a better one by the same painter, he sold or gave away the discard. He knew the contents of his house from cellar to garret—roved over it a good deal in his many lonely hours.

He came downstairs a few minutes before seven and from force of habit strolled through the rooms on a tour of inspection. In keeping with his sense of personal dignity, he always put on his dinner coat in the evening, even when he was alone. He rang and asked the smartly capped and aproned maid who responded whether his daughter was at home.

"Miss Leila went to the Country Club this afternoon, sir, and hasn't come in yet. She said she was dining here."

"Thank you," he replied colorlessly, and turned to glance over some new books neatly arranged on a table at the side of the living-room. A clock struck seven and on the last solemn stroke the remote titter of an electric bell sent the maid to the door.

"Mr. and Mrs. Shepherd Mills," the girl announced in compliance with an established rule, which was not suspended even when Mills's son and daughter-in-law were the guests.

"Shep fairly dragged me!" Mrs. Mills exclaimed as she greeted her father-in-law. "He's in such terror of being late to one of your feasts! I know I'm a fright." She lifted her hand to her hair with needless solicitude; it was perfectly arranged. She wore an evening gown of sapphire blue chiffon,—an effective garment; she knew that it was effective. Seeing that he was eyeing it critically, she demanded to know what he thought of it.

"You're so fastidious, you know! Shep never pays any attention to my clothes. It's a silly idea that women dress only for each other; it's for captious men like you that we take so much trouble."

"You're quite perfectly turned out, I should say," Mills remarked. "That's a becoming gown. I don't believe I've seen it before."

Her father-in-law was regarding her quizzically, an ambiguous smile playing about his lips. She was conscious that he never gave her his whole approval and she was piqued by her failure to evoke any expressions of cordiality from him. Men usually liked her, or at least found her amusing, and she had never been satisfied that Franklin Mills either liked her or thought her clever. It was still a source of bitterness that Mills had objected strongly to Shepherd's marrying her. His objections she attributed to snobbery; for her family was in nowise distinguished, and Constance, an only child, had made her own way socially chiefly through acquaintances and friendships formed in the Misses Palmers' school, a local institution which conferred a certain social dignity upon its patrons.

She had never been able to break down Mills's reserves, and the tone which she had adopted for her intercourse with him had been arrived at after a series of experiments in the first year of her marriage. He suffered this a little stolidly. There was a point of discretion beyond which she never dared venture. She had once tried teasing him about a young widow, a visitor from the South for whom he had shown some partiality, and he hadn't liked it, though he had taken the same sort of chaff from others in her presence with perfect good nature.

Shepherd, she realized perfectly, was a disappointment to his father. Countless points of failure in the relationship of father and son were manifest to her, things of which Shepherd himself was unconscious. It was Mills's family pride that had prompted him to make Shepherd president of the storage battery company, and the same vanity was responsible for the house he had given Shepherd on his marriage—a much bigger house than the young couple needed. He expected her to bear children that the continuity of the name might be unbroken, but the thought of bearing children was repugnant to her. Still, the birth of an heir, to take the name of Franklin Mills, would undoubtedly heighten his respect for her—diminish the veiled hostility which she felt she aroused in him.

"Where's Leila?" asked Shepherd as dinner was announced and they moved toward the dining-room.

"She'll be along presently," Mills replied easily.

"Dear Leila!" exclaimed Constance. "You never disciplined her as you did Shep. Shep would go to the stake before he'd turn up late."

"Leila," said Mills a little defensively, "is a law unto herself."

"That's why we all love the dear child!" said Constance quickly. "Not for worlds would I change her."

To nothing was Mills so sensitive as to criticism of Leila, a fact which she should have remembered.

As they took their places Mills asked her, in the impersonal tone she hated, what the prospects were for a gay winter. She was on the committee of the Assembly, whose entertainments were a noteworthy feature of every season. There, too, was the Dramatic Club, equally exclusive in its membership, and Constance was on the play committee. Mills listened with interest, or with the pretense of interest, as she gave him the benefit of her knowledge as to the winter's social programme.

They were half through the dinner when Leila arrived. With a cheerful "Hello, everybody," she flung off her wrap and without removing her hat, sank into the chair Shepherd drew out for her.

"Sorry, Dada, but Millie and I played eighteen holes this afternoon; got a late start and were perfectly starved when we finished and just had to have tea. And some people came along and we got to talking and it was dark before we knew it."

"How's your game coming on?" her father asked.

"Not so bad, Dada. Millie's one of these lazy players; she doesn't care whether she wins or loses, and I guess I'm too temperamental to be a good golfer."

"I thought Millie was pretty strong on temperament herself," remarked Shepherd.

"Well, Millie is and she isn't. She's not the sort that flies all to pieces when anything goes wrong."

"Millie's a pretty fine girl," declared Shepherd.

"Millicent really has charm," remarked Constance, though without enthusiasm.

"Millie's a perfect darling!" said Leila. "She's so lovely to her father and mother! They're really very nice. Everybody knocks Doc Harden, but he's not a bad sort. It's a shame the way people treat them. Mrs. Harden's a dear, sweet thing; plain and sensible and doesn't look pained when I cuss a little." She gave her father a sly look, but he feigned inattention. "Dada, how do you explain Millie?"

"Well, I don't," replied Mills, with a broad smile at the abruptness of the question. "It's just as well that everything and everybody on this planet can't be explained and don't have to be. I've come to a time of life when I'm a little fed up on things that can be reduced to figures. I want to be mystified!"

Leila pointed her finger at him across the table.

"I'll say you like mystery! If there was ever a human being who just had to have the facts, you're it! I know because I've tried hiding milliners' bills from you."

"Well, I usually pay them," Mills replied good-humoredly. "Now that you've spoken of bills, I'd like to ask you——"

"Don't!" Leila ejaculated, placing her hands over her ears with simulated horror. "I know what you're going to say. You're going to ask why I bought that new squirrel coat. Well, winter's coming and it's to keep me from freezing to death."

"Well, the house is well heated," Mills replied dryly. "The answer is for you to spend a little time at home."

Leila was a spoiled child and lived her own life with little paternal interference. After Mills had failed utterly to keep her in school, or rather to find any school in which she would stay, he had tried tutors with no better results. He had finally placed her for a year in New York with a woman who made a business of giving the finishing touches to the daughters of the provincial rich. There were no lessons to learn which these daughters didn't want to learn, but Leila had heard operas and concerts to a point where she really knew something of music, and she had acquired a talent that greatly amused her father for talking convincingly of things she really knew nothing about. He found much less delight in her appalling habit of blurting out things better left unsaid, and presumably foreign to the minds of well-bred young women.

Her features were a feminized version of her father's; she was dark like him and with the same gray eyes; but here the resemblance ended. She was alert, restless, quick of speech and action. The strenuous life of her long days was expressing itself in little nervous twitchings of her hands and head. Her father, under his benignant gaze, was noting these things now.

"I hope you're staying in tonight, Leila?" he said. "It seems to me you're not sleeping enough."

"Well, no, Dada. I was going to the Claytons'. I told Fred Thomas he might come for me at nine."

"Thomas?" Mills questioned. "I don't know that I'd choose him for an escort."

"Oh, Freddy's all right!" Leila replied easily. "He's always asking me to go places with him, and I'd turned him down until I was ashamed to refuse any more."

"I think," said her father, "it might be as well to begin refusing again. What about him, Shep?"

"He's a good sort, I think," Shepherd replied after a hasty glance at his wife. "But of course——"

"Of course, he's divorced," interposed Constance, "and he hasn't been here long. But people I know in Chicago say he was well liked there. What is it he has gone into, Shep?"

"He came here to open a branch of a lumber company—a large concern, I think," Shepherd replied. "I believe he *has* been divorced, Father, if that's what's troubling you."

"Oh, he told me all about the divorce!" interposed Leila imperturbably. "His wife got crazy about another man and—biff! Don't worry, Dada; he isn't dangerous."

III

When they had gone upstairs to the library for coffee, Leila lighted a cigarette and proceeded to open some letters that had been placed on a small desk kept in the room for her benefit. She perched herself on the desk and read aloud, between whiffs of her cigarette, snatches of news from a letter. Shepherd handed her a cup and she stirred her coffee, the cigarette hanging from her lip. Constance feigned not to notice a shadow of annoyance on her father-in-law's face as Leila, her legs dangling, occasionally kicked the desk frame with her heels.

"By the way, Leila," said Constance, "the Nelsons want to sell their place at Harbor Hills. They haven't been there for several years, you know. It's one of the best locations anywhere in Michigan. It would solve the eternal summer problem for all of us—so accessible and a marvelous view—and you could have all the water sports you wanted. And they say the new clubhouse is a perfect dream."

Shepherd Mills's cup tottered in its saucer with a sharp staccato. He had warned his wife not to broach the matter of purchasing the northern Michigan cottage, which she had threatened to do for some time and had discussed with Leila in the hope of enlisting her as an ally for an effective assault upon Mills.

"It's a peach of a place, all right," Leila remarked. "I wonder if the yacht goes with the house. I believe I could use that yacht. Really, Dada, we ought to have a regular summer place. I'm fed up on rented cottages. If we had a house like the Nelsons' we could all use it."

She had promised Constance to support the idea, but her sister-in-law had taken her off guard and she was aware that she hadn't met the situation with quite the enthusiasm it demanded. Mills was lighting a cigar in his usual unhurried fashion. He knew that Constance was in the habit of using Leila as an advocate when she wanted him to do something extraordinary, and Leila, to his secret delight, usually betrayed the source of her inspiration.

"What do the Nelsons want for the property?" he asked, settling himself back in his chair.

"I suppose the yacht isn't included," Constance answered. "They're asking seventy thousand for the house, and there's a lot of land, you know. The Nelsons live in Detroit and it would be easy to get the details."

"You said yourself it was a beautiful place when you were there last summer," Leila resumed, groping in her memory for the reasons with which Constance had fortified her for urging the purchase. "And the golf course up there is a wonder, and the whole place is very exclusive—only the nicest people."

"I thought you preferred the northeast coast," her father replied. "What's sent you back to fresh water?"

"Oh, Dada, I just have to change my mind sometimes! If I kept the same idea very long it would turn bad—like an egg."

Constance, irritated by Leila's perfunctory espousal of the proposed investment, tried to signal for silence. But Leila, having undertaken to implant in her father's mind the desirability of acquiring the cottage at Harbor Hills, was unwilling to drop the subject.

"Poor old Shep never gets any vacation to amount to anything. If we had a place in Michigan he could go up every week-end and get a breath of air. We all of us could have a perfectly grand time."

"Who's all?" demanded her father. "You'd want to run a select boarding house, would you?"

"Well, not exactly. But Connie and I could open the place early and stay late, and we'd hope you'd be with us all the time, and Shep, whenever he could get away."

"Shep, I think this is only a scheme to shake you and me for the summer. Connie and Leila are trying to put something over on us. And of course we can't stand for any such thing."

"Of course, Father, the upkeep of such a place is considerable," Shepherd replied conciliatingly.

"Yes; quite as much as a town house, and you'd never use it more than two or three months a year. By the way, Connie, do you know those Cincinnati Marvins Leila and I met up there?"

Connie knew that her father-in-law had, with characteristic deftness, disposed of the Harbor Hills house as effectually as though he had roared a refusal. Shepherd, still smarting under the rejection of his plan for giving his workmen a clubhouse, marveled at the suavity with which his father eluded proposals that did not impress him favorably. He wondered at times whether his father was not in some degree a superman who in his judgments and actions exercised a Jovian supremacy over the rest of mankind. Leila, finding herself bored by her father's talk with Constance about the Marvins, sprang from the table, stretched herself lazily and said she guessed she would go and dress.

When she reached the door she turned toward him with mischief in her eyes. "What are you up to tonight, Dada? You might stroll over and see Millie! The Claytons didn't ask her to their party."

"Thanks for the hint, dear," Mills replied with a tinge of irony.

"I think I'll go with you," said Constance, as Leila impudently kissed her fingers to her father and turned toward her room. "Whistle for me at eight-thirty, Shep."

Both men rose as the young women left the room—Franklin Mills was punctilious in all the niceties of good manners—but before resuming his seat he closed the door. There was something ominous in this, and Shepherd nervously lighted a cigarette. He covertly glanced at his watch to fix in his mind the amount of time he must remain with his father before Constance returned. He loved and admired his wife and he envied her the ease with which she ignored or surmounted difficulties.

Connie made mistakes in dealing with her father-in-law and Shepherd was aware of this, but his own errors in this respect only served to strengthen his reliance on the understanding and sympathy of his wife, who was an adept in concealing disappointment and discomfiture. When Shepherd was disposed to complain of his father, Connie was always consoling. She would say:

"You're altogether too sensitive, Shep. It's an old trick of fathers to treat their sons as though they were still boys. Your father can't realize that you're grown up. But he knows you stick to your job and that you're anxious to please him. I suppose he thought you'd grow up to be just like himself; but you're not, so it's up to him to take you as the pretty fine boy you are. You're the steadiest young man in town and you needn't think he doesn't appreciate that."

Shepherd, fortifying himself with a swift recollection of his wife's frequent reassurances of this sort, nevertheless wished that she had not run off to gossip with Leila. However, the interview would be brief, and he played with his cigarette while he waited for his father to begin.

"There's something I've wanted to talk with you about, Shep. It will take only a minute."

"Yes, father."

"It's about Leila"—he hesitated—"a little bit about Constance, too. I'm not altogether easy about Leila. I mean"—he paused again—"as to Connie's influence over your sister. Connie is enough older to realize that Leila needs a little curbing as to things I can't talk to her about as a woman could. Leila doesn't need to be encouraged in extravagance. And she likes running about well enough without being led into things she might better let alone. I'm not criticizing Connie's friends, but you do have at your house people I'd rather Leila didn't know—at least not to be intimate with them. As a concrete example, I don't care for this fellow Thomas. To be frank, I've made some inquiries about him and he's hardly the sort of person you'd care for your sister to run around with."

Shepherd, blinking under this succession of direct statements, felt that some comment was required.

"Of course, father, Connie wouldn't take up anyone she didn't think perfectly all right. And she'd never put any undesirable acquaintances in Leila's way. She's too fond of Leila and too deeply interested in her happiness for that."

"I wasn't intimating that Connie was consciously influencing Leila in a wrong way in that particular instance. But Leila is very impressionable. So far I've been able to eliminate young men I haven't liked. I'm merely asking your cooperation, and Connie's, in protecting her. She's very headstrong and rather disposed to take advantage of our position by running a little wild. Our friends no doubt make allowances, but people outside our circle may not be so tolerant."

"Yes, that's all perfectly true, father," Shepherd assented, relieved and not a little pleased that his father appeared to be criticizing him less than asking his assistance.

"For another thing," Mills went on. "Leila has somehow got into the habit of drinking. Several times I've seen her when she'd had too much. That sort of thing won't do!"

"Of course not! But I'm sure Connie hasn't been encouraging Leila to drink. She and I both have talked to her about that. I hoped she'd stop it before you found it out."

"Don't ever get the idea that I don't know what's going on!" Mills retorted tartly. "Another thing I want to speak of is Connie's way of getting Leila to back her schemes—things like that summer place, for example. We don't need a summer place. The idea that you can't have a proper vacation is all rubbish. I urged you all summer to take Connie East for a month."

"I know you did. It was my own fault I didn't go. Please don't think we're complaining; Connie and I get a lot of fun just motoring. And when you're at the farm we enjoy running out there. I think, Father, that sometimes you're not—not—quite just to Connie."

"Not just to her!" exclaimed Mills, with a lifting of the brows. "In what way have I been unjust to her?"

Shepherd knew that his remark was unfortunate before it was out of his mouth. He should have followed his habit of assenting to what his father said without broadening the field of discussion. He was taken aback by his father's question, uttered with what was, for Franklin Mills, an unusual display of asperity.

"I only meant," Shepherd replied hastily, "that you don't always"—he frowned—"you don't quite give Connie credit for her fine qualities."

"Quite the contrary," Mills replied. "My only concern as her father-in-law is that she shall continue to display those qualities. I realize that she's a popular young woman, but in a way you pay for that, and I stand for it and make it possible for you to spend the money. Now don't jump to the conclusion that I'm intimating that you and Connie wouldn't have just as many friends if you spent a tenth of what you're spending now. Be it far from me, my boy, to discredit your value and Connie's as social factors!"

Mills laughed to relieve the remark of any suspicion of irony. There was nothing Shepherd dreaded so much as his father's ironies. The dread was the greater because there was always a disturbing uncertainty as to what they concealed.

"About those little matters I mentioned," Mills went on, "I count on you to help."

"Certainly, father. Connie and I both will do all we can. I'm glad you spoke to me about it."

"All right, Shep," and Mills opened the door to mark the end of the interview.

IV

In Leila's room Constance had said, the moment they were alone:

"Well, you certainly gummed it!"

"Oh, shoot! Dada wouldn't buy that Nelson place if it only cost a nickel."

"Well, you didn't do much to advance the cause!"

"See here," said Leila, "one time's just as good as another with Dada. I knew he'd never agree to it. I only spoke of it because you gave me the lead. You never seem to learn his curves."

"If you'd backed me up right we could have got him interested and won him over. Anybody could see that he was away off tonight—even more difficult than usual!"

"Oh, tush! You and Shep make me tired. You take father too seriously. All you've got to do with him is just to kid him along. Let's have a little drink to drown our troubles."

"Now, Leila——"

Leila had drawn a hat-box from the inner recesses of a closet and extracted from it a quart bottle of whiskey.

"I'm all shot to hell and need a spoonful of this stuff to pep me up! Hands off, old thing! Don't touch—Leila scream!" Constance had tried to seize the bottle.

"Leila, *please* don't drink! The Claytons are having everybody of any consequence at this party and if you go reeking of liquor all the old tabbies will babble!"

"Well, darling, let them talk! At least they will talk about both of us then!"

"Who's talking about me?" Constance demanded.

"Be calm, dearest! You certainly wore the guilty look then. Let's call it quits —I've got to dress!"

She poured herself a second drink and restored the bottle to its hiding place.

CHAPTER SIX

I

Several interviews with Freeman had resulted in an arrangement by which Bruce was to enter the architect's office immediately. As Henderson had predicted, Mrs. Freeman was a real power in her husband's affairs. She confided to Bruce privately that, with all his talents, Bill lacked tact in dealing with his clients and he needed someone to supply this deficiency. And the office was a place of confusion, and Bill was prone to forgetfulness. Bruce, Mrs. Freeman thought, could be of material assistance in keeping Bill straight and extricating him from the difficulties into which he constantly stumbled in his absorption in the purely artistic side of his profession. Bruce was put to work on tentative sketches and estimates for a residence for a man who had no very clear idea of what he wanted nor how much he wanted to spend.

Bruce soon discovered that Freeman disliked interviews with contractors and the general routine necessary to keep in touch with the cost of labor and materials. When he was able to visualize and create he was happy, but tedious calculations left him sulky and disinclined to work. Bruce felt no such repugnance; he had a kind of instinct for such things, and was able to carry in his head a great array of facts and figures.

On his first free evening after meeting Millicent Harden at the Country Club he rang the Harden doorbell, and as he waited glanced toward the Mills' house in the lot adjoining. He vaguely wondered whether Franklin Mills was within its walls.

He had tried to analyze the emotions that had beset him that night when he had taken the hand of the man he believed to be his father. There was something cheap and vulgar in the idea that blood speaks to blood and that possibly Mills had recognized him by some sort of intuition. But Bruce rejected this as preposterous, a concession to the philosophy of ignorant old women muttering scandal before a dying fire. Very likely he had been wrong in fancying that Mills had taken any special note of him. And there was always his mother's assurance that Mills didn't know of his existence. Mills probably had the habit of eyeing people closely; he shouldn't have permitted himself to be troubled by that. He was a man of large affairs, with faculties trained to the quick inspection and appraisment of every stranger he met....

The middle-aged woman who opened the door was evidently a member of the household and he hastily thrust into his pocket the card he had taken out, stated his name and asked if Miss Harden was at home.

"Yes, Millie's home. Just come in, Mr. Storrs, and I'll call her."

But Millicent came into the hall without waiting to be summoned.

"I'm so glad to see you, Mr. Storrs!" she said, and introduced him to her mother, a tall, heavily built woman with reddish hair turning gray, and a friendly countenance.

"I was just saying to Doctor Harden that I guessed nobody was coming in tonight when you rang. You simply can't keep a servant in to answer the bell in the evening. You haven't met Doctor Harden? Millie, won't you call your papa?"

Millicent opened a door that revealed a small, cozy sitting-room and summoned her father—a short, thick-set man with a close-trimmed gray beard, who came out clutching a newspaper.

"Shan't we all go into the library?" asked Millicent after the two men had been introduced and had expressed their approval of the prolonged fine weather.

"You young folks make yourselves comfortable in the library," said Mrs. Harden. "I told Millie it was too warm for a fire, but she just has to have the fireplace going when there's any excuse, and this house does get chilly in the fall evenings even when it's warm outside."

Harden was already retreating toward the room from which he had been drawn to meet the caller, and his wife immediately followed. Both repeated their expressions of pleasure at meeting Bruce; but presumably, in the accepted fashion of American parents when their daughters entertain callers, they had no intention of appearing again.

Millicent snapped on lights that disclosed a long, high-ceilinged room finished in dark oak and fitted up as a library. A disintegrating log in the broad fireplace had thrown out a puff of smoke that gave the air a fleeting pungent scent.

The flooring was of white and black tiles covered with oriental rugs in which the dominant dark red brought a warmth to the eye. Midway of the room stood a grand piano, and beyond it a spiral stair led to a small balcony on which the console of an organ was visible. Back of this was a stained glass window depicting a knight in armor—a challenging, militant figure. Even as revealed only by the inner illumination, its rich colors and vigorous draughtsmanship were clearly suggested. And it was wholly appropriate, Bruce decided, and altogether consonant with the general scheme of the room. Noting his interest, Millicent turned a switch that lighted the window from a room beyond with the effect of vitalizing the knight's figure, making him seem indeed to be gravely riding, with lance in rest, along the wall.

"Do pardon me!" Bruce murmured, standing just inside the door and glancing about with frank enjoyment of the room's spaciousness. The outer lines of the somewhat commonplace square brick house had not prepared him for this. The room presented a mingling of periods in both architecture and furnishing, but the blending had been admirably done.

"Forgive me for staring," he said as he sat down on a divan opposite her with the hearth between them. "I'm not sure even yet that I'm in the twentieth century!"

"I suppose it is a queer jumble; but don't blame the architect! He, poor wretch, thought we were perfectly crazy when we started, but I think before he got through he really liked it."

"I envy him the fun he had doing it! But someone must have furnished the inspiration. I'm going to assume that it was mostly you."

"You may if you'll go ahead and criticize—tear it all to pieces."

"I'd as soon think of criticizing Chartres, Notre Dame, or the hand that rounded Peter's dome!" Bruce exclaimed. "Alas that our acquaintance is so brief! I want to ask you all manner of questions—how you came to do it— and all that."

"Well, first of all one must have an indulgent father and mother. I'm reminded occasionally that my little whims were expensive."

"I dare say they were! But it's something to have a daughter who can produce a room like this."

He rose and bowed to her, and then turning toward the knight in the window, gravely saluted.

"I'm not so sure," he said as he sat down, "that the gentleman up there didn't have something to do with it."

"Please don't make too much of him. Everyone pays me the compliment of thinking him Galahad, but I think of him as the naughty Launcelot. I read a book once on old French glass and I just had to have a window. And the organ made this room the logical place for it. Papa calls this my chapel and refuses to sit in it at all. He says it's too much like church!"

"Ah! But that's a tribute in itself! Your father realizes that this is a place for worship—without reference to the knight."

She laid her forefinger against her cheek, tilted her head slightly, mocking him with lips and eyes.

"Let me think! That was a pretty speech, but of course you're referring to that bronze Buddha over there. Come to think of it, papa does rather fancy him."

When she smilingly met his gaze he laughed and made a gesture of despair.

"That was a nice bit of side-stepping! I'm properly rebuked. I see my own worshiping must be done with caution. But the room is beautiful. I'm glad to know there's such a place in town."

"I did have a good time planning and arranging it. But there's nothing remarkable about it after all. It's merely what you might call a refuge from reality—if that means anything."

"It means a lot—too much for me to grasp all at once."

"You're making fun of me! All I meant was that I wanted a place to escape into where I can play at being something I really am not. We all need to do that. After all, it's just a room."

"Of course that's just what it isn't! It's superb. I've already decided to spend a lot of time here."

"You may, if you won't pick up little chance phrases I let fall and frighten me with them. I have a friend—an awful highbrow—and he bores me to death exclaiming over things I say and can't explain and then explaining them to me. But—why aren't you at the Claytons' party?"

"I wasn't asked," he said. "I don't know them."

"I know them, but I wasn't asked," she replied smilingly.

"Well, anyhow, it's nicer here, I think."

Bruce remembered what Henderson had said about the guarded social acceptance of the patent medicine manufacturer and his family; but Millicent evidently didn't resent her exclusion from the Claytons' party. Social differentiations, Bruce imagined, mattered little to this girl, who was capable of fashioning her own manner of life, even to the point of building a temple for herself in which to worship gods of her own choosing. When he expressed interest in her modeling, which Dale Freeman had praised, Millicent led the way to a door opening into an extension of the library beyond the knight's window, that served her as a studio. It was only a way of amusing herself, she said, when he admired a plaque of a child's profile she confessed to be her work. The studio bore traces of recent use. Damp cloths covered several unfinished figures. There was a drawing-board in one corner and scattered among the casts on the wall were crayon sketches, merely notes, she explained, tacked up to preserve her impressions of faces that had interested her.

He was struck by her freedom from pretense; when he touched on something of which she was ignorant or about which she was indifferent, she did not scruple to say so. Her imaginative, poetical side expressed itself with healthy candor and frequent flashes of girlish enthusiasm. She was wholly natural, refreshingly spontaneous in speech, with no traces of pedantry or conceit even in discussing music, in which her training had gone beyond the usual amateur's bounds.

"You haven't been to see Leila yet? She asked you to call, and if you don't go she'll think it's because of that little unpleasantness on the river. Leila's altogether worth while."

Bruce muttered something about having been very busy. He had determined never to enter Franklin Mills's house, and he was embarrassed by Millicent's intimation that Leila might take it amiss that he ignored her invitation.

"Leila's a real person," Millicent was saying. "Her great trouble is in trying to adjust herself to a way of life that doesn't suit her a little bit."

"You mean——" he began and paused because he didn't know at all what she meant.

"I mean that living in a big house and going to teas and upholding the dignity of a prominent and wealthy family bores her to distraction. Her chief trouble is her way of protesting against the kind of life she's born to. It's screamingly funny, but Leila just hates being rich, and she's terribly bored at having so much expected of her as her father's daughter."

"His standard, then, is so high?" Bruce ventured, curious as to what further she might say of her neighbor.

"Oh, Mr. Mills is an interesting man, and he worships Leila; but she worries and puzzles him. It isn't just the difference between age and youth——" She paused, conscious perhaps of the impropriety of discussing her neighbor with a comparative stranger, but Bruce's gravely attentive face prompted her to go on. "He's one of those people we meet sometimes who don't seem—how can one put it?—they don't seem quite at ease in the world."

"Yes," he said slowly, "but—where all the conditions of happiness are given —money, position, leisure to do as you please—what excuse has anyone for not finding happiness? You'd conclude that there was some fundamental defect——"

"And when you reach that conclusion you're not a bit better off!" she interrupted. "You're back where you started. Oh, well!" she said, satisfied now that she had said quite enough about her neighbor and regretting that she had mentioned him at all, "it's too bad happiness can't be bought as you buy records to play on a machine and have nothing to do but wind it up and listen. You have to do a little work yourself."

"We've all got to play in the band—that's the idea!" he laughed, and to escape from the thought of Mills, asked her whether she ever played for an ignorant heathen like himself.

"You're probably a stern critic," she replied, "but I'll take a chance. If you don't mind I'll try the organ. Papa and Mamma always like me to play some old pieces for them before they go to bed. Afterwards I'll do some other things."

In a moment she was in the balcony with the knight towering above her, but he faded into the shadows as she turned off the lights in the studio below. Bruce's eyes at once became attentive to her golden head and clearly limned profile defined by the lamp over the music rack. She seemed suddenly infinitely remote, caught away into a world of legendary and elusive things. The first reedy notes of the organ stole eerily through the room as though they too were evoked from an unseen world.

The first things she played were a concession to her parents' taste, but she threw into them all the sentiment they demanded—the familiar airs of "Annie Laurie," "Ben Bolt," and "Auld Lang Syne." She played them without flourishes, probably in deference to the preferences of the father and mother who were somewhere listening. To these she added old revival songs—"Beulah Land," and "Pull for the Shore"—these also presumably favorites of the unseen auditors. He watched her aureoled head, the graceful movement of her arms and shoulders as she gave herself to her task with complete absorption. She was kind to these parents of hers; possibly it was through her music that she really communicated with them, met them on ground of their simpler knowledge and aspirations.

He was conscious presently of the faint ring of a bell, followed by the murmur of voices in the hall. Someone entered the room and sat down quietly behind him. Millicent, who had paid no heed to him since mounting to the organ, was just beginning the Tannhäuser overture. She followed this with passages from Lohengrin and Parsifal and classical liturgical music touched with a haunting mystery....

She came down slowly into the room as though the spell of the music still held her.

"I shan't say anything—it might be the wrong word," he said as he went to meet her. "But it was beautiful—very beautiful!"

"You were a good listener; I felt that," she replied.

He had forgotten that there had been another listener until she smilingly waved her hand to someone behind him.

"So I had two victims—and didn't know it! Patient sufferers! Mr. Mills, you and Mr. Storrs have met—I needn't introduce you a second time."

It was Franklin Mills, then, exercising a neighbor's privilege, who had arrived in the middle of the recital and taken a seat by the door.

"Mr. Storrs is a perfect listener," Mills was saying as he shook hands with Bruce. "He didn't budge all the time you were playing."

Mills's easy, gracious manners, the intimacy implied in his chaffing tone as he complained that she played better when she didn't know he was in the house, irritated Bruce. He had been enjoying himself so keenly, the girl's talk had so interested him and he had been so thrilled and lifted by her music that Mills's appearance was like a profanation.

They were all seated now, and Millicent spoke of a book Mills had sent her which it happened Bruce had read, and she asked his opinion of it before expressing her own. Very likely Mills was in the habit of sending her books. She said that she hadn't cared greatly for the book—a novel that discussed the labor question. The author evidently had no solution of his own problem and left the reader in the air as to his purpose.

"Maybe he only meant to arouse interest—stir people up and leave the solution to others," Bruce suggested.

"That was the way I took it," said Mills. "The fact is, nobody has any solution short of a complete tearing down of everything. And that," he added with a smile and a shrug, "would be very uncomfortable."

"For us—yes," Millicent replied quickly. "But a good many of our millions would probably welcome a chance to begin over again."

"What with," Mills demanded, "when everything had been smashed?"

"Oh, they'd be sure to save something out of the wreck!" Millicent replied.

"Well," Mills remarked, "I'm hoping the smash won't come in my day. I'm too old to go out with a club to fight for food against the mob."

"You want us to say that you're *not* too old," laughed Millicent; "but we're not going to fall into that trap!"

"But—what *is* going to happen?" asked Bruce.

"Other civilizations!" Mills replied, regarding the young man with an intent look. "We've had a succession of them, and the world's about due to slip back into chaos and perhaps emerge again. It's only the barbarians who never change; they know they'll be on top again if they just wait."

"What an optimist you are!" cried Millicent. "But you don't really believe such things."

"Of course I do," Mills answered with a broad smile.

She made it necessary for Bruce to assist her in combating Mills's hopeless view of the future, though she bore the main burden of the opposition herself. Mills's manner was one of good-natured indulgence; but Bruce was wondering whether there was not a deep vein of cynicism in the man. Mills was clever at fencing, and some of the things he said lightly no doubt expressed real convictions.

Bruce was about to take his leave when Mills with assumed petulance declared that the fire had been neglected and began poking the embers. Carefully putting the poker and tongs back in the rack, he lounged toward the door, paused halfway and said good-night formally, bowing first to one and then the other.

"Come in again sometime!" Millicent called after him.

"Is that impudence?" Mills replied, reappearing from the hall with his coat and hat. In a moment the door closed and they heard the sound of his stick on the walk outside.

"He's always like that," Millicent remarked after a moment of silence. "It's understood that he may come in when I'm playing and leave when he pleases. Sometimes when I'm at the organ he sits for an hour without my knowing he's here. It made me nervous at first—just remembering that he *might* be here; but I got over that when I found that he really enjoyed the playing. I'm sorry he didn't stay longer and really talk; he wasn't at his best tonight."

Bruce made the merest murmur of assent, but something in Mills's quizzical, mocking tone, the very manner of his entrance into the house, affected him disagreeably.

He realized that he was staying too long for a first call, but he lingered until they had regained the cheery note with which the evening began, and said good night.

<h1 style="text-align:center">II</h1>

When he reached the street Bruce decided to walk the mile that lay between the Hardens' and his apartment. His second meeting with Franklin Mills had left his mind in tumult. He was again beset by an impulse to flee from the town, but this he fought and vanquished.

Happiness and peace were not to be won by flight. In his soldiering he had never feared bodily injury, and at times when he had speculated as to the existence of a soul he had decided that if he possessed such a thing he would not suffer it to play the coward. But this unexpected meeting at the Hardens', which was likely to be repeated if he continued his visits to the house, had shaken his nerve more than he liked to believe possible. Millicent evidently admired Mills, sympathized with him in his loneliness, was flattered perhaps by his visits to her home in search of solace and cheer, or whatever it was Mills sought.

The sky was overcast and a keen autumn wind whipped the overhanging maples as Bruce strode homeward with head bent, his hands thrust deep into the pockets of his overcoat. He hummed and whistled phrases of the Parsifal, with his thoughts playing about Millicent's head as she had sat at the organ with the knight keeping watch above her. After all, it was through beautiful things, man-made and God-made, as his mother had taught him, that life found its highest realizations. In this idea there was an infinite stimulus. Millicent had found for herself this clue to happiness and was a radiant proof of its efficacy. It had been a privilege to see her in her own house, to enjoy contact with her questioning, meditative mind, and to lose himself in her entrancing music.

The street was deserted and only a few of the houses he passed showed lights. Bruce experienced again, as often in his night tramps during the year of his exile, a happy sense of isolation. He was so completely absorbed in his thoughts that he was unaware of the propinquity of another pedestrian who was slowly approaching as though as unheedful as he of the driving wind and the first fitful patter of rain. They passed so close that their arms touched. Both turned, staring blankly in the light of the street lamps, and muttered confused apologies.

"Oh, Storrs!" Franklin Mills exclaimed, bending his head against the wind.

"Sorry to have bumped into you, sir," Bruce replied, and feeling that nothing more was required of him, he was about to go on, but Mills said quickly:

"We're in for a hard rain. Come back to my house—it's only half a dozen blocks—and I'll send you home."

There was something of kindly peremptoriness in his tone, and Bruce, at a loss for words with which to refuse, followed, thinking that he would walk a block to meet the demands of courtesy and turn back. Mills, forging ahead rapidly, complained good-naturedly of the weather.

"I frequently prowl around at night," he explained; "I sleep better afterwards."

"I like a night walk myself," Bruce replied.

"Not afraid of hold-ups? I was relieved to find it was you I ran into. My daughter says I'm bound to get sandbagged some night."

At the end of the first block both were obliged to battle against the wind, which now drove the rain in furious gusts through the intersecting streets. In grasping his hat, Mills dropped his stick, and after picking it up, Bruce took hold of his arm for their greater ease in keeping together. It would, he decided, be an ungenerous desertion to leave him now, and so they arrived after much buffeting at Mills's door.

"That's a young hurricane," said Mills as he let himself in. "When you've dried out a bit I'll send you on in my car."

In response to his ring a manservant appeared and carried away their hats and overcoats to be dried. Mills at once led the way upstairs to the library, where a fire had been kindled, probably against the master's return in the storm.

"Sit close and put your feet to the blaze. I think a hot drink would be a help."

Hot water and Scotch were brought and Mills laughingly assured Bruce that he needn't be afraid of the liquor.

"I had it long before Prohibition. Of course, everybody has to say that!"

In his wildest speculations as to possible meetings with his father, Bruce had imagined nothing like this. He was not only in Franklin Mills's house, but the man was graciously ministering to his comfort. And Bruce, with every desire to resist, to refuse these courteous offices, was meekly submitting. Mills, talking easily, with legs stretched to the fire, sipped his drink contentedly while the storm beat with mounting fury round the house.

"I think my son said you had been in the army; I should say that the experience hadn't done you any harm," Mills remarked in his pleasant voice.

"Quite the contrary, sir. The knocking about I got did me good."

"I envy you young fellows the experience; it was a ghastly business, but it must mean a lot in a man's life to have gone through it."

In response to a direct question Bruce stated concisely the nature of his service. His colorless recital of the bare record brought a smile to Mills's face.

"You're like all the young fellows I've talked with—modest, even a little indifferent about it. I think if I'd been over there I should do some bragging!"

Still bewildered to find himself at Mills's fireside, Bruce was wondering how soon he could leave; but Mills talked on in leisurely fashion of the phenomenal growth of the town and the opportunities it offered to young men. Bruce was ashamed of himself for not being more responsive; but Mills seemed content to ramble on, though carefully attentive to the occasional remarks Bruce roused himself to make. Bruce, with ample opportunity, observed Mills's ways—little tricks of speech, the manner in which he smoked—lazily blowing rings at intervals and watching them waver and break—an occasional quick lifting of his well-kept hand to his forehead.

It was after they had been together for half an hour that Bruce noted that Mills, after meeting his gaze, would lift his eyes and look intently at something on the wall over the bookcases—something immediately behind Bruce and out of the range of his vision. It seemed not to be the unseeing stare of inattention; but whatever it was, it brought a look of deepening perplexity—almost of alarm—to Mills's face. Bruce began to find this upward glance disconcerting, and evidently aware that his visitor was conscious of it, Mills got up and, with the pretence of offering his guest another cigarette, reseated himself in a different position.

"I must run along," said Bruce presently. "The storm is letting up. I can easily foot it home."

"Not at all! After keeping you till midnight I'll certainly not send you out to get another wetting. There's still quite a splash on the windows."

He rang for the car before going downstairs, and while he was waiting for the chauffeur to answer on the garage extension of the house telephone, Bruce, from the fireplace, saw that it must have been a portrait—one of a number ranged along the wall—that had invited Mills's gaze so frequently. It was the portrait of a young man, the work of a painstaking if not a brilliant artist. The clean-shaven face, the long, thick, curly brown hair, and the flowing scarf knotted under a high turn-over collar combined in an effect of quaintness.

There was something oddly familiar in the young man's countenance. In the few seconds that Mills's back was turned Bruce found himself studying it, wondering what there was about it that teased his memory—what other brow and eyes and clean-cut, firm mouth he had ever seen were like those of the young man who was looking down at him from Franklin Mills's wall. And then it dawned upon him that the face was like his own—might, indeed, with a different arrangement of the hair, a softening of certain lines, pass for a portrait of himself.

Mills, turning from the telephone, remarked that the car was on the way.

"Ah!" he added quickly, seeing Bruce's attention fixed on the portrait, "my father, at about thirty-five. There's nothing of me there; I take after my mother's side of the house. Father was taller than I and his features were cleaner cut. He died twenty years ago. I've always thought him a fine American type. Those other——"

Bruce lent polite attention to Mills's comments on the other portraits, one representing his maternal grandfather and another a great-uncle who had been killed in the Civil War. When they reached the lower floor Mills opened the door of a reception room and turned on the frame lights about a full-length portrait of a lady in evening dress.

"That is Mrs. Mills," he said, "and an excellent likeness."

He spoke in sophisticated terms of American portraiture as they went to the hall where the servant was waiting with Bruce's hat and coat. A limousine was in the porte-cochère, and Mills stood on the steps until Bruce got in.

"I thank you very much, Mr. Mills," Bruce said, taking the hand Mills extended.

"Oh, I owe you the thanks! I hope to see you again very soon!"

Mills on his way to his room found himself clinging to the stair rail. When he had closed the door he drew his hand slowly across his eyes. He had spoken with Marian Storrs's son and the young man by an irony of nature had the countenance, the high-bred air of Franklin Mills III. It was astounding, this skipping for a generation of a type! It seemed to Mills, after he had turned off the lights, that his father's eyes—the eyes of young Storrs—were still fixed upon him with a disconcerting gravity.

CHAPTER SEVEN

I

In the fortnight following his encounter with Mills at the Hardens', and the later meeting that same night in the storm, Bruce had thrown himself with fierce determination into his work. There must be no repetitions of such meetings; they added to his self-consciousness, made him ill at ease even when walking the streets in which at a turn of any corner he might run into Mills.

He had never known that he had a nerve in his body, but now he was aware of disturbing sensations, inability to concentrate on his work, even a tremor of the hands as he bent over his drawing-board. His abrupt change from the open road to an office in some measure accounted for this and he began going to a public golf links on Saturday afternoons and Sundays, and against the coming of winter he had his name proposed for membership in an athletic club.

He avoided going anywhere that might bring him again in contact with the man he believed to be his father. Shepherd Mills he ran into at the University Club now and then, and he was not a little ashamed of himself for repelling the young man's friendly overtures. Shepherd, evidently feeling that he must in some way explain his silence about the clubhouse, for which Bruce had made tentative sketches, spoke of the scheme one day as a matter he was obliged to defer for the present.

"It's a little late in the season to begin; and father's doubtful about it—thinks it might cause feeling among the men in other concerns. I hadn't thought of that aspect of the matter——"

Shepherd paused and frowned as he waited for Bruce to offer some comment on the abandonment of the project. It was none of Bruce's affair, but he surmised that the young man had been keenly disappointed by his father's refusal.

"Oh, well, it doesn't matter!" Bruce remarked as though it were merely a professional matter of no great importance. But as he left Shepherd he thought intently about the relations of the father and son. They were utterly irreconcilable natures. Having met Franklin Mills, sat at his fireside, noted with full understanding the man's enjoyment of ease and luxury, it was not difficult to understand his lack of sympathy with Shepherd's radical tendencies. Piecing together what he had heard about Mills from Henderson and Millicent Harden with his own estimate, Bruce was confident that whatever else Franklin Mills might be he was no altruist.

After he left Shepherd Bruce was sorry that he had been so brusque. He might at least have expressed his sympathy with the young man's wish to do something to promote the happiness of his workmen. The vitality so evident in Franklin Mills's vigorous figure, and his perfect poise, made Shepherd appear almost ridiculous in contrast.

Bruce noted that the other young men about the club did not treat Shepherd quite as one of themselves. When Shepherd sat at the big round table in the grill he would listen to the ironic give and take of the others with a pathetic eagerness to share in their good fellowship, but unable to make himself quite one of them. This might have been due, Bruce thought, to the anxiety of Shepherd's contemporaries—young fellows he had grown up with—to show their indifference to the fact that he was the son of the richest man in town. Or they felt, perhaps, that Shepherd was not equal to his opportunities. Clearly, however, no one ever had occasion to refer to Shepherd Mills as the typical young scion of a wealthy family whose evil ways were bound to land him in the poorhouse or the gutter.

In other circumstances Bruce would have felt moved to make a friend of Shepherd, but the fact that they were of the same blood haunted him like a nightmare.

II

As the days went by, Bruce fell prey to a mood common to sensitive men in which he craved talk with a woman—a woman of understanding. It was Saturday and the office closed at noon. He would ask Millicent to share his freedom in a drive into the country; and without giving himself time to debate the matter, he made haste to call her on the telephone.

Her voice responded cheerily. Leila had just broken an engagement with her for golf and wouldn't he play? When he explained that he wasn't a member of a club and the best he could do for her would be to take her to a public course, she declared that he must be her guest. The point was too trivial for discussion; the sooner they started the better, and so two o'clock found them both with a good initial drive on the Faraway course.

"Long drives mean long talks," she said. "We begin at least with the respect of our caddies. You'll never guess what I was doing when you called up!"

"At the organ, or in the studio putting a nose on somebody?"

"Wrong! I was planting tulip bulbs. This was a day when I couldn't have played a note or touched clay to save my life. Ever have such fits?"

"I certainly do," replied Bruce.

Each time he saw her she was a little different—today he was finding her different indeed from the girl who had played for him, and yet not the girl of his adventure on the river or the Millicent he had met at the Country Club party. There was a charm in her variableness, perhaps because of her habitual sincerity and instinctive kindness. He waited for her to putt and rolled his own ball into the cup.

"Sometimes I see things black; and then again there *does* appear to be blue sky," he said.

"Yes; but that's not a serious symptom. If we didn't have those little mental experiences we wouldn't be interesting to ourselves!"

"Great Scott! *Must* we be interesting to ourselves?"

"Absolutely!"

"But when I'm down in the mouth I don't care whether I'm interesting or not!"

"Nothing in it! Life's full of things to do—you know that! I believe you're just trying to psychoanalyze me!"

"I swear I'm not! I was in the depths this morning; that's why I called you up!"

"Now——" She carefully measured a short approach and played it neatly. "Oh, you didn't want to see me socially, so to speak; you just wanted someone to tell your troubles to! Is that a back-handed compliment?"

"Rather a confession—do you hate it?"

"No—I rather like that."

With an artistic eye she watched him drive a long low ball with his brassie. His tall figure, the free play of arms and shoulders, his boyish smile when she praised the shot, contributed to a new impression of him. He appeared younger than the night he called on her, when she had thought him diffident, old-fashioned and stiffly formal.

As they walked over the turf with a misty drizzle wetting their faces fitfully it seemed to both that their acquaintance had just begun. When he asked if she didn't want to quit she protested that she was dressed for any weather. It was unnecessary to accommodate himself to her in any way; she walked as rapidly as he; when she sliced her ball into the rough she bade him not follow her, and when she had gotten into the course again she ran to join him, as though eager not to break the thread of their talk. The thing she was doing at a given moment was, he judged, the one thing in the world that interested her. The wind rose presently and blew the mist away and there was promise of a clearing sky.

"You've brought the sun back!" he exclaimed. "Something told me you had influence with the weather."

"I haven't invoked any of my gods today; so it's just happened."

"Your gods! You speak as though you had a list!"

"Good gracious! You promised me once not to pick me up and make me explain myself."

"Then I apologize. I can see that it isn't fair to make a goddess explain her own divinity."

"Oh-o-o-o," she mocked him. "You get zero for that!"

She was walking along with her hands thrust into the pockets of her sweater, the brim of her small sport hat turned up above her face.

"But seriously," she went on, "out of doors is the best place to think of God. The churches make religion seem so complicated. We can't believe in a God we can't imagine. Where there's sky and grass it's all so much simpler. The only God I can feel is a spirit hovering all about, watching and loving us—the God of the Blue Horizons. I can't think of Him as a being whose name must be whispered as children whisper of terrifying things in the dark."

"The God of the Blue Horizons?" He repeated the phrase slowly. "Yes; the world has had its day of fear—anything that lifts our eyes to the blue sky is good—really gives us, I suppose, a sense of the reality of God...."

They had encountered few other players, but a foursome was now approaching them where the lines of the course paralleled.

"Constance Mills and George Whitford; I don't know the others," said Millicent.

Mrs. Mills waved her hand and started toward them, looking very fit in a smart sport suit. Idly twirling her driver, she had hardly the air of a zealous golfer.

"Ah!" she exclaimed. "Aren't we the brave ones? Scotch blood! Not afraid of a little moisture. Mr. Storrs! I know now why you've never been to see me—you're better occupied. It's dreadful to be an old married woman. You see what happens, Millicent! I warn you solemnly against marriage. Yes, George—I'm coming. Nice to meet you, even by chance, Mr. Storrs. By-by, Millie."

"You've displeased her ladyship," Millicent remarked. "You ought to go to see her."

"I haven't felt strongly moved," Bruce replied.

"She doesn't like being ignored. Of course nobody does, but Mrs. Mills demands to be amused."

"Is she being amused now?" Bruce asked.

"I wish Leila could have heard that!"

"Doesn't Leila like her sister-in-law?"

"Yes, of course she does, but Constance is called the most beautiful and the best dressed woman in town and the admiration she gets goes to her head a little bit. George Whitford seems to admire her tremendously. Leila has a sense of humor that sees right through Constance's poses."

"Doesn't Leila pose just a little herself?"

"You might say that she does. Just now she's affecting the fast young person pose; but I think she's about through with it. She's really the finest girl alive, but she kids herself with the idea that she's an awful devil. Her whole crowd are affected by the same bug."

"I rather guessed that," said Bruce. "Let me see—was that five for you?"

III

When they reached the clubhouse Millicent proposed that they go home for the tea which alone could fittingly conclude the afternoon. The moment they entered the Harden hall she lifted her arms dramatically.

"Jumbles!" she cried in a mockery of delight. "Mother has been making jumbles! Come straight to the kitchen!"

In the kitchen they found Mrs. Harden, her ample figure enveloped in a gingham apron of bright yellow checks that seemed to fill the immaculate white kitchen with color. Bruce was a little dismayed by his sudden precipitation into the culinary department of the establishment. Millicent began piling a plate with warm jumbles; a maid appeared and began getting the tea things ready. Mrs. Harden, her face aglow from its recent proximity to the gas range, explained to Bruce that it was the cook's afternoon out and at such times she always liked to cook something just to keep her hand in. She was proud of the kitchen with its white-tiled walls and flooring and glittering utensils. The library and the organ belonged to Millie, she said, but Doctor Harden had given her free swing to satisfy her own craving for an up-to-date kitchen.

Bruce's heart warmed under these revelations of the domestic sanctuary. Mrs. Harden's motherliness seemed to embrace the world and her humor and sturdy common sense were strongly evident. She regaled Bruce with a story of a combat she had lately enjoyed with a plumber. She warned him that if he would succeed as an architect he must be firm with plumbers.

Alone in the living-room with their tea, Millicent and Bruce continued to find much to discuss. She was gay and serious by turns, made him talk of himself, and finding that this evidently was distasteful to him, she led the way back to impersonal things again.

"Why go when there will be dinner here pretty soon?" she asked when he rose.

"Because I want to come back sometime! I want some more jumbles! It's been a great afternoon for me. I do like the atmosphere of this house—kitchen and everything. And the outdoors was fine—and you——"

"I hoped you'd remember I was part of the scenery!"

"I couldn't forget it if I wanted to—and I don't! Do you suppose we could do it all over again—sometime when you're not terribly busy?"

"Oh, I'll try to bear another afternoon with you!"

"Or we might do a theater or a movie?"

"Even that is possible."

He didn't know that she was exerting herself to send him away cheerful. When he said soberly, his hand on the door, "You don't know how much you've helped me," she held up her finger warningly.

"Not so serious! Always cheerful!—that's the watchword!"

"All right! You may have to say that pretty often."

Her light laugh, charged with friendliness, followed him down the steps. She had made him forget himself, lifted him several times to heights he had never known before. He was sorry that he had not asked her further about the faith to which she had confessed, her God of the Blue Horizons. The young women he had known were not given to such utterances,—certainly not while playing very creditable golf! Her phrase added majesty to the universe, made the invisible God intelligible and credible. He felt that he could never again look at the heavens without recalling that phrase of hers. It wakened in him the sense of a need that he had never known before. It was as if she had interpreted some baffling passage in a mysterious book and clarified it. He must see her again; yes, very often he must see her.

But on his way home a dark thought crossed his mind: *"What would Millicent say if she knew?"*

CHAPTER EIGHT

I

Two weeks later Bud Henderson sought Bruce at Freeman's office. Bruce looked up from his desk with a frown that cleared as he recognized his friend. With his cap pushed back on his head and buttoned up in a long ulster, Henderson eyed him stolidly and demanded to know what he was doing.

"Going over some specifications; I might say I'm at work, if you knew what the word means."

"Thanks for the compliment, but it's time to quit," Henderson replied, taking a cigarette from a package on Bruce's desk. "I happen to know your boss is playing handball this moment at the Athletic and he'll never know you've skipped. I haven't liked a certain look in your eye lately. You're sticking too close to your job. Bill is pleased to death with your work, so you haven't a thing to worry about. Get your bonnet and we'll go out and see what we can stir up."

"I'm in a frame of mind to be tempted. But I ought to finish this stuff."

"Don't be silly," replied Bud, who was prowling about the room viewing the framed plans and drawings on the walls, peering into cabinets, unrolling blue prints merely to fling them aside with a groan of disgust.

"My God! It doesn't seem possible that Bill Freeman would put his name to such things!"

"Don't forget this is a *private* office, Mr. Henderson. What's agitating your bean?"

"Thought I'd run you up to the art institute to look at some Finnish work they're showing. Perhaps it's Hottentotish; or maybe it's Eskimo art. We've got to keep in touch with the world art movement." Henderson yawned.

"Try again; I pant for real excitement," said Bruce, who was wondering whether his friend really had noticed signs of his recent worry. Henderson, apparently intent upon a volume of prints of English country houses, swung round as Bruce, in putting on his overcoat, knocked over a chair. He crossed the room and laid his hands on Bruce's broad shoulders.

"I say, old top; this will never do! You're nervous; you're damned nervous. Knocking over chairs—and you with the finest body known in modern times! I watched you the other day eating your lunch all alone at the club—you didn't know I was looking at you. Your expression couldn't be accounted for even by that bum club lunch. Now if it's money——"

"Nothing of the kind, Bud!" Bruce protested. "You'll have me scared in a minute. There's nothing the matter with me. I'm all right; I just have to get readjusted to a new way of living; that's all."

"Well, as you don't thrill to the idea of viewing works of art, I'll tell you what I'm really here for. I'm luring you away to sip tea with a widow!"

"A widow! Where do you get the idea that I'm a consoler of widows?"

"This one doesn't need consoling! Helen Torrence is the name; relict of the late James B. deceased. She's been away ever since you lit in our midst and just got home. About our age and not painful to look at. Jim Torrence was a good fifty when he met her, at White Sulphur or some such seat of opulence, and proudly brought her home for local inspection. The gossips forcibly removed most of her moral character, just on suspicion, you understand—but James B.'s money had a soothing effect and she got one foot inside our social door before he passed hence three years ago and left her the boodle he got from his first wife. Helen's a good scout. It struck me all of a heap about an hour ago that she's just the girl to cheer you up. I was just kidding about the art stuff. I telephoned Helen I was coming, so we're all set."

"Ah! I see through the whole game! You're flirting with the woman and want me for a blind in case Maybelle finds you out."

"Clever! The boy's clever! But—listen—I never try to put anything over on Maybelle. A grand jury hasn't an all-seeinger eye than Mrs. Bud Henderson. Let's beat it!"

On the drive uptown Henderson devoted himself with his usual thoroughness to a recital of the history of Mrs. Torrence. The lady's social status lay somewhere between the old and the new element, Bud explained.

The president of the trust company that administered her affairs belonged to the old crowd—the paralytic or angina pectoris group, as Bud described it, and his wife and daughters just *had* to be nice to Torrence's wife or run a chance of offending her and losing control of the estate. On the other hand her natural gaiety threw her toward the camps of the newer element who were too busy having a good time to indulge in ancestor worship.

Henderson concluded his illuminative exposition of Mrs. Torrence's life history as they reached the house. They were admitted by a colored butler who took their coats and flung open a door that revealed a spacious living-room.

"Helen!" exclaimed Henderson dramatically.

It was possible that Mrs. Torrence had prepared for their entrance by posing in the middle of the room with a view to a first effect, an effect to which her quick little step as she came forward to meet them contributed. Her blue tea gown, parted a little above the ankles, invited inspection of her remarkably small feet adorned with brilliant buckles. She was short with a figure rounded to plumpness and with fluffy brown hair, caught up high as though to create an illusion as to her stature. Her complexion was a clear brilliant pink; her alert small eyes were a greenish blue. Her odd little staccato walk was in keeping with her general air of vivacity. She was all alive, amusingly abrupt, spontaneous, decisive.

"Hello! Bud, the old reliable! Mr. Storrs! Yes; I *had* been hoping for this!"

She gave a hand to each and looked up at Bruce, who towered above her, and nodded as though approving of him.

"This is delightful! A new man! Marvelous!"

As she explained that she had been away since June and was only just home, Bruce became aware that Henderson had passed on and was standing by a tea table indulging in his usual style of raillery with a young woman whose voice even before he looked at her identified her as Constance Mills.

"You know Mrs. Mills? Of course! If you'd only arrived this morning you'd know Connie. Not to know Connie is indeed to be unknown."

Constance extended her hand from the divan on which she was seated behind the tea table—thrust it out lazily with a minimum of effort.

"Oh—the difficult Mr. Storrs! I'm terribly mortified to be meeting you in a friend's house and not in my own!"

"To meet you anywhere——" began Bruce, but she interrupted him, holding him with her eyes.

"——would be a pleasure! Of course! I know the formula, but I'm not a debutante. You didn't like me that night we met at Dale Freeman's, and I was foolish enough to think I'd made an impression!"

"Let's tell him the truth," said Henderson, helping himself to a slice of cinnamon toast. "Bruce, I bet a hundred cigarettes with Connie I could deliver you here and I win!"

"Not a word of truth in that!" declared Constance. "Bud's such a liar!"

Mrs. Torrence said they must have tea, and Henderson protested that tea was not to be thought of. Tea, he declared, was extremely distasteful to him; and Bruce always became ill at the sight of it.

"But when I told Connie you were bringing Mr. Storrs she said he was terribly proper and for me not to dare mention cocktails."

"Now, Helen, I didn't say just that! What I meant, of course, was that I hoped that Mr. Storrs wasn't too proper," said Constance.

"Proper!" Bruce caught her up. "This is an enemy's work. Bud, I suspect you of this dastardly assault on my character!"

"Not guilty!" Bud retorted. "The main thing right now is that we're all peevish and need martinis. What's the Volstead signal, Helen?"

"Three rings, Bud, with a pause between the first and second."

The tea tray was removed and reappeared adorned with all the essentials for the concoction of cocktails. When the glasses were filled and all had expressed their satisfaction at the result, Henderson detained the negro butler for a conference on dice throwing. He seated himself on the floor the better to receive the man's instructions. The others taunted him for his inaptitude. The butler retired finally with five dollars of Bud's money, a result attained only after the spectators were limp with laughter.

"You're a scream, Bud! A perfect scream!" and Mrs. Torrence refilled the glasses.

She took Bud to the dining-room to exhibit a rare Japanese screen acquired in her travels, and Bruce found himself alone with Constance. She pointed to her glass, still brimming, and remarked:

"Please admire my abstemiousness! One is my limit."

"Let me see; did I really have three?" asked Bruce as he sat down beside her.

"I want to forget everything this afternoon," she began. "I feel that I'd like to climb the hills of the unattainable, be someone else for a while."

"Oh, we all have those spells," he replied. "That's why Prohibition's a failure."

"But life is a bore at times," she insisted. "Maybe you're one of the lucky ones who never go clear down. A man has his work—there's always that ____"

"Hasn't woman got herself everything—politics, business, philanthropy? You don't mean to tell me the new woman is already pining for her old slavery! I supposed you led a complete and satisfactory existence!"

"A pretty delusion! I just pretend, that's all. There are days when nothing seems of the slightest use. I thought there might be something in politics, but after I'd gone to a few meetings and served on a committee or two it didn't amuse me any more. I played at being a radical for a while, but after you've scared all your friends a few times with your violence it ceases to be funny. The only real joy I got out of flirting with socialism was in annoying my father-in-law. And I had to give that up for fear he'd think I was infecting Shep with my ideas."

II

A tinge of malice was perceptible in her last words, but she smiled instantly to relieve the embarrassment she detected in his face. He was not sure just how she wanted him to take her. The unhappiness she had spoken of he assumed to be only a pose with her—something to experiment with upon men she met on gray afternoons in comfortable houses over tea and cocktails. Mrs. Shepherd Mills might be amusing, or she might easily become a bore. The night he met her at the Freemans' he had thought her probably guileless under her mask of sophistication. She was proving more interesting than he had imagined, less obvious; perhaps with an element of daring in her blood that might one day get the better of her. She was quite as handsome as he remembered her from the meeting at the Freemans' and she indubitably had mastered the art of dressing herself becomingly.

He was watching the play of the shadow of her picture hat on her face, seeking clues to her mood, vexed that he had permitted himself to be brought into her company, when she said:

"I'm not amusing you! Please forgive me. I can't help it if I'm a little *triste*. Some little devilish imp is dancing through my silly head. If I took a second glass——"

Bruce answered her look of inquiry with a shake of the head.

"Are you asking my advice? I positively refuse to give it; but if you command me, of course——"

He rose, took the glass, and held it high for her inspection.

"The man tempts me——" she said pensively.

"The man doesn't tempt you. We'll say it's the little imp. Mrs. Mills, do you want this cocktail or do you not?"

"It might cheer me up a little. I don't want you to think me stupid; I know I'm terribly dull!"

She drank half the cocktail and bade him finish it.

"Oh, certainly!" he replied and drained the glass. "Now, under the additional stimulus, we can proceed with the discussion. What were we talking about, anyhow?"

"It doesn't matter. Life offers plenty of problems. How many people do you really think are happy—really happy? Now Bud's always cheerful; he and Maybelle are happy—remarkably so, I think. Helen Torrence—well, I hesitate to say whether she's really happy or not; she always appears gay, just as you see her today; and it's something to be able to give the impression, whether it's false or not."

"Yes; it's well to make a front," Bruce replied, determined to keep a frivolous tone with her. "The Freemans enjoy themselves; they're quite ideally mated, I'd say."

"Yes, they're making a success of their lives. Dale and Bill are always cheerful. Now there's dear old Shep——"

"Well, of course he's happy. How could he be otherwise?"

"You're not taking me seriously at all! I'm disappointed. I was terribly blue today; that's why I plotted with Bud to get you here—I shamelessly confess that I want to know you better."

"Come now! You're just kidding!"

"You're incorrigible. I'm that rarest of beings—a frank woman. You refuse to come to my house, presumably because you don't like me, so I have to trap you here."

"How you misjudge me! I haven't been around because I've been busy; I belong to the toiling masses!"

"You have time for Miss Harden; you two seemed ever so chummy on the golf course. Of course, I can't compete with Millie—she's so beautiful and so artistic—so many accomplishments. But you ought to be considerate of a poor thing like me. I'm only sorry I have so little to offer. I really thought you would be a nice playmate; but——"

"A playmate? Aren't we playing now?—at least you are playing with me!"

"Am I?" she asked.

She bent toward him with a slight, an almost imperceptible movement of her shoulders, and her lips parted tremulously in a wistful smile of many connotations. She was not without her charms; she was a very pretty woman; and there was nothing vulgar in her manner of exercising her charms. Bruce touched her hand, gently clasped it—a slender, cool hand. She made no attempt to release it; and it lay lingering and acquiescent in his clasp. He raised it and kissed the finger tips.

"You really understand me; I knew you would," she murmured. "It's terrible to be lonely. And you are so big and strong; you can help me if you will ——"

"I have no right to help you," he said. "It's part of the game in this funny world that we've got to help ourselves."

"But if you knew I needed you——"

"Ah, but you don't!" he replied.

Bud tiptoed in with a tray containing highball materials and placed it on the tea table. He urged them in eloquent pantomime to drink themselves to death and tiptoed out again. Bruce, wondering if he dared leave, hoped the interruption would serve to change the current of his talk with Constance, when she said:

"Shep speaks of you often; he likes you and really Shep's ever so interesting."

"Yes," Bruce answered, "he has ideas and ideals—really thinks about things in a fine way."

He did not care to discuss Shepherd Mills with Shepherd's wife, even when, presumably, she was merely making talk to create an atmosphere of intimacy.

"Shep isn't a cut-up," she went on, "and he doesn't know how to be a good fellow with men of his own age. And he's so shy he's afraid of the older men. And his father—you've met Mr. Mills? Well, Shep doesn't seem able to get close to his father."

"That happens, of course, between fathers and sons," Bruce replied. "Mr. Mills——"

He paused, took a cigarette from his case and put it back. He was by turns perplexed, annoyed, angry and afraid—afraid that he might in some way betray himself.

"Mr. Mills is a curious person," Constance went on. "He seems to me like a man who lives alone in a formal garden with high walls on four sides and has learned to ignore the roar of the world outside—a prisoner who carries the key of his prison-house but can't find the lock!"

Bruce bent his head toward her, intent upon her words. He hadn't thought her capable of anything so imaginative. Some reply was necessary; he would make another effort to get rid of a subject that both repelled and fascinated him.

"I suppose we're all born free; if we find ourselves shut in it's because we've built the walls ourselves."

"How about my prison-house?" she asked. "Do you suppose I can ever escape?"

"Why should you? Don't you like your garden?"

"Not always; no! It's a little stifling sometimes!"

"Then push the walls back a little! It's a good sign, isn't it, when we begin to feel cramped?"

"You're doing a lot better! I begin to feel more hopeful about you. You really could be a great consolation to me if—if you weren't so busy!"

"I really did appreciate your invitation. I'll be around very soon."

After all, he decided, she was only flirting with him; her confidences were only a means of awakening his interest, stirring his sympathy. She had probably never loved Shepherd, but she respected his high-mindedness and really wanted to help him. The depression to which she confessed was only the common ennui of her class and type; she needed occupation, doubtless children would solve her problem to some extent. Her life ran too smooth a course, and life was not meant to be like that....

He was impatient to leave, but Mrs. Torrence and Henderson had started a phonograph and were dancing in the hall. Constance seemed unmindful of the noise they were making.

"Shall we join in that romp?" asked Bruce.

"Thanks, no—if you don't mind! I suppose it's really time to run along. May I fix a drink for you? It's too bad to go away and leave all that whisky!"

The music stopped in the midst of a jazzy saxophone wail and Mrs. Torrence and Henderson were heard noisily greeting several persons who had just come in.

"It's Leila," said Constance, rising and glancing at the clock. "She has no business being here at this time of day."

"Hello, Connie! Got a beau?"

Leila peered into the room, struck her hands together and called over her shoulder:

"Come in, lads! See what's here! Red liquor as I live and breathe! Oh, Mr. What's-your-name——"

"Mr. Storrs," Constance supplied.

"Oh, of course! Mr. Storrs—Mr. Thomas and Mr. Whitford!"

Bruce had heard much of Whitford at the University Club, where he was one of the most popular members. He had won fame as an athlete in college and was a polo player of repute. A cosmopolitan by nature, he had traveled extensively and in the Great War had won honorable distinction. Having inherited money he was able to follow his own bent. It was whispered that he entertained literary ambitions. He was one of the chief luminaries of the Dramatic Club, coached the players and had produced several one-act plays of his own that had the flavor of reality. He was of medium height and looked the soldier and athlete. Women had done much to spoil him, but in spite of his preoccupation with society, men continued to like George, who was a thoroughly good fellow and a clean sportsman.

Whitford entered at once into a colloquy with Constance. Thomas, having expressed his pleasure at meeting Bruce, was explaining to Mrs. Torrence how he and Whitford had met Leila downtown.

"Liar!" exclaimed Leila, who was pouring herself a drink. "You did nothing of the kind. We met at the Burtons' and Nellie gave us a little drink—just a tweeney, stingy little drink."

The drink she held up for purposes of illustration was not infinitesimal. Mrs. Torrence said that everyone must have a highball and proceeded to prepare a drink for Thomas and Whitford.

"You and Connie are certainly the solemn owls," she remarked to Bruce. "Anyone would have thought you were holding a funeral in here. Say when, Fred. This is real Bourbon that Jim had for years. You'll never see anything like it."

"Bruce," cried Henderson, "has Connie filled you with gloom? She gets that way sometimes, but it doesn't mean anything. A little of this stuff will set you up. This bird, Storrs, always did have glass legs," he explained to

Thomas; "he can drink gallons and be ready to converse with bishops. Never saw such a capacity! If I get a few more Maybelle will certainly hand it to me when I get home."

Constance walked round the table to Leila, who had drunk a glass of the Bourbon to sample it and, satisfied of its quality, was now preparing a highball.

"No more, Leila!" said Constance, in a low tone. The girl drew back defiantly.

"Go away, Connie! I need just one more."

"You had more than you needed at the Burtons'. Please, Leila, be sensible. Helen, send the tray away."

"Leila's all right!" said Thomas, but at a sign from Mrs. Torrence he picked up the tray and carried it out.

"I don't think it pretty to treat me as though I were shot when I'm not," said Leila petulantly. She walked to the end of the room and sat down with the injured air of a rebellious child.

"Leila, do you know what time it is?" demanded Constance. "Your father's having a dinner and you've got to be there."

"I'm going to be there! There's loads of time. Everybody sit down and be comfortable!" Leila composedly sipped her glass as though to set an example to the others. Thomas had come back and Constance said a few words to him in a low tone.

"Oh, shucks! I know what you're saying. Connie's telling you to take me home," said Leila. She turned her wrist to look at her watch—frowned in the effort of focusing upon it and added with a shrug: "There's all the time in the world. If you people think you can scare me you've got another guess coming. It's just ten minutes of six; dinner's at seven-thirty! I've got to rest a little. You all look so ridiculous standing there glaring at me. I'm no white mouse with pink eyes!"

"Really, dear," said Mrs. Torrence coaxingly, walking toward Leila with her hands outstretched much as though she were trying to make friends with a reluctant puppy. "Do run along home like a good girl!"

Leila apparently had no intention of running along home like a good little girl. She dropped her glass—empty—and without warning caught the astounded lady tightly about the neck.

"Step-mother! Dear, nice step-mamma!" she cried. "Nice, dear, sweet, kind step-mamma! Helen's going to be awful good to poor little Leila. Helen not be bad step-mamma like story books; Helen be sweet, kind step-mamma and put nice, beautiful gin cocktails in baby's bottle!"

As she continued in cooing tones Leila stroked her captive's cheek and kissed her with a mockery of tenderness. Henderson and Thomas were shouting with laughter; Constance viewed the scene with lofty disdain; Whitford was mildly amused; Bruce, wishing himself somewhere else, withdrew toward the door, prepared to leave at the earliest possible moment. When at last Mrs. Torrence freed herself she sank into a chair and her laughter attained a new pitch of shrillness.

"Leila, you'll be the death of me!" she gasped when her mirth had spent itself.

"Leila will be the death of all of us," announced Constance solemnly.

"Oh, I don't know!" said Leila, straightening her hat composedly at the mantel mirror.

"Too bad Leila's 'step-mama' couldn't have heard that!" sighed Henderson.

"Now, Leila," said Constance severely, "do run along home. Please let me take you in my car; you oughtn't to drive in the condition you're in."

The remark was not fortunate. Leila had discovered a box of bonbons and was amusing herself by tossing them into the air and trying to catch them in her mouth. She scored one success in three attempts and curtsied to an imaginary audience.

"My condition!" she said, with fine scorn. "I wish you wouldn't speak as though I were a common drunk!"

"Anyone can see that you're not fit to go home. Your father will be furious."

"Not if I tell him I've been with you!" Leila flung back.

"Say, Leila!" began Henderson, ingratiatingly. "We're old pals, you and I—let's shake this bunch. I'll do something nice for you sometime."

"What will you do?" Leila demanded with provoking deliberation.

"Oh, something mighty nice! Maybelle and I will give you a party and you can name the guests."

"Stupid!" she yawned. "Your hair's mussed, Helen. You and Bud have been naughty."

"Your behavior isn't ladylike," said Thomas. "The party's getting rough! Come on, let's go."

"Oh, I'm misbehaving, am I? Well, I guess my conduct's as good as yours! Where do you get this stuff that I'm a lost lamb? Even an expert like you, Freddy, wouldn't call me soused. I'm just little bit tipsy—that's all! If I had a couple more highballs——"

III

By a signal passed from one to the other they began feigning to ignore her. Constance said she was going; Bud, Whitford and Thomas joined Bruce at the door where he was saying good-night to Mrs. Torrence. Leila was not so tipsy but that she understood what they were doing.

"Think you can freeze me out, do you? Well, I'm not so easily friz! Mr. What's-your-name——" She fixed her eyes upon Bruce detainingly.

"Storrs," Bruce supplied good-naturedly.

"You're the only lady or gentleman in this room. I'm going to ask you to take me home!"

"Certainly, Miss Mills!"

With a queenly air she took his arm. Henderson ran forward and opened the door, the others hanging back, silent, afraid to risk a word that might reopen the discussion and delay her departure.

"Shall I drive?" Bruce asked when they reached the curb.

"Yes, thanks; if you don't mind."

"Home?" he inquired as he got her car under way.

"I was just doing a little thinking," she said deliberatingly. "It will take only five minutes to run over to that little cafeteria on Fortieth Street. Some coffee wouldn't be a bad thing; and would you mind turning the windshield —I'd like the air."

"A good idea," said Bruce, and stepped on the gas. The car had been built for Leila's special use and he had with difficulty squeezed himself into the driver's seat; but he quickly caught the hang of it. He stopped a little beyond the cafeteria to avoid the lights of the busy corner and brought out a container of hot coffee and paper cups.

"Like a picnic, isn't it?" she said. "You won't join me?"

She sipped the coffee slowly while he stood in the street beside her.

"There!" she said. "Thank you, ever so much. Quarter of seven? Forty-five minutes to dress! Just shoot right along home now. Would you mind driving over to the boulevard and going in that way? The air certainly feels good."

"Nothing would please me more," he said, giving her a quick inspection as they passed under the lights at a cross-street. She was staring straight ahead, looking singularly young as she lay back with her hands clasped in her lap.

"Constance was furious!" she said suddenly. "Well, I suppose she had a right to be. I had no business getting lit."

"Well, strictly speaking, you shouldn't do it," he said. It was not the time nor place and he was not the proper person to lecture her upon her delinquencies. But he had not been displeased that she chose him to take her home, even though the choice was only a whim.

"You must think me horrid! This is the second time you've seen me teed up too high."

"I've seen a lot of other people teed up much higher! You're perfectly all right now?"

"Absolutely! That coffee fixed me; I'm beginning to feel quite bully. I can go home now and jump into my joy rags and nobody will ever be the wiser. This is an old folks' party, but Dada always wants to exhibit me when he feeds the nobility—can you see me?"

Her low laugh was entirely reassuring as to her sobriety, and he was satisfied that she would be able to give a good account of herself at her father's table.

"Just leave the car on the drive," she said as they reached the house. "Maybe I can crawl up to my room without Dada knowing I'm late. I'm a selfish little brute—to be leaving you here stranded! Well, thanks awfully!"

He walked with her to the entrance and she was taking out her key when Mills, in his evening clothes, opened the door.

"Leila! You're late!" he exclaimed sharply. "Where on earth have you been?"

"Just gadding about, as usual! But I'm in plenty of time, Dada. Please thank Mr. Storrs for coming home with me. Good-night and thank you some more!"

She darted into the house, leaving Bruce confronting her father.

"Oh, Mr. Storrs!" The emphasis on the name was eloquent of Mills's surprise that Bruce was on his threshold. Bruce had decided that any explanations required were better left to Leila, who was probably an adept in explanations. He was about to turn away when Mills stepped outside.

"We're entertaining tonight," he said pleasantly. "I was a little afraid something had happened to my daughter."

A certain dignity of utterance marked his last words—my daughter. He threw into the phrase every possible suggestion of paternal pride.

Bruce, halfway down the steps, paused until Mills had concluded his remark. Then lifting his hat with a murmured good-night, he hurried toward the gate. An irresistible impulse caused him to look back. Mills remained just inside the entry, his figure clearly defined by the overhead lights, staring toward the street. Seeing Bruce look back, he went quickly into the house and the heavy door boomed upon him.

Bruce walked to the nearest street car line and rode downtown for dinner. The fact that Mills was waiting at the door for his daughter was not without its significance, hinting at a constant uneasiness for her safety beyond ordinary parental solicitude. What Constance had said that afternoon about Mills came back to him. He was oppressed by a sense of something tragic in Mills's life—the tragedy of a failure that wore outwardly the guise of success.

In spite of a strong effort of will to obliterate these thoughts he found his memory dragging into his consciousness odd little pictures of Mills—fragmentary snapshots, more vivid and haunting than complete portraits: the look Mills gave him the first time they met at the Country Club; Mills's shoulders and the white line of his collar above his dinner coat as he left the Hardens'; and now the quick change from irritation to relief and amiable courtesy when he admitted Leila.

Henderson and Millicent and now today Constance had given him hints of Mills's character, and Bruce found himself trying to reconcile and unify their comments and fit them into his own inferences and conclusions. The man was not without his fascinations as a subject for analysis. Behind that gracious exterior there must be another identity either less noble or finer than the man the world knew.... Before he slept, Bruce found it necessary to combat an apprehension that, if he continued to hear Mills dissected and analyzed, he might learn to pity the man.

<h1 style="text-align:center">IV</h1>

That evening when Shepherd Mills went home he found Constance seated at her dressing table, her heavy golden-brown hair piled loosely upon her head, while her maid rubbed cold cream into her throat and face. She espied him in the mirror and greeted him with a careless, "Hello, Shep. How did the day go with you?"—the question employed by countless American wives in saluting their husbands at the end of a toilsome day.

"Oh, pretty good!" he replied. No husband ever admits that a day has been wholly easy and prosperous.

She put out her hand for him to kiss and bade him sit down beside her. He was always diffident before the mysteries of his wife's toilet. He glanced at the gown laid across a chair and surveyed the crystal and silver on the dressing table with a confused air as though he had never seen them before.

The room denoted Constance Mills's love of luxury, and incidentally her self-love. The walls on two sides were set in mirrors that reached from ceiling to floor. The furniture, the rugs, the few pictures, the window draperies had been chosen with an exquisite care and combined in an evocation of the spirit of indolence. There was a much be-pillowed divan across one corner, so placed that when she enjoyed a siesta Constance could contemplate herself in the mirrors opposite. Scents—a mingling of faint exotic odors—hung upon the air.

She was quick to note that something was on Shepherd's mind and half from curiosity, half in a spirit of kindness, dismissed the maid as quickly as possible.

"You can hook me up, Shep. I'll do my hair myself. I won't need you any more, Marie. Yes—my blue cloak. Now, little boy, go ahead and tell me what's bothering you."

Shepherd frowned and twisted his mustache as he sat huddled on the divan.

"It's about father; nothing new, just our old failure to understand each other. It's getting worse. I never know where I stand with him."

"Well, does anyone?" Constance asked serenely. "You really mustn't let him get on your nerves. There are things you've got to take because we all do; but by studying him a little and practicing a little patience you'll escape a lot of worry."

"Yes," he assented eagerly. "You know he just pretends that I'm the head of the plant; Fields is the real authority there. It's not the president but the vice-president who has the say about things. Father consults Fields constantly. He doesn't trust me—I'm just a figurehead."

"Fields is such an ass," remarked Constance with a shrug of her shapely shoulders. "An utterly impossible person. Why not just let him do all the explaining to your father? If any mistakes are made at the plant, then it's on him."

"But that's not the way of it," Shepherd protested plaintively. "He gets the praise; I get the blame."

"Oh, well, you can't make your father over. You ought to be glad you're not of his hard-boiled variety. You're human, Sheppy, and that's better than being a magnificent iceberg."

"Father doesn't see things; he doesn't realize that the world's changing," Shepherd went on stubbornly. "He doesn't see that the old attitude toward labor won't do any more."

"He'll never see it," said Constance. "Things like that don't hit him at all. He's like those silly people who didn't know there was anything wrong in France till their necks were in the guillotine."

"I told you about that clubhouse I wanted to build for our people on the Milton farm? I hate to give that up. It would mean so much to those people. And he was all wrong in thinking it would injure the property. I think it's only decent to do something for them."

"Well, how can you do it without your father?" she asked, shifting herself for a better scrutiny of her head in the mirror.

"You know that little tract of land—about twenty acres, back of the plant? I could buy that and put the clubhouse there. I have some stock in the Rogers Trust Company I can sell—about two hundred shares. It came to me through mother's estate. Father has nothing to do with it. The last quotation on it is two hundred. What do you think of that?"

"Well, I think pretty well of it," said Constance. "Your father ought to let you build the clubhouse, but he has a positive passion for making people uncomfortable."

"I suppose," continued Shepherd dubiously, "if I go ahead and build the thing—even with my own money—he would be angry. Of course there may be something in his idea that if we do a thing of this kind it would make the workmen at other plants restless——"

"Piffle!" exclaimed Constance. "That's the regular old stock whimper of the back-number. You might just as well say that it would be a forward step other employers ought to follow!"

"Yes, there's that!" he agreed, his eyes brightening at the suggestion.

"If you built the house on your own land the storage battery company wouldn't be responsible for it in any way."

"Certainly not!" Shepherd was increasingly pleased that she saw it all so clearly.

She had slipped on her gown and was instructing him as to the position of the hooks.

"No; the other side, Shep. That's right. There's another bunch on the left shoulder. Now you've got it! Thanks ever so much."

He watched her admiringly as she paraded before the mirrors to make sure that the skirt hung properly.

"If there's to be a row——" he began as she opened a drawer and selected a handkerchief.

"Let there be a row! My dear Shep, you're always too afraid of asserting yourself. What could he do? He might get you up to his office and give you a bad quarter of an hour; but he'd respect you more afterwards if you stood to your guns. His vanity and family pride protect you. Catch him doing anything that might get him into the newspapers—not Franklin Mills!"

Relieved and encouraged by her understanding and sympathy, he explained more particularly the location of the property he proposed buying. It was quite as convenient to the industrial colony that had grown up about the storage battery plant as the Milton land his father had declined to let him use. The land was bound to appreciate in value, he said.

"What if it doesn't!" exclaimed Constance with mild scorn. "You'll have been doing good with your money, anyhow."

"You think, then, you'd go ahead—sell the stock and buy the land? It's so late now, maybe I'd better wait till spring?"

"That might be better, Shep, but use your own judgment. You asked your father to help and he turned you down. Your going ahead will have a good effect on him. He needs a jar. Now run along and dress. You're going to be late for dinner."

"Yes, I know," he said, rising and looking down at her as she sat turning over the leaves of a book. "Connie——"

"Yes, Shep," she murmured absently; and then, "Oh, by the way, Shep, I was at Helen's this afternoon."

"Helen Torrence's? What was it—a tea?"

"In a manner of speaking—tea! Dramatic Club business. George Whitford was there—he's concentrating on theatricals. George is such a dear!"

"One of the best fellows in the world!" said Shep.

"He certainly is!" Constance affirmed.

"Connie——" he stammered and took her hand. "Connie—you're awfully good to me. You know I love you——"

"Why, of course, you dear baby!" She lifted her head with a quick, reassuring smile. "But for goodness' sake run along and change your clothes!"

V

When his guests had gone, Mills, as was his habit, smoked a cigar and discussed the dinner with Leila. He was aware that in asking her to join him on such occasions of state he was subjecting her to a trying ordeal, and tonight he was particularly well pleased with her.

"They all enjoyed themselves, Dada; you needn't worry about that party!" Leila remarked, smoking the cigarette she had denied herself while the guests remained.

"I think they did; thank you very much for helping me."

Leila had charm; he was always proud of an opportunity to display her to her mother's old friends, whose names, like his own, carried weight in local history. His son was a Shepherd; Leila, he persuaded himself, was, with all her waywardness and little follies, more like himself. Leila looked well at his table, and her dramatic sense made it possible for her to act the rôle of the daughter of the house with the formality that was dear to him. Whenever he entertained he and Leila received the guests together, standing in front of Mrs. Mills's portrait. People who dared had laughed about this, speculating as to the probable fate of the portrait in case Mills married again.

"I'd got nervous about you when you were so late coming," Mills was saying. "That's how I came to be at the door. I'd just called Millicent to see if you were over there."

"Foolish Dada! Don't I always turn up?" she asked, kicking off her slippers. "I'd been fooling around all afternoon, and I hate getting dressed and waiting for a party to begin."

"I've noticed that," Mills replied dryly. "Just what did you do all day? Your doings are always a mystery to me."

"Well—let me see—I went downtown with Millie this morning, and home with her for lunch, and we talked a while and I ran out to the Burtons' and there were some people there and we gassed; and then I remembered I hadn't seen Mrs. Torrence since she got home, so I took a dash up there. And Connie was there, and Bud Henderson came up with Mr. Storrs and we had tea and Mr. Storrs was coming this way so I let him drive me home."

This, uttered with smooth volubility, was hardly half the truth. She lighted a fresh cigarette and blew a series of rings while waiting to see whether he would crossexamine her, as he sometimes did.

"Constance was there, was she? Anyone else?"

"Fred Thomas and Georgy Whitford blew in just as I was leaving."

"So? I shouldn't have thought Mrs. Torrence would be interested in them."

"Oh, she isn't!" replied Leila, who hadn't intended to mention Thomas or Whitford. "Connie was trying to talk Helen into taking a perfectly marvelous part in a new play the Dramatic Club's putting on soon, and they are in it, too. Highbrow discussion; it bored me awfully—Mr. Storrs and I managed to escape together. Oh, dear, I'm sleepy!"

"Does this Storrs go about among people you know?" Mills asked, extending his arm to the ash tray.

"Oh, I think so, Dada! He was in college with Bud Henderson, you know, and is in Mr. Freeman's office. Dale's crazy about him. You could hardly say he's pushing himself. Millie and I met him at the Faraway Club—didn't you meet him that same night? I asked him to call and he hasn't and he *has* been to see Millie. I guess the joke's on me!"

"I saw him again at the Hardens'," Mills remarked carelessly. "And ran into him afterwards when I was strolling around, and I brought him back with me to get out of the storm. It was the night of the Claytons' party."

"Then you know as much about him as I do," said Leila indifferently. "I think, Dada, if you don't mind, I'll seek the hay."

He stood to receive her good-night kiss. When he heard her door close he took several turns across the room before resuming his cigar. He sat down in the chair in which he had sat the night he brought Bruce into the house. Magazines and books were within easy reach of his hand, but he was not in a mood to read. He lifted his eyes occasionally to the portrait of his father on the opposite wall. It might have seemed that he tried to avoid it, averting his gaze to escape the frank, steady eyes. But always the fine face drew him back. When he got up finally and walked to the door it was with a hurried step as if the room or his meditations had suddenly become intolerable.

CHAPTER NINE

I

The morning after his dinner party Franklin Mills rose at eight o'clock. He had slept badly, an unusual thing with him, and he found little satisfaction in an attempt to account for his wakefulness on the score of something he had eaten. As he shaved he found that he was not performing the familiar rite automatically as usual. He tried a succession of blades and became impatient when they failed to work with their usual smoothness.... Perhaps he was smoking too much, and he made a computation of the number of cigars and cigarettes he had smoked the day before, and decided that he had exceeded his usual allowance by a couple of cigars.

The mental exercise necessary to reach this conclusion steadied him. He had no intention of breaking, as some of his friends and contemporaries had broken, from sheer inattention to the laws of health. He attained a degree of buoyancy as he dressed by thinking of his immunity from the cares that beset most men. No other man in town enjoyed anything like his freedom. He had not dreaded age because he never thought of himself as old. And yet the years were passing.

He must study means of deferring old age. Marriage might serve to retard the march of time. The possibility of remarrying had frequently of late teased his imagination. Leila would leave him one of these days; he must have a care that she married well. Mills had plans for Carroll's future; Carroll would be a most acceptable son-in-law. Leila had so far shown no interest in the secretary, but Leila had the Mills common sense; when it came to marrying, Leila would listen to reason.

He called his man to serve breakfast in his room, read the morning paper, inspected his wardrobe and indicated several suits to be pressed.

From his south window he viewed the Harden house across the hedge. Millicent was somewhere within.... It might be a mistake to marry a girl as young as Millicent. He knew of men who had made that mistake, but

Millicent was not to be measured by ordinary standards. With all the charm of youth, she was amazingly mature; not a feather-brained girl who would marry him for his money. There was the question of her family, her lack of social background; but possibly he magnified the importance of such things. His own standing, he argued, gave him certain rights; he could suffer nothing in loss of dignity by marrying Millicent. It gave a man the appearance of youth to be seen with a young wife. Helen Torrence would not do; she lacked the essential dignity, and her background was far too sketchy—no better than the Hardens'. He had settled that....

The remembrance of the young architect's head superimposed upon the portrait of Franklin Mills III caused him an uneasiness which he was not able to dispel by a snap of the fingers. Any attempt to learn what had prompted Storrs to choose for his residence the city so long sacred to the Mills family might easily arouse suspicions. The portrait in itself was a menace. People were such fools about noting resemblances! If his sister, Alice Thornberry, met Storrs she might remark upon his resemblance to their father. And yet she was just as likely to note the removal of the picture if he relegated it to the attic....

By the time he had interviewed the house servants and driven to the office Mills had passed through various moods ranging from his habitual serenity and poise to apprehension and foreboding. This puzzled him. Why should he, the most equable of men, suddenly fall a prey to moods? He put on a pair of library glasses that he kept in his desk, though he usually employed a pince-nez at the office—a departure that puzzled Carroll, who did not know that Mills, in the deep preoccupation of the morning, had left his pocket case at home. Mills, in normal circumstances, was not given to forgetfulness. Aware that something was amiss, Carroll made such reports and suggestions as were necessary with more than his usual economy of words.

"Doctor Lindley telephoned that he'd be in to see you at eleven. You have no engagements and I told him all right."

"Lindley? What does Lindley want?" Mills demanded, without looking up from a bank statement he was scanning.

"He didn't say, sir; but as you always see him———"

"I don't know that I care to see him today," Mills mumbled. Mills rarely mumbled; his speech was always clean-cut and definite.

Carroll, listening attentively to his employer's instructions as to answering letters and sending telegraphic orders for the sale of certain stocks, speculated as to what had caused Mills's unwonted irascibility.

A few minutes after eleven word was passed from the office boy to the stenographer and thence from Carroll to Mills that the Reverend Doctor Lindley was waiting.

Mills detained Carroll rather unnecessarily to discuss matters of no immediate moment. This in itself was surprising, as the rector of St. Barnabas, the oldest and richest church in town, had heretofore always been admitted without delay. The Mills family had been identified with St. Barnabas from pioneer times and Doctor Lindley was entertained frequently by Mills, not only at home but at the men's luncheons Mills gave at his clubs for visiting notables.

"Ah, Mills! Hard at it!" exclaimed the minister cheerfully. He was short, rotund and bald, with a large face that radiated good nature. A reputation for breadth of view and public spirit had made him, in the dozen years of his pastorate, one of the best liked men in town. He gave Mills a cordial handshake, asked after Leila and assured Mills that he had never seen him looking better.

Lindley was a dynamic person and his presence had the effect of disturbing the tranquility of the room. Mills wished now that he hadn't admitted the rector of St. Barnabas, with his professional good cheer and optimism. He remembered that Lindley always wanted something when he came to the office. If it proved to be help for a negro mission St. Barnabas maintained somewhere, Mills resolved to refuse to contribute. He had no intention of encouraging further the idea that he could be relied upon to support all of Lindley's absurd schemes for widening the sphere of the church. It was a vulgar idea that a sinner should prostrate himself before an imaginary God and beg for forgiveness. Where sin existed the main thing was to keep it decently out of sight. But the whole idea of sin was repellent. He caught himself up sharply. What had he to do with sin?

But outwardly Mills was serene; Lindley was at least a diversion, though Mills reflected that someone ought to warn him against his tendency to obesity. A fat man in a surplice was ridiculous, though Mills hadn't seen Lindley in vestments since the last fashionable wedding. At the reception following the wedding Mills remembered that he had been annoyed by Lindley's appetite; more particularly by a glimpse of the rector's plump hand extended for a second piece of cake—cake with a thick, gooey icing.

Mills wondered what he had ever seen that was likable in the rector, who certainly suggested nothing of apostolic austerity. Lindley threw back his coat, disclosing a gold cross suspended from a cord that stretched across his broad chest. Mills's eyes fixed upon the emblem disapprovingly as he asked his visitor to have a cigar.

"No, thanks, Mills; I never smoke so early in the day—found it upset me. Moderation in all things is my motto. I missed you at the Clayton party the other night; a brilliant affair. Dear Leila was there, though, and Shepherd and his charming wife, to represent your family. Margaret and I left early." The clergyman chuckled and lowering his voice continued: "I've heard— I've heard *whispers* that later on the party got quite gay! I tell you, Mills, the new generation is stepping high. All the more responsibility for the forces that make for good in this world! I was saying to the bishop only the other day that the church never before faced such perplexities as now!"

"Why do you say perplexities?" asked Mills in the quiet tone and indulgent manner of an expert cross-examiner who is preparing pitfalls for a witness.

"Ah, I see you catch at the word! It's become a serious question what the church dare do! There's the danger of offending; of estranging its own membership."

"Yes, but why is it a danger?" Mills persisted.

The minister was surprised at these questions, which were wholly foreign to all his previous intercourse with Mills. His eyes opened and shut quickly. The Reverend Stuart Lindley was known as a man's man, a clergyman who viewed humanity in the light of the twentieth century and was particularly discerning as to the temptations and difficulties that beset twentieth century business men.

"My dear Mills," he said ingratiatingly, "you know and I know that this is an age of compromise. We clergymen are obliged to temper our warnings. The wind, you know, no longer blows on the lost sheep with the violence it once manifested, or at least the sheep no longer notice it!" A glint in Mills's eyes gave him pause, but he went on hurriedly. "In certain particulars we must yield a little without appearing to yield. Do you get my point?"

"Frankly, I don't know that I do," Mills replied bluntly. "You preach that certain things are essential to the salvation of my soul. What right have you to compromise with me or anyone else? You either believe the Gospel and the creeds that are used every day in our churches or you don't. I didn't mean to start a theological discussion; I was just a little curious as to what you meant by perplexities, when the obligation is as plain as that table."

"But—you see the difficulties! We have a right to assume that God is perfectly aware of all that goes on in His world and that the changing times are only a part of His purpose."

"Well, yes," Mills assented without enthusiasm. "But I was thinking of what you and the church I was born into declare to be necessary to the Christian life. I go to church rarely, as you know, but I'm fairly familiar with the New Testament. I've got a copy with the words of Jesus printed in bold type, so you can't miss His meaning. He was pretty explicit; His meaning hits you squarely in the eye!"

"But, my dear friend, above all He preached tolerance! He knew human frailty! There's the great secret of His power."

"Oh, that's all true!" said Mills, with courteous forbearance. "But you know very well that few of us—no—I'll admit that *I* don't live the Christian life except where it's perfectly easy and convenient. Why talk of the perplexities of the ministry when there's no excuse for any of us to mistake His teachings? You either preach Jesus or you don't! We lean heavily on His tolerance because we can excuse ourselves with that; it's only an alibi. But what of His courage? Whatever I may think of Him—divine or merely a foolish idealist—He did die for His convictions! It occurs to me sometimes that He's served nowadays by a pretty cowardly lot of followers. Oh—not you, my friend!—I don't mean anyone in particular—except myself! Probably there are other men who think much as I do, but we don't count. We pay to keep the churches going, but we don't want to be bothered about our duty to God. *That's* a disagreeable subject!"

He ended with a smile that was intended to put Lindley at ease.

"You are absolutely right, Mills!" declared the minister magnanimously. "But as a practical man you realize that there *are* embarrassments in the way of doing our full duty."

"No; truly, I don't!" Mills retorted. "We either do it or we don't. But please don't think I meant to quiz you or be annoying. I wouldn't offend you for anything in the world!"

"My dear *Mills*!" cried the clergyman with the disdain demanded by so monstrous a suggestion.

"It never occurred to me before," Mills went on, his good humor only faintly tinged with irony, "it never struck me in just this way before, but I suppose if you were to preach to your congregation just what Jesus preached you'd empty the church."

"Well, of course——" began Lindley, with difficulty concealing his surprise at the dogged fashion in which Mills was pursuing the subject.

"Of course you can't do it!" With a bland smile Mills finished the sentence for him. "Jesus is the Great Example of a perfect life; but do we any of us really want to live as He lived?"

"Ah, Mills, we can only approximate perfection; that's the best we can hope for!"

"Thank you! There's some consolation in that!" Mills laughed. "But if we really took the teachings of Jesus literally we wouldn't be sitting here; we'd be out looking up people who need shelter, food, cheer. As it is I'm not bothering my head about them. I pay others to do that—Carroll hands me a list of organizations he considers worthy of assistance and all I do is to sign the checks—ought to be ashamed of myself, oughtn't I?"

"Well, now, Mills," Lindley laughed pleasantly, "that's a matter I leave to your own conscience."

"But you oughtn't to! It's your duty to tell me that instead of riding up to a comfortable club today to eat luncheon with a couple of bankers I ought first to be sure that every man, woman and child in the community is clothed and fed and happy.”

“What would you do if I did?” Lindley demanded, bending forward and regarding Mills fixedly.

“I’d tell you to go to the Devil!”

“There you are!” cried Lindley with a gesture of resignation. “You know your duty to your neighbor as well as I do. The affair isn’t between you and me, after all, my dear friend—it’s between you and God!”

“God?” Mills repeated the word soberly, his eyes turning to the window and the picture it framed, of a sky blurred by the smoke of factory chimneys. “I wonder——” he added, half to himself.

Lindley was puzzled and embarrassed, uncertain whether to try to explain himself further. His intuitions were keen and in his attempt to adjust himself to a new phase of Mills’s character he groped for an explanation of the man’s surprising utterances. There had been something a little wistful in Mills’s use of the word *God*. Lindley was sincerely eager to help where help was needed, but as he debated whether Mills really had disclosed any need that he could satisfy, Mills ended the matter by saying a little wearily:

“What was it you wanted to see me about, Lindley?”

“It’s about the Mills memorial window in St. Barnabas; the transept wall’s settled lately and pulled the window out of plumb. Some of the panels are loose. The excavations for the new building across the alley caused the disturbance. Now that the building’s up we’ll hope the worst is over. That’s one of the finest windows in the West. The figure of our Lord feeding the multitude is beautifully conceived. I had Freeman look at it and he says we’ll have to get an expert out from New York to take care of it properly. The vestry’s hard up as usual, but I felt sure you’d want us to have the job well done——”

“Certainly, Lindley. Go ahead and send me the bill. Of course I’m glad to take care of it.”

II

Mills was himself again. The mention of the Mills memorial window had touched his pride. The window not only symbolized the miraculous powers of Jesus, but quite concretely it visualized for the congregation of St. Barnabas the solid worth and continuity of the house of Mills.

He detained Lindley, gave him a chance to tell a story, made sure before he permitted him to go that the minister had not been wounded by anything he had said. He had come out pretty well in his talk with the minister; it did no harm to ruffle the complacency of a man like Lindley occasionally. But he wanted to guard against a return of the vexatious thoughts with which the day had begun.

A ride would set him up and he would find some cheerful companions to join him at the farm. Usually he planned his parties ahead, but the day was too fine to let pass. He rang for Carroll, his spirits already mounting at the thought of escaping from town.

"I believe I'll run out to Deer Trail this afternoon. I'll ask some people who like to ride to join me. Will you call Mrs. Freeman, Mrs. Torrence, Leila and Miss Harden? I'll be glad to have you go if you can arrange it—I'll leave it all to you. As to men, try Doctor Armstrong, Mr. Turner, Ralph Burton—say that I'll send machines to take them out unless they prefer using their own cars. You'll look after that?"

"Yes, sir."

"Oh, yes; if Shep calls up tell him I'll see him later about those battery plant matters. I want to talk to Fields first...."

"Yes; I understand, sir."

"Let me see; this was the day Freeman was to meet me out there to look over the superintendent's house. I've promised Jackson to make the addition he wants this fall. Freeman's probably forgotten it—he has a genius for forgetting engagements, and I'd overlooked your memorandum till just now. Freeman hates a horse, but if he goes it will only take a few minutes to show him what's wanted."

CHAPTER TEN

I

Bruce was finding his association with Freeman increasingly agreeable. The architect, amusingly indifferent and careless as to small things, was delighted to find that his new subordinate was not afraid to assume responsibility and grateful that Bruce was shielding him from the constant pecking of persons who called or telephoned about trivial matters.

"By the way, Storrs, can you run into the country this afternoon?" Freeman asked. "I promised Franklin Mills I'd meet him at his farm to look at the superintendent's house. I've put him off several times and now that Brookville man's coming in to talk house and I've got to see him. There's not much to do but get data and make my apologies to Mills. Mrs. Freeman just called up to say she's going out there to ride. Mills is having a party, so he'll get through with you quickly. I don't want him to think me indifferent about his work. He's been a loyal client."

"Yes, certainly," Bruce replied, reluctant to trouble Freeman by refusing, but not relishing another meeting with Mills.

"Everybody knows where Deer Trail is—you'll have no trouble finding it. I think he said he'd be there by two-thirty. Listen carefully to what he says, and I'll take the matter up with him tomorrow. Now about the specifications for that Sterling house——"

It was thus that Bruce found himself at Deer Trail Farm on the afternoon of the day that Mills was giving his riding party. Mills, with whom punctuality was a prime virtue, came down the steps in his riding clothes and good-naturedly accepted Bruce's excuses in Freeman's behalf.

"Freeman's a busy man, of course, and a job like this is a good deal of a nuisance. You can get the idea just as well. Can you ride a horse?"

Bruce, whose eyes had noted with appreciation the horses that had been assembled in the driveway, said that he could.

"All right, then; we'll ride over. It's nearly a mile and we'll save time."

He let Bruce choose a horse for himself from a dozen or more thoroughbreds, watched him mount with critical but approving eyes, and they set off over a road that led back through the fields. Mills sat a horse well; he had always ridden, he explained as they traversed the well-made gravel road at a trot. Finding that Bruce knew something of the American saddle stocks, he compared various breeds, calling attention to the good points of the horses they were riding.

When they reached the superintendent's house Bruce found that what was required was an extension that would provide the family with additional sleeping rooms. He took measurements, made notes, suggested a few difficulties, and in reply to Mills's questions expressed his belief that the addition could be made without spoiling the appearance of the house.

"I suppose I really ought to tear it down and build a new house, but this hundred acres right here has been in my family a long time and the place has associations. I hate to destroy it."

"I can understand that," said Bruce, busy with his notebook. "I think I have all the data Mr. Freeman will need, sir."

As they rode back Mills talked affably of the country; spoke of the history and traditions of the neighborhood, and the sturdy character of the pioneers who had settled the region.

"I used to think sometimes of moving East—settling somewhere around New York. But I've never been able to bring myself to it. This is my own country right here. Over there—you notice that timber?—well, I'll never cut that. This whole region was forest in the early days. I've kept that strip of woodland as a reminder of the men who broke through the wilderness with nothing but their rifles and axes."

"They were a great race," Bruce remarked....

Mills called attention to a young orchard he had lately planted, and to his conservatories, where he amused himself, he said, trying to produce a new rose.

"Won't you stay and join in the ride?" he asked as they dismounted. "I can fit you out with breeches and puttees. I'd be delighted to have you."

"Thanks, but I must get into town," Bruce replied.

"Well, if you must! Please don't let Freeman go to sleep on this job!"

Bruce, glad that his duty had been performed so easily, was starting toward his car when a familiar voice hailed him from the broad pillared veranda.

"Why the hurry? Aren't you in this party?"

He swung round to find Millicent Harden, dressed for the saddle, standing at the edge of the veranda a little apart from the animated group of Mills's other guests. As he walked toward her she came down the steps to meet him. The towering white pillars made a fitting frame for her. Here, as in the library of her own house, the ample background served to emphasize her pictorial effectiveness. Her eyes shone with happy expectancy.

"I don't care if you are here on business, you shouldn't be running away! On a day like this nobody should be in town."

"Somebody has to work in this world. How are the organ and the noble knight?"

"Both would be glad to welcome you. Leila's growing superstitious about you; she says you're always saving her life. Oh, she confessed everything about last night!—how you ministered to her and set her on her father's doorstep in fine shape. And she's going to be a good girl now. We must see that she is!"

At this moment Leila detached herself from the company on the veranda and called his attention to the fact that Mrs. Freeman was trying to bow to him. Mills, who had been discussing the fitness of one of the horses with his superintendent, announced that he was ready to start.

"I wish you were coming along," said Leila; "there's scads of horses. We'd all adore having you!"

"I'd adore coming!" Bruce answered. "But I've really got to skip."

"I'll tell Dada to ask you another time. Dada isn't at all bad when you know him, is he, Millie?"

"Oh, one learns to tolerate him!" said Millicent teasingly.

"You might like driving through the farm—good road all the way from that tall elm down there," suggested Leila, "and it takes you through our woods. The maples are putting on their pink bonnets. There's a winding stretch over yonder that's a little wild, but it's interesting, and you can't get lost. It would be a shame to dash back to town without seeing something of this gorgeous day!"

"All right, thanks; I'll try it," said Bruce.

With his roadster in motion he wondered dejectedly whether there was any way of remaining in the town and yet avoiding Franklin Mills and his family. But the sight of Millicent had heartened him. The glowing woodlands were brighter for his words with her. He wished he might have taken her away from Mills and his party and ridden alone with her in the golden haze of the loveliest of autumn afternoons....

Suddenly when he was beyond the Deer Trail boundaries and running along slowly he came upon a car drawn up close to the stake-and-rider fence that enclosed a strip of woodland. His quiet approach over the soft winding road had not been noted by the two occupants of the car, a man and a woman.

Two lovers, presumably, who had sought a lonely spot where they were unlikely to be observed, and Bruce was about to speed his car past them when the woman lifted her head with an involuntary cry of surprise that caused him, quite as involuntarily, to turn his gaze upon her. It was Constance Mills; her companion was George Whitford.

"Hello, there!" Whitford cried, and Bruce stopped his car and got out. "Mrs. Mills and I are out looking at the scenery. We started for the Faraway Club, but lost interest."

"Isn't this a heavenly day?" remarked Mrs. Mills with entire serenity. "George and I have been talking poetry—an ideal time for it!" She held up a book. "Yeats—he's so marvelous! Where on earth are you wandering to?"

"I've been to Deer Trail—a little errand with Mr. Mills for my boss."

"Oh, is Mr. Mills at the farm? What is it—a party?" she asked carelessly.

"Yes, Miss Mills, Miss Harden, Mrs. Torrence and Mrs. Freeman are there to ride—I didn't make them all out."

"It sounds quite gay," she said languidly. "I've thought a lot about our talk yesterday. You evidently delivered Leila home without trouble. It was awfully sweet of you, I'm sure. I don't believe we'll go in to the farm, George. I think a crowd of people would bore me today, and we must get back to town."

Whitford started his car, and as they moved away Constance leaned out and smiled and waved her hand. Bruce stood for a moment gazing after them, deep in thought. Constance Mills, he decided, was really a very clever woman.

II

After his visit to Deer Trail Farm Bruce found himself in a cynical humor with reference to his own life and the lives of the people with whom he had lately come in contact. Nothing was substantial or definite. He read prodigiously—poetry and philosophy, and the latest discussions of the problems of the time; caught in these an occasional gleam. It seemed centuries ago that he had walked in the Valley of the Shadow in France. The tragedy of war seemed as nothing weighed against the tragedy of his own life.

Why had she told him? was a question he despairingly asked himself. His mother had had no right to go out of the world leaving him to carry the burden her confession had laid upon him. Then again, with a quickening of his old affection for her, he felt that some motive, too fine and high for his understanding, had impelled her to the revelation....

He had settled himself to read one evening when Henderson, always unexpected in his manifestations of sociability, dropped in at his apartment.

"Maybelle's at Shep Mills's rehearsing in a new Dramatic Club show, so I romped up here hoping to catch you in. I guessed you'd be here laughing heartily all to yourself. I've cut the booze; honest I have. My bootlegger strolled in today, but I kissed him good-bye forever. So don't offer me any licker; my noble resolution isn't so strong that I mightn't yield to a whisper from the devil."

"You're safe! There's nothing stronger on the premises than a tooth wash warranted not to remove the enamel."

Henderson picked up the book Bruce had been reading, "A World in Need of God," and ran his eye over the chapter headings.

"'The Unlit Lamp,' 'The Descent Perilous,' 'Untended Altars'—so you've got it too, have you?"

"I've got the book, if that's what you mean," Bruce replied. "I paid two dollars for it. It's a gloomy work; no wonder the author put it out anonymously."

"It's a best seller," Henderson replied mournfully as he seated himself and drew out his pipe. "The world is nervous about itself—doesn't know whether to repent and be good or stroll right along to the fiery pit. Under my stoical exterior, Bruce, old boy, I trouble a good deal about the silly human race. That phrase, 'The Descent Perilous,' gives me a chill. If I'd edited that book I'd have made it 'The Road to Hell is Easy' and drawn a stirring picture of the universe returning to chaos to the music of jazzy bands. People seem anxious to be caught all lit up when our little planet jumps the track and runs amuck. But there really are a few imbeciles, like the chap who produced that book, who're troubled about the whole business. We all think we're playing comedy rôles, but if we'd just take a good square look at ourselves in the mirror we'd see that we're made up for tragedy."

"Lordy! Hear the boy talk! If I'd known you were coming I'd have hidden the book."

"There's a joke! I've been in several prosperous homes lately where I got a glimpse of that joyous work stuck under the sofa pillows. Everybody's afraid to be caught with it—afraid it points to a state of panic in the purchaser. It's the kind of thing folks read and know it's all true, and get so low in their minds they pull the old black bottle from its hiding place and seek alcoholic oblivion."

"I bought the thing as a matter of business. If all creation's going to shoot the chutes I want to be prepared. It's silly for me to get all set to build houses for people if the world's coming to an end."

"By Jove, when the crash comes I'm going to be stuck with a lot of Plantagenets!"

"But this chap thinks the world can be saved! He says in the mad rush to find some joy in life we're forgetting God. The spiritual spark growing dim —all that sort of thing."

"Um-m." Henderson took the pipe from his mouth and peered into the bowl. "Now on this spiritual dope, I'm a sinner—chock full of sin, original and acquired. I haven't been to church since my wedding except to a couple of funerals—relations where I couldn't dodge the last sad rites. Cheerless, this death stuff; sort o' brings you up with a jerk when you think of it. Most of us these days are frantically trying to forget man's inevitable destiny by running as wild as we dare—blindfolded. It isn't fashionable to be serious about anything. I tell you, my boy, I could count on the fingers of one hand all the people I know who ever take a good square look at life."

"Oh, not as bad as that!" said Bruce, surprised at Henderson's unwonted earnestness. "There must be a lot of people who are troubled about the state of their souls—who have some sort of ideals but are ashamed to haul them out!"

"Ashamed is the word!" Henderson affirmed. "We're afraid of being kidded if anybody sneaks up on us and catches us admiring the Ten Commandments or practicing the Christian virtues! Now I know the rattle of all the skeletons in all the closets in this town. If they all took a notion to trot up and down our main thoroughfares some moonlit evening they'd make quite a parade. You understand I'm not sitting in judgment on my fellow man; I merely view him at times like this, when I'm addressing a man of intellect like you, with a certain cheerful detachment. And I see things going on—and I take part in them—that I deplore. I swear I deplore them; particularly," he went on with a grim smile, "on days when I'm suffering from a severe case of hang-overitis."

"You must have been on a roaring tear last night. You have all the depressing symptoms."

"A cruel injustice! I'm never terribly wicked. I drink more than I need at times and I flirt occasionally to keep my hand in. Maybelle doesn't mind if I wander a little, but when she whistles I'm right back at my own fireside pretending nothing happened."

"I'll wager you do!" laughed Bruce.

"Right now," Henderson went on, "I can see a few people we both know who are bound to come a cropper if they don't mind their steps. There's Connie Mills. Not a bad sort, Connie, but a little bit too afraid she isn't having as much fun as she's entitled to. And Shep—the most high-minded, unselfish fellow I know—he, poor nut, just perishing for somebody to love him!"

"What sort of a chap's George Whitford?" Bruce asked.

"First class," Bud answered promptly. "A real fellow; about the best we've got. Something of the soldier of fortune about him. A variety of talents; brilliant streak in him. Why do you ask? George getting on your preserves?"

"Lord, no! I was just wondering whether you'd knock him. I like him myself."

"Well, nearly everyone does. He appeals to the imagination. Just a little too keen about women, however, for his own good."

A buzzer sounded and Bruce went to the telephone by which visitors announced themselves from the hall below.

"Mr. Carroll? Certainly; come right up!"

"Carroll? Didn't know you were so chummy with him," Henderson grumbled, not pleased by the interruption.

"I run into him at the club occasionally. He's been threatening to drop in some evening. Seems to be a nice chap."

"Oh, yes, Carroll's all right!" Bud grinned. "We might proceed with our discussion of the Millses. Arthur ought to know a few merry facts not disclosed to the general public. He wears the mask of meekness, but that's purely secretarial, so to speak."

Carroll, having reached the apartment, at once began bantering Henderson about the Plantagenet Bud had lately sold him.

"I'm another Plantag victim," said Bruce. "Bud's conscience is hurting him; he's moaning over the general depravity of the world."

"He should worry!" said Carroll. "The Plantagenet's shaken my faith in Heaven."

III

Carroll, Bruce knew, was a popular man in town, no doubt deriving special consideration from his association with Mills. His name was written into local history almost as far back as that of the Mills family. In giving up the law to become Mills's right-hand man it was assumed that he had done so merely for the benefit to be derived from contact with a man of Mills's importance. He dabbled somewhat in politics, possibly, it was said, that he might be in a position to serve Mills when necessary in frustrating any evil designs of the State or the municipal government upon Mills's interests.

Bruce had wondered a little when Carroll intimated his purpose to look him up; he had even speculated as to whether Mills might not have prompted this demonstration of friendliness for some purpose of his own. But Carroll bore all the marks of a gentleman; he was socially in demand and it was grossly ungenerous to think that his call had any motive beyond a wish to be courteous to a new member of the community.

Carroll was tall and slender, with light brown hair and deep-set blue eyes. His clean-shaven face was rather deeply lined for a man of his years; there was something of the air of a student about him. But when he spoke it was in the crisp, incisive tones of an executive. A second glance at his eyes discovered hints of reserve strength. Serving an exacting man had not destroyed his independence and self-respect. On the whole a person who knew what he was about, endowed with brains and not easily to be trampled upon or driven.

"You mustn't let Bud fool you about our home town. Most anything he says is bound to be wrong; it's temperamental with him. But you know him of old; I needn't tell you what a scoundrel he is."

"Certainly not! You can't room with a man for four years without knowing all his weaknesses."

"Yes, I certainly know all yours," Henderson retorted. "But he isn't a bad fellow, Arthur. We must marry him off and settle him in life. I already see several good chances to plant him."

"You'd better let Maybelle do that," replied Carroll. "Your judgment in such delicate matters can't be trusted."

"Perhaps I'd better leave the room while you make a choice for me," said Bruce.

"What would you think of Leila Mills as a fitting mate for him?" asked Henderson.

"Excellent," Carroll affirmed. "It's about time Leila was married. You've met Miss Mills, haven't you, Storrs?"

"Yes; several times," said Bruce. He suspected Bud of turning the conversation upon Leila merely to gratify his passion for gossip.

"Of course you've got the first call, Arthur," said Henderson with cheerful impudence. "The town is getting impatient waiting for you to show your hand."

"I'm sorry to keep my fellow citizens waiting," Carroll replied. "Of course there are always Miss Mills's wishes to consider."

"Oh, well, there *is* that! Bruce, with his known affection for the arts, may prefer the lovely Millicent. He's not worth troubling about as a competitor. Well, I must skip back to Maybelle! Wait till I get downstairs before you begin knocking me!"

"Don't be in a rush," said Bruce.

"Oh, I'll go now!" said Bud as he lounged out. "I want you to have plenty of time to skin me properly!"

"Bud's a mighty good fellow," said Carroll when they were alone. "He and Maybelle give a real tang to our social affairs. I suppose we have Bud to thank for bringing you here."

"Oh, not altogether!" Bruce replied. "I was alone in the world and my home town hadn't much to offer an architect."

"Your profession does need room. I was born right here and expect to be buried among my ancestors. Let me see—did I hear that you're from the East?"

The question on its face was courteously perfunctory; Mills would certainly not have done anything so clumsy, Bruce reflected, as to send Carroll to probe into his history.

"I'm an Ohioan—born in Laconia," he replied.

"Not really! I have an uncle and some cousins there. Just today we had a letter at the office from Laconia, an inquiry about a snarl in the title to some property. Mr. Mills's father—of the same name—once had some interests there—a stave factory, I think it was. Long before your day, of course. He bought some land near the plant—the Millses have always gone in strong for real estate—thinking he might need it if the business developed. Mr. Mills was there for a while as a young man. Suppose he didn't like the business, and his father sold out. I was there a year ago visiting my relations and I met some Bruces—Miss Carolyn Bruce—awfully jolly girl—related to you?"

"My cousin. Bruce was my mother's name."

"The old saying about the smallness of the world! Splendid girl—not married yet?"

"Not when I heard from her last week."

"We might drive over there sometime next spring and see her."

"Fine. Carolyn was always a great pal of mine. Laconia's a sociable town. Everybody knows everybody else; it's like a big family. We can't laugh so gaily at the small towns; they've got a lot that's mighty fine. I sometimes think our social and political regeneration has got to begin with the small units."

"I say that sometimes to Mr. Mills," Carroll continued. "But he's of the old ultra-conservative school; a pessimist as to the future, or pretends to be. He really sees most things pretty straight. But men of his sort hate the idea of change. They prefer things as they are."

"I think we all want the changes to come slowly—gradual evolution socially and politically," Bruce ventured. "That's the only safe way. The great business of the world is to find happiness—get rid of misery and violence and hatred. I'm for everything that moves toward that end."

"I'm with you there," Carroll replied quickly.

Bruce's liking for Carroll increased. Mills's secretary was not only an agreeable companion but he expressed views on many questions that showed knowledge and sound reasoning. He referred to Mills now and then, always with respect but never with any trace of subserviency. Bruce, now that his fear had passed, was deriving a degree of courage merely from talking with Carroll. Carroll, in daily contact with Mills, evidently was not afraid of him. And what had he, Bruce Storrs, to fear from Franklin Mills? There could not have been any scandal about Mills's affair with his mother or she herself would probably have mentioned it; or more likely she would never have told him her story. Carroll's visit was reassuring every way that Bruce considered it.

"I got a glimpse of you at Deer Trail the other day," Carroll was saying. "You were there about the superintendent's house—Mr. Mills spoke of you afterward—said you seemed to know your business. He's not so hard to please as many people think—only"—Carroll smiled—"it's always safer to do things his way."

"I imagine it is!" Bruce assented.

Carroll remained until the clock on the mantel chimed twelve.

"I hope you've enjoyed this as much as I have!" he said. "If there's anything I can do for you, give me a ring. Mr. Mills is a regular client of Freeman's. We'll doubtless meet in a business way from time to time."

CHAPTER ELEVEN

I

On a Sunday afternoon a fortnight later Bruce, having been reproved by Dale Freeman for his recent neglect of her, drove to the architect's house. He had hoped to see Millicent there and was disappointed not to find her.

"You expected to see someone in particular!" said Dale. "I can tell by the roving look in your eye."

"I was merely resenting the presence of these other people. My eyes are for you alone!"

"What a satisfactory boy you are! But it was Millicent, wasn't it?"

"Lady, lady! You're positively psychic! Do you also tell fortunes?"

"It's easy to tell yours! I see a beautiful blonde in your life! Sorry I can't produce Millie today. She's not crazy about my Sunday parties; she hates a crowd. I must arrange something small for you two. You must meet that girl who just came in alone—the one in the enchanting black gown. She's a Miss Abrams, a Jewess, very cultivated—lovely voice."

The rooms were soon crowded. Bruce was still talking to Miss Abrams when he caught sight of Shepherd and Constance Mills, who had drifted in with Fred Thomas. A young man with a flowing tie and melancholy dark eyes claimed Miss Abrams's attention and Bruce turned to find Shepherd at his elbow.

"Just the man I wanted to see!" Shepherd exclaimed. "Let's find a place where we can talk."

"Not so easy to find!" said Bruce. However, he led the way to Freeman's den, which had not been invaded, wondering what Franklin Mills's son could have to say to him.

"Do pardon me for cornering you this way," Shepherd began. "I looked for you several days at the club, but you didn't show up."

"I've been too busy to go up there for luncheon," Bruce replied. "You could always get track of me at the office."

"Yes, but this was—is—rather confidential for the present." Shepherd, clasping and unclasping his hands in an attempt to gain composure, now bent forward in his chair and addressed Bruce with a businesslike air. "What I want to talk to you about is that clubhouse for our workmen. You know I mentioned it some time ago?"

"Yes; I remember," Bruce replied, surprised that Shepherd still had the matter on his mind.

"It's troubled me a good deal," said Shepherd, with the earnestness that always increased his stammering. "I've felt that there's a duty—a real duty and an opportunity there. You know how it is when you get a thing in your head you can't get rid of—can't argue yourself out of?"

"Those perplexities are annoying. I'd assumed that you'd given the thing up."

"Well, I thought I had! But I'm determined now to go on. There's a piece of land I can get that's just the thing. That neighborhood is so isolated—the people have no amusements unless they come to town. I'd like to go ahead so they can have some use of the house this winter."

Bruce nodded his sympathy with the idea.

"Now since I talked with you I've found some pictures of such houses. I've got 'em here." He drew from his pocket some pages torn from magazines. "I think we might spend a little more money than I thought at first would be available. We might go thirty thousand to get about what's in this house I've marked with a pencil."

Bruce scrutinized the pictures and glanced over the explanatory text.

"The idea seems to be well worked out. There are many such clubhouses scattered over the country. You'd want the reading room and the play room for children and all those features?"

"Yes; and I like the idea of a comfortable sitting-room where the women can gather and do their sewing and that sort of thing. And I'd like you to do this for me—begin getting up the plans right away."

Shepherd's tone was eager; his eyes were bright with excitement.

"But, Mr. Mills, I can hardly do that! I'm really only a subordinate in Mr. Freeman's office. It would be hardly square for me to take the commission —at least not without his consent."

Shepherd, who had not thought of this, frowned in his perplexity. Since his talk with Constance he had been anxious to get the work started before his father heard of it; and he had been hoping to run into Bruce somewhere to avoid visiting Freeman's office. He felt that if he had an architect who sympathized with the idea everything would be simplified. His father and Freeman met frequently, and Freeman, blunt and direct, was not a man who would connive at the construction of a building, in which presumably Franklin Mills was interested, without Mills's knowledge.

His sensitive face so clearly indicated his disappointment that Bruce, not knowing what lay behind this unexpected revival of the clubhouse plan, said, with every wish to be kind:

"Very likely Mr. Freeman would be glad to let me do the work—but I'd rather you asked him. I'd hate to have him think I was going behind his back to take a job. You can understand how I'd feel about it."

"I hadn't thought of that at all!" said Shepherd sincerely. "And of course I respect your feeling." Then with a little toss of the head and a gesture that expressed his desire to be entirely frank, he added: "You understand I'm doing this on my own hook. I think I told you my father thought it unwise for the battery company to do it. But I'm going ahead on my own responsibility—with my own money."

"I see," said Bruce. "It's fine of you to want to do it."

"I've *got* to do it!" said Shepherd, slapping his hand on his knee. "And of course my father and the company being out of it, it's no one's concern but my own!"

The door was open. Connie Mills's laugh for a moment rose above the blur of talk in the adjoining rooms. Shepherd's head lifted and his lips tightened as though he gained confidence from his wife's propinquity. Mrs. Freeman appeared at the door, demanding to know if they wanted tea, and noting their absorption withdrew without waiting for an answer.

It was clear enough that Shepherd meant to put the scheme through without his father's consent, even in defiance of his wishes. The idea had become an obsession with the young man; but his sincere wish to promote the comfort and happiness of his employees spoke for so kind and generous a nature that Bruce shrank from wounding him. Seeing Bruce hesitate, Shepherd began to explain the sale of his trust stock to obtain the money, which only increased Bruce's determination to have nothing to do with the matter.

"Why don't you take it up with Mr. Carroll?" Bruce suggested. "He might win your father over to your side."

"Oh, I couldn't do that! Carroll, you know, is bound to take father's view of things. Father will be all right about it when it's all done. Of course after the work starts he'll know, so it won't be a secret long. I'm going ahead as a little joke on him. I think he'll be tickled to know I've got so much initiative!"

He laughed in his quick, eager way, hoping that he had made this convincing. Bruce, from his observation of Franklin Mills, was not so sanguine as to the outcome. Mills would undoubtedly be very angry. On the face of it he would have a right to be. And one instinctively felt like shielding Shepherd Mills from his own folly.

"If you really want my advice," said Bruce after a moment's deliberation, "I'd take a little more time to this. Before you could get your plans we'll be having rough weather. I'd wait till spring, when you can develop your grounds and complete the whole thing at once. And it would be just as well to look around a bit—visit other cities and get the newest ideas."

"You think that? I supposed there'd be time to get the foundations in if I started right away."

"I wouldn't risk it; in fact I think it would be a serious mistake."

"Well, you are probably right," assented Shepherd, though reluctantly, and there was a plaintive note in his voice. "Thanks ever so much. I guess I'll take your advice. I'll let it go till spring."

"Damon and Pythias couldn't look more brotherly!" Constance Mills stood at the doorway viewing them with her languid smile. "It peeves me a good deal, Mr. Storrs, that you prefer my husband's society to mine."

“This is business, Connie,” Shepherd said. “We’ve just finished.”

“Let’s say the party is just beginning,” said Bruce. “I was just coming out to look you up.”

“I can’t believe it! But Leila just telephoned for us to come out to Deer Trail and bring any of Dale’s crowd who look amusing. That includes you, of course, Mr. Storrs. Everyone’s gone but Helen Torrence and Fred Thomas and Arthur Carroll. Mr. Mills is at the farm; it’s a fad of his to have Sunday supper in the country. Leila hates it and sent out an S. O. S., so we can’t desert her. No, Mr. Storrs, you can’t duck! Millicent is there—that may add to the attractions!”

This with a meaningful glance at Bruce prompted him to say that Miss Harden’s presence hardly diminished the attractions of the farm. There was real comedy in his inability to extricate himself from the net in which he constantly found himself enmeshed with the members of the house of Mills.

In discussing who had a car and who hadn’t, Freeman said his machine was working badly, to which Shepherd replied that there was plenty of room in his limousine for the Freemans and any others who were carless.

“Mr. Storrs will want to take his car,” said Constance. “He oughtn’t really to drive out alone——”

“Not alone, certainly not!” Bruce replied. “I shall be honored if you will drive with me!”

II

“You didn’t mind?” asked Constance when Bruce got his car under way.

“You mean do I mind driving you out? Please don’t make me say how great the pleasure is!”

“You’re poking fun at me; you always do!”

“Never! Why, if I followed my inclinations I’d come trotting up to your house every day. But it wouldn’t do. You know that!”

“But I wouldn’t want you to do that—not unless you——”

There was a bridge to cross and the pressure of traffic at the moment called for care in negotiating it.

"What were you saying?" he asked as they turned off the brilliantly lighted boulevard. The town lay behind and they moved through open country.

"You know," she said, "I gave you the sign that I wanted to be friends. I had a feeling you knew I needed——"

"What?" he demanded, curious as to the development of her technic.

"Oh, just a little attention! I've tried in every way to tell you that I'm horribly lonely."

"But you oughtn't to be!" he said, vaguely conscious that they were repeating themselves.

"Oh, I know what you think! You think I ought to be very content and happy. But happiness isn't so easy! We don't get it just by wishing."

"I suppose it's the hardest thing in the world to find," he assented.

It was now quite dark and the stars hung brilliant in the cloudless heavens. In her fur coat, with a smart toque to match, Constance had not before seemed so beguiling. His meeting with her in the lonely road with George Whitford and her evident wish not to be seen that day by Franklin Mills or the members of his riding party had rather shaken his first assumption that she could be classified as a harmless flirt. Tonight he didn't care particularly. If Franklin Mills's daughter-in-law wanted to flirt with him he was ready to meet her halfway.

"It's strange, but you know I'm not a bit afraid of you. And the other evening when the rest of us couldn't do a thing with Leila she chose you to take her home. You have a way of inspiring confidence. Shep picks you out, when he hardly knows you, for confidential talks. I've been trying to analyze your—fascinations."

"Oh, come now! Your husband thought I might help him in a small perplexity—purely professional. Nothing to that! And your young sister-in-law was cross at the rest of you that day at Mrs. Torrence's and out of pique chose me to take her home."

"But *I* trust you!"

“Maybe you shouldn’t!”

“Well, that afternoon you caught me out here with Mr. Whitford I knew you wouldn’t tell on me. George was a trifle nervous about it. I told him you were the soul of discretion.”

“But—I didn’t see you! I didn’t see you at all! I’m blind in both eyes and I can be deaf and dumb when necessary!”

“Oh, I knew you wouldn’t rush over town telling on me! It’s really not that! It’s because I knew you wouldn’t that I’m wondering what—*what*—it is that makes even your acquaintances feel that they can rely on you. You know you’re quite a wonderful person. Leila and Millicent were talking about you only yesterday. Not schoolgirl twaddle, but real appreciation!”

“That’s consoling! I’m glad of their good opinion. But you—what did *you* say?”

“Oh, I said I thought you were disagreeable and conceited and generally unpleasant!” She turned toward him with her indolent laugh. “You *know* I wouldn’t say anything unkind of you.” This in so low a tone that it was necessary for him to bend his head to hear. His cheek touched the furry edge of her hat thrillingly.

“It seems strange, our being together this way,” she said. “I wish we hadn’t a destination. I’d like to go right on—and on——”

“That would be all right as long as the gas held out!”

“You refuse to take me seriously!”

“I seem doomed to say the wrong thing to you! You’ll have to teach me how to act and what to say.”

“But I’d rather be the pupil! There are many things you could teach me!”

“Such as——”

“There’s always love!” she replied softly, lingering upon the word; and again it was necessary to bend down to hear. She lifted her face; he felt rather than saw her eyes meeting his. Her breath, for a fleeting instant on his cheek, caused him to give hurried consideration to the ancient question whether a woman who is willing should be kissed or whether delicate ethical questions should outweigh the desirability of the kiss prospective.

He kissed her—first tentatively on the cheek and then more ardently on the lips. She made no protest; he offered no apology. Both were silent for some time. When she spoke it was to say, with serene irrelevance:

"How smoothly your car runs! It increases my respect for the Plantagenet."

"Oh, it's very satisfactory; some of Bud's claims for it are really true!"

Bruce was relieved; but he was equally perplexed. It was an ungallant assumption that any man might, in like circumstances, kiss Constance Mills. On the other hand it eased his conscience to find that she evidently thought so little of it. She had been quite willing to be kissed.... She was a puzzling person, this young woman.

III

The Freemans and the others who had started with them had taken short cuts and were already at the house. They passed through an entry hall into a big square living-room. It was a fit residence for the owner of the encompassing acres and Bruce felt the presence of Franklin Mills before he saw him. This was the kind of thing Mills would like. The house was in keeping with the fertile land, the prize herds, the high-bred horses with which he amused himself.

Mills welcomed the newcomers with a bluff heartiness, as though consciously or unconsciously he adopted a different tone in the country and wished to appear the unobtrusive but hospitable lord of the manor. Leila joined him as he talked a moment to Constance and Bruce.

"You see you can't dodge me! Awfully glad you came. Millie's here somewhere and I think old Bud Henderson will drop in later."

"There'll be supper pretty soon," said Mills. "We're just waiting for everybody to get here. I think you know everyone. It's a pleasure to see you here, Mr. Storrs. Please make yourself at home. Constance, see that Mr. Storrs has a cocktail."

The members of the company gathered about the fire began twitting Constance and Bruce about the length of time it had taken them to drive out. They demanded to know what Connie had talked to him about. He answered them in kind, appealing to Constance to confirm his assertion that they had taken the most expeditious route. They had discussed the political conditions in Poland, he declared.

"Come with me," said Mrs. Torrence, drawing him away. "I want to talk to you! I'm sorry things happened as they did on your first call. I don't want you to get the idea that my house is a place where I pull nothing but rough parties! Please think better of me than that!"

"Heavens, woman! Such a thought never entered my head! I've been thinking seriously of coming back! I need some more of your spiritual uplift!"

"Good! There's more of that Bourbon! But I wanted to say that I was sorry Leila came to my house as she did. That is a problem—not a serious problem, but the child needs a little curbing. She has one good friend— Millicent Harden—that tall, lovely girl standing over there. Do you know Millie?"

"Oh, yes; I've even played golf with her!"

"My! You really have an eye! Well, you might come to call on me! I'm a trifle old to be a good playmate for you; but you might take me on as a sort of aunt—not too old to be unsympathetic with youth. When nothing better offers, look me up!"

"I'd been thinking seriously of falling in love with you! Nothing is holding me back but my natural diffidence!"

She raised her hand warningly.

"Go no further! I can see that you've been well trained. But it isn't necessary to jolly me. I'm not half the fool I look. My self-respect didn't want you to get the idea that I'm a wild woman. I was worried that evening about Leila—she has a heart of gold, but I don't dare take any special interest in her for the absurd reason—what do you think?—I've been suspected of having designs on—our host!"

She laughed merrily. Her mirth was of the infectious sort; Bruce laughed with her; one had to, even when the provocation was slight.

"One doesn't talk of one's host," she said with a deep sigh, "but I was talked about enough when I married Mr. Torrence; I'll never try it again. But why am I taking you into my confidence? Merely that I want you to know my house isn't a booze shop all the time! I'm going to keep my eye on you. If I see you wandering too close to the rifle pits, I'll warn you! May I?"

"Of course you may!" said Bruce, conscious of an honest friendliness in this proffer, but not at once finding words to express his appreciation. "Tell me, do I look as though I might be gassed?"

"I don't know whether you're susceptible or not. But I like you! I'm going to prove it by doing you a favor. Come with me!"

The supper was a buffet affair and the butler was distributing plates and napkins. At one side of the room Franklin Mills was talking to Millicent. Bruce had glanced at them occasionally, thinking with a twinge how young Mills looked tonight, noting how easily he seemed to be holding the girl's interest, not as a man much older but as a contemporary. And he had everything to offer—his unassailable social position and the wealth to support it. As he crossed the room beside Mrs. Torrence, accommodating his long stride to her pattering step, he saw a frown write itself fleetingly on Mills's brow. Millicent—in a soft blue Jersey sport dress, with a felt hat of the same shade adorned with a brilliant pheasant's wing—kept her eyes upon Mills until he had finished something he was saying.

"What's it all about?" demanded Mrs. Torrence, laying her hand upon Millicent's arm. "We knew you two were talking of something confidential and important; that's why we're interrupting you."

"Oh, we're discussing the horrors of Sunday—and whether it should be abolished!" said Millicent. "And Mr. Mills won't be serious!"

"Sunday's always a hard day," remarked Mrs. Torrence. "I'm always worn out trying to decide whether to go to church or stay at home."

"And today?" asked Mills.

"I went! The sermon was most disagreeable. Doctor Lindley told us we all know our duty to God and can't pretend that we don't!"

"Is that what he preached?" asked Mills with a vague smile. "What do you think of the proposition?"

"The man's right! But it doesn't make me any happier to know it," Mrs. Torrence replied. "Next Sunday I'll stay in bed."

She took Mills away for the avowed purpose of asking his private counsel in spiritual matters.

"Isn't she nice?" said Millicent.

"I'm bound to think so; she arranged this for me!"

"Did she?" asked Millicent with feigned innocence. "She did it neatly!"

"She promised to be my friend and then proved it," Bruce said, and then added, "I'm not so sure our host quite liked being taken away."

"How foolish of you! He can always see me!" she replied indifferently. "Don't scorn your food! It is of an exceeding goodness. Bring me up to date a little about yourself. Any more dark days?"

"No-o-o."

She laughed at the prolongation of his denial.

"Come now! I'm beginning to think I'm of no use to you!"

"Right now I'm as happy as a little lark!" he declared.

She had begun to suspect that he had known unhappiness. A love affair perhaps. Or it might have been the war that had taken something of the buoyancy of youth out of him. She was happy in the thought that she was able to help him. He was particularly responsive to a kind of humor she herself enjoyed, and they vied with each other in whimsical ridicule of the cubists in art and the symbolists in literature.

... The guests were redistributing themselves and she suggested that he single out Leila for a little attention.

"Don't have prejudices! There's nothing in that," she said.

"I haven't a prejudice against Miss Mills!"

"Not so formal! I'll give you permission to call her Leila! She'll like it!"

"But you haven't told me I might call you——"

"Millicent let it be!"

"Well, little one, how's your behavior!" demanded Leila when Bruce found her.

"Bad!" Bruce replied in her own key.

"My example, I suppose. I've heard that I'm a bad influence in the community. Let's sit. You and I have got to have an understanding some day; why not now?"

"All right, but don't get too deep—Leila!"

"That's good! I didn't suppose you knew my name. Millie's put you up to that."

"She did. I hope you like it."

"Intensely! Are you falling in love with Millie?"

"That's a secret. If I said I was, what would you say?"

"Atta boy! But—I don't think she is in love with you."

"Your penetration does you credit! I had thought of her as perishing for the hour when I would again dawn upon her sight!"

"You're going good! Really, though, she admits that she likes you ever so much."

"Is that the reason why you think she doesn't love me?"

"Of course! I'm in love myself. I'm simply wild about Freddy Thomas! But I'd die before I'd admit the awful fact to my dearest friend! That's love!"

"How about your Freddy? Is he aware of your infatuation?"

"That's the wonderful part. You see, it's a secret. No one knows it but just Freddy and me!"

"Oh, I see! You pretend to hate Freddy but really you love him?"

"You're a thinker! What would you say if I told you I had a cute little flask upstairs and asked you to meet me in the pantry and have a little nip just to celebrate this event? I had only one cocktail; my dearest Dada saw to that!"

"I'd meet you in the pantry and confiscate the flask!"

She regarded him fixedly for a moment, and her tone and manner changed abruptly.

"You know about life, people, things; I know you do! It's in your eyes, and I'd know it if Millie hadn't said so. Do you really think it is disgraceful for me to get—well, soused—as you've seen me several times? Dada and my aunts lecture me to death—and I hate it—but, well—what do you think?"

Her gravity demanded kindness. He felt infinitely older; she seemed very like a child tonight—an impulsive, friendly child.

"I think I'd cut it out. There's no good in it—for you or anyone else."

"I'll consider that," she replied slowly; then suddenly restless, she suggested that they go into the long enclosed veranda that connected the house with the conservatories.

As they walked back and forth—Leila in frivolous humor now—Bruce caught a glimpse of her father and Millicent just inside the conservatory door. They were talking earnestly. Evidently they had paused to conclude some matter they had been discussing before returning to the house. Millicent held three roses in her hand and lifted them occasionally to her face.

<h1 style="text-align:center">IV</h1>

Still beset by uncertainties as to whether he would increase his chances of happiness by marrying again, Mills was wondering just how a man of his years could initiate a courtship with a girl of Millicent Harden's age. It must be managed in such a way as to preserve his dignity—that must be preserved at all hazards. They had been walking through the conservatory aisles inspecting his roses, which were cultivated by an expert whose salary was a large item of the farm budget. Millicent was asking questions about the development of new floral types and he was answering painstakingly, pleased by her interest.

"It's unfortunate that the human species can't be improved as easily. At least we don't see our way to improving it," he remarked.

He had never thought her so beautiful as now; her charm was rather enhanced by her informal dress. It would be quite possible for him to love her, love her even with a young man's ardor.

"Oh, patience, sir!" she smiled. "Evolution is still going on."

"Or going back! There's our old quarrel!" he laughed. "We always seem to get into it. But your idea that we're not creatures of chance—that there's some unseen power back of everything we call life—that's too much for me. I can understand Darwin—but you!"

"Honestly, now, are you perfectly satisfied to go on thinking we're all creatures of chance?"

"Sometimes I am and then again I'm not!" he replied with a shrug. "I can't quite understand why it is that with everything we have, money and the ability to amuse ourselves, we do at times inquire about that Something that never shows itself or gives us a word."

"Oh, but He does!" She held up the three perfect roses Mills had plucked for her. "He shows Himself in all beautiful things. They're all trying to tell us that the Something we can't see or touch has a great deal to do with our lives."

"Millie," he said in a tone of mock despair, tapping her hand lightly, "you're an incorrigible mystic!"

They were interrupted by a knock on the glass door, which swung open, disclosing Leila and Bruce.

"Mr. Storrs and I are dying of curiosity! You've been talking here for ages!" cried Leila.

"Millie's been amusing herself at my expense," said Mills. "Mr. Storrs, I wish you'd tell me sometime what Miss Harden means when she reaches into the infinite and brings down——"

"Roses!" laughed Millicent.

V

His glimpse of Franklin Mills and Millicent at the conservatory door affected Bruce disagreeably. The fact that the two had been discussing impersonal matters did not lessen his resentment. Millicent with Mills's roses in her hand; Mills courteously attentive, addressing the girl with what to Bruce was a lover-like air, had made a picture that greatly disturbed him.

Very likely, with much this same air, with the same winning manner and voice, Mills had wooed his mother! He saw in Mills a sinister figure—a man who, having taken advantage of one woman, was not to be trusted with another. The pity he had at times felt for Mills went down before a wave of jealous anger and righteous indignation. The man was incapable of any true appreciation of Millicent; he was without wit or soul to penetrate to the pure depths of the girl's nature.

"You two are always talking about things I don't understand!" Leila said to them; and led Bruce on through the conservatories, talking in her inconsequential fashion.

When they returned to the house someone had begun playing old-fashioned games—blindman's buff, drop the handkerchief and London Bridge. When these ceased to amuse, the rugs were cleared away and they danced to the phonograph. Mills encouraged and participated in all this as if anxious to show that he could be as young as the youngest. And what occasion could be more fitting than an evening in his handsome country house, with his children and their friends about him!

With Millicent constantly before his eyes, entering zestfully into all these pleasures, Bruce recovered his tranquillity. For the thousandth time he convinced himself that he was not a weakling to suffer specters of the past and forebodings of the future to mar his life. He danced with Millicent; seized odd moments in which to talk to her; tried to believe that she had a particular smile for him....

"I wonder if you'd drive me in?" asked Mrs. Torrence when the party began to break up.

"I'd been counting on it!" said Bruce promptly.

Constance came along and waived her rights to his escort, as she and Shepherd were taking the Freemans home.

"I believe we're a little better acquainted than we were," she said meaningfully.

"It seemed to me we made a little headway," Bruce replied.

"Come and see me soon! You never can tell when I'll need a little consoling."

"That was a good party," Mrs. Torrence began as Bruce got his car in motion. "Mr. Mills is two or three different men. Sometimes I think he consciously assumes a variety of rôles. He's keen about this country gentleman stuff—unassuming grandeur and all that! But meet him out at dinner in town tomorrow night and you'd never think him capable of playing drop the handkerchief! Makes you wonder just which is the real Mills."

"Maybe we all lead two or three existences without knowing it," Bruce remarked.

"We do! We do, indeed!" the little woman cheerfully agreed. "All except me. I'm always just the same and too much of that!"

"Well, you always come up with a laugh and that helps. Please let me into the secret."

"My dear boy, I learned early in life to hide my tears. Nobody's interested in a cry-baby. And minding my own business saves a lot of bother. I think I've acquired that noble trait!"

"That's genius!" exclaimed Bruce.

"But—in your case I may not do it! I like you, you know."

"Am I to believe that?" he asked seriously.

"I hope you'll believe it. I offered at the beginning of the evening to be your friend until death do us part; I've done some thinking since. I do think occasionally, though you'd never guess it."

"It's an old trick of the world to be mistrustful of thinkers. I've suffered from it myself."

"Listen to me, young man! I've got my eye on you. I suggested to Connie that it would be simpler for her to go in with Shep. I love Connie; she's always been nice to me. But Connie's not just a safe chum for you. Your fascinations might be a trifle too—too——"

"Too," he supplied mockingly, "much for me?"

"Don't be silly! Connie's a young woman of charm, and she likes to use it. And you're not without a little of the same ingredient. You may be nice and friendly with Connie—*and* Shep—but you mustn't forget that there is Shep.

Shep's a nice, dear boy. I'm strong for Shepherd. I could cry when I see how much in love he is with Connie! And of course she doesn't love him in any such way. She sort o' mothers and pets him. She still has her grand love affair before her. Isn't this nasty of me to be talking of her in this fashion! But I don't want you to be the victim. One drive alone with her is enough for you in one evening!"

"Oh, but——"

"Oh, all the buts! We haven't been talking of her at all! Aren't the shadows of that tall tree interesting?"

The shadows of the tall tree were not particularly interesting, but Bruce, speculating a little as to what Mrs. Torrence would say if she knew he had kissed Constance on the drive out, was guiltily glad that she had concluded what he felt to be a well-meant warning against getting in too deep with Mrs. Shepherd Mills.

"You've got a big future," Mrs. Torrence remarked later. "Nothing's going to spoil it. But socially, walk softly. This is a city of illusions. It's the fashion to pretend that everybody's awfully good. Of course everybody isn't! But it's better to fall in with the idea. I'm just giving you the hint. Take Franklin Mills for your model. Always know the right people and do the right thing. There's a man who never sinned in all his life. You're lucky to have caught his eye so soon! I saw him watching you tonight—with approval, I mean. He's a man of power. I advise you to cultivate him a little."

"Oh, my knowing him is just a matter of chance," Bruce replied indifferently.

"He's the most interesting man in town and all the more so because he's puzzling—not all on the surface. An unusual person. And to think he has a daughter like Leila and a son like Shep! I love them both; they're so unlike him! You wouldn't know them for the same breed. One couldn't love *him*, you know; he's far too selfish and self-satisfied for that!"

CHAPTER TWELVE

I

As Bruce was driving past the Mills's residence one evening several weeks later, Carroll hailed him. Mills, it appeared, had driven out with Carroll and the limousine waited at the curb to carry the secretary on home. Carroll asked Bruce whether he would go with him to a lecture at the art institute the following night; a famous painter was to speak and it promised to be an interesting occasion. Mills lingered while the young men arranged to meet at the club for dinner before the lecture, and Bruce was about to climb back into his car when Mills said detainingly:

"Storrs, won't you have pity on me? Carroll's just refused to dine with me. My daughter's going out and there's just myself. Do you think you could stand it?"

"The soil of the day is upon me!" said Bruce. "But——"

He very much wished to refuse, but the invitation was cordially given, and taken by surprise, he was without a valid excuse for declining.

"You don't need to dress and you may leave the moment you're bored," said Mills amiably.

"Sorry, but I've got to run," said Carroll. "I'll send your car right back, Mr. Mills. Thank you. I envy you two your quiet evening!"

Mills led the way upstairs, opened the door of one of the bedrooms and turned on the lights.

"The room's supposed to be in order—it's my son's old room. Ring if you don't find what you want."

Bruce closed the door and stared about him.

Shepherd's old room! It was a commodious chamber, handsomely furnished. The bath was a luxurious affair. As he drew off his coat Bruce's mind turned back to his little room in the old frame house in Laconia; the snowy window draperies his mother always provided, and the other little tributes of her love, fashioned by her own hands, that adorned the room in which he had dreamed the long, long dreams of youth. Through the dormer windows he had heard the first bird song in the spring, and on stormy nights in winter had sunk to sleep to the north wind's hoarse shout through the elms and maples in the yard.

"My son's room!" Franklin Mills had said carelessly as he turned away. The phrase still rang in Bruce's ears. Mills could not know; he could not even suspect! No man would be callous enough to make such a remark if he believed he was uttering it to an unrecognized child of his own blood.

Bruce laved his face and brushed his hair and went down the hall to the library where Mills had taken him on the memorable night they met in the storm. The portrait which had so disturbed Mills still hung in its place. Bruce turned his back on it and took up the evening newspapers.

A maid appeared to say that Mr. Mills was answering a long-distance call, but would be free in a moment; and a little later the butler came in with a tray and began concocting a cocktail. While this was in preparation a low whistle from the door caused Bruce to glance round. Leila was peering at him, her head alone being visible.

"I thought you were a burglar!" she whispered.

Bruce pointed to the servant, who was solemnly manipulating the shaker, and beckoned her to enter.

"Briggs! You lied to me again!" she said severely as she swept into the room. "You told me there wasn't a drop in the house!"

"It was the truth, Miss Leila, when I told you," the man replied gravely. "A friend of Mr. Mills left this at the door this morning."

"I don't believe it! It was more likely a friend of mine. I say, little one, how do I look?"

"Queenly," Bruce replied. "If you were more beautiful my eyes couldn't bear it."

"Cut it! Am I really all right?"

"I'd be ashamed if I didn't know it!"

"Good boy! You have a taste!"

She was charming indeed in her evening gown, which he praised in ignorant terms that she might correct him. She remained standing, drawing on her gloves, and explaining that she was dining at the Tarletons and wasn't highly edified at the prospect. Her going was a concession to her father. The Tarletons had a young guest whose grandfather had once been a business associate of her Grandfather Mills; hence she must sacrifice herself.

"Dad's keen about the old family stuff. Just look at those grand old relics up there." She indicated the line of family portraits with a disdainful gesture. "I come in and make faces at them when I feel naughty. I can't tell my grandfathers apart, and don't want to!"

"How lacking in piety!" said Bruce, who could have pointed out her Grandfather Mills! He bestowed a hasty glance at the portrait, satisfied that Leila at least would never detect her ancestor's resemblance to himself. The servant, having sufficiently agitated the cocktails, withdrew. Leila, waiting till the door to the back stairs closed, began advancing with long steps and a rowdyish swagger toward the tray.

"Alone with a cocktail! And I'm going to a dry party! Hist!" She bent her head toward the door, her hand to her ear. "What's the Colonel doing?" she asked.

"At the telephone; he'll be here any minute."

"Quick! Fill that glass—that's the good sport!"

"Service for two only! You wouldn't rob *me*!"

"Please—I don't want my gloves to reek of gin—please!"

"You can't touch that tray—you can't touch that shaker! You're hypnotized!" he declared solemnly.

"Oh, tush!" With a quick movement she tried to grasp the shaker; but he caught her hand, held it a moment, then let it fall to her side while he smiled into her bright, eager eyes.

"In the name of all your ancestors I forbid you!" he said.

"You wouldn't trust me with one?" she demanded, half defiant, half acquiescing.

"Not tonight, when you're meeting old family friends and all that!"

"Pshaw!" She stamped her foot. "I can stop at half a dozen houses and get a drink——"

"But you won't; really you won't!"

"What's it to you—why should you care?" she demanded, looking him straight in the eyes.

"Aren't we friends?" he asked. "A friend wouldn't give it to you. See! You don't really want it at all—it was just an hallucination!"

"Oh, no!" she said, puckering her face and scowling her abhorrence of the idea while her eyes danced merrily. "I just *dreamed* I wanted it. Well, score one for you, old top! You're even nicer than I thought you were!"

"Leila, haven't you *gone* yet?" exclaimed Mills, appearing suddenly in the room.

"No, Dada! I was just kidding Bruce a little. Hope you have a nice dinner! Don't be too solemn, and don't scold your guest the way you do me. Yes, I've got my key and every little thing. Good-night. Come and see me sometime, Bruce." She lifted her face for her father to kiss, paused in the doorway to shake her fist at Bruce and tripped down the hall singing.

"Do pardon me for keeping you waiting," said Mills. "I had a New York call and the connection was bad. Let's see what we have here——"

"Allow me, sir——"

As Bruce gave the drinks a supplemental shake Mills inspected the two glasses, ostensibly to satisfy himself that the housekeeping staff had properly cared for them, but really, Bruce surmised, to see whether Leila had been tippling.

II

When they went down to the dining-room Bruce found it less of an ordeal than he had expected to sit at Mills's table. Mills was a social being; his courtesy was unfailing, and no doubt he was sincere in his expressions of gratitude to Bruce for sharing his meal.

The table was lighted by four tapers in tall candlesticks of English silver. The centerpiece was a low bowl of pink roses, the product of the Deer Trail conservatories. Mills, in spite of his austere preferences in other respects, deferred to changing fashions in the furnishing of his table, to which he gave the smart touch of a sophisticated woman. It was a way of amusing himself, and he enjoyed the praise of the women who dined with him for his taste, the discrimination he exercised in picking up novelties in exclusive New York shops. Even when alone he enjoyed the contemplation of precious silver and crystal, and the old English china in which he specialized. He invited Bruce's attention, as one connoisseur to another, to the graceful lines and colors of the water glasses—a recent acquisition. The food was excellent, but doubtless no better than Mills ate every night, whether he dined alone or with Leila. The courses were served unhurriedly; Franklin Mills was not a man one could imagine bolting his food. Again Bruce found his dislike ebbing. The idea that the man was his father only fleetingly crossed his mind. If Mills suspected the relationship he was an incomparable actor....

"I've never warmed to the idea that America should be an asylum for the scum of creation; it's my Anglo-Saxon conceit, I suppose. You have the look of the old American stock——"

"I suppose I'm a pretty fair American," Bruce replied. "My home town is Laconia—settled by Revolutionary soldiers; they left their imprint. It's a patriotic community."

"Oh, yes; Laconia! Carroll was telling me that had been your home. He has some relatives there himself."

"Yes, I know them," Bruce said, meeting Mills's gaze carelessly. "The fact is I know, or used to know, nearly everybody in the town."

"Carroll may have told you that I had some acquaintance with the place myself. That was a long time ago. I went there to look after some business interests for my father. It was a part of my apprenticeship. I seem to recall people of your name; Storrs is not so common—?"

"My father was John Storrs—a lawyer," said Bruce in the tone of one stating a fact unlikely to be of particular interest.

"Yes; John Storrs——" Mills repeated musingly. "I recall him very well—and his wife—your mother—of course. Delightful people. I've always remembered those months I spent there with a particular pleasure. For the small place Laconia was then, there was a good deal doing—dances and picnics. I remember your mother as the leading spirit in all the social affairs. Is she——"

"Father and mother are both gone. My mother died a little more than a year ago."

"I'm very sorry," Mills murmured sympathetically. "For years I had hoped to go back to renew old acquaintances, but Laconia is a little inaccessible from here and I never found it possible."

Whether Mills had referred to his temporary residence in Laconia merely to show how unimportant and incidental it was in his life remained a question. But Bruce felt that if Mills could so lightly touch upon it, he himself was equal to gliding over it with like indifference. Mills asked with a smile whether Gardner's Grove was still in existence, that having been a favorite picnic ground, an amateurish sort of country club where the Laconians used to have their dances. The oak trees there were the noblest he had ever seen. Bruce expressed regret that the grove was gone....

Mills was shrewd; and Bruce was aware that the finely formed head across the table housed a mind that carefully calculated all the chances of life even into the smallest details. He wondered whether he had borne himself as well as Mills in the ordeal. The advantage had been on Mills's side; it was his house, his table. Possibly he had been waiting for some such opportunity as this to sound the son of Marian Storrs as to what he knew—hoped perhaps to surprise him into some disclosure of the fact if she had ever, in a moment of weakness or folly, spoken of him as other than a passing acquaintance.

"We'll go down to the billiard room to smoke," Mills remarked at the end of the dinner. "We'll have our coffee there."

Easy chairs and a davenport at one end of the billiard room invited to comfort. On the walls were mounted animal heads and photographs of famous horses.

"Leila doesn't approve of these works of art," said Mills, seeing Bruce inspecting them. "She thinks I ought to move them to the farm. They do look out of place here. Sit where you like."

He half sprawled on the davenport as one who, having dined to his satisfaction and being consequently on good terms with the world, wishes to set an example of informality to a guest. Bruce wondered what Mills did on evenings he spent alone in the big house; tried to visualize the domestic scene in the years of Mrs. Mills's life.

"You see Shepherd occasionally?" Mills asked when the coffee had been served. "The boy hasn't quite found himself yet. Young men these days have more problems to solve than we faced when I was your age. Everything is more complicated—society, politics, everything. Maybe it only seems so. Shep's got a lot of ideas that seem wild to me. Can't imagine where he gets them. Social reforms and all that. I sometimes think I made a mistake in putting him into business. He might have been happier in one of the professions—had an idea once he wanted to be a doctor, but I discouraged it. A mistake, perhaps."

Mills's manner of speaking of Shepherd was touched with a certain remoteness. He appeared to invite Bruce's comment, not in a spirit of sudden intimacy, but as if he were talking with a man of his own years who was capable of understanding his perplexities. It seemed to Bruce in those few minutes that he had known Franklin Mills a very long time. He was finding it difficult to conceal his embarrassment under equivocal murmurs. But he pulled himself together to say cordially:

"Shepherd is a fine fellow, Mr. Mills. You can't blame him for his idealism. There's a lot of it in the air."

"He was not cut out for business," Mills remarked. "Business is a battle these days, and Shep isn't a fighter."

"Must the game be played in that spirit?" asked Bruce with a smile.

"Yes, if you want to get anywhere," Mills replied grimly. "Shall we do some billiards?"

III

Mills took his billiards seriously. It was, Bruce could see, a pastime much to his host's taste; it exercised his faculties of quick calculation and deft execution. Mills explained that he had employed a professional to teach him. He handled the cue with remarkable dexterity; it was a pleasure to watch the ease and grace of his playing. Several times, after a long run, he made a wild shot, unnecessarily it seemed, and out of keeping with his habitual even play. Bud Henderson had spoken of this peculiarity. Bruce wondered whether it was due to fatigue or to the intrusion upon Mills's thoughts of some business matter that had caused a temporary break in the unity of eye and hand. Or it might have been due to some decision that had been crystallizing in his subconsciousness and manifested itself in this odd way. Mills was too good a player to make a fluke intentionally, merely to favor a less skillful opponent. He accepted his ill fortune philosophically. He was not a man to grow fretful or attempt to explain his errors.

"We're not so badly matched," he remarked when they finished and he had won by a narrow margin. "You play a good game."

"You got the best there was in me!" said Bruce. "I rarely do as well as that."

"Let's rest and have a drink." Mills pressed a button. "I'm just tired enough to want to sit awhile."

Bruce had expected to leave when the game was ended, but Mills gave him no opportunity. He reestablished himself on the davenport and began talking more desultorily than before. For a time, indeed, Bruce carried the burden of the conversation. Some remark he let fall about the South caused Mills to ask him whether he had traveled much in America.

"I've walked over a lot of it," Bruce replied. "That was after I came back from the little splurge overseas. Gave myself a personally conducted tour, so to speak. Met lots of real tramps. I stopped to work occasionally—learned something that way."

Mills was at once interested. He began asking questions as to the living conditions of the people encountered in this adventure and the frame of mind of the laborers Bruce had encountered.

"You found the experience broadening, of course. It's a pity more of us can't learn of life by direct contact with the people."

Under Mills's questioning the whole thing seemed to Bruce more interesting than he had previously thought it. The real reason for his long tramp—the fact that he had taken to the road to adjust himself to his mother's confession that he was the son of a man of whom he had never heard—would probably have given Mills a distinct shock.

"I wish I could have done that myself!" Mills kept saying.

Bruce was sorry that he had stumbled into the thing. Mills was sincerely curious; it was something of an event to hear first-hand of such an experience. His questions were well put and required careful answers. Bruce found himself anxious to appear well in Mills's eyes. But Mills was leading toward something. He was commenting now on the opportunities open to young men of ability in the business world, with Bruce's experiences as a text.

"A professional man is circumscribed. There's a limit to his earning power. Most men in the professions haven't the knack of making money. They're usually unwise in the investments they make of their savings."

"But they have the joy of their work," Bruce replied quickly. "We can't measure their success just by their income."

"Oh, I grant you that! But many of the doors of prosperity and happiness are denied them."

"But others are open! Think of the sense of service a physician must feel in helping and saving. And even a puttering architect who can't create masterpieces has the fun of doing his small jobs well. He lives the life he wants to live. There are painters and musicians who know they can never reach the high places; but they live the life! They starve and are happy!"

Bruce bent forward eagerly, the enthusiasm bright in his eyes. He had not before addressed Mills with so much assurance. The man was a materialist; his standards were fixed in dollars. It was because he reckoned life in false terms that Shepherd was afraid of him.

"Oh, don't misunderstand me! I realize the diversity of talents that are handed out to us poor mortals. But if you were tempted to become a painter, say, and you knew you would never be better than second-rate, and at the same time you were pretty sure you could succeed in some business and live comfortably—travel, push into the big world currents and be a man of mark—what would you do?”

“Your question isn’t fair, because it’s not in the design of things for us to see very far ahead. But I’ll answer! If I had a real urge to paint I’d go to it and take my chance.”

“That’s a fine spirit, Storrs; and I believe you mean it. But——”

Mills rose and, thrusting his hands into his trousers’ pockets, walked across the room, his head bent, and then swung round, took the cigar from his lips and regarded the ash fixedly.

“Now,” he said, “don’t think me ungracious”—he smiled benignantly—“but I’m going to test you. I happen right now to know of several openings in financial and industrial concerns for just such a young man as you. They are places calling for clear judgment and executive talent such as I’d say you possess. The chances of getting on and up would be good, even if you had no capital. Would you care to consider these places?”

The smile had faded from his face; he waited gravely, with a scarcely perceptible eagerness in his eyes, for the answer.

“I think not, sir. No, Mr. Mills, I’m quite sure of it.” And then, thinking that his rejection of the offer was too abrupt and not sufficiently appreciative, Bruce added: “You see, I’m going to make a strong effort to get close to the top in my profession. I may fall off the ladder, but—I’ll catch somewhere! I have a little money—enough to tide me over bad times—and I know I’d be sorry if I quit right at the start. It’s kind of you to make the suggestion. I assure you I’m grateful—it’s certainly very kind of you!”

“Oh, I’m wholly selfish in suggesting it! In my various interests we have trouble finding young men of the best sort. I know nothing of your circumstances, of course; but I thought maybe a promising business opening would appeal to you. On the whole”—Mills was still standing, regarding Bruce fixedly as though trying to accommodate himself to some newly discovered quality in his guest—“I like to see a young man with confidence in his own powers. Yours is the spirit that wins. I hope you won’t take it amiss that I broached the matter. You have your engaging personality to blame for that!”

"I'm glad to know it isn't a liability!" said Bruce; and this ended the discussion.

IV

He left the house with his mind in confusion as to the meaning of Mills's offer. He drove about for an hour, pondering it, reviewing the whole evening from the first mention of Laconia to the suggestion, with its plausible inadvertence, that business openings might be found for him. Mills was hardly the man to make such a proposition to a comparative stranger without reason. The very manner in which he had approached the subject was significant. *Mills knew!* If he didn't know, at least his suspicions were strongly aroused. Either his conscience was troubling him and he wished to quiet it by a display of generosity, or he was anxious to establish an obligation that would reduce to the minimum the chance that any demand might be made upon him. Bruce was glad to be in a position to refuse Mills's help; his mother's care and self-denial had made it unnecessary for him to abase himself by accepting Mills's bounty.

He wished he knew some way of making Mills understand that he was in no danger; that any fears of exposure he might entertain were groundless. His pride rose strong in him as he reviewed his hours spent with Mills. He had not acquitted himself badly; he had forced Mills to respect him, and this was a point worth establishing. When finally he fell asleep it was with satisfaction,—a comforting sense of his independence and complete self-mastery.

CHAPTER THIRTEEN

I

Mills, too, though lately mistrustful of his own emotions, was well satisfied with the result of the long evening. He had spoken of Marian Storrs to Marian's son and the effect had been to strengthen his belief that the young man knew nothing that could in any way prove annoying. He was a little sorry that he had suggested finding a business opening for Storrs; but decided that on the whole he had managed the matter in a manner to conceal his real purpose. Bruce had said that he was not wholly dependent upon his earnings for a livelihood, and this in itself was reassuring and weighed strongly against the possibility of his ever asserting any claim even if he knew or suspected their relationship.

In his careful study of Bruce at their various meetings Mills had been impressed increasingly by the young man's high-mindedness, his self-confidence and fine reticences, the variety and range of his interests. Ah, if only Shepherd were like that! It was a cruel fate that had given him a son he could never own, who had drifted across the smooth-flowing current of his life to suggest a thousand contrasts with Shepherd Mills—Shep with his pathetically small figure, his absurd notions of social equality and his inability to grasp and deal with large affairs!

Ugly as the fact was, Bruce Storrs was a Mills; it wasn't merely in the resemblance to the portrait of Franklin Mills III that this was evident. Young Storrs's mental processes were much like those of the man who was, to face it frankly, his grandfather. Bruce Storrs, who had no right to the Mills name, was likely to develop those traits that had endeared Franklin Mills III to the community—traits that nature, with strange perversity, had failed utterly to transmit to his lawful son.

Mills, in his new security, pondered these things with a degree of awe. The God in whom he had much less faith than in a protective tariff or a sound currency system might really be a more potent agent in mundane affairs than he, Franklin Mills, who believed in nothing very strongly that couldn't be reduced to figures, had ever thought possible.

As winter gripped the town Mills was uneasy in the thought that he wasn't getting enough out of life. Even with eight million dollars and the tastes of a cultivated gentleman, life was paying inadequate dividends. And there across the hedge lived Millicent. He would marry Millicent; but there were matters to be arranged first....

Millicent was the most beautiful young woman he knew, and she had brains and talents that added enormously to her desirability. Against this was the fact that the Hardens had risen out of nowhere, and Millicent's possession of a father and mother could not be ignored. Their very simplicity and the possession of the homely parochial virtues so highly valued in the community by Mills and his generation made it possible to do something toward giving them a social status.

Discreet inquiry revealed the consoling fact that Nathaniel Harden was taxed on approximately a million dollars' worth of property. Not for nothing had he applied himself diligently for twenty-five years to the manufacture of the asthma cure! He was also the creator of a hair tonic, a liver accelerator and a liniment that were almost as well established in the proprietary drug market as the asthma remedy. Mills was amazed to find that there was so much money in the business.

Harden had not brought his laboratory with him when he moved to the city, but it was still under his own direction. Fortunately, as Mills viewed the matter, the business was conducted under a corporate title, that of the International Medical Company, which was much less objectionable than if it bore Harden's name, though the doctor's picture did, regrettably, adorn the bottles in which the world-famous asthma cure was offered and exposed for sale.

In his investigations Mills found that Harden had invested his money in some of the soundest of local securities. It spoke well for the Doctor's business acumen that he owned stock in the First National Bank, which Mills controlled. A vacancy occurring in the directorate, Mills caused Harden to be elected to the board. Harden was pleased but not overcome by the honor. Mrs. Harden manifested a greater pleasure and expressed herself to Mills with characteristic heartiness.

Mills, after much careful consideration, gave a dinner for Doctor and Mrs. Harden—made it appear to be a neighborly affair, though he was careful to ask only persons whose recognition of the Hardens was likely to add to their prestige. Mills had rather dreaded seeing Harden in a dress suit, but the Doctor clad in social vestments was nothing to be ashamed of. He revealed a sense of humor and related several stories of a former congressman from his old district that were really funny. Mrs. Harden looked as well and conducted herself with quite as much ease as the other women present. No one would have guessed that she made salt-rising bread once a week for her husband's delectation and otherwise continued, in spite of her prosperous state, to keep in close touch with her kitchen.

After giving the dinner Mills waited a little before venturing further in his attempt to lift the social sky line for the Hardens. Much as he disliked Constance, he was just the least bit afraid of her. Constance was not stupid, and he was not blind to the fact that she wielded a certain influence. His daughter-in-law could easily further his plans for imparting dignity to the Hardens. And he foresaw that if he married again it would be Connie, not Shepherd or Leila, who would resent the marriage as a complicating circumstance when the dread hour arrived for the parceling of his estate. Leila would probably see little more than a joke in a marriage that would make her best friend her stepmother.

"Why isn't Millie in the Dramatic Club?" he asked Leila one day when they were dining alone together.

"Not so easy, Dada. I talked to some of the membership committee about it last spring and I have a sneaking idea that they don't want her. Not just that, of course; it's not Millie but the patent medicine they can't swallow. I think the club's a bore myself. There's a bunch of girls in it—Connie's one of them—who think they're Ethel Barrymores and Jane Cowlses, and Millie, you know, might be a dangerous rival. Which she would be, all right! So they kid themselves with the idea that the club really stands for the real old graveyard society of our little village and that they've got to be careful who gets by."

"How ridiculous!" Mills murmured.

"Silly! I do hate snobs! Millie isn't asked to a lot of the nicest parties just because she's new in town. Doctor Harden's guyed a good deal about his fake medicines. I don't see anything wrong with Doc myself." Leila bent her head in a quick way she had when mirth seized her. "Bud Henderson says the Harden hair tonic's the smoothest furniture polish on the market."

Mills laughed, but not heartily. The thought of Henderson's ridicule chilled him. Henderson entertained a wide audience with his humor; he must be cautious....

II

Leila was an impossible young democrat, utterly devoid of the sense of social values. He must make an ally of Constance. Connie always wanted something; it was one of Connie's weaknesses to want things. Connie's birthday falling in the second week in December gave him a hint. Leila had mentioned the anniversary and reminded her father that he usually made Connie a present. Connie expected presents and was not satisfied with anything cheap.

Mills had asked a New York jeweler to send out some pearls from which to make a selection for a Christmas present for Leila. They were still in his vault at the office. He chose from the assortment a string of pearls with a diamond pendant and bestowed it upon his daughter-in-law on the morning of her birthday. He had made her handsome presents before, but nothing that pleased her so much as this.

While Connie's gratitude was still warm, Mills found occasion to mention Millicent one evening when he was dining at Shepherd's. Leila had been asked to some function to which Millicent was not bidden. Mills made the very natural comment that it was unfortunate that Millicent, intimate as she was with Leila, could not share all her pleasures; the discrimination against the Hardens' daughter was unjust. Quick to see what was expected of her, Constance replied that it was Millicent's own fault that she hadn't been taken up more generally. It was perhaps out of loyalty to her parents that she had not met more responsively the advances of women who, willing to accept Millicent, yet couldn't quite see her father and mother in the social picture. Now that she thought of it, Constance herself had never called on Mrs. Harden, but she would do so at once. There was no reason at all why Millicent shouldn't be admitted to the Dramatic Club; she would see to that. She thought the impression had got around that Millicent was, if not

Bohemian in her sympathies, at least something of a nonconformist in her social ideas. It was her artistic nature, perhaps.

"That's nonsense," said Mills. "There isn't a better bred girl in town. She's studious, quite an intellectual young woman—but that's hardly against her. I always feel safe about Leila when I know she and Millicent are together. And her father and mother are really very nice—unpretentious, kindly people. Of course the patent medicine business isn't looked on with great favor—but——"

"But—it's about as respectable as canning our native corn or cutting up pigs," Constance suggested.

She was bewildered to find Mills, who had looked askance at her own claims to social recognition because her father's real estate and insurance business was rather insignificant, suddenly viewing the asthma cure so tolerantly. However, a father-in-law who gave her valuable presents must be humored in his sudden manifestation of contempt for snobbery. This was the first time Mills had ever shown any disposition to recognize her social influence. No matter what had caused his change of heart, it was flattering to her self-esteem that he was, even so indirectly, asking her aid. She liked Millicent well enough and gladly promised to help her along.

When Mills left she asked Shepherd what he thought was in the wind; but he failed to be aroused by the suggestion that his father might be thinking of marrying Millicent. His father would never marry again, Shepherd insisted; certainly not unless he found a woman of suitable age, for companionship and to promote his comfort when Leila was settled.

"You don't know your father any better than I do, Shep. He always has a motive for everything he does—you may be sure of that!"

"Father means to be just and kind," said Shepherd, half-heartedly, as if he were repeating a formula in which he didn't believe.

"When he's moved to be generous he certainly lets go with a free hand," Constance remarked. "That necklace wasn't cheap. I'm afraid it wasn't just a spontaneous outburst of affection for me. I think I owe it to Millicent!"

"Oh, father likes you, Connie. You're foolish to think he doesn't," Shepherd replied defensively.

"I think your father's getting nervous about Leila. He's set his heart on having Carroll in the family. But Arthur's too old. Leila ought to marry a younger man. Your father's been suspecting me of promoting her little affair with Freddy Thomas—I've seen it in his eye. But I don't think she's serious about that. She says she's crazy about him, but as she tells everyone, it doesn't mean anything."

"Thomas—no," Shepherd replied slowly. "I shouldn't be for that myself. I don't like the idea of her marrying a divorced man. Arthur would be quite fine, I think. He's a gentleman and he understands Leila. The man who marries her has got to understand her—make a lot of allowances."

Constance smiled her amusement at his display of sagacity.

"Wrong again, Shep! Leila will settle down and be the tamest little matron in town. She seems to have cut out her drinking. That was more for effect than anything else. She's got about all the fun to be had out of making people think her a perfect little devil. By the way, speaking of marrying men, that young Storrs is a nice fellow—rather impressive. I think Leila's a little tempted to try her hand at flirting with him. She was at the Henderson's yesterday afternoon and Bud was shaking up some cocktails. Mr. Storrs came in and Leila refused to drink. She joked about it, but said he had made her promise to quit. He's not a prig, but he knows the danger line when he sees it."

"Yes—yes," Shepherd assented eagerly. "He's one of the most attractive men I ever met. He's the kind of fellow you'd trust with anything you've got!"

"Yes—and be safe," Constance replied. "He's hardly likely to do anything rash."

They came again, as they often did, to a discussion of Franklin Mills.

"Your father's the great unaccountable," sighed Constance. "I long since gave up trying to understand him. He's a master hand at dodging round things that don't strike him just right. The way he turned down your clubhouse scheme was just like him; and the way he spurned my little suggestion about buying a summer place. By the way, what are you doing about the clubhouse? I thought you were selling your Rogers Trust stock to get money to build it. You haven't weakened, have you, Shep?"

"No! certainly not. I'm going ahead as soon as the weather opens up. I sold my stock yesterday and I mean to do the thing right. When I was in Chicago last week I looked at a number of community houses and got a lot of ideas."

"Well, don't get cold feet. That thing has worried you a lot. I'd do it or I'd forget it."

"Oh, I'm going to do it all right!" Shepherd replied jauntily. He greatly wished her to think him possessed of the courage and initiative to carry through large projects no matter how formidable the opposition.

CHAPTER FOURTEEN

I

Franklin Mills was now on better terms with himself than at any time since Bruce Storrs's appearance in town. Open weather had made it possible for him to go to Deer Trail once or twice a week for a ride, and he walked several miles every day. Leila had agreed to accompany him on a trip to Bermuda the first of February. In his absence the machinery he had set in motion would be projecting the Hardens a little further into the social limelight without his appearing to be concerned in it.

He was hoping that the trip would serve effectually to break off Thomas's attentions to Leila, and that within the next year he would see her engaged to Carroll. Leila couldn't be driven; to attempt to force the thing would be disastrous. But the thought of her marrying Thomas, a divorced man, was abhorrent, while Carroll was in all ways acceptable. What Shepherd lacked in force and experience, Carroll would bring into the family. Mills was annoyed that he had ever entertained a thought that he could be denied anything in life that he greatly coveted, or deprived of the comfort and peace he had so long enjoyed. He would prolong his Indian Summer; his last years should be his happiest.

He enjoyed the knowledge that he exercised, with so little trouble to himself, a real power in the community. In a directors' meeting no one spoke with quite his authoritative voice. No other business man in town was so thoroughly informed in finance and economics as he. He viewed the life of his city with the tranquil delight of a biologist who in the quiet of his laboratory studies specimens that have been brought to the slide without any effort on his own part. And Mills liked to see men squirm—silly men who overreached themselves, pretentious upstarts who gestured a great deal with a minimum of accomplishment. Blessed with both brains and money, he derived the keenest satisfaction in screening himself from contact with the vulgar while he participated in the game like an invisible master chess player....

Doctor Lindley had asked him to come in to St. Barnabas to look at the Mills Memorial window, which had been restored with Mills's money. He stopped on his way to the office a few days before Christmas and found Lindley busy in his study. They went into the church and inspected the window, which was quite as good as new. While they were viewing it Mrs. Torrence came in, her vivacity subdued to the spirit of the place. She was on a committee to provide the Christmas decorations.

"You're just the man I want to see," she said to Mills. "I was going to call you up. There's some stuff in your greenhouses I could use if you don't mind."

"Anything I've got! Tell me what you want and I'll have the people at the farm deliver it."

"That's fine! I knew you'd be glad to help. The florists are such robbers at Christmas." She scribbled a memorandum of her needs on an envelope and left them.

Mills stood with his hand resting on the Mills pew for a last glance at the transept window. The church, which had survived all the changes compelled by the growth of the city, was to Mills less of a holy place than a monument to the past. His grandfather and father had been buried from the church; here he had been married, and here Shepherd and Leila had been baptized. Leila would want a church wedding.... His thoughts transcribed a swift circle; then, remembering that the rector was waiting, he followed him into the vestry.

"Can't you come in for a talk?" asked Lindley after Mills had expressed his gratification that the window had been repaired so successfully.

"No; I see there are people waiting for you." Mills glanced at a row of men and women of all ages—a discouraged-looking company ranged along the wall outside the study door. One woman with a shawl over her head coughed hideously as she tried to quiet a dirty child. "These people want advice or other help? I suppose there's no end to your work."

"It's my business to help them," the rector replied. "They're all strangers—I never saw any of them before. I rather like that—their sense of the church standing ready to help them."

"If they ask for money, what do you do?" asked Mills practically. "Is there a fund?"

"Well, I have a contingency fund—yes. Being here in the business district, I have constant calls that I don't feel like turning over to the charity society. I deal with them right here the best I can. I make mistakes, of course."

"How much have you in hand now?" Mills asked bluntly. The bedraggled child had begun to whimper, and the mother, in hoarse whispers, was attempting to silence it.

"Well, I did have about four dollars," laughed Lindley, "but Mrs. Torrence handed me a hundred this morning."

"I'll send you a check for a thousand for these emergency cases. When it gets low again, let me know."

"That's fine, Mills! I can cheer a good many souls with a thousand dollars. This is generous of you, indeed!"

"Oh—Lindley!" Mills had reached the street door when he paused and retraced his steps. "Just a word—sometime ago in my office I talked to you in a way I've regretted. I'm afraid I wasn't quite—quite just, to you and the church—to organized religion. I realize, of course, that the church——"

"The church," said Lindley smilingly, "the church isn't these walls; it's here!" He tapped his breast lightly. "It's in your heart and mine."

"That really simplifies the whole thing!" Mills replied, and with a little laugh he went on to his office.

He thought it fine of the minister to give audience to the melancholy suppliants who sought him for alms and counsel. He didn't envy Lindley his job, but it had to be done by someone. Lindley was really a very good fellow indeed, Mills reflected—a useful man in the community, and not merely an agreeable table companion and witty after-dinner speaker.

II

Before he read his mail Mills dispatched the check for a thousand dollars by special messenger. It was a pleasure to help Lindley in his work. A man who had to deal with such unpleasant specimens of humanity as collected at

Lindley's door shouldn't be disregarded. He remembered having seen Lindley driving about in a rattletrap machine that was a disgrace to the parish and the town. It was a reflection upon St. Barnabas that its rector was obliged to go about his errands in so disreputable a car.

When Carroll came in with some reports Mills told him to see Henderson and order a Plantagenet for Lindley to be delivered at the clergyman's house Christmas morning.

Carroll reported a court decision in Illinois sustaining the validity of some municipal bonds in which Mills had invested.

"Christmas presents coming in early," Mills remarked as he read the telegram. "I thought I was stung there."

He approved of the world and its ways. It was a pretty good world, after all; a world in which he wielded power, as he liked to wield it, quietly, without subjecting himself to the fever and fret of the market place. Among other memoranda Carroll had placed on his desk was a list of women—old friends of Mrs. Mills—to whom he had sent flowers every Christmas since her death. The list was kept in the office files from year to year to guard against omissions. Sentiment. Mills liked to believe himself singularly blessed with sentiment. He admired himself for this fidelity to his wife's old friends. They probably spoke to one another of these annual remembrances as an evidence of the praiseworthy feeling he entertained for the old times.

"You told me to keep on picking up Rogers Trust whenever it was in the market," said Carroll. "Gurley called up yesterday and asked if you wanted any more. I've got two hundred shares here—paid three eighteen. They're closing the transfer books tomorrow so I went ahead without consulting you."

"That part of it's all right," Mills remarked, scanning the certificate. "Who's selling this?"

"It was in Gurley's name—he'd bought it himself."

"A little queer," Mills remarked. "There were only a few old stockholders who had blocks of two hundred—Larsen, Skinner, Saintsbury; and Shep and Leila had the same amount. None of them would be selling now. Suppose you step over to the Trust Company and see where Gurley got this.

It makes no particular difference—I'm just a little curious. There's been no talk about the merger—no gossip?"

"Nothing that I've heard. I'm pretty sure Gurley had no inkling of it. If he had, of course he wouldn't have let go at the price he asked."

When Carroll went out Mills took a turn across the floor. Before resuming his chair he stood for a moment at the window looking off toward the low hills vaguely limned on the horizon. His mood had changed. He greatly disliked to be puzzled. And he was unable to account for the fact that Gurley, a broker with whom he rarely transacted any business, had become possessed of two hundred shares of Roger Trust just at this time.

Larsen, Skinner and Saintsbury were all in the secret of the impending merger with the Central States Company. There was Shepherd; he hadn't told Shepherd, but there had been no reason why he should tell Shepherd any more than he would have made a confidante of Leila, who probably had forgotten that she owned the stock. Having acquired two-thirds of the Rogers shares, all that was necessary was to call a meeting of the stockholders and put the thing through in accordance with the formula already carefully prepared by his lawyers.

When Carroll came back he placed a memorandum on Mills's desk and started to leave the room.

"Just a moment, Carroll"—Mills eyed the paper carefully. "So it was Shep who sold to Gurley—is that right?"

"Yes," Carroll assented. "Gurley only held it a day before he offered it to me."

"Shepherd—um—did Shep tell you he wanted to sell?"

"No; he never mentioned it," Carroll replied, not relishing Mills's inquiries.

"Call Shep and tell him to stop in this afternoon on his way home, and—Carroll"—Mills detained his secretary to impress him with his perfect equanimity—"call Mrs. Rawlings and ask how the Judge is. I understand he's had a second stroke. I hate to see these older men going——"

"Yes, the Judge has been a great figure," Carroll replied perfunctorily.

Carroll was troubled. He was fond of Shepherd Mills, recognized the young man's fine qualities and sympathized with his high aims. There was something pitiful in the inability of father and son to understand each other. And he was not deceived by Franklin Mills's characteristic attempt to conceal his displeasure at Shepherd's sale of the stock.

It was evident from the manner in which the stock had passed through Gurley's hands that Shepherd wished to hide the fact that he was selling. Poor Shep! There could have been no better illustration of his failure to understand his father than this. Carroll had watched much keener men than Shepherd Mills attempt to deceive Franklin Mills. Just why Shepherd should have sold the stock Carroll couldn't imagine. Constance had, perhaps, been overreaching herself. No matter what had prompted the sale, Mills would undoubtedly make Shepherd uncomfortable about it—not explosively, for Mills never lost his perfect self-control—but with his own suave but effective method. Carroll wished there were something he could do to save Shep from the consequences of his folly in attempting to hide from Franklin Mills a transaction so obviously impossible of concealment.

III

Shepherd entered his father's office as he always did, nervous and apprehensive.

"Well, Father, how's everything with you today?" he asked with feigned ease.

"All right, Shep," Mills replied pleasantly as he continued signing letters. "Everything all right at the plant?"

"Everything running smoothly, Father."

"That's good." Mills applied the blotter to the last signature and rang for the stenographer. When the young woman had taken the letters away Mills filled in the assignment on the back of the certificate of stock in the Rogers Company which Carroll had brought him that morning and pushed it across the desk.

"You seem to have sold your two hundred shares in the Rogers Trust, Shep —the two hundred you got from your mother's estate."

"Why, yes, Father," Shepherd stammered, staring at the certificate. There was no evidence of irritation in his father's face; one might have thought that Mills was mildly amused by something.

"You had a perfect right to dispose of it, of course. I'm just a trifle curious to know why you didn't mention it to me. It seemed just a little—a little—unfriendly, that's all."

"No, Father; it wasn't that!" Shepherd replied hastily.

It had not occurred to him that his father would discover the sale so soon. While he hadn't in so many words asked Gurley to consider the transaction a confidential matter, he thought he had conveyed that idea to the broker. He felt the perspiration creeping out on his face; his hands trembled so that he hid them in his pockets. Mills, his arms on the desk, was playing with a glass paper weight.

"How much did Gurley give you for it?" he asked.

"I sold it at two seventy-five," Shepherd answered. The air of the room seemed weighted with impending disaster. An inexorable fate had set a problem for him to solve, and his answers, he knew, exposed his stupidity. It was like a nightmare in which he saw himself caught in a trap without hope of escape.

"It's worth five hundred," said Mills with gentle indulgence. "But Gurley, in taking advantage of you, blundered badly. I bought it from him at three eighteen. And just to show you that I'm a good sport"—Mills smiled as he reflected that he had never before applied the phrase to himself—"I'm going to sell it back to you at the price Gurley paid you. And here's a blank check,—we can close the matter right now."

Mills pretended to be looking over some papers while Shepherd wrote the check, his fingers with difficulty moving the pen. A crisis was at hand; or was it a crisis? His fear of his father, his superstitious awe of Franklin Mills's supernatural prescience numbed his will. The desk seemed to mark a wide gulf between them. He had frequently rehearsed, since his talk with Constance, the scene in which he would defend the building of the clubhouse for the battery employees; but he was unprepared for this discovery of his purpose. He had meant to seize some opportunity, preferably when he could drive his father to the battery plant and show him the foundations of the clubhouse, for disclosing the fact that he was going ahead, spending his own money. It hadn't occurred to him that Gurley might sell the stock to his father. He had made a mess of it. He felt himself cowering, weak and ineffectual, before another of those velvety strokes with which his father was always able to defeat him.

"You'd better go in early tomorrow and get a new certificate; they're closing the transfer books. The Rogers is merging with the Central States—formal announcement will be made early in the new year. The combination will make a powerful company. The Rogers lately realized very handsomely on some doubtful securities that had been charged off several years ago. It was known only on the inside. Gurley thought he was making a nice turn for himself, but you see he wasn't so clever after all!"

Shepherd shrank further into himself. It was he who was not clever! He hoped to be dismissed like a presumptuous schoolboy caught in an attempt to evade the rules. Franklin Mills, putting aside the crystal weight, had taken up the ivory paper knife and was drawing it slowly through his shapely, well-kept hands.

"I suppose it's none of my business, Shep, but just why did you sell that stock? It was absolutely safe; and I thought that as it came to you from your mother, and her father had been one of the original incorporators, you would have some sentiment about keeping it. You're not embarrassed in any way, are you? If you're not able to live within your income you ought to come to me about it. You can hardly say that I haven't always stood ready to help when you ran short."

"Well, no, Father; it wasn't that. The fact is—well, to tell the truth——"

Mills was always annoyed by Shepherd's stammering. He considered it a sign of weakness in his son; something akin to a physical blemish. Shepherd frowned and with a jerk of the head began again determinedly, speaking slowly.

"I wanted to build that clubhouse for the factory people. I felt that they deserved it. You refused to help; I couldn't make you understand how I felt about it. I meant to build it myself—pay for it with my own money. So I sold my Rogers stock. I thought after I got the thing started you wouldn't object. You see——"

Shepherd's eyes had met his father's gaze, bent upon him coldly, and he ceased abruptly.

"Oh, that's why you sold! My dear boy, I'm surprised and not a little grieved that you should think of doing a thing like that. It's not—not quite ——"

"Not quite straight!" Shepherd flung the words at him, a gleam of defiance in his eyes. "Well, all right! We'll say it wasn't square. But I did it! And you've beaten me. You've shown me I'm a fool. I suppose that's what I am. I don't see things as you do; I wanted to help those people—give them a little cheer—brighten their lives—make them more contented! But you couldn't see that! You don't care for what I think; you treat me as though I were a stupid child. I'm only a figurehead at the plant. When you ask me questions about the business you do it just to check me up—you've already got the answers from Fields. Oh, I know it! I know what a failure I am!"

He had never before spoken so to his father. Amazed that he had gotten through with it, he was horror struck. He sank back in his chair, waiting for the sharp reprimand, the violent retort he had invited. It would have been a relief if his father had broken out in a violent tirade. But Mills had never been more provokingly calm.

"I'm sorry, Shep, that you have this bitterness in your heart." Mills's tone was that of a man who has heard forbearingly an unjust accusation and proceeds patiently to justify himself. "I wouldn't have you think I don't appreciate your feeling about labor; that's fine. But I thought you accepted my reasons for refusing. I've studied these things for years. I believe in dealing justly with labor, but we've got to be careful about mixing business and philanthropy. If you'll just think it over you'll see that for yourself. We've got to be sensible. I'm old-fashioned, I suppose, in my way of thinking, but——"

His deprecatory gesture was an appeal to his son to be merciful to a sire so hopelessly benighted. Shepherd had hardly taken in what his father said. Once more it was borne in upon him that he was no match for his father. His anger had fallen upon Franklin Mills as impotently as a spent wave breaking upon a stone wall.

"Well, I guess that's all," he said faintly.

"One thing more, Shep. There's another matter I want to speak of. It's occurred to me the past year that you are not happy at the battery plant. Frankly, I don't believe you're quite adapted to an industrial career. The fact is you're just a little too sensitive, too impressionable to deal with labor." Mills smiled to neutralize any sting that might lurk in the remark. "I think you'd be happier somewhere else. Now I want someone to represent me in the trust company after the merger goes into effect. Carroll is to be the vice-president and counsel, perhaps ultimately the president. Fleming did much to build up the Rogers and he will continue at the head of the merged companies for the present. But he's getting on in years and is anxious to retire. Eventually you and Carroll will run the thing. I never meant for you to stay in the battery plant—that was just for the experience. Fields will take your place out there. It's fitting that you should be identified with the trust company. I've arranged to have you elected a vice-president when we complete the reorganization next month—a fine opportunity for you, Shep. I hope this meets with your approval."

Shepherd nodded a bewildered, grudging assent. This was the most unexpected of blows. In spite of the fact that his authority at the battery plant was, except as to minor routine matters, subordinate to that of Fields, he enjoyed his work. He had made many friends among the employees and found happiness in counseling and helping them in their troubles. He would miss them. To go into a trust company would mean beginning a new apprenticeship in a field that in no way attracted him. He felt humiliated by the incidental manner of his dismissal from one place and appointment to another.

His father went on placidly, speaking of the bright prospects of the trust company, which would be the strongest institution of the kind in the State. There were many details to be arranged, but the enlargement of the Rogers offices to accommodate the combined companies was already begun, and Shepherd was to be ready to make the change on the first of February. Before he quite realized it his father had glided away from the subject and was speaking of social matters—inquiring about a reception someone was giving the next night. Shepherd picked up his hat and stared at it as though not sure that it belonged to him. His father walked round the desk and put out his hand.

"You know, Shep, there's nothing I have so much at heart as the welfare of my children. You married the girl you wanted; I've given you this experience in the battery company, which will be of value to you in your new position, and now I'm sure you'll realize my best hopes for you in what I believe to be a more suitable line of work. I want you always to remember it of me that I put the happiness of my children before every other consideration."

"Yes, Father."

Shepherd passed out slowly through the door that opened directly into the hall and, still dazed, reached the street. He wandered about, trying to remember where he had parked his car. The city in which he was born had suddenly become strange to him. He dreaded going home and confessing to Constance that once more he had been vanquished by his father. Constance would make her usual effort to cheer him, laugh a little at the ease with which his father had frustrated him; tell him not to mind. But her very good humor would be galling. He knew what she would think of him. He must have time to think before facing Constance. If he went to the club it would be to look in upon men intent upon their rhum or bridge, who would give him their usual abstracted greeting. They cared nothing for him: he was only the son of a wealthy father who put him into jobs where he would do the least harm!

<h1 style="text-align:center">IV</h1>

He must talk to someone. His heart hungered for sympathy and kindness. If his father would only treat him as he would treat any other man; not as a weakling, a bothersome encumbrance! There was cruelty in the reflection that, envied as no doubt he was as the prospective heir to a fortune and the inheritor of an honored name, there was no friend to whom he could turn in his unhappiness. He passed Doctor Lindley, who was talking animatedly to two men on a corner. A man of God, a priest charged with the care of souls; but Shepherd felt no impulse to lay his troubles before the rector of St. Barnabas, much as he liked him. Lindley would probably rebuke him for rebelling against his father's judgments. But there must be someone....

His heart leaped as he thought of Bruce Storrs. The young architect, hardly more than an acquaintance, had in their meetings impressed him by his good sense and manliness. He would see Storrs.

The elevator shot him up to Freeman's office. Bruce, preparing to leave for the day, put out his hand cordially.

"Mr. Freeman's gone; but won't you sit and smoke?"

"No, thanks. Happened to be passing and thought I'd look in. Maybe you'll join me in a little dash into the country. This has been an off day with me—everything messy. I suppose you're never troubled that way?"

Bruce saw that something was amiss. Shepherd's attempt to give an air of inadvertence to his call was badly simulated.

"That's odd!" Bruce exclaimed. "I'm a little on edge myself! Just thinking of walking a few miles to pull myself together. What region shall we favor with our gloomy presences?"

"That is a question!" Shepherd ejaculated with a mirthless laugh; and then striking his hands together as he recalled where he had parked his car, he added: "Let's drive to the river and do our walking out there. You won't mind—sure I'm not making myself a nuisance?"

"Positive!" Bruce declared, though he smothered with some difficulty a wish that Shepherd Mills would keep away from him.

It was inconceivable that Shepherd had been drinking, but he was clearly laboring under some strong emotional excitement. In offering his cigarette case as they waited for the elevator, his hand shook. Bruce adopted a chaffing tone as they reached the street, making light of the desperate situation in which they found themselves.

"We're two nice birds! All tuckered out by a few hours' work. That's what the indoor life brings us to. Henderson got off a good one about the new traffic rules—said they've got it fixed now so you can't turn anywhere in this town till you get to the cemetery. Suppose the ancient Egyptians had a lot of trouble with their chariots—speed devils even in those days!"

Shepherd laughed a little wildly now and then at Bruce's efforts at humor. But he said nothing. He drove the car with what for him was reckless speed. Bruce good-naturedly chided him, inquiring how he got his drag with the police department; but he was trying to adjust himself to a Shepherd Mills he hadn't known before....

They crossed a bridge and Shepherd stopped the car at the roadside. "Let's walk," he said tensely. "I've got to talk—I've *got* to talk."

"All right, we'll walk and talk!" Bruce agreed in the tone of one indulging a child's whims.

"I wanted to come to the river," Shepherd muttered. "I like being where there's water."

"Many people don't!" Bruce said, thinking his companion was joking.

"A river is kind; a river is friendly," Shepherd added in the curious stifled voice of one who is thinking aloud. "Water always soothes me—quiets my nerves"—he threw his hand out. "It seems so free!"

It was now dark and the winter stars shone brightly over the half-frozen stream. Bruce remembered that somewhere in the neighborhood he had made his last stop before entering the city; overcome his last doubt and burned his mother's letters that he had borne on his year-long pilgrimage. And he was here again by the river with the son of Franklin Mills!

Intent upon his own thoughts, he was hardly conscious that Shepherd had begun to speak, with a curious dogged eagerness, in a high strained voice that broke now and then in a sob. It was of his father that Shepherd was speaking—of Franklin Mills. He was a disappointment to his father; there was no sympathy between them. He had never wanted to go into business but had yielded in good spirit when his father opposed his studying medicine. At the battery plant he performed duties of no significance; the only joy he derived from the connection was in the friendship of the employees, and he was now to be disciplined for wanting to help them. His transfer to the trust company was only a punishment; in the new position he would merely repeat his experience in the factory—find himself of less importance than the office boy.

They paced back and forth at the roadside, hardly aware of occasional fast-flying cars whose headlights fell upon them for a moment and left them again to the stars. When the first passion of his bitter indignation had spent itself, Shepherd admitted his father's generosity. There was no question of money; his father wished him to live as became the family dignity. Constance was fine; she was the finest woman alive, he declared with a quaver in his voice. But she too had her grievances; his father was never fair to Constance. Here Shepherd caught himself up sharply. It was the widening breach between himself and his father that tore his heart, and Constance had no part in that.

"I'm stupid; I don't catch things quickly," he went on wearily. "But I've tried to learn; I've done my best to please father. But it's no good! I give it up!"

Bruce, astounded and dismayed by this long recital, was debating what counsel he could offer. He could not abandon Shepherd Mills in his dark hour. The boy—he seemed only that tonight, a miserable, tragic boy—had opened his heart with a child's frankness. Bruce, remembering his own unhappy hours, resolved to help Shepherd Mills if he could.

Their stay by the river must not be prolonged; Shepherd was shivering with cold. Bruce had never before been so conscious of his own physical strength. He wished that he might confer it upon Shepherd—add to his stature, broaden the narrow shoulders that were so unequal to heavy burdens! It was, he felt, a critical hour in Shepherd Mills's life; the wrong word might precipitate a complete break in his relations with his father. Franklin Mills, as Bruce's imagination quickened under the mystical spell of the night, loomed beside them—a shadowy figure, keeping step with them on the dim bank where the wind mourned like an unhappy spirit through the sycamores.

"I had no right to bother you; you must think me a fool," Shepherd concluded. "But it's helped me, just to talk. I don't know why I thought you wouldn't mind——"

"Of course I don't mind!" Bruce replied, and laid his hand lightly on Shepherd's shoulder. "I'm pleased that you thought of me; I want to help. Now, old man, we're going to pull you right out of this! It's disagreeable to fumble the ball as we all do occasionally. But this isn't so terrible! That was a fine idea of yours to build a clubhouse for the workmen: but on the other hand there's something to be said for your father's reasons against it. And frankly, I think you made a mistake in selling your stock without speaking to him first. It wasn't quite playing the game."

"Yes; I can see that," Shepherd assented faintly. "But you see I'd got my mind on it; and I wanted to make things happier for those people."

"Of course you did! And it's too bad your father doesn't feel about it as you do. But he doesn't; and it's one of the hardest things we have to learn in this world, that we've got to accommodate ourselves very often to other people's ideas. That's life, old man!"

"I suppose you're right; but I do nothing but blunder. I never put anything over."

"Oh, yes, you do! You said a bit ago your father didn't want you to marry the girl you were in love with; but you did! That scored for you. And about the clubhouse, it's hard to give it up; but we passionate idealists have got to learn to wait! Your day will come to do a lot for humanity."

"No! I'm done! I'm going away; I want a chance to live my own life. It's hell, I tell you, never to be free; to be pushed into subordinate jobs I hate. By God, I won't go into the trust company!"

The oath, probably the first he had ever uttered, cut sharply into the night. To Bruce it hinted of unsuspected depths of passion in Shepherd's nature. The sense of his own responsibility deepened.

Shepherd, surprised and ashamed of his outburst, sought and clutched Bruce's hand.

"Steady, boy!" said Bruce gently. "You'll *take* the job and you'll go into it with all the pep you can muster! It offers you a bigger chance than the thing you've been doing. All kinds of people carry their troubles to a trust company. Such institutions have a big benevolent side,—look after widows and orphans and all that sort of thing. If you want to serve humanity you couldn't put yourself in a better place! I'm serious about that. And with Carroll there you'll be treated with respect; you can raise the devil if anybody tries any foolishness! Why, your father's promoting you—showing his confidence in a pretty fine way. He might better have told you of his plans earlier—I grant that—but he probably thought he'd save it for a surprise. It was pretty decent of him to sell you back your stock. A mean, grasping man would have kept it and swiped the profit. You've got to give him credit for trying to do the square thing by you."

"It was a slap in the face; he meant to humiliate me!" cried Shepherd stubbornly.

"All right; assume he did! But don't be humiliated!"

"You'd stand for it? You wouldn't make a row?" demanded Shepherd quaveringly.

"No: decidedly no!"

"Well, I guess you're right," Shepherd replied after a moment's silence. "It doesn't seem so bad the way you put it. I'm sorry I've kept you so long. I'll never forget this; you've been mighty kind."

"I think I've been right," said Bruce soberly.

He was thinking of Franklin Mills—his father and Shepherd's. There was something grotesque in the idea that he was acting as a conciliator between Franklin Mills and this son who had so little of the Mills iron in his blood. The long story had given him still another impression of Mills. It was despicable, his trampling of Shepherd's toys, his calm destruction of the boy's dreams. But even so, Bruce felt that his advice had been sound. A complete break with his father would leave Shepherd helpless; and public opinion would be on the father's side.

Shepherd struck a match and looked at his watch.

"It's nearly seven!" he exclaimed. "Connie won't know what's become of me! I think she's having a Dramatic Club rehearsal at the house tonight."

"That's good. We'll stop at the first garage and you can telephone her. Tell her you're having dinner with me at the club. And—may I say it?—never tell her of your bad hour today. That's better kept to ourselves."

"Of course!"

With head erect Shepherd walked to the car. His self-confidence was returning. Before they reached the club his spirits were soaring. He was even eager to begin his work with the trust company.

After a leisurely dinner he drove Bruce home. When he said good-night at the entrance to the apartment house he grasped both Bruce's hands and clung to them.

"Nothing like this ever really happened to me before," he said chokingly. "I've found a friend!"

They remained silent for a moment. Then Bruce looked smilingly into Shepherd's gentle, grateful eyes and turned slowly into the house. The roar of Shepherd's car as it started rose jubilantly in the quiet street.

CHAPTER FIFTEEN

I

Duty was a large word in Franklin Mills's lexicon. It pleased him to think that he met all his obligations as a parent and a citizen. In his own cogitations he was well satisfied with his handling of his son Shepherd. Shepherd had needed just the lesson he had given him in the matter of the sale of the Rogers Trust Company stock. Mills, not knowing that Bruce Storrs was responsible for Shepherd's change of mind, was highly pleased that his son had expressed his entire satisfaction with his transfer from the battery plant to the new trust company.

The fact that Shepherd was now eager to begin his new work and evidently had forgotten all about the community house project increased Mills's contentment with his own wisdom and his confidence in his ability to make things happen as he wanted them to happen. Shepherd was not so weak; he was merely foolish, and being foolish, it was lucky that he had a father capable of checking his silly tendencies. The world would soon be in a pretty mess if all the sons of rich men were to begin throwing their money to the birds. In the trust company Shepherd would learn to think in terms of money without the emotional disturbances caused by contact with the hands that produced it. Shepherd, Mills felt, would be all right now. Incidentally he had taught the young man not to attempt to play tricks on him— something which no one had ever tried with success.

The social promotion of the Hardens was proceeding smoothly, thanks to Connie's cooperation. Mrs. Harden had been elected a member of the Orphan Asylum board, which in itself conferred a certain dignity. Leila and Connie had effected Millicent's election to the Dramatic Club. These matters were accomplished without friction, as Mills liked to have things done. Someone discovered that Doctor Harden's great-grandfather, back in the year of the big wind, had collected more bounties for wolf scalps than had ever been earned by any other settler in Jackson County, and the Doctor was thereupon admitted to fellowship in the Pioneer Society. The Hardens did not climb; they were pushed up the ladder, seemingly by unseen hands, somewhat to their own surprise and a little to their discomfiture.

II

The only cloud on Mills's horizon was his apprehension as to Leila's future. Mills was increasingly aware that she couldn't be managed as he managed Shepherd. He had gone as far as he dared in letting Carroll know that he would be an acceptable son-in-law, and he had perhaps intimated a little too plainly to Leila the desirability of such an arrangement. Carroll visited the house frequently; but Leila snubbed him outrageously. When it pleased her to accept his attentions it was merely, Mills surmised, to allay suspicion as to her interest elsewhere. It was his duty to see that Leila married in keeping with her status as the daughter of the house of Mills.

In analyzing his duty with respect to Leila, it occurred to Mills that he might have been culpable in not laying more stress upon the merits of religion in the upbringing of Leila. She had gone to Sunday school in her earliest youth; but churchgoing was not to her taste. He was unable to remember when Leila had last attended church, but never voluntarily within his recollection. She needed, he decided, the sobering influence of religion. God, in Mills's speculations, was on the side of order, law and respectability. The church frowned upon divorce; and Leila must be saved from the disgrace of marrying a divorced man. Leila needed religion, and the idea broadened in Mills's mind until he saw that probably Constance and Shepherd, too, would be safer under the protecting arm of the church.

The Sunday following Christmas seemed to Mills a fitting time for renewing the family's acquaintance with St. Barnabas. When he telephoned his invitation to Constance, carefully putting it in the form of a suggestion, he found his daughter-in-law wholly agreeable to the idea. She and Shepherd would be glad to breakfast with him and accompany him to divine worship. When he broached the matter to Leila she did not explode as he had expected. She took a cigarette from her mouth and expelled the smoke from her lungs.

"Sure, I'll go with you, Dada," she replied.

He had suggested nine as a conservative breakfast hour, but Constance and Shepherd were fifteen minutes late. Leila was considerably later, but appeared finally, after the maid had twice been dispatched to her room. Having danced late, she was still sleepy. At the table she insisted on scanning the society page of the morning newspaper. This annoyed Mills, particularly when in spreading out the sheet she upset her water glass, with resulting deplorable irrigation of the tablecloth and a splash upon Connie's smart morning dress that might or might not prove permanently disfiguring. Mills hated a messy table. He also hated criticism of food. Leila's complaint that the scalloped sweetbreads were too dry evoked the pertinent retort that if she hadn't been late they wouldn't have been spoiled.

"I guess that'll hold me for a little while," she said cheerfully. "I say, Dada, what do we get for going to church?"

"You'll get what you need from Doctor Lindley," Mills replied, frowning at the butler, who was stupidly oblivious of the fact that the flame under the percolator was threatening a general conflagration. Shepherd, in trying to clap on the extinguisher, burned his fingers and emitted a shrill cry of pain. All things considered, the breakfast was hardly conducive to spiritual uplift.

It was ten minutes after eleven when the Millses reached St. Barnabas and the party went down the aisle pursued by an usher to the chanting of the *Venite, exultemus Domino*. The usher, caught off guard, was guiltily conscious of having a few minutes before filled the Mills pew with strangers in accordance with the rule that reserved seats for their owners only until the processional. Mills, his silk hat on his arm, had not foreseen such a predicament. He paused in perplexity beside the ancestral pew in which five strangers were devoutly reinforcing the chanting of the choir, happily unaware that they were trespassers upon the property of Franklin Mills.

The courteous usher lifted his hand to indicate his mastery of the situation and guided the Mills party in front of the chancel to seats in the south transept. This maneuver had the effect of publishing to the congregation the fact that Franklin Mills, his son, daughter-in-law and daughter, were today breaking an abstinence from divine worship which regular attendants knew to have been prolonged.

Constance, Leila and Shepherd knelt at once; Mills remained standing. A lady behind him thrust a prayer book into his hand. In trying to find his glasses he dropped the book, which Leila, much diverted, recovered as she rose. This was annoying and added to Mills's discomfiture at being planted in the front seat of the transept where the whole congregation could observe him at leisure.

However, by the time the proper psalms for the day had been read he had recovered his composure and listened attentively to Doctor Lindley's sonorous reading of the lessons. His seat enabled him to contemplate the Mills memorial window in the north transept, a fact which mitigated his discomfort at being deprived of the Mills pew.

Leila stifled a yawn as the rector introduced as the preacher for the day a missionary bishop who had spent many years in the Orient. Mills had always been impatient of missionary work among peoples who, as he viewed the matter, were entitled to live their lives and worship their gods without interference by meddlesome foreigners. But the discourse appealed strongly to his practical sense. He saw in the schools and hospitals established by the church in China a splendid advertisement of American good will and enterprise. Such philanthropies were calculated to broaden the market for American trade. When Doctor Lindley announced that the offerings for the day would go to the visitor to assist in the building of a new hospital in his far-away diocese, Mills found a hundred dollar bill to lay on the plate....

III

As they drove to Shepherd's for dinner he good-naturedly combated Constance's assertion that Confucius was as great a teacher as Christ. Leila said she'd like to adopt a Chinese baby; the Chinese babies in the movies were always so cute. Shepherd's philanthropic nature had been deeply impressed by the idea of reducing human suffering through foreign missions. He announced that he would send the bishop a check.

"Well, I claim it was a good sermon," said Leila. "That funny old bird talked a hundred berries out of Dada."

When they reached the table, Mills reproved Leila for asserting that she guessed she was a Buddhist. She confessed under direct examination that she knew nothing about Buddhism but thought it might be worth taking up sometime.

"Millie says there's nothing in the Bible so wonderful as the world itself," Leila continued. "Millie has marvelous ideas. Talk about miracles—she says the grass and the sunrise are miracles."

"Millie is such a dear," Constance murmured in a tone that implied a lack of enthusiasm for grass and sunrises.

"Millicent has a poetic nature," Mills remarked, finding himself self-conscious at the mention of Millicent. Millicent's belief in a Supreme Power that controls the circling planets and guides the destinies of man was interesting because Millicent held it and talked of it charmingly.

"*Did* you see that outlandish hat Mrs. Charlie Felton was sporting?" Leila demanded with cheerful irrelevance. "I'll say it's some hat! She ought to hire a blind woman to buy her clothes."

"I didn't see anything the matter with her hat," remarked Shepherd.

"You *wouldn't,* dear!" said Constance.

"Who's Charlie Felton?" asked Mills. "It seemed to me I didn't know a dozen people in church this morning."

"Oh, the Feltons have lately moved here from Racine, Fond du Lac or St. Louis—one of those queer Illinois towns."

"Those towns may be queer," said her father gently. "But they are not in Illinois."

"Oh, well, give them to Kansas, then," said Leila, who was never disturbed by her errors in geography or any other department of knowledge. "You know," she continued, glad the conversation had been successfully diverted from religion, "that Freddy Thomas was in college with Charlie Felton and Freddy says Mrs. Felton isn't as bad as her hats."

Mills frowned. Shepherd laughed at this more joyously than the remark deserved and stammeringly tried to cover up the allusion to Thomas. It was sheer impudence for Leila to introduce into the Sunday table talk a name that could only irritate her father; but before Shepherd could make himself articulate Mills looked up from his salad.

"*Freddy?* I didn't know you were so intimate with anyone of that name."

This was not, of course, strictly true. Leila always referred to Thomas as Freddy; she found a mischievous delight in doing so before her father. Since she became aware of her father's increasing displeasure at Thomas's attentions and knew that the young man's visits at the house were a source of irritation, she had been meeting Thomas at the homes of one or another of her friends whose discretion could be relied on, or at the public library or the Art Institute—it was a joke that Leila should have availed herself of these institutions for any purpose! Constance in giving her an admonitory prod under the table inadvertently brushed her father-in-law's shin.

"I meant Mr. Frederick Thomas, Dada," Leila replied, her gentle tone in itself a species of impudence.

"I hope you are about done with that fellow," said Mills, frowning.

"Sure, Dada, I'm about through with him," she replied with intentional equivocation.

"I should think you would be! I don't like the idea of your name being associated with his!"

"Well, it isn't, is it?"

Mills disliked being talked back to. His annoyance was increased by the fact that he had been unable to learn anything detrimental to Thomas beyond the fact that the man had been divorced. The decree of divorce, he had learned in Chicago, was granted to Thomas though his wife had brought the suit. While not rich, Thomas was well-to-do, and when it came to the question of age, Arthur Carroll was a trifle older. But Leila should marry Carroll. Carroll was ideally qualified to enter the family by reason of his familiarity with its history and traditional conservatism. He knew and respected the Franklin Mills habit of mind, and this in itself was an asset. Mills had no intention of being thwarted in his purpose to possess Carroll as a son-in-law....

Gloom settled over the table. Mills, deeply preoccupied, ate his dessert in silence. Leila presented a much more serious and pressing problem than foreign missions. Constance strove vainly to dispel the cloud. Leila alone seemed untroubled; she repeated a story that Bud Henderson had told her which was hardly an appropriate addendum for a missionary sermon. Her father rebuked her sternly. If there was anything that roused his ire it was a risqué story.

"One might think," he said severely, "that you were brought up in a slum from the way you talk. The heathen are not all in China!"

"Well, it is a funny story," Leila persisted. "I told it to Doctor Harden and he almost died laffin'. Doc certainly knows a joke. You're not angry—not really, terribly angry at your 'ittle baby girl, is 'ou, Dada?"

"I most certainly am!" he retorted grimly. A moment later he added: "Well, let's go to Deer Trail for supper. Connie, you and Shep are free for the evening, I hope?"

"We'll be glad to go, of course," Constance replied amiably.

IV

The Sunday evening suppers at Deer Trail were usually discontinued after Christmas, and Leila was taken aback by the announcement. Her father had not, she noted, shown his usual courtesy in asking her if she cared to go. She correctly surmised that the proposed flight into the country was intended as a disciplinary measure for her benefit. She had promised to meet Thomas at the Burtons' at eight o'clock, and he could hardly have hit upon anything better calculated to awaken resentment in her young breast. She began to consider the hazards of attempting to communicate with Thomas to explain her inability to keep the appointment. As there were to be no guests, the evening at Deer Trail promised to be an insufferably dull experience and she must dodge it if possible.

"Oh, don't let's do that!" she said. "It's too cold, Dada. And the house is always drafty in the winter!"

"Drafty!" Her father stared at her blandly. The country house was steam-heated and this was the first time he had ever heard that it was drafty. The suggestion of drafts was altogether unfortunate. "Had you any engagement for this evening?" he asked.

"Oh, I promised Mrs. Torrence I'd go there for supper—she's having some people in to do some music. It's just an informal company, but I hate dropping out."

Constance perceptibly shuddered.

"When did she give this invitation?" asked Mills, with the utmost urbanity.

"Oh, I met her downtown yesterday. It's no great matter, Dada. If you're making a point of it, I'll be glad to go to the farm!"

"Mrs. Torrence must be a quick traveler," her father replied, entirely at ease. "I met her myself yesterday morning. She was just leaving for Louisville and didn't expect to be back until Tuesday."

"How funny!" Leila ejaculated, though she had little confidence in her ability to give a humorous aspect to her plight. She bent her head in the laugh of self-derision which she had frequently employed in easing her way out of similar predicaments with her father. This time it merely provoked an ironic smile.

Mills, from the extension telephone in the living room, called Deer Trail to give warning of the approach of four guests for supper; there was no possible escape from this excursion. Thomas filled Leila's thoughts. He had been insisting that they be married before the projected trip to Bermuda. The time was short and she was uncertain whether to take the step now or postpone it in the hope of winning her father's consent in the intimate association of their travels.

Today Mills's cigar seemed to be of interminable length. As he smoked he talked in the leisurely fashion he enjoyed after a satisfactory meal, and Constance never made the mistake of giving him poor food. He had caught Leila in a lie—a stupid, foolish lie; but no one would have guessed that it had impressed him disagreeably or opened a new train of suspicions in his mind. Constance was admiring his perfect self-restraint; Franklin Mills, no matter what else he might or might not be, was a thoroughbred.

"If you don't have to stop at home, Leila, we can start from here," he said —"at three o'clock."

"Yes, Dada. I'm all set!" she replied.

Constance and Shepherd left the room and Leila was prepared for a sharp reprimand, but her father merely asked whether she had everything necessary for the Bermuda trip. He had his steamer reservation and they would go to New York a few days ahead of the sailing date to see the new plays and she could pick up any little things she needed.

"Arthur's going East at the same time. We have some business errands in New York," he continued in a matter of course tone.

She was aware that he had mentioned Carroll with special intention, and it added nothing to her peace of mind.

"That's fine, Dada," she said, reaching for a fresh cigarette. "Arthur can take me to some of the new dancing places. Arthur's a good little hopper."

She felt moved to try to gloss over her blunder in pretending to have an engagement that evening with Helen Torrence, but her intuitions warned her that the time was not fortunate for the practice of her familiar cajoleries upon her father. She realized that she had outgrown her knack of laughing herself out of her troubles; and she had never before been trapped so neatly. Like Shepherd, she felt that in dealing with her father she never knew what was in his mind until he laid his cards on the table—laid them down with the serenity of one who knows thoroughly the value of his hand.

She was deeply in love with Thomas and craved sympathy and help; but she felt quite as Shepherd always did, her father's remoteness and the closing of the common avenues of communication between human beings. He had always indulged her, shown kindness even when he scolded and protested against her conduct; but she felt that his heart was as inaccessible as a safety box behind massive steel doors. On the drive to Deer Trail she took little part in the talk, to which Shepherd and Constance tried, with indifferent success, to impart a light and cheery tone. When they reached the country house, which derived a fresh picturesqueness from the snowy fields about it, Mills left them, driving on to the stables for a look at his horses.

"Well, that was some break!" exclaimed Constance the moment they were within doors. "Everybody in town knows Helen is away. You ought to have known it yourself! I never knew you to do anything so clumsy as that!"

"Oh, shoot! I didn't want to come out here today. It's a bore; nobody here and nothing to do. And I object to being punished like a child!"

"You needn't have lied to your father; that was inexcusable," said Constance. "If you've got to do such a thing, please don't do it when I'm around!"

"See here, sis," began Shepherd with a prolonged sibilant stutter, "let's be frank about this! You know this thing of meeting Fred Thomas at other people's houses is no good. You've got to stop it! Father would be terribly cut up if he found you out. You may be sure he suspects something now, after that foolish break about going to Helen Torrence's."

"Well, I haven't said I was going to meet anyone, have I?" Leila demanded defiantly.

"You don't have to. There are other people just as clever as you are," Constance retorted, jerking off her gloves.

"I can't imagine what you see in Thomas," Shepherd persisted.

"I don't care if you don't. It's my business what I see in him." Leila nervously lighted a cigarette. "Freddy's a fine fellow; father doesn't know a thing against him!"

"If you marry him you'll break father's heart," Shepherd declared solemnly.

"His heart!" repeated Leila with fine contempt. "You needn't think he's going to treat me as he treats you. I won't stand for it! How about that clubhouse you wanted to build—how about this sudden idea of taking you out of the battery business and sticking you into the trust company? You didn't want to change, did you? He didn't ask you if you wanted to move, did he? I'll say he didn't! That's dada all over—he doesn't ask you; he tells you! And I'm not a child to be sent to bed whenever his majesty gets peevish."

"Don't be ridiculous!" said Constance with a despairing sigh. "You're going to make trouble for all of us if you don't drop Freddy!"

"You tell *me* not to make trouble!"

Leila's eyes flashed her scorn of the idea and something more. Her words had the effect of bringing a deep flush to Constance's face. Constance walked to the fire and sat down. There was no counting on Leila's discretion; and if she eloped with Thomas the town would hum with talk about the whole Mills family.

"Now, Leila," began Shepherd, who had not noticed his wife's perturbation or understood the nature of the spiteful little stab that caused it. "You'd better try to square yourself with father."

"I see myself trying! You two make me tired! Please don't talk to me any more!"

V

She waited until Constance and Shepherd had found reading matter and were settled before the fireplace, and then with the remark that she wanted to fix her hair, went upstairs; and after closing a door noisily to allay suspicions, went cautiously down the back stairs to the telephone in the butler's pantry. Satisfying herself by a glance through the window that her father was still at the stables, she called Thomas's number and explained her inability to go to the Burtons' where they had planned to meet. Happy to hear his voice, she talked quite as freely as though speaking to him face to face, and his replies over the wire soothed and comforted her....

"No, dear; there'd only be a row if you asked father now. You'll have to take my word for that, Freddy."

"I'm not so sure of that—if he knows you love me!"

"Of course I love you, Freddy!"

"Then let us be married and end all this bother. You're of age; there's nothing to prevent us. I'd a lot rather have it out with your father now. I know I can convince him that I'm respectable and able to take care of you. I've got the record of the divorce case; there's nothing in it I'm ashamed of."

"That's all right enough; but the very mention of it would make him furious. We've talked of this a hundred times, Freddy, and I'm not going to let you make that mistake. We're going to wait a little longer!"

"You won't go back on me?"

"Never, Freddy!"

"You might meet someone on the trip you'd like better. I'm going to be terribly nervous about you!"

"Then you don't trust me! If you don't trust me you don't love me!"

"Don't be so foolish. I'm mad about you. And I'm sick of all this sneaking round for a chance to see you!"

"Be sensible, dear; it's just as hard for me as it is for you. And people *are* talking!"

In her absorption she had forgotten the importance of secrecy and the danger of being overheard. The swing doors had creaked several times, but she had attributed this to suction from an open window in the kitchen. Constance and Shepherd would wonder at her absence; the talk must not be prolonged.

"I've got to go!" she added hurriedly.

"Say you care—that you're not just putting me off——"

"I love you, Freddy! Please be patient. Remember, I love you with all my heart! Yes, always!"

As she hung up the receiver she turned round to face her father. He had entered the house through the kitchen and might or might not have heard part of her dialogue with Thomas. But she was instantly aware that her last words, in the tense, lover-like tone in which she had spoken them, were enough to convict her.

"Hello, Dada! How's the live stock?" she asked with poorly feigned carelessness as she hung the receiver on the hook.

Mills, his overcoat flung over his arm, his hat pushed back from his forehead, eyed her with a cold stare.

"Why are you telephoning here?" he demanded.

"No reasons. I didn't want to disturb Connie and Shep. They're reading in the living-room."

"That's very thoughtful of you, I'm sure!"

"I thought so myself," she replied, and took a step toward the dining-room door. He flung out his arm arrestingly.

"Just a moment, please!"

"Oh, hours—if you want them!"

"I overheard some of your speeches. To whom were you speaking—tell me the truth!"

"Don't be so fierce about it! And do take off your hat! You look so funny with your hat stuck on the back of your head that way!"

"Never mind my hat! It will be much better for you not to trifle with me. Who was on the other end of that telephone?"

"What if I don't tell you?" she demanded.

"I want an answer to my question! You told me one falsehood today; I don't want to hear another!"

"Well, you won't! I was talking to Mr. Frederick V. Thomas!"

"I thought as much. Now I've told you as plainly as I know how that you've got to drop that fellow. He's a scoundrel to force his attentions on you. I haven't wanted to bring matters to an issue with you about him. I've been patient with you—let him come to the house and go about with you. But you've not played fair with me. When I told you I didn't like his coming to the house so much you began meeting him when you thought I wouldn't know it—that's a fact, isn't it?"

"Yes, Dada—only a few times, though."

"May I ask what you mean by that? That a girl brought up as you have been, with every advantage and indulgence, should be so basely ungrateful as to meet a man I disapprove of—meet him in ways that show you know you're doing a wrong thing—is beyond my understanding. It's contemptible; it's close upon the unpardonable!"

"Then why don't you act decently about it?" She lifted her head and met his gaze unwaveringly. "If you didn't hear what I said I'll tell you! I told him I love him; I've promised to marry him."

"Well, you won't marry him!" he exclaimed, his voice quavering in his effort to restrain his anger. "A man who's left a wife somewhere and plays upon the sympathy of a credulous young girl like you is a contemptible hound!"

"All right, then! He's a contemptible hound!"

Her insolence, her refusal to cower before him, increased his anger. His time-tried formula for meeting emergencies by superior strategy—the method that worked so well with his son—was of no use to him here. He had lost a point in letting her see that for once in his life his temper had got the better of him. He had been too tolerant of her faults; the bills for his indulgence were coming in now—a large sheaf of them. She must be handled with care—with very great caution, indeed; thus far in his life he had got what he wanted, and it was not for a girl whom he saw only as a spoiled child to circumvent him.

But he realized at this moment that Leila was no longer a child. She was not only a woman, but a woman it would be folly to attempt to drive or frighten. He was alarmed by the composure with which she waited for the further disclosure of his purposes, standing with her back against the service shelf, eyeing him half hostilely, half, he feared, with a hope that he would carry the matter further and open his guard for a thrust he was not prepared to parry. He was afraid of her, but she must not know that he was afraid.

He took off his hat and let it swing at arm's length as he considered how to escape with dignity from the corner into which she had forced him. Sentiment is a natural refuge of the average man when other resources fail. He smiled benevolently, and with a quick lifting of the head remarked:

"This isn't the way for us to talk to each other. We've always been the best of friends; nothing's going to change that. I trust your good sense—I trust"—here his voice sank under the weight of emotion—"I trust your love for me—your love for your dear mother's memory—to do nothing to grieve me, nothing that would hurt her."

"Yes, Dada," she said absently, not sure how far she could trust his mood. Then she walked up to him and drew her hand across his cheek and gave his tie a twitch. He drew his arm about her and kissed her forehead.

"Let this be between ourselves," he said. "I'll go around and come in the front way."

She went up the back stairs and reappeared in the living-room, whistling. Constance and Shepherd were still reading before the fire where she had left them.

After supper—served at the dining-room table tonight—Leila was unwontedly silent, and the attempts of Constance and Shepherd to be gay were sadly deficient in spontaneity. Mills's Sunday, which had begun with high hopes, had been bitterly disappointing. Though outwardly tranquil and unbending a little more than usual, his mind was elsewhere.

<h1 style="text-align:center">VI</h1>

The happy life manifestly was not to be won merely by going to church. At the back of his mind, with all his agnosticism, he had entertained a superstitious belief that in Christianity there was some secret of happiness revealed to those who placed themselves receptively close to the throne of grace. This was evidently a mistake; or at least it was clear from the day's experience that the boon was less easy of attainment than he had believed.

He recalled what the rector of St. Barnabas had said to him the morning he had gone in to inspect the Mills window—that walls do not make the church, that the true edifice is within man's own breast. Lindley shouldn't say things like that, to perplex the hearer, baffle him, create a disagreeable uneasiness! This hint of a God whose tabernacle is in every man's heart was displeasing. Mills didn't like the idea of carrying God around with him. To grant any such premise would be to open the way for doubts as to his omnipotence in his own world; and Franklin Mills was not ready for that. He groped for a deity who wouldn't be a nuisance, like a disagreeable guest in the house, upsetting the whole establishment! God should be a convenience, subject to call like a doctor or a lawyer. But how could a man reach Lindley's God, who wasn't in the church at all, but within man himself?

In his pondering he came back to his own family. He didn't know Shepherd; he didn't know Leila. And this was all wrong. He knew Millicent Harden better than he knew either of his children.

He had friends who were good pals with their children, and he wondered how they managed it. Maybe it was the spirit of the age that was the trouble. It was a common habit to fix responsibility for all the disturbing moral and social phenomena of the time on the receding World War, or the greed for gain, or the diminished zeal for religion. This brought him again to God; uncomfortable—the reflection that thought in all its circling and tangential excursions does somehow land at that mysterious door.... Leila must be dealt with. She was much too facile in dissimulation. He was confident that no other Mills had ever been like that.

When they reached home he followed Leila into her room. He took the cigarette she offered him and sat down in the low rocking chair she pulled out for him—a befrilled feminine contrivance little to his taste. Utterly at a loss as to how he could most effectively reprimand her for her attempted deception and give her to understand that he would never countenance a marriage with Thomas, he was relieved when she took the initiative.

"I *was* naughty, Dada!" she said. "But Freddy was going over to the Burtons' tonight and I had told him I'd be there—that's all. I wasn't just crazy about going to the farm."

She held a match for him, extinguished it with a flourish, and after lighting her own cigarette dropped down on the chaise longue with a weary little sigh. If she had remained standing or had sat down properly in a chair, his rôle as the stern, aggrieved parent would have been simpler. Leila was so confoundedly difficult, so completely what he wished she was not!

"About this Thomas——" he began.

"Oh, pshaw! Don't you bother a little tiny bit about him. I'm just teasing him along."

"I must say your talk over the telephone sounded pretty serious to me!"

"Oh, bunk! All the girls talk to men that way these days—it doesn't mean anything!"

"What's that? You say the words you used don't *mean* anything?"

"Not a thing, Dada. If you'd tell a man you didn't love him he'd be sure to think you did!"

"A dangerous idea, I should think."

"Oh, no! Everything's different from what it was when you were young!"

"Yes; I've noticed that!" he replied drily. "But seriously, Leila, this meeting a man—a man we know little about—at other people's houses won't do! You ought to have more self-respect and dignity than that!"

"You're making too much of it, Dada! It's happened only two or three times. I thought you were sore about Freddy's coming here so much, and I *have* met him other places—always perfectly proper places!"

"I should hope so!" he exclaimed with his first display of spirit. "But you can't afford to go about with him. You've got to remember the community has a right to expect the best of you. You should think of your dear mother even if you don't care for me!"

"Now, Dada!" She leveled her arm at him, the smoking cigarette in her slim fingers. "Don't be silly; you *know* I adore you; I've always been perfectly crazy about you!"

She spoke in much the same tone she would have used in approving of a new suit of clothes he had submitted for inspection.

"Now, I have your promise——" he said, sitting up alertly in his chair.

"Promise, Dada?" she inquired, her thoughts far afield. "Oh, about Freddy! Well, if you'll be happier I promise you now never to marry him. Frankly— *frankly*—I'm not going to marry anybody right away. When I get ready I'll probably marry Arthur if some widow doesn't snatch him first. But please don't crowd me, Dada! If there *is* anything I hate it's being crowded!"

"Nobody's crowding you!" he said, feeling that she was once more eluding him.

"Then don't push!" she laughed.

"Let's not have any more nonsense," he said. "I think you do a lot of things just to annoy me. It isn't fair!"

"Why, Dada!" she exclaimed in mock astonishment. "I thought you liked being kidded. I kid all your old friends and it tickles 'em to death."

"Go to bed!" he retorted, laughing in spite of himself.

She mussed his hair before kissing him good-night, but even as he turned away he could see that her thoughts were elsewhere.

VII

Behind his own door, as he thought it over, the interview was about as unsatisfactory as an interview could be. She had kept it in her own hands, left him no opening for the eloquent appeal he had planned or the severe scolding she deserved. He wished he dared go back and put his arms about her and tell her how deeply he loved her. But he lacked the courage; she wouldn't understand it. It was the cruelest of ironies that he dare not knock at his child's door to tell her how precious she was to him.

That was the trouble—he didn't know how to make her understand! As he paced the floor, he wondered whether anyone in all the world had ever loved him! Yes, there was Marian Storrs; and, again, the woman who had been his wife. Beyond question each had, in her own way, loved him; but both were gathered into the great company of the dead. That question, as to whether anyone had ever loved him, reversed itself: in the whole course of his life had he, Franklin Mills, ever unselfishly loved anyone? This was the most disagreeable question that had forced itself upon Franklin Mills's attention in a long time. As he tried to go to sleep it took countless forms in the dark, till the room danced with interrogation marks.

He turned on the lights and got up. After moving about restlessly for a time he found himself staring at his reflection in the panel mirror in the bathroom door. It seemed to him that the shadow in the glass was not himself but the phantom of a man he had never known.

CHAPTER SIXTEEN

I

At Christmas Bruce had sent Millicent a box of flowers, which she had acknowledged in a cordial little note, but he had not called on her, making the excuse to himself that he lacked time. But the real reason was a fear that he had begun to care too much for her. He must not allow himself to love her when he could never marry her; he could never ask any woman to take a name to which he had no honest right.

But if he hadn't seen Millicent he heard of her frequently. He was established as a welcome visitor at all times at the Freemans' and the Hendersons'. The belated social recognition of the Hardens, in spite of the adroitness with which Mills had inspired it, had not gone unremarked.

There was, Bud said, always some reason for everything Mills did; and Maybelle, who knew everything that was said and done in town, had remarked in Bruce's hearing that the Hardens' social promotion was merely an item in Mills's courtship of Millicent.

"I'll wager he doesn't make it! Millicent will never do it," was Maybelle's opinion, expressed one evening at dinner.

"Why not?" Bruce asked, trying to conceal his suspicion that the remark was made for his own encouragement.

"Oh, Millie's not going to throw herself away on an old bird like Frank Mills. She values her youth too much for that."

"Oh, you never can tell," said Bud provokingly. "Girls have done it before this."

"But not girls like Millicent!" Maybelle flung back.

"That's easy," Bud acquiesced. "There never was a girl like Millie—not even you, Maybelle, much as I love you. But all that mazuma and that long line of noble ancestors; not a spot on the whole bloomin' scutcheon! I wonder if Mills is really teasing himself with the idea that he has even a look-in!”

“What you ought to do, Bruce, is to sail in and marry Millie yourself,” said Maybelle. “Dale and I are strong for you!”

“Thanks for the compliment!” exclaimed Bruce. “You and Dale want me to enter the race in the hope of seeing Mills knocked out! No particular interest in me! You don’t want me to win half as much as you want the great Mills to lose. Alas! And this is friendship!”

“The idea warms my sporting blood,” said Bud. “Once the struggle begins we’ll post the bets on the club bulletin. I’ll start with two to one on you, old top!”

“I’m surprised at Connie—she seems to be helping on the boosting of the Hardens,” said Maybelle. “It must occur to her that it wouldn’t help her own fortunes to have a healthy young stepmother-in-law prance into the sketch. When Frank Mills passes on some day Connie’s going to be all set to spend a lot of his money. Connie’s one of the born spenders.”

“That’s all well enough,” remarked Bud. “But just now Connie’s only too glad to have Mills’s attention directed away from her own little diversions. She and George Whitford——”

“Bud!” Maybelle tapped her water glass sharply. “Remember, boys, these people are our friends!”

“Not so up-stage, darling!” said Bud. “I’m sure we’ve been talking only in a spirit of loving kindness!”

“Honorable men and women—one and all!” said Bruce.

“Absolutely!” Bud affirmed, and the subject was dropped.

A few nights later Bruce was obliged to listen to similar talk at the Freemans’, though in a different key. Mrs. Freeman was indignant that Mills should think of marrying Millicent.

“There’s just one right man in the world for every woman,” she declared. “And the right man for Millicent is you, Bruce Storrs!”

Bruce met her gaze with mock solemnity.

"Please don't force me into a hasty marriage! Here I am, a struggling young architect who will soon be not so young. Give me time to become self-supporting!"

"Of course Millie will marry you in the proper course of things," said Freeman. "If that girl should throw herself away on Franklin Mills she wouldn't be Millie. And she is very much Millie!"

"Heavens!" exclaimed his wife. "The bare thought of that girl, with her beauty, her spiritual insight, her sweetness, linking herself to that—that ——"

"This talk is all bosh!" interrupted Freeman. "I doubt if Mills ever sees Millicent alone. These gossips ought to be sent to the penal farm."

"Oh, I think they've seen each other in a neighborly sort of way," said Mrs. Freeman. "Mills is a cultivated man and Millicent's music and modeling no doubt really interest him. I ran in to see her the other morning and she's been doing a bust of Mills—she laughed when I asked her about it and said she had hard work getting sitters and Mr. Mills is ever so patient."

The intimacy implied in this kindled Bruce's jealousy anew. Dale Freeman, whose prescience was keen, saw a look in his face that gave her instant pause.

"Mr. Mills and Leila are leaving in a few days," she remarked quickly. "I don't believe he's much of a success as a matchmaker. It's been in the air for several years that Leila must marry Arthur Carroll, but he doesn't appear to be making any headway."

"Leila will do as she pleases," said Freeman, who was satisfied with a very little gossip. "Bruce, how do you feel about tackling that Laconia war memorial?"

Bruce's native town was to build a museum as a memorial to the soldiers in all her wars, from the Revolutionary patriots who had settled the county to the veterans of the Great War. Freeman had encouraged Bruce to submit plans, which were to be passed on by a jury of the highest distinction. Freeman kept strictly to domestic architecture; but Bruce's ideas about the memorial had impressed him by their novelty. His young associate had, he saw, a natural bent for monumental structures that had been increased by the contemplation of the famous memorials in Europe. They went into the

Freemans' study to talk over the specifications and terms of the competition, and by midnight Bruce was so reassured by his senior's confidence that it was decided he should go to work immediately on his plans.

"It would be splendid, Bruce!" said Dale, who had sewed during the discussion, throwing in an occasional apt comment and suggestion. "The people of Laconia would have all the more pride in their heroes if one of them designed the memorial. It's not big enough to tempt the top-notchers in the profession, but if you land it it will push you a long way up!"

"Yes; it would be a big thing for you," Freeman added. "You'd better drop your work in the office and concentrate on it...."

Undeterred by the cold, Bruce drove daily into the country, left his car and walked—walked with a new energy begotten of definite ambition and faith in his power of achievement. To create beautiful things: this had been his mother's prayer for him. He would do this for her; he would create a thing of beauty that should look down forever upon the earth that held her dust.

The site of the proposed building was on the crest of a hill on the outskirts of Laconia and within sight of its main street. Bruce had known the spot all his life and had no trouble in visualizing its pictorial possibilities. The forest trees that crowned the hill would afford a picturesque background for an open colonnade that he meant to incorporate in his plans.

Walking on clear, cold nights he fancied that he saw on every hilltop the structure as it would be, with the winds playing through its arches and wistful young moons coming through countless years to bless it anew with the hope and courage of youth.

II

On Shep's account rather than because of any interest he felt in Constance, Bruce had twice looked in at the Shepherd Mills's on Constance's day at home.

Constance made much of the informality of her "days," but they were, Bruce thought, rather dull. The girls and the young matrons he met there gave Mrs. Shep the adoration her nature demanded; the few men who dropped in were either her admirers or they went in the hope of meeting other young women in whom they were interested. On the first of these occasions Bruce had found Leila and Fred Thomas there, and both times George Whitford was prominent in the picture.

Thomas was not without his attractions. His cherubic countenance and the infantile expression of his large myopic blue eyes made him appear younger than his years. The men around the University Club said he had a shrewd head for business; the women of the younger set pronounced him very droll, a likely rival of Bud Henderson for humor. It was easy to understand why he was called Freddy; he had the look of a Freddy. And Bruce thought it quite natural that Leila Mills should fancy him.

Constance's attempts to attract the artistic and intellectual on her Thursdays had been a melancholy failure; such persons were much too busy, and it had occurred to the musicians, literary aspirants and struggling artists in town that there was something a little patronizing in her overtures. Her house was too big; it was not half so agreeable as the Freemans', and of course Freeman was an artist himself and Dale was intelligently sympathetic with everyone who had an idea to offer. As Bud Henderson put it, Dale could mix money and social position with art and nobody thought of its being a mixture, whereas at Constance's you were always conscious of being either a sheep or a goat. Connie's upholstery was too expensive, Bud thought, and her sandwiches were too elaborate for the plebeian palates of goats inured to hot ham in a bun in one-arm lunch rooms.

Gossip, like death, loves a shining mark, and Mrs. Shepherd Mills was too conspicuous to escape the attention of the manufacturers and purveyors of rumor and scandal. The parochial habit of mind dies hard in towns that leap to cityhood, and the delights of the old time cosy gossip over the back fence are not lightly relinquished. Bruce was appalled by the malicious stories he heard about people he was beginning to know and like. He had heard George Whitford's name mentioned frequently in connection with Connie's, but he thought little of it. He had, nevertheless, given due weight to Helen Torrence's warning to beware of becoming one of Connie's victims.

There was a good deal of flirting going on among young married people, Bruce found, but it was of a harmless sort. Towns of two and three hundred thousand are too small for flirtations that pass the heavily mined frontiers of discretion. Even though he had weakly yielded to an impulse and kissed Connie the night he drove her from the Freemans' to Deer Trail, he took it for granted that it had meant no more to her than it had to him. And he assumed that on the earlier afternoon, when he met Connie and Whitford on the road, Whitford had probably been making love to Connie and Connie had not been unwilling to be made love to. There were women like that, he knew, not infrequently young married women who, when the first ardor of marriage has passed, seek to prolong their youth by re-testing their charm for men. Shepherd Mills was hardly a man to inspire a deep love in a woman of Connie's temperament; it was inevitable that Connie should have her little fling.

On his way home from one of his afternoon tramps Bruce was moved to make his third call at the Shepherd Mills's. It was not Connie's day at home, but she had asked him to dinner a few nights earlier when it was impossible for him to go and he hadn't been sure that she had accepted his refusal in good part. He was cold and tired—happily tired, for the afternoon spent in the wintry air had brought the solution of several difficult questions touching the Laconia memorial. His spirit had won the elation which workers in all the arts experience when hazy ideas begin to emerge into the foreground of consciousness and invite consideration in terms of the tangible and concrete.

He would have stopped at the Hardens' if he had dared; lights shone invitingly from the windows as he passed, but the Mills house, with its less genial façade, deterred him. The thought of Millicent was inseparable from the thought of Mills....

He hadn't realized that it was so late until he had rung the bell and looked at his watch under the entry light. The maid surveyed him doubtfully, and sounds of lively talk from within gave him pause. He was about to turn away when Constance came into the hall.

"Oh, pleasantest of surprises!" she exclaimed. "Certainly you're coming in! There's no one here but old friends—and you'll make another!"

"If it's a party, I'm on my way," he said hesitatingly.

"Oh, it's just Nellie Burton and George Whitford—nothing at all to be afraid of!"

At this moment Mrs. Burton and Whitford exhibited themselves at the living-room door in proof of her statement.

"Bully!" cried Whitford. "Of course Connie knew you were coming!"

"I swear I didn't!" Constance declared.

"No matter if you did!" Whitford retorted.

Mrs. Burton clasped her hands devoutly as Bruce divested himself of his overcoat. "We were just praying for another man to come in—and here you are!"

"And a man who's terribly hard to get, if you ask me!" said Constance. "Come in to the fire. George, don't let Mr. Storrs perish for a drink!"

"He shall have gallons!" replied Whitford, turning to a stand on which the materials for cocktail making were assembled. "We needed a fresh thirst in the party to give us a new excuse. 'Stay me with flagons'!"

"Now, *Bruce*," drawled Constance. "*Did* I ever call you *Bruce* before? Well, you won't mind—say you don't mind! Shep calls you by your first name, why not I?"

"This one is to dear old Shep—absent treatment!" said Mrs. Burton as she took her glass.

"Shep's in Cincinnati," Constance was explaining. "He went down on business yesterday and expected to be home for dinner tonight—but he wired this forenoon that he has to stay over. So first comes Nellie and then old George blows in, and we were wishing for another man to share our broth and porridge."

"My beloved hubby's in New York; won't you be my beau, Mr. Storrs?" asked Mrs. Burton.

"*Bruce!*" Constance corrected her.

"All right, then, Bruce! I'm Nellie to all the good comrades."

"Yes, Nellie," said Bruce with affected shyness. He regarded them amiably as they peppered him with a brisk fire of questions as to where he had been and why he made himself so inaccessible.

Mrs. Burton he knew but slightly. She was tall, an extreme blonde and of about Constance's age. Like Constance, she was not of the older order of the local nobility. Her father had been a manufacturer of horsedrawn vehicles, and when the arrival of the gasoline age destroyed his business he passed through bankruptcy into commercial oblivion. However, the law of compensations operated benevolently in Nellie's favor. She married Dick Burton, thereby acquiring both social standing and a sound financial rating. She was less intelligent than Constance, but more daring in her social adventures outside the old conservative stockade.

"George brought his own liquor," said Constance. "We have him to thank for this soothing mixture. Shep's terribly law-abiding; he won't have the stuff on the place. Bruce, you're not going to boast of other engagements; you'll dine right here!"

"That's all settled!" remarked Whitford cheerfully.

"If Bruce goes he takes me with him!" declared Mrs. Burton. "I'm not going to be left here to watch you two spoon. I'm some little spooner myself!"

"You couldn't drive me from this house," protested Bruce.

"There spoke a real man!" cried Constance, and she rang for the maid to order the table set for four.

Mrs. Burton, whom Bruce had met only once before, became confidential when Constance and Whitford went to the piano in the reception parlor, where Whitford began improvising an air to some verses he had written.

"Constance is always so lucky! All the men fall in love with her. George has a terrible case—writes poems to Connie's eyes and everything!"

"Every woman should have her own poet," said Bruce. "I couldn't make a rhyme to save my life!"

"Oh, well, do me something in free verse; you don't need even an idea for that!"

"Ah, the reality doesn't need metrical embellishment!"

"Thanks so much; I ought to have something clever to hand back to you. Constance always know just what to say to a man. I have the courage, but I haven't the brains for a first-class flirt."

"Men are timid creatures," he said mournfully. "I haven't the slightest initiative in these matters. You are charming and the light of your eyes was stolen from the stars. Does that have the right ring?"

"Well, hardly! You're not intense enough! You make me feel as though I were a freak of some kind. Oh, George——"

"Yes, Nellie——" Whitford answered from the piano.

"You must teach Bruce to flirt. His education's been neglected."

"He's in good hands now!" Whitford replied.

"Oh, Bruce is hopeless!" exclaimed Connie, who was seated beside Whitford at the piano. "I gave him a try-out and he refused to play!"

"Then I give up right now!" Mrs. Burton cried in mock despair.

Bruce half suspected that she and Whitford had not met at Constance's quite as casually as they pretended. But it was not his affair, and he was not averse to making a fourth member of a party that promised at least a little gaiety.

Mrs. Burton was examining him as to the range of his acquaintance in the town, and what had prompted him to settle there, and what he thought of the place—evoking the admission (always expected of newcomers) that it was a place singularly marked by its generous hospitality—when she asked with a jerk of the head toward Constance and Whitford:

"What would you do with a case like that?"

"What would I do with it?" asked Bruce, who had been answering her questions perfunctorily, his mind elsewhere. Constance and Whitford, out of sight in the adjoining room, were talking in low tones to the fitful accompaniment of the piano. Now and then Constance laughed happily.

"It really oughtn't to go on, you know!" continued Mrs. Burton. "Those people are *serious*! But—what is one to do?"

"My dear Nellie, I'm not a specialist in such matters!" said Bruce, not relishing her evident desire to discuss their hostess.

"Some of their friends—I'm one of them—are *worried*! I know Helen Torrence has talked to Constance. She really ought to catch herself up. Shep's so blind—poor boy! It's a weakness of his to think everyone perfectly all right!"

"It's a noble quality," remarked Bruce dryly. "You don't think Shep would object to this party?"

"There's the point! Connie isn't stupid, you know! She asked me to come just so she could keep George for dinner. And being a good fellow, I came! I'm ever so glad you showed up. I might be suspected of helping things along! But with you here the world might look through the window!"

"Then we haven't a thing to worry about!" said Bruce with finality.

"It's too bad," she persisted, "that marriage isn't an insurance of happiness. Now George and Constance are ideally suited to each other; but they never knew it until it was too late. I wish he'd go to Africa or some far-off place. If he doesn't there's going to be an earthquake one of these days."

"Well, earthquakes in this part of the world are never serious," Bruce remarked, uncomfortable as he found that Constance's friend was really serious and appealing for his sympathy.

"You probably don't know Franklin Mills—no one does, for that matter— but with his strict views of things there'd certainly be a big smash if *he* knew!"

"Well, of course there's nothing for him to know," said Bruce indifferently.

The maid came in to announce dinner and Constance and Whitford reappeared.

"George has been reciting lovely poetry to me," said Constance. "Nellie, has Bruce kept you amused? I know he *could* make love beautifully if he only *would*!"

"He's afraid of me—or he doesn't like me," said Mrs. Burton—"I don't know which!"

"He looks guilty! He looks terribly guilty. I'm sure he's been making love to you!" said Constance dreamily as though under the spell of happy memories. "We'll go in to dinner just as we are. These informal parties are always the nicest."

III

Whitford was one of those rare men who are equally attractive to both men and women. Any prejudice that might have been aroused in masculine minds by his dilettantism was offset by his adventures as a traveler, hunter and soldier.

"Now, heroes," began Mrs. Burton, when they were seated, "tell us some war stories. I was brought up on my grandfather's stories of the Civil War, but the boys we know who went overseas to fight never talk war at all!"

"No wonder!" exclaimed Whitford. "It was only a little playful diversion among the nations. That your idea, Storrs?"

"Nothing to it," Bruce assented. "We had to go to find out that the French we learned in school was no good!"

Whitford chuckled and told a story of an encounter with a French officer of high rank he had met one wet night in a lonely road. The interview began with the greatest courtesy, became violent as neither could make himself intelligible to the other, and then, when each was satisfied of the other's honorable intentions, they parted with a great flourish of compliments. Bruce capped this with an adventure of his own, in which his personal peril was concealed by his emphasis on the ridiculous plight into which he got himself by an unauthorized excursion through a barbed wire entanglement for a private view of the enemy.

"That's the way they all talk!" said Connie admiringly. "You'd think the whole thing had been a huge joke!"

"You've got to laugh at war," observed Whitford, "it's the only way. It's so silly to think anything can be proved by killing a lot of people and making a lot more miserable."

"You laugh about it, but you might both have been killed!" Mrs. Burton expostulated.

"No odds," said Whitford, "except—that we'd have missed this party!"

They played bridge afterward, though Whitford said it would be more fun to match dollars. The bridge was well under way when the maid passed down the hall to answer the bell.

"Just a minute, Annie!" Constance laid down her cards and deliberated.

"What's the trouble, Connie? Is Shep slipping in on us?" asked Mrs. Burton.

"Hardly," replied Constance, plainly disturbed by the interruption. "Oh, Annie, don't let anyone in you don't know."

They waited in silence for the opening of the door.

In a moment Franklin Mills's voice was heard asking if Mr. and Mrs. Mills were at home.

"Um!" With a shrug Constance rose hastily and met Mills at the door.

"I'd like to see you just a moment, Connie," he said without prelude.

Whitford and Bruce had risen. Mills bowed to them and to Mrs. Burton, but behind the mask of courtesy his face wore a haggard look.

Constance followed him into the hall where their voices—Mills's low and tense—could be heard in hurried conference. In a moment Constance went to the hall telephone and called a succession of numbers.

"The club—Freddy Thomas's rooms——" muttered Whitford. "Wonder what's up——"

They exchanged questioning glances. Whitford idly shuffled and reshuffled the cards.

"He's looking for Leila. Do you suppose——" began Mrs. Burton in a whisper.

"You're keeping score, aren't you, Storrs?" asked Whitford aloud.

They began talking with forced animation about the game to hide their perturbation over Mills's appearance and his evident concern as to Leila's whereabouts.

"Mr. Thomas is at the club," they heard Constance report. "He dined there alone."

"You're sure Leila's not been here—she's not here now?" Mills demanded irritably.

"I haven't seen Leila at all today," Constance replied with patient deliberation. "I'm so sorry you're troubled. She's probably stopped somewhere for dinner and forgotten to telephone."

"She usually calls me up. That's what troubles me," Mills replied, "not hearing from her. There's no place else you'd suggest?"

"No——"

"Thank you, Connie. Shep's still away?"

"Yes. He'll be back tomorrow."

Mills paused in the doorway and bowed to the trio at the card table. "I'm sorry I interrupted your game!" he said, forcing a smile. "Do pardon me!"

He turned up the collar of his fur-lined coat and fumbled for the buttons. There seemed to Bruce a curious helplessness in the slow movement of his fingers.

Constance followed him to the outer door, and as it closed upon him walked slowly back into the living room.

"That's a pretty how-d'ye-do! Leila ought to have a whipping! It's after eight and nothing's been seen of her since noon. But she hasn't eloped— that's one satisfaction! Freddy's at the club all right enough."

"She's certainly thrown a scare into her father," remarked Mrs. Burton. "He looked positively ill."

"It's too bad!" ejaculated Whitford. "I hope she hasn't got soused and smashed up her car somewhere."

"I wish Freddy Thomas had never been born!" cried Constance impatiently. "Leila and her father have been having a nasty time over him. And she had cut drinking and was doing fine!"

"Is there anything we can do?—that's the question," said Whitford, taking a turn across the floor.

Bruce was thinking hard. What might Leila do in a fit of depression over her father's hostility toward Thomas?...

"I think maybe——" he began. He did not finish, but with sudden resolution put out his hand to Constance. "Excuse me, won't you? It's just possible that I may be able to help."

"Let me go with you," said Whitford quickly.

"No, thanks; Mr. Mills may come back and need assistance. You'd better stay. If I get a clue I'll call up."

It was a bitter night, the coldest of the year, and he drove his car swiftly, throwing up the windshield and welcoming the rush of cold air. He thought of his drive with Shepherd to the river, and here he was setting forth again in a blind hope of rendering a service to one of Franklin Mills's children!...

On the unlighted highway he had difficulty in finding the gate that opened into the small tract on the bluff above the boathouse where he had taken Leila and Millicent on the summer evening when he had rescued them from the sandbar. Leaving his car at the roadside, he stumbled down the steps that led to the water. He paused when he saw lights in the boathouse and moved cautiously across the veranda that ran around its land side. A vast silence hung upon the place.

He opened the door and stood blinking into the room. On a long couch that stretched under the windows lay Leila, in her fur coat, with a rug half drawn over her knees. Her hat had slipped to the floor and beside it lay a silver flask and an empty whisky bottle. He touched her cheek and found it warm; listened for a moment to her deep, uneven breathing, and gathered her up in his arms.

He reached the door just as it opened and found himself staring into Franklin Mills's eyes—eyes in which pain, horror and submission effaced any trace of surprise.

"I—I followed your car," Mills said, as if an explanation of his presence were necessary. "I'm sure—you are very—very kind——"

He stepped aside, and Bruce passed out, carrying the relaxed body tenderly. As he felt his way slowly up the icy steps he could hear Mills following.

The Mills limousine stood by the gate and the chauffeur jumped out and opened the door. No words were spoken. Mills got into the car slowly, unsteadily, in the manner of a decrepit old man. When he was seated Bruce placed Leila in his arms and drew the carriage robe over them. The chauffeur mounted to his place and snapped off the tonneau lights, and Bruce, not knowing what he did, raised his hand in salute as the heavy machine rolled away.

CHAPTER SEVENTEEN

I

The day following his discovery of Leila Mills in the boathouse, Bruce remained in his apartment. He was not a little awed by the instinct that had led him to the river—the unlikeliest of places in which to seek the runaway girl. The poor little drugged body lying there in the cold room; her deep sigh and the touch of her hand on his face as he took her up, and more poignantly the look in Franklin Mills's face when they met at the door, remained with him, and he knew that these were things he could never forget....

There was more of superstition and mysticism in his blood than he had believed. Lounging about his rooms, staring down at the bleak street as it whitened in a brisk snowfall, his thoughts ranged the wide seas of doubt and faith. Life was only a corridor between two doors of mystery. Petty and contemptible seemed the old familiar teachings about God. Men were not rejecting God; they were merely misled as to his nature. The spirit of man was only an infinitesimal particle of the spirit that was God. No other person he had ever talked with had offered so reasonable a solution of the problem as Millicent.

Again he went over their talk on the golf course. Millicent had the clue—the clue to a reality no less tangible and plausible because it was born of unreality. And here was the beginning of wisdom: to abandon the attempt to explain all things when so manifestly life would become intolerable if the walls of mystery through which man moves were battered down. As near as he was able to express it, the soul required room—all infinity, indeed, as the playground for its proper exercise. The freer a man's spirit the greater its capacity for loving and serving its neighbor souls. Somewhere in the illimitable horizons of which Millicent dreamed it was imaginable that Something august and supreme dominated the universe—Something only belittled by every attempt to find a name for it....

Strange reflections for a healthy young mind in a stalwart, vigorous young body! Bruce hardly knew himself today. The scent of Leila's hair as he bore her out of the boathouse had stirred a tenderness in his heart that was strange to him. He hoped Franklin Mills had dealt leniently with Leila. He had no idea what the man would do or say after finding his daughter in such a plight. He considered telephoning Mills's house to ask about her, but dismissed the thought. His duty was discharged the moment he gave her into her father's keeping; in all the circumstances an inquiry would be an impertinence.

Poor Leila! Poor, foolish, wilful, generous-hearted little girl! Her father was much too conspicuous for her little excursions among the shoals of folly to pass unremarked. Bruce found himself excusing and defending her latest escapade. She had taken refuge in the oblivion of alcohol as an escape from her troubles.... Something wrong somewhere. Shep and Leila both groping in the dark for the door of happiness and getting no help from their father in their search—a deplorable situation. Not altogether Franklin Mills's fault; perhaps no one's fault; just the way things happen, but no less tragic for all that.

Bruce asked the janitor to bring in his meals, content to be alone, looking forward to a long day in which to brood over his plans for the memorial. He was glad that he had not run away from Franklin Mills. It was much better to have remained in the town, and more comfortable to have met Mills and the members of his family than to have lived in the same community speculating about them endlessly without ever knowing them. He knew them now all too well! Even Franklin Mills was emerging from the mists; Bruce began to think he knew what manner of man Mills was. Shepherd had opened his own soul to him; and Leila—Bruce made allowances for Leila and saw her merits with full appreciation. One thing was certain: he did not envy Franklin Mills or his children their lot; he coveted nothing they possessed. He thanked his stars that he had had the wit to reject Mills's offer to help him into a business position of promise; to be under obligation of any sort to Franklin Mills would be intolerable. Through the afternoon he worked desultorily on his sketches of the Laconia memorial, enjoying the luxury of undisturbed peace. He began combining in a single drawing his memoranda of details; was so pleased with the result in crayon that he began a pen and ink sketch and was still at this when Henderson appeared, encased in a plaid overcoat that greatly magnified his circumference.

"What's responsible for this!" Bruce demanded.

"Thanks for your hearty greeting! I called your office at five-minute intervals all day and that hard-boiled telephone girl said you hadn't been there. All the clubs denied knowledge of your whereabouts, so I clambered into my palatial Plantagenet and sped out, expecting to find you sunk in mortal illness. You must stop drinking, son."

"That's a good one from you! Please don't sit on those drawings!"

"My mistake. You're terribly peevish. By the way—what was the row last night about Leila Mills?" Bud feigned deep interest in a cloisonné jar that stood on the table.

"Well, what was?" asked Bruce. "I might have known you had something up your sleeve."

"Oh, the kid disappeared yesterday long enough to give her father heart failure. Mills called Maybelle to see if she was at our house; Maybelle called Connie, and Connie said you'd left a party at her house to chase the kidnappers. Of course I'm not asking any questions, but I do like to keep pace with the local news."

"I'll say you do!" Bruce grinned at him provokingly. "Did they catch the kidnappers?"

"Well, Connie called Maybelle later to say that Leila was all safe at home and in bed. But even Connie didn't know where you found the erring lambkin."

"You've called the wrong number," Bruce said, stretching himself. "I didn't find Miss Leila. When I left Connie's I went to the club to shoot a little pool."

"You certainly lie like a gentleman! Come on home with me to dinner; we're going to have corn beef and cabbage tonight!"

"In other words, if you can't make me talk you think Maybelle can!"

"You insult me! Get your hat and let's skip!"

"No; I'm taking my nourishment right here today. Strange as it may seem—I'm working!"

"Thanks for the hint! Just for that I hope the job's a failure."

II

Bruce was engrossed at his drawing-board when, at half past eight, the tinkle of the house telephone startled him.

"Mr. Storrs? This is Mr. Mills speaking—may I trouble you for a moment?"

"Yes; certainly. Come right up, Mr. Mills!"

There was no way out of it. He could not deny himself to Mills. Bruce hurriedly put on his coat, cleared up the litter on his table, straightened the cushions on the divan and went into the hall to receive his guest. He saw Mills's head and shoulders below; Mills was mounting slowly, leaning heavily upon the stair rail. At the first landing—Bruce's rooms were on the third floor—Mills paused and drew himself erect. Bruce stepped inside the door to avoid embarrassing his caller on his further ascent.

"It's a comfort not to have all the modern conveniences," Mills remarked graciously when Bruce apologized for the stairs. "Thank you, no; I'll not take off my coat. You're nicely situated here—I got your number from Carroll; he can always answer any question."

His climb had evidently wearied him and he twisted the head of his cane nervously as he waited for his heart to resume its normal beat. There was a tired look in his eyes and his face lacked its usual healthy color. If Mills had come to speak of Leila, Bruce resolved to make the interview as easy for him as possible.

"Twenty-five years ago this was cow pasture," Mills remarked. "My father owned fifty acres right here when I was a boy. He sold it for twenty times its original cost."

Whatever had brought Franklin Mills to Bruce's door, the man knew exactly what he had come to say, but was waiting until he could give full weight to the utterance. In a few minutes he was quite himself, and to

Bruce's surprise he rose and stood, with something of the ceremonial air of one about to deliver a message whose nature demanded formality.

"Mr. Storrs, I came to thank you for the great service you rendered me last night. I was in very great distress. You can understand my anxious concern; so I needn't touch upon that. Words are inadequate to express my gratitude. But I can at least let you know that I appreciate what you did for me—for me and my daughter."

He ended with a slight inclination of the head.

"Thank you, Mr. Mills," said Bruce, taking the hand Mills extended. "I hope Miss Mills is quite well."

"Quite, thank you."

With an abrupt change of manner that dismissed the subject Mills glanced about the room.

"You bring work home? That speaks for zeal in your profession. Aren't the days long enough?"

"Oh, this is a little private affair," said Bruce, noting that Mills's gaze had fallen upon the drawings propped against the wall. It was understood between him and the Freemans that his participation in the Laconia competition was to be kept secret; but he felt moved to explain to Mills the nature of the drawings. The man had suffered in the past twenty-four hours —it would be ungenerous to let him go without making some attempt to divert his thoughts from Leila's misbehavior.

"This may interest you, Mr. Mills; I mean the general proposition—not my little sketches. Only—it must be confidential!"

"Yes; certainly," Mills smiled a grave assent. "Perhaps you'd rather not tell me—I'm afraid my curiosity got the better of my manners."

"Oh, not that, sir! Mr. and Mrs. Freeman know, of course; but I don't want to have to explain my failure in case I lose! I'm glad to tell you about it; you may have some suggestions."

Mills listened as Bruce explained the requirements of the Laconia memorial and illustrated with the drawings what he proposed to offer.

"Laconia?" Mills repeated the name quickly. "How very interesting!"

"You may recall the site," Bruce went on, displaying a photograph of the hilltop.

"I remember the place very well; there couldn't be a finer site. I suppose the town owns the entire hill? That's a fine idea—to adjust the building to that bit of forest; the possibilities are enormous for effective handling. There should be a fitting approach—terraces, perhaps a fountain directly in front of the entrance—something to prepare the eye as the visitor ascends——"

"That hadn't occurred to me!" said Bruce. "It would be fine!"

Mills, his interest growing, slipped out of his overcoat and sat down in the chair beside the drawing board.

"Those colonnades extending at both sides give something of the effect of wings—buoyancy is what I mean," he remarked. "I like the classical severity of the thing. Beauty can be got with a few lines—but they must be the right ones. Nature's a sound teacher there."

Bruce forgot that there was any tie between them; Laconia became only a place where a soldiers' memorial was to be constructed. Mills's attitude toward the project was marked by the restraint, the diffidence of a man of breeding wary of offending but eager to help. Bruce had seen at once the artistic value of the fountain. He left Mills at the drawing table and paced the floor, pondering it. The look of weariness left Mills's face. He was watching with frankly admiring eyes the tall figure, the broad, capable shoulders, the finely molded head, the absorbed, perplexed look in the handsome face. Not like Shep; not like any other young man he knew was this Bruce Storrs. He had not expected to remain more than ten minutes, but he was finding it difficult to leave.

Remembering that he had a guest, Bruce glanced at Mills and caught the look in his face. For a moment both were embarrassed.

"Do pardon me!" Bruce exclaimed quickly. "I was just trying to see my way through a thing or two. I'm afraid I'm boring you."

Mills murmured a denial and took a cigarette from the box Bruce extended.

"How much money is there to spend on this? I was just thinking that that's an important point. Public work of this sort is often spoiled by lack of funds."

"Three hundred thousand is the limit. Mr. Freeman warns me that it's hardly enough for what I propose, and that I've got to do some trimming."

He drew from a drawer the terms of the competition and the specifications, and smoked in silence while Mills looked them over.

"It's all clear enough. It's a joint affair—the county does half and the rest is a popular subscription?"

"Yes; the local committee are fine people; too bad they haven't enough to do the thing just right," Bruce replied. "Of course I mean the way I'd like to do it—with your idea of the fountain that I'd rejoice to steal!"

"That's a joke—that I could offer a trained artist any suggestion of real value!"

Bruce was finding his caller a very different Franklin Mills from the man he had talked with in the Jefferson Avenue house, and not at all the man whom, in his rôle of country squire, he had seen at Deer Trail. Mills was enjoying himself; there was no question of that. He lighted a cigar—the cigar he usually smoked at home before going to bed.

"You will not be known as a competitor; your plans will go in anonymously?" he inquired.

"Yes; that's stipulated," Bruce replied.

Returning to the plans—they seemed to have a fascination for Mills—one of his questions prompted Bruce to seize a pencil and try another type of entrance. Mills stood by, watching the free swift movement of the strong hand.

"I'm not so sure that's better than your first idea. I've always heard that a first inspiration is likely to be the best—providing always that it is an inspiration! I'd give a lot if I could do what you've just done with that pencil. I suppose it's a knack; you're born with it. You probably began young; such talent shows itself early."

"I can't remember a time when I didn't like to fool with a pencil. My mother gave me my first lessons. She had a very pretty talent—sketched well and did water colors—very nice ones, too. That's one of them over there—a corner of our garden in the old home at Laconia."

Mills walked slowly across the room to look at a framed water color that hung over Bruce's writing table.

"Yes; I can see that it's good work. I remember that garden—I seem to remember this same line of hollyhocks against the brick wall."

"Oh, mother had that every year! Her flowers were famous in Laconia."

"And that sun-dial—I seem to remember that, too," Mills observed meditatively.

"Mother liked that sort of thing. We used to sit out there in the summer. She made a little festival of the coming of spring. I think all the birds in creation knew her as friend. And the neighbor children came in to hear her read—fairy stories and poetry. We had jolly good times there—mother and I!"

"I'm sure you did," said Mills gravely.

As he stepped away from the table his eyes fell upon the photograph of a young woman in a silver frame. He bent down for a closer inspection. Bruce turned away, walked the length of the room and glanced round to find Mills still regarding the photograph.

"My mother, as she was at about thirty," Bruce remarked.

"Yes; I thought so. Somewhat older than when I knew her, but the look of youth is still there."

"I prefer that to any other picture of her I have. She refused to be photographed in her later years—said she didn't want me to think of her as old. And she never was that—could never have been."

"I can well believe it," said Mills softly. "Time deals gently with spirits like hers."

"No one was ever like her," said Bruce with feeling. "She made the world a kindlier and nobler place by living in it."

"And you're loyal to the ideal she set for you! You think of her, I'm sure, in all you do—in all you mean to do."

"Yes, it helps—it helps a lot to feel that somewhere she knows and cares."

Mills picked up a book, scanned the title page unseeingly and threw it down.

"I've just about killed an evening for you," he said with a smile and put out his hand cordially. "My chauffeur is probably frozen."

"You've been a big help!" replied Bruce. "It's been fine to have you here. I'll see Mr. Freeman tomorrow and go over the whole thing again. He may be able to squeeze the fountain out of the appropriation! May I tell him it's your idea?"

"Oh, no! No, indeed! Just let my meddlesomeness be a little joke between us. I shall be leaving town shortly and may not see you again for several months. So good-bye and good luck!"

Bruce walked downstairs with him. At the entrance they again shook hands, as if the good will on both sides demanded this further expression of amity.

III

A brief item in the "Personal and Society" column of an afternoon newspaper apprised Bruce a few days later of the departure of Mr. Franklin Mills and Miss Leila Mills for the Mediterranean, they having abandoned their proposed trip to Bermuda for the longer voyage. Bruce wondered a little at the change of plans, suspecting that it might in some degree be a disciplinary measure for Leila's benefit, a scheme for keeping her longer under her father's eye. He experienced a curious new loneliness at the thought of their absence and then was impatient to find himself giving them a second thought. A month earlier he would have been relieved by the knowledge that Mills was gone and that the wide seas rolled between them. An amazing thing, this! To say they were nothing to him did not help now as in those first months after he had established himself in Mills's town. They meant a good deal to him and perhaps he meant something to them. It was very odd indeed how he and the Millses circled about each other.

As he put down the newspaper a note was brought to him at his apartment by Mills's chauffeur. It read:

> Dear Bruce: You said I might; I can't just Mr. Storrs you! Trunks at the station and Dada waiting at the front door. I couldn't bear the idea of writing you a note you'd read while I was still in town—so please consider that I'm throwing you a kiss from the tail end of the observation car. I could never, never

have had the courage to *say* my thanks to you—if I tried I'd cry and make a general mess of it. But—I want you to *know* that I do appreciate it—what you did—in saving my life and every little thing! I'd probably have died all right enough in the frightful cold if you hadn't found me. I really didn't know till yesterday, when I wormed it out of Dada, just how it all happened! I'm simply crushed! I promise I'll never do such a thing again. Thank you *loads*, and be sure I'll never forget. I wish you were my big brother; I'd just adore being a nice, good little sister to you. Love and kisses, from

Leila.

He reread it a dozen times in the course of the evening. It was so like the child—the perverse, affectionate child—that Leila was. *"I wish you were my big brother."* The sentence had slipped from her flying pen thoughtlessly, no doubt, but it gave Bruce a twinge. Shep did not know; Leila did not know! and yet for both of these children of Franklin Mills he felt a fondness that was beyond ordinary friendship. Shep could never be, in the highest sense, a companion of his father; Mills no doubt loved Leila, but he loved her without understanding. Her warm, passionate heart, the very fact that she and Shep were the children of Franklin Mills made life difficult for them. Either would have been happier if they had not been born into the Mills caste. The Mills money and the Mills position were an encumbrance against which more or less consciously they were in rebellion.

CHAPTER EIGHTEEN

I

It was ten days later that a communication from the Laconia War Memorial Association gave warning that the stipulations for the contesting architects were being altered, and in another week Bruce received the supplemental data sent out to all the contestants. The amount to be expended had been increased by an unexpected addition to the private subscriptions.

In one of his first fits of homesickness Bruce had subscribed for the Laconia Examiner to keep in touch with affairs in his native town. The paper printed with a proud flourish the news of the augmentation of the fund. One hundred thousand dollars had been contributed through a New York trust company by "a citizen" whose identity for good and sufficient reasons was not to be disclosed. The trust company's letter as quoted in the Examiner recited that the donation was from a "patriotic American who, recognizing the fine spirit in which Laconia had undertaken the memorial and the community's desire that it should be an adequate testimony to the valor and sacrifice of American youth, considered it a high privilege to be permitted to assist."

Mills! Though the Laconia newspaper was evidently wholly at sea as to the identity of the contributor, Bruce was satisfied that Mills was the unknown donor. And he resented it. The agreeable impression left by Mills the evening they discussed the plans was dispelled by this unwarranted interference. Bruce bitterly regretted having taken Mills into his confidence. Mills's interest had pleased him, but he had never dreamed that the man might feel moved to add to the attractiveness of the contest by a secret contribution to the fund. He felt strongly moved to abandon the whole thing and but for the embarrassment of explaining himself to Freeman he would have done so. But the artist in him prevailed. Mills had greatly broadened the possibilities of the contest and in a few days Bruce fell to work with renewed enthusiasm.

He was living in Laconia again, so engrossed did he become in his work. He dined with Carroll now and then, enjoyed long evenings at the Freemans' and kept touch with the Hendersons; but he refused so many invitations to the winter functions that Dale protested. He dropped into the Central States Trust Company now and then to observe Shep in his new rôle of vice-president. Shep was happier in the position than he had expected to be. Carroll was seeing to it that he had real work to do, work that was well within his powers. He had charge of the savings department and was pleased when his old friends among the employees of the battery plant looked him up and opened accounts. The friends of the Mills family, where they took note of Shep's transfer at all, saw in it a promotion.

Bruce, specially importuned by telephone, went to one of Constance's days at home, which drew a large attendance by reason of the promised presence of an English novelist whose recent severe criticism of American society and manners had made him the object of particular adoration to American women readers. Bud Henderson, who had carried a flask to the tea, went about protesting against the consideration shown the visitor. If, he said, an American writer criticized American women in any such fashion he would be lynched, but let an Englishman do it and women would steal the money out of their children's banks to buy his books and lecture tickets. So spake Bud. If Bud had had two flasks he would have broken up the tea; restricted as he was, his protest against the Briton took the form of an utterly uncalled for attack upon the drama league delivered to an aunt of Maybelle's who was president of the local society—a strong Volsteadian who thought Bud vulgar, which at times Bud, by any high social standard, indubitably was. However, if amid so many genuflections the eminent Briton was disturbed by Bud's evil manners or criticisms, Bud possibly soothed his feelings by following him upstairs when the party was dispersing and demonstrating the manner in which American law is respected by drawing flasks from nine out of fifteen overcoats laid out on Constance's guest room bed and pouring half a pint of excellent bourbon into the unresisting man of letters.

This function was only an interlude in the city's rather arid social waste. The local society, Bruce found, was an affair of curiously close groupings. The women of the ancestral crowd were so wary of the women who had floated in on the tide of industrial expansion that one might have thought the newcomers were, in spite of their prosperity, afflicted with leprosy....

While Bruce might bury himself from the sight of others who had manifested a friendly interest in him, Helen Torrence was not so easily denied. She had no intention of going alone to the February play of the Dramatic Club. She telephoned Bruce to this effect and added that he must dine with her that evening and take her to the club. Bud had already sent him an admission card with a warning not to come if anything better offered, such as sitting up with a corpse—this being Bud's manner of speaking of the organization whose politics he dominated and whose entertainments he would not have missed for a chance to dine with royalty.

Bruce, having reached the Torrence house, found Millicent there.

"You see what you get for being good!" cried Helen, noting the surprise and pleasure in Bruce's face as he appeared in her drawing room.

"I thought you'd probably run when you saw me," said Millicent. "You passed me at the post office door yesterday and looked straight over my head. I never felt so small in my life."

"Post office?" Bruce repeated. "I haven't been near the place for weeks!"

"That will do from you!" warned Helen. "We all thought you'd be a real addition to our sad social efforts here, but it's evident you don't like us. It's very discouraging. You were at Connie's, though, to hear her lion roar. I saw you across the room. Connie always gets the men! Your friend Bud insulted everybody there; I see him selling any more Plantagenets!"

"Bud's patriotism leads him astray sometimes; that's all. Any more scolding, Millicent?" Bruce asked. "Let me see—we had arrived at the stage of first names, hadn't we?"

"Yes, Bruce! But after the long separation it might be as well to go back to the beginning. As for scolding, let's consider that we've signed an armistice."

"I don't like the military lingo; it sounds as though there had been war between us."

"Dear me!" Helen interposed mournfully. "You're not going to spend the whole evening in preliminaries! Let's go out to dinner."

After they were seated Bruce was still rather more self-conscious than was comfortable. Nothing had happened; or more truthfully, nothing had happened except that he had been keeping away from Millicent because of Franklin Mills. She evidently was not displeased to see him again. He had not realized how greatly he had missed her till her voice touched chords that had vibrated at their first meeting. Her eyes had the same steady light and kindled responsively to any demand of mirth; her hair had the same glint of gold. He marveled anew at her poise and ease. Tonight her gown, of a delicate shade of crimson, seemed a subdued reflection of her bright coloring. He floundered badly in his attempts to bring some spirit to the conversation. It seemed stupid to ask Millicent about her music or inquire how her modeling was coming on or what she had been reading. He listened with forced attention while she and Helen compared notes on recent social affairs in which they had participated.

"Millie, you don't really like going about—teas and that sort of thing," said Helen. "I know you don't. All you girls who have ideas are like that."

"Ideas! Dearest Helen, are you as easily deceived as that! Sometimes there are things I'd rather do than go to parties! Does one really have to keep going to avoid seeming queer?"

"I go because I haven't the brains to do anything else. I like wandering with the herd. It just thrills me to get into a big jam. And I suppose I show myself whenever I'm asked for fear I'll be forgotten!"

"My sole test of a social function is whether they feed me standing or sitting," said Bruce when appealed to. "I can bear anything but that hideous sensation that my plate is dripping."

"That's why men hate teas," observed Helen. "It's because of the silly refreshments no one wants and everybody must have or the hostess is broken-hearted."

"That's probably where jailers got the idea of forcible feeding," Millicent suggested.

"At the Hendersons'," Bruce added, "only the drinks are compulsory. Bud's social symbol is the cocktail-shaker!"

"Everybody drinks too much;" said Helen, "except us. Bruce, help yourself to the sherry."

"What is a perfect social occasion?" Bruce asked. "My own ideas are a little muddled, but you—Helen?"

"If you must know the truth—there is no such thing! However, you might ask Millicent; she's an optimist."

"A perfect time is sitting in the middle of the floor in my room cutting paper dolls," Millicent answered. "I'm crazy about it. Leila says it's the best thing I do."

"Do you ever exhibit your creations?" asked Bruce solicitously.

"We've got her in a trap now," exclaimed Helen. "Millie takes her paper dolls to the sick children in the hospitals. I know, because the children told me. I was at the City Hospital the other day and peeped into the children's ward. Much excitement—a vast population of paper dolls dressed in the latest modes. The youngsters were so tickled! They said a beautiful lady had brought them—a most wonderful, beautiful lady. And she was going to come back with paper and scissors and show them just how they were made!"

"They're such dear, patient little angels," murmured Millicent. "You feel better about all humanity when you see how much courage there is in the world. It's a pretty brave old world after all."

"It's the most amazing thing about life," said Bruce, "that so many millions rise up every morning bent on doing their best. You'd think the whole human race would have given up the struggle long ago and jumped into the sea. But no! Poor boobs that we are, we go whistling right along. Frankly, I mean to hang on a couple of weeks longer. Silly old world—but—it has its good points."

"Great applause!" exclaimed Helen, satisfied now that her little party was not to prove an utter failure. These were two interesting young people, she knew, and she was anxious to hear their views on matters about which she troubled herself more than most people suspected.

"I've wondered sometimes," Millicent said, "what would happen if the world could be made altogether happy just once by a miracle of some kind, no heartache anywhere; no discomfort! How long would it last?"

"Only till some person among the millions wanted something another one had; that would start the old row over again," Bruce answered.

"I see what you children mean," said Helen seriously. "Selfishness is what makes the world unhappy!"

"Now—we're getting in deep!" Bruce exclaimed. "Millicent always swims for the open water."

"Millie ought to go about lecturing; telling people to be calm, to look more at the stars and less at their neighbors' new automobiles. I believe that would do a lot of good," said Helen.

"A splendid idea!" Bruce declared, laughing into Millicent's eyes. "But what a sacrifice of herself! A wonderful exhibition of unselfishness, but _____"

"I'd be stoned to death!"

"You'd be surer of martyrdom if you told them to love their neighbors as themselves," said Helen. "Seriously now, that's the hardest thing there is to do! Love my neighbor as myself! Me! Why, on one side my neighbor's children snowball my windows; on the other side there's a chimney that ruins me paying cleaner's bills. Perhaps you'd speak to them for me, Millie?"

"See here!" exclaimed Millicent. "Where do you get this idea of using me as a missionary and policeman! I don't feel any urge to reform the world! I'm awful busy tending to my own business."

"Oh, all right," said Bruce with a sigh of resignation. "Let the world go hang, then, if you won't save it!"

Helen was dressing the salad, and Bruce was free to watch Millicent's eyes as they filled with dreams. As at other times when some grave mood touched her, it seemed that she became another being, exploring some realm alien to common experience. He glanced at her hands, folded quietly on the edge of the table, and again at her dream-filled eyes. Hers was the repose of a nature schooled in serenity. The world might rage in fury about her, but amid the tempest her soul would remain unshaken....

Helen, to whom silence was always disturbing, looked up, but stifled an apology for the unconscionable time she was taking with the salad when she saw Millicent's face, and Bruce's intent, reverent gaze fixed upon the girl.

"Saving the world!" Millicent repeated deliberatingly. "I never quite like the idea. It rather suggests—doesn't it?—that some new machinery or method must be devised for saving it. But the secret came into the world ever so long ago—it was the ideal of beauty. A Beautiful Being died that man might know the secret of happiness. It had to be that way or man would never have understood or remembered. It's not His fault that his ideas have been so confused and obscured in the centuries that have passed since He came. It's man's fault. The very simplicity of His example has always bewildered man; it was too good to be true!"

"But, Millie," said Helen with a little embarrassed laugh, "does the world really want to live as Jesus lived? Or would it admire people who did? Somebody said once that Christianity isn't a failure because it's never been tried. Will it *ever* be tried—does anyone care enough?"

"Dear me! What have I gotten into?" Millicent picked up her fork and glanced at them smilingly. "Bruce, don't look so terribly solemn! Why, people are trying it every day, at least pecking at it a little. I've caught you at it lots of times! While we sit here, enjoying this quite wonderful salad, scores of people are doing things to make the world a better place to live in —safer, kinder and happier. I saw a child walk out of the hospital the other day who'd been carried in, a pitiful little cripple. It was a miracle; and if you'd seen the child's delight and the look in the face of the doctor whose genius did the work, you'd have thought the secret of Jesus is making some headway!"

"And knowing the very charming young woman named Millicent who found that little crippled girl and took her to the hospital. I'd have thought a lot more things!"

"I never did it!" Millicent cried.

"She's always up to such tricks!" Helen informed Bruce. "Paper dolls are only one item of Millie's good works."

"Be careful!" Millicent admonished. "I could tell some stories on you that might embarrass you terribly." She turned to Bruce with a lifting of the brows that implied their hostess's many shameless excursions in philanthropy.

"How grand it would be if we could all talk about serious things—life, religion and things like that—as Millie does," remarked Helen. "Most people talk of religion as though it were something disgraceful."

"Or they take the professional tone of the undertaker telling a late pallbearer where to sit," Bruce added, "and the pallbearer is always deaf and insists on getting into the wrong place and sitting on someone's hat."

"How jolly! Anything to cheer up a funeral," said Helen. "Go on, Millie, and talk some more. You're a lot more comforting than Doctor Lindley."

"The Doctor's fine," said Millicent spiritedly. "I don't go to church because half of me is heathen, I suppose." She paused as though a little startled by the confession. "There are things about churches—some of the hymns, the creed, the attempts to explain the Scriptures—that don't need explaining— that rub me the wrong way. But it isn't fair to criticize Doctor Lindley or any other minister who's doing the best he can to help the world when the times are against him. No one has a harder job than a Christian minister of his training and traditions who really knows what's the trouble with the world and the church but is in danger of being burned as a heretic if he says what he thinks."

"People can't believe any more, can they, what their grandfathers believed? It's impossible—with science and everything," suggested Helen vaguely.

"Why should they?" asked Millicent. "I liked to believe that God moves forward with the world. He has outgrown His own churches; it's their misfortune that they don't realize it. And Jesus, the Beautiful One, walks through the modern world weighted down with a heavier cross than the one he died on—bigotry, intolerance, hatred—what a cruel thing that men should hate one another in His name! I've wondered sometimes what Jesus must think of all the books that have been written to explain Him— mountains of books! Jesus is the only teacher the world ever had who got His whole story into one word—a universal word, an easy word to say, and the word that has inspired all the finest deeds of man. He rested His case on that, thinking that anything so simple would never be misunderstood. At the hospital one day I heard a mother say to her child, a pitiful little scrap who was doomed to die, 'I love you so!' and the wise, understanding little baby said, 'Me know you do.' I think that's an answer to the charge that Christianity is passing out. It can't, you see, because it's founded on the one thing in the world that can never die."

The room was very still. The maid, who had been arrested in the serving of the dinner by a gesture from Helen, furtively made the sign of the cross. The candle flames bent to some imperceptible stirring of the quiet air. Bruce experienced a sense of vastness, of the immeasurable horizons of Millicent's God and a world through which the Beautiful One wandered still, symbolizing the ineffable word of His gospel that was not for one people, or one sect, not to be bound up into one creed, but written into the hearts of all men as their guide to happiness. It seemed to him that the girl's words were part of some rite of purification that had cleansed and blessed the world.

"I hadn't thought of it in quite that way," said Bruce thoughtfully.

Helen was a wise woman and knew the perils of anticlimax. She turned and nodded to the maid.

"Please forgive me! I've been holding back the dinner!" Millicent exclaimed. "You must always stop me when I begin riding the clouds. Bruce, are you seeing Dale Freeman these days? Of course you are! Helen, we must study Dale more closely. She knows how to bring Bruce running!"

"I cheerfully yield to Dale in everything," said Helen. "I must watch the time. They promise an unusually good show tonight—three one-act pieces and one of them by George Whitford; he and Connie are to act in it."

"Connie ought to be a star," Millicent remarked, "she gives a lot of time to theatricals."

"There's just a question whether Connie and George Whitford are not— well, getting up theatricals does make for intimacy!" said Helen. "I wish George had less money! An idle man—particularly a fascinating devil like George—is a dangerous playmate for a woman like Connie!"

"Oh, but Connie's a dear!" exclaimed Millicent defensively. "Her position isn't easy. A lot of the criticism you hear of her is unjust."

"A lot of the criticism you hear of everybody is unjust," Bruce ventured.

"Oh, we have a few people here who pass for respectable but start all the malicious gossip in town," Helen observed. "They're not all women, either! I suspect Mort Walters of spreading the story that Connie and George are having a big affair, and that Mr. Mills gave Connie a good combing about it before he went abroad!"

"Ridiculous!" murmured Millicent.

"Of course," Helen went on. "We all know why Leila's father dragged her away. But Connie ought really to have a care. It's too bad Shep isn't big enough to give Walters a thrashing. The trouble with Walters is that he tried to start a little affair with Connie himself and she turned him down cold. Pardon me, are we gossiping?"

"Of course not!" laughed Millicent.

"Just whetting our appetites for anything new that offers at the club," said Bruce. "I'm glad I'm a new man in town; I can listen to all the scandal without being obliged to take sides."

"Millie! You hate gossip," said Helen, "so please talk about the saints so I won't have a chance to chatter about the sinners."

"Don't worry," said Bruce. "If there were no sinners the saints wouldn't know how good they are!"

"We'd better quit on that," said Helen. "It's time to go!"

<h1 style="text-align:center">II</h1>

At the hall where the Dramatic Club's entertainments were given they met Shepherd Mills, who confessed that he had been holding four seats in the hope that they'd have pity on him and not let him sit alone.

"I've hardly seen Connie for a week," he said. "This thing of having a wife on the stage is certainly hard on the husband!"

The room was filled to capacity and there were many out of town guests, whom Shep named proudly as though their presence were attributable to the fact that Connie was on the program.

Whitford, in his ample leisure, had been putting new spirit into the club, and the first two of the one-act plays that constituted the bill disclosed new talent and were given with precision and finish. Chief interest, however, lay in the third item of the bill, a short poetic drama written by Whitford himself. The scene, revealed as the curtain rose, was of Whitford's own designing—the battlements of a feudal castle, with a tower rising against a sweep of blue sky. The set transcended anything that the club had seen in its long history and was greeted with a quick outburst of applause. Whitford's name passed over the room, it seemed, in a single admiring whisper. George was a genius; the town had never possessed anyone comparable to George Whitford, who distinguished himself alike in war and in the arts of peace and could afford to spend money with a free hand on amateur theatricals.

His piece, "The Beggar," written in blank verse, was dated vaguely in the Middle Ages and the device was one of the oldest known to romance. A lord of high degree is experiencing the time-honored difficulty in persuading his daughter of the desirability of marriage with a noble young knight whose suit she has steadfastly scorned. The castle is threatened; the knight's assistance is imperatively needed; and the arrival of messengers, the anxious concern of the servitors, induce at once an air of tensity.

In the fading afternoon light Constance Mills, as the princess, who has been wandering in the gardens, makes her entrance unconcernedly and greets her distracted lover with light-hearted indifference. She begins recounting a meeting with a beggar minstrel who has beguiled her with his music. She provokingly insists upon singing snatches of his songs to the irritated knight, who grows increasingly uneasy over the danger to the beleagured castle. As the princess exits the beggar appears and engages the knight in a colloquy, witty and good-humored on the vagrant's part, but marked by the knight's mounting anger. Whitford, handsome, jaunty, assured, even in his rags, with his shrewd retorts evokes continuous laughter.

A renewed alarm calls the knight away, leaving the beggar thrumming his lute. The princess reappears to the dimming of lights and the twinkle in the blue background of the first tremulous star. The beggar, who of course is the enemy prince in disguise, springs forward as she slips out of her cloak and stands forth in a flowing robe in shimmering white. Her interchange with the beggar passes swiftly from surprise, indifference, scorn, to awakened interest and encouragement.

No theatre was ever stilled to an intenser silence. The audacity of it, the folly of it! The pictorial beauty of the scene, any merit it possessed as drama, were lost in the fact that George Whitford was making love to Constance Mills. No make-believe could have simulated the passion of his wooing in the lines that he had written for himself, and no response could have been informed with more tenderness and charm than Constance brought to her part.

Whitford was declaiming:

> "My flower! My light, my life! I offer thee
> Not jingling coin, nor lands, nor palaces,
> But yonder stars, and the young moon of spring,
> And rosy dawns and purple twilights long;
> All singing streams, and their great lord the sea—
> With these I'd thee endow."

And Constance, slowly lifting her head, an enthralling picture of young trusting love, replied:

> "I am a beggar in my heart!
> My soul hath need of thee! Teach me thy ways,
> And make me partner in thy wanderings,
> And lead me to the silver springs of song,
> I would be free as thou art, roam the world,
> Away from clanging war, by murmuring streams,
> Through green cool woodlands sweet with peace and love....
> Wilt thou be faithful, wilt thou love me long?"

To her tremulous pleading he pledged his fealty and when he had taken her into his arms and kissed her they exited slowly. As they passed from sight his voice was heard singing as the curtain fell.

The entire cast paraded in response to the vociferous and long continued applause, and Whitford and Constance bowed their acknowledgments together and singly. Cries of "author" detained Whitford for a speech, in which he chaffed himself and promised that in appreciation of their forbearance in allowing him to present so unworthy a trifle, which derived its only value from the intelligence and talent of his associates, he would never again tax their patience.

As the lights went up Bruce, turning to his companions, saw that Shepherd was staring at the stage as though the players were still visible. Helen, too, noticed the tense look in Shep's face, and touched him lightly on the arm. He came to with a start and looked about quickly, as if conscious that his deep preoccupation had been observed.

"It was perfectly marvelous, Shep! Connie was never so beautiful, and she did her part wonderfully!"

"Yes; Connie was fine! They were all splendid!" Shep stammered.

"I've seen her in plays before, but nothing to match tonight," said Helen. "You'll share her congratulations—it's a big night for the family!"

They had all risen, and Millicent and Bruce added their congratulations— Shep smiling but still a little dazed, his eyes showing that he was thinking back—trying to remember, in the way of one who has passed through an ordeal too swiftly for the memory fully to record it.

"Constance was perfectly adorable!" said Millicent sincerely.

"Yes, yes!" Shep exclaimed. "I had no idea, really. She has acting talent, hasn't she?"

The question was not perfunctory; he was eager for their assurance that they had been watching a clever piece of acting.

The room was being cleared for the dancing, and others near by were expressing their admiration for his wife. Helen seized a moment to whisper to Bruce:

"It rather knocked him. Be careful that he doesn't run away. George ought to be shot—Heaven knows there's been enough talk already!"

"The only trouble is that they were a little too good, that's all," said Bruce. "That oughtn't to be a sin—when you remember what amateur shows usually are!"

"It's not to laugh!" Helen replied. "Shep's terribly sensitive! He's not so stupid but he saw that George was enjoying himself making love to Connie."

"Well, who wouldn't enjoy it!" Bruce answered.

The dancing had begun when Constance appeared on the floor. She had achieved a triumph and it may have been that she was just a little frightened now that it was over. As she held court near the stage, smilingly receiving congratulations, she waved to Shep across the crowd.

"Was I so very bad?" she asked Bruce. "I was terribly nervous for fear I'd forget my lines."

"But you didn't! It was the most enthralling half hour I ever spent. I'm proud to know you!"

"Thank you, Bruce. Do something for me. These people bore me; tell Shep to come and dance with me. Yes—with you afterwards."

Whether it was kindness or contrition that prompted this request did not matter. It sufficed that Connie gave her first dance to Shep and that they glided over the floor with every appearance of blissful happiness. Whitford was passing about, paying particular attention to the mothers of debutantes, quite as unconcernedly as though he had not given the club its greatest thrill....

As this was Millicent's first appearance since her election to the club, her sponsors were taking care that she met such of the members as had not previously been within her social range. Franklin Mills's efforts to establish the Hardens had not been unavailing. Bruce, watching her as she danced with a succession of partners, heard an elderly army officer asking the name of the golden-haired girl who carried herself so superbly.

Bruce was waiting for his next dance with her and not greatly interested in what went on about him, when Dale Freeman accosted him.

"Just look at the girl! Seeing her dancing just like any other perfectly healthy young being, you'd never think she had so many wonderful things in her head and heart. Millie's one of those people who think with their hearts as well as their brains. When you find that combination, sonny, you've got something!"

"Um—yes," he assented glumly.

Dale looked up at him and laughed. "I'll begin to suspect you're in love with her now if you act like this!"

"The suspicion does me honor!" he replied.

"Oh, I'm not going to push you! I did have some idea of helping you, but I see it's no use."

"Really, none," he answered soberly. And for a moment the old unhappiness clutched him....

At one o'clock he left the hall with Helen and Millicent.

"I suppose the tongues will wag for a while," Helen sighed wearily. "But you've got to hand it to Constance and George! They certainly put on a good show!"

At the Harden's Bruce took Millicent's key and unlocked the door.

"I've enjoyed this; it's been fine," she said and put out her hand.

"It was a pretty full evening," he replied. "But there's a part of it I've stored away as better than the plays—even better than my dances with you!"

"I know!" she said. "Helen's salad!"

"Oh, better even than that! The talk at the table—your talk! I must thank you for that!"

"Oh, please forget! I believe I'd rather you'd remember our last dance!"

She laughed light-heartedly and the door closed.

"They've done it now!" exclaimed Helen as the car rolled on. "Why will people be such fools! To think they had to go and let the whole town into the secret!"

"Cease worrying! If they'd really cared anything for each other they couldn't have done it."

"George would—it was just the dare-devil sort of thing that George Whitford *would* do!"

"Well, you're not troubled about me any more!" he laughed. "A little while ago you thought Connie had designs on me! Has it got to be someone?"

"That's exactly it! It's got to be someone with Connie!"

But when he had left her and was driving on to his apartment it was of Millicent he thought, not of Constance and Whitford. It was astonishing

how much freer he felt now that the Atlantic rolled between him and
Franklin Mills.

III

Bruce, deeply engrossed in his work, was nevertheless aware that the
performance of "The Beggar" had stimulated gossip about Constance Mills
and Whitford. Helen Torrence continued to fret about it; Bud Henderson
insisted on keeping Bruce apprised of it; Maybelle deplored and Dale
Freeman pretended to ignore. The provincial mind must have exercise, and
Bruce was both amused and disgusted as he found that the joint appearance
of Constance and Whitford in Whitford's one-act play had caused no little
perturbation in minds that lacked nobler occupation or were incapable of
any very serious thought about anything.

It had become a joke at the University Club that Bruce, who was looked
upon as an industrious young man, gave so much time to Shepherd Mills.
There was a doglike fidelity in Shep's devotion that would have been
amusing if it hadn't been pathetic. Bud Henderson said that Shep trotted
around after Bruce like a lame fox terrier that had attached itself to an
Airedale for protection.

Shep, inspired perhaps by Bruce's example, or to have an excuse for
meeting him, had taken up handball. As the winter wore on this brought
them together once or twice a week at the Athletic Club. One afternoon in
March they had played their game and had their shower and were in the
locker room dressing.

Two other men came in a few minutes later and, concealed by the lockers,
began talking in low tones. Their voices rose until they were audible over
half the room. Bruce began to hear names—first Whitford's, then
unmistakably Constance Mills was referred to. Shep raised his head as he
caught his wife's name. One of the voices was unmistakably that of Morton
Walters, a young man with an unpleasant reputation as a gossip. Bruce
dropped a shoe to warn the men that they were not alone in the room. But
Walters continued, and in a moment a harsh laugh preluded the remark:

"Well, George takes his pleasure where he finds it. But if I were Shep Mills
I certainly wouldn't stand for it!"

Shep jumped up and started for the aisle, but Bruce stepped in front of him and walked round to where Walters and a friend Bruce didn't know were standing before their lockers.

"I beg your pardon, Mr. Walters, but may I remind you that this is a gentleman's club?"

"Well, no; you may not!" Walters retorted hotly. He advanced toward Bruce, his eyes blazing wrathfully.

The men, half clothed, eyed each other for a moment.

"We don't speak of women in this club as you've been doing," said Bruce. "I'm merely asking you to be a little more careful."

"Oh, you're criticizing my manners, are you?" flared Walters.

"Yes; that's what I'm doing. They're offensive. My opinion of you is that you're a contemptible blackguard!"

"Then that for your opinion!"

Walters sprang forward and dealt Bruce a ringing slap in the face. Instantly both had their fists up. Walters's companion grasped him by the arm, begging him to be quiet, but he flung him off and moved toward Bruce aggressively.

They sparred for a moment warily; then Walters landed a blow on Bruce's shoulder.

"So you're Mrs. Mills's champion, are you?" he sneered.

Intent upon the effect of his words, he dropped his guard. With lightning swiftness Bruce feinted, slapped his adversary squarely across the mouth and followed with a cracking blow on the jaw that sent him toppling over the bench. His fall made considerable noise, and the superintendent of the club came running in to learn the cause of the disturbance. Walters, quickly on his feet, was now struggling to shake off his friend. Several other men coming in stopped in the aisle and began chaffing Walters, thinking that he and Bruce were engaged in a playful scuffle. Walters, furious that his friend wouldn't release him, began cursing loudly.

"Gentlemen, this won't do!" the superintendent admonished. "We can't have this here!"

"Mr. Walters," said Bruce when Walters had been forced to sit down, "if you take my advice you'll be much more careful of your speech. If you want my address you'll find it in the office!"

He went back to Shep, who sat huddled on the bench by his locker, his face in his hands. He got up at once and they finished dressing in silence. Walters made no further sign, though he could be heard blustering to his companion while the superintendent hovered about to preserve the peace.

Shep's limousine was waiting—he made a point of delivering Bruce wherever he might be going after their meetings at the club—and he got into it and sat silent until his house was reached. He hadn't uttered a word; the life seemed to have gone out of him.

Bruce walked with him to the door and said "Good night, Shep," as though nothing had happened. Shep rallied sufficiently to repeat the good-night, choking and stammering upon it. Bruce returned to the machine and bade the chauffeur take him home.

He did no work that night. Viewed from any angle, the episode was disagreeable. Walters would continue to talk—no doubt with increased viciousness. Bruce wasn't sorry he had struck him, but as he thought it over he found that the only satisfaction he derived from the episode was a sense that it was for Shep that he had taken Walters to task. Poor Shep! Bruce wished that he did not so constantly think of Shep in commiserative phrases....

Bud Henderson, who was in the club when the row occurred, informed Bruce that the men who had been in the locker room were good fellows and that the story was not likely to spread. It was a pity, though, in Bud's view, that the thing had to be smothered, for Walters had been entitled to a licking for some time and the occurrence would make Bruce the most popular man in town.

"If the poor boob had known how you used to train with that middle-weight champ in Boston during our bright college years he wouldn't have slapped you! I'll bet his jaw's sore!"

Bruce was not consoled. He wished the world would behave itself; and in particular he wished that he was not so constantly, so inevitably, as it seemed, put into the position of aiding and defending the house of Mills.

CHAPTER NINETEEN

I

Bruce worked at his plans for the Laconia memorial determinedly and, he hoped, with inspiration. He looked in at the Hardens' on a Sunday afternoon and found Millicent entertaining several callow youths—new acquaintances whom she had met at the functions to which Mills's cautious but effective propaganda had admitted her. Bruce did not remain long; he thought Millicent was amused by his poorly concealed disappointment at not finding her alone. But he was deriving little satisfaction from his self-denial in remaining away and grew desperate for a talk with her. He made his next venture on a wild March night, and broke forth in a pæan of thanksgiving when he found her alone in the library.

"You were deliciously funny when you found me surrounded! Those were nice boys; they'd just discovered me!"

"They had the look of determined young fiends! I knew I couldn't stay them out. But I dare 'em to leave home on a night like this!"

"Oh, I know! You're afraid of competition! After you left that Sunday mamma brought in ginger cookies and we popped corn and had a grand old time!"

"It sounds exciting. But it was food for the spirit I needed; I couldn't have stood it to see them eat!"

"Just for that our pantry is closed to you forever—never a cookie! Those boys were vastly pleased to meet you. They knew you as a soldier of the Republic and a crack handball player—not as an eminent architect. That for fame! By the way, you must be up to something mysterious. Dale gave me just a tiny hint that you're working on something prodigious. But of course I don't ask to be let into the secret!"

"The secret's permanent if I fail!" he laughed.

He was conscious that their acquaintance had progressed in spite of their rare meetings. Tonight she played for him and talked occasionally from the organ—running comment on some liturgical music with which she had lately been familiarizing herself. Presently he found himself standing beside her; there seemed nothing strange in this—to be standing where he could watch her hands and know the thrill of her smile as she invited his appreciation of some passage that she was particularly enjoying....

"What have you been doing with your sculpting? Please bring me up to date on everything," he said.

"Oh, not so much lately. You might like to see some children's heads I've been doing. I bring some of the little convalescents to the house from the hospital to give them a change."

"Lucky kids!" he said. "To be brought here and played with."

"Why not? They're entitled to all I have as much as I am."

"Revolutionist! Really, Millicent, you must be careful!"

Yes; no matter how little he saw of her, their amity and concord strengthened. Sometimes she looked at him in a way that quickened his heartbeat. As they went down from the organ his hand touched hers and he thrilled at the fleeting contact. A high privilege, this, to be near her, to be admitted to the sanctuary of her mind and heart. She had her clichés; harmony was a word she used frequently, and colors and musical terms she employed with odd little meanings of her own.

In the studio she showed him a plaque of her mother's head which he knew to be creditable work. His praise of it pleased her. She had none of the amateur's simpering affectation and false modesty. She said frankly she thought it the best thing she had done.

"I know mamma—all her expressions—and that makes a difference. You've got to see under the flesh—get the inner light even in clay. I might really get somewhere if I gave up everything else," she said pensively as they idled about the studio.

"Yes; you could go far. Why not?"

"Oh, but I'd have to give up too much. I like life—being among people; and I have my father and mother. I think I'll go on just as I am. If I got too serious about it I might be less good than now, when I merely play at it...."

In their new familiarity he made bold to lift the coverings of some of her work that she thought unworthy of display. She became gay over some of her failures, as she called them. She didn't throw them away because they kept her humble.

On a table in a corner of the room stood a bust covered with a cloth to which they came last.

"Another *magnum opus*?" he asked carelessly. She lifted the cloth and stood away from it.

"Mr. Mills gave me some sittings. But this is my greatest fizzle of all; I simply couldn't get him!"

The features of Franklin Mills had been reproduced in the clay with mechanical fidelity; but unquestionably something was lacking. Bruce studied it seriously, puzzled by its deficiencies.

"Maybe you can tell me what's wrong," she said. "It's curious that a thing can come so close and fail."

"It's a true thing," remarked Bruce, "as far as it goes. But you're right; there's something that isn't there. If you don't mind, it's dead—there's— there's no life in it."

Millicent touched the clay here and there, suggesting points where the difficulty might lie. She was so intent that she failed to see the changing expression on Bruce's face. He had ceased to think of the clay image. Mills himself had been in the studio, probably many times. The thought of this stirred the jealousy in Bruce's heart—Millicent and Mills! Every kind and generous thought he had ever entertained for the man was obliterated by this evidence that for many hours he had been there with Millicent. But she, understanding nothing of this, was startled when he flung round at her.

"I think I can tell you what's the matter," he said in a tone harsh and strained. "The fault's not yours!"

"No?" she questioned wonderingly.

"The man has no soul," he said, as though he were pronouncing sentence of death.

That Millicent should have fashioned this counterfeit of Mills, animated perhaps by an interest that might quicken to love, was intolerable. Passion possessed him. Lifting the bust, he flung it with a loud crash upon the tile floor. He stared dully at the scattered fragments.

"God!" he turned toward her with the hunger of love in his eyes. "I—I—I'm sorry—I didn't mean to do that!"

He caught her hand roughly; gently released it, and ran up the steps into the library.

Millicent remained quite still till the outer door had closed upon him. She looked down at the broken pieces of the bust, trying to relate them to the cause of his sudden wrath. Then she knelt and began mechanically, patiently, picking up the fragments. Suddenly she paused. Her hands relaxed and the bits of clay fell to the floor. She stood up, her figure tense, her head lifted, and a light came into her eyes.

II

He had made a fool of himself: this was Bruce's reaction to the sudden fury that had caused him to destroy Millicent's bust of Franklin Mills. He would never dare go near her again; and having thus fixed his own punishment, and being very unhappy about it, a spiteful fate ordained that he should meet her early the next morning in the lobby of the Central States Trust Company, where, out of friendly regard for Shepherd Mills, he had opened an account.

"So—I'm not the only early riser!" she exclaimed, turning away from one of the teller's windows as he passed. "This is pay day at home and I'm getting the cook's money. I walked down—what a glorious morning!"

"Cook—money?" he repeated stupidly. There was nothing extraordinary in the idea that she should be drawing the domestic payroll. Her unconcern, the deftness with which she snapped her purse upon a roll of new bills and dropped it into a bead bag were disconcerting. Her eyes turned toward the door and he must say something. She was enchanting in her gray fur coat and feathered hat of vivid blue; it hadn't been necessary for her to say that she had walked four miles from her house to the bank; her glowing cheeks were an eloquent advertisement of that.

"Please," he began eagerly. "About last night—I made a dreadful exhibition of myself. I know—I mean that to beg your forgiveness——"

"Is wholly unnecessary!" she finished smilingly. "The bust was a failure and I had meant to destroy it myself. So please forget it!"

"But my bad manners!"

She was making it too easy for his comfort. He wished to abase himself, to convince her of his contrition.

"Well," she said with a judicial air, "generally speaking, I approve of your manners. We all have our careless moments. I've been guilty myself of upsetting bric-a-brac that I got tired of seeing in the house."

"You ought to scold me—cut my acquaintance."

"Who'd be punished then?" she demanded, drawing the fur collar closer about her throat.

"I might die!" he moaned plaintively.

"An irreparable loss—to the world!" she said, "for which I refuse to become responsible." She took a step toward the door and paused. "If I may refer to your destructive habits, I'll say you're some critic!" She left him speculating as to her meaning. To outward appearances, at least, she hadn't been greatly disturbed by the smashing of Mills's image.

When he had concluded his errand he went to the enclosure where the company's officers sat to speak to Shep, whom he had been avoiding since the encounter with Walters at the Athletic Club. Shep jumped up and led the way to the directors' room.

"You know," he began, "I don't want to seem to be pursuing you, but"—he was stammering and his fine, frank eyes opened and shut quickly in his agitation—"but you've got to know how much I appreciate——"

"Now, old man," Bruce interrupted, laying his hand on Shep's shoulder, "let's not talk of ancient history."

Shep shook his head impatiently.

"No, by George! You've *got* to take my thanks! It was bully of you to punch that scoundrel's head. I ought to have done it myself, but——" He held out his arms, his eyes measuring his height against Bruce's tall frame, and grinned ruefully.

"I didn't give you a chance, Shep," said Bruce, drawing himself onto the table and swinging his legs at ease. "I don't believe that bird's been looking for me; I've been right here in town."

"I guess he won't bother you much!" exclaimed Shep with boyish pride in his champion's prowess. "You certainly gave him a good one!"

"He seemed to want it," replied Bruce. "I couldn't just kiss him after he slapped me!"

"I told Connie! I didn't care for what Walters said—you understand—but I wanted Connie to know what you did—for her!"

His eyes appealed for Bruce's understanding. But Bruce, who had hoped that Shep wouldn't tell Connie, now wished heartily that Shep would drop the matter.

"You made too much of it! It wasn't really for anyone in particular that I gave Walters that little tap—it was to assert a general principle of human conduct."

"We'll never forget it," declared Shep, not to be thwarted in his expression of gratitude. "That anyone should speak of Connie—*Connie*—in that fashion! Why, Connie's the noblest girl in the world! You know that, the whole world knows it!"

He drew back and straightened his shoulders as though daring the world to gainsay him.

"Why, of course, Shep!" Bruce replied quietly. He drew a memorandum from his pocket and asked about some bonds the trust company had advertised and into which he considered converting some of the securities he had left with his banker at Laconia which were now maturing. Shep, pleased that Bruce was inviting his advice in the matter, produced data from the archives in confirmation of his assurance that the bonds were gilt-edge and a desirable investment. Bruce lingered, spending more time than was necessary in discussing the matter merely to divert Shep's thoughts from the Walters' episode.

III

Bruce had never before worked so hard; Freeman said that the designer of the Parthenon had been a loafer in comparison. After a long and laborious day he would drive to the Freemans with questions about his designs for the memorial that he feared to sleep on. Dale remarked to her husband that it was inspiring to see a young man of Bruce's fine talent and enthusiasm engrossed upon a task and at the same time in love—an invincible combination.

Carroll had kept in mind the visit to Laconia he had proposed and they made a week-end excursion of it in May. Bruce was glad of the chance to inspect the site of the memorial, and happier than he had expected to be in meeting old friends. It was disclosed that Carroll's interest in Bruce's cousin was not quite so incidental as he had pretended. Mills's secretary had within the year several times visited Laconia, an indication that he was not breaking his heart over Leila.

Bruce stole away from the hotel on Sunday morning to visit his mother's grave. She had lived so constantly in his thoughts that it seemed strange that she could be lying in the quiet cemetery beside John Storrs. There was something of greatness in her or she would never have risked the loss of his respect and affection. She had trusted him, confident of his magnanimity and love. Strange that in that small town, with its brave little flourish of prosperity, she had lived all those years with that secret in her heart, perhaps with that old passion tormenting her to the end. She had not been afraid of him, had not feared that he would despise her. "O soul of fire within a woman's clay"—this line from a fugitive poem he had chanced upon in a newspaper expressed her. On his way into town he passed the old home, resenting the presence of the new owner, who could not know what manner of woman had dwelt there, sanctified its walls, given grace to the garden where the sun-dial and the flower beds still spoke of her.... Millicent was like Marian. Very precious had grown this thought, of the spiritual kinship of his mother and Millicent.

Traversing the uneven brick pavements along the maple arched street, it was in his mind that his mother and Millicent would have understood each other. They dreamed the same dreams; the garden walls had not shut out Marian Storrs's vision of the infinite. A church bell whose clamorous peal was one of his earliest recollections seemed subdued today to a less insistent note by the sweetness of the spring air. Old memories awoke. He remembered a sermon he had heard in the church of the sonorous bell when he was still a child; the fear it had wakened in his heart—a long noisy discourse on the penalties of sin, the horror in store for the damned. And he recalled how his mother had taken his hand and smiled down at him there in the Storrs pew—that adorable smile of hers. And that evening as they sat alone in the garden on the bench by the sun-dial she had comforted him and told him that God—her God—was not the frightful being the visiting minister had pictured, but generous and loving. Yes, Millicent was like Marian Storrs....

After this holiday he fell upon his work with renewed energy—but he saw Millicent frequently. It was much easier to pass through the Harden gate and ring the bell now that the windows of the Mills house were boarded up. Mrs. Harden and the doctor made clear their friendliness—not with parental anxiety to ingratiate themselves with an eligible young man, but out of sincere regard and liking.

"You were raised in a country town and all us folks who were brought up in small towns speak the same language," Mrs. Harden declared. She conferred the highest degree of her approval by receiving him in the kitchen on the cook's day out, when she could, in her own phrase, putter around all she pleased. Millicent, enchantingly aproned, shared in the sacred rites of preparing the evening meal on these days of freedom, when there was very likely to be beaten biscuit, in the preparation of which Bruce was duly initiated.

Spring repeated its ancient miracle in the land of the tall corn. A pleasant haven for warm evenings was the Harden's "back yard" as the Doctor called it, though it was the most artistic garden in town, where Mrs. Harden indulged her taste in old-fashioned flowers; and there was a tea house set in among towering forest trees where Millicent held court. Bruce appearing late, with the excuse that he had been at work, was able to witness the departure of Millicent's other "company" as her parents designated her visitors, and enjoy an hour with her alone. Their privacy was invaded usually by Mrs. Harden, who appeared with a pitcher of cooling drink and plates of the cakes in which she specialized. She was enormously busy with her work on the orphan asylum board. She was ruining the orphans, the

Doctor said; but he was proud of his wife and encouraged her philanthropies. He was building a hospital in his home town—thus, according to Bud Henderson, propitiating the gods for the enormity of his offense against medical ethics in waxing rich off the asthma cure. The Doctor's sole recreation was fishing; he had found a retired minister, also linked in some way with the Hardens' home town, who shared his weakness. They frequently rose with the sun and drove in Harden's car to places where they had fished as boys. Bruce had known people like the Hardens at Laconia. Even in the big handsome house they retained their simplicity, a simplicity which in some degree explained Millicent. It was this quality in her that accounted for much—the sincerity and artlessness with which she expressed beliefs that gained sanctity from her very manner of speaking of them.

On a June night he put into the mail his plans for the memorial and then drove to the Hardens'. Millicent had been playing for some callers who were just leaving.

"If you're not afraid of being moonstruck, let's sit out of doors," she suggested.

"It's a habit—this winding up my day here! I've just finished a little job and laid it tenderly on the knees of the gods."

"Ah, the mysterious job is done! Is it anything that might be assisted by a friendly thought?"

"Just a bunch of papers in the mail; that's all."

They talked listlessly, in keeping with the langurous spirit of the night. The Mills house was plainly visible through the shrubbery. In his complete relaxation, his contentment at being near Millicent, Bruce's thoughts traveled far afield while he murmured assent to what she was saying. The moonlit garden, its serenity hardly disturbed by the occasional whirr of a motor in the boulevard, invited to meditation, and Millicent was speaking almost as though she were thinking aloud in her musical voice that never lost its charm for him.

"It's easy to believe all manner of strange things on a night like this! I can even imagine that I was someone else once upon a time...."

"Go right on!" he said, rousing himself, ready for the game which they often played like two children. He turned to face her. "I have a sneaking idea that a thousand years ago at this minute I was sitting peacefully by a well in an oasis with camels and horses and strange dark men sleeping round me; that same lady moon looking down on the scene, making the sandy waste look like a field of snow."

"That sounds dusty and hot! Now me—I'm on a galley ship driving through the night; a brisk cool wind is blowing; a slave is singing a plaintive song and the captain of the rowers is thumping time for them to row by and the moon is shining down on an island just ahead. It's all very jolly! We're off the coast of Greece somewhere, I think."

"I suppose that being on a ship while I'm away off in a desert I really shouldn't be talking to you. I couldn't take my camel on your yacht!"

"There's telepathy," she suggested.

"Thanks for the idea! If we've arrived in this pleasant garden after a thousand-year journey I certainly shan't complain!"

"It wouldn't profit you much if you did! And besides, my feelings would be hurt!" she laughed softly. "I do so love the sound of my own voice—I wonder if that's because I've been silent a thousand years!"

"I hope you weren't, for—I admire your voice! Looking at the stars does make you think large thoughts. If they had all been flung into space by chance, as a child scatters sand, we'd have had a badly scrambled universe by this time—it must be for something—something pretty important."

"I wonder...." She bent forward, her elbow on the arm of the chair, her hand laid against her cheek. "Let's pretend we can see all mankind, from the beginning, following a silken cord that Some One ahead is unwinding and dropping behind as a guide. And we all try to hold fast to it—we lose it over and over again and stumble over those who have fallen in the dark places of the road—then we clutch it again. And we never quite see the leader, but we know he is there, away on ahead trying to guide us to the goal——"

"Yes," he said eagerly, "the goal——"

"Is happiness! That's what we're all searching for! And our Leader has had so many names—those ahead are always crying back a name caught from those ahead of them—down through the ages. But it helps to know that many are on ahead clutching the cord, not going too fast for fear the great host behind may lose their hope and drop the cord altogether!"

"I like that; it's bully! It's the life line, the great clue——"

"Yes, yes," she said, "and even the half gods are not to be sneered at; they've tangled up the cord and tied hard knots in it—— Oh, dear! I'm soaring again!"

There had been some question of her going away for the remainder of the summer, and he referred to this presently. He was hoping that she would go before the return of Mills and Leila. The old intimacy between the two houses would revive: it might be that Millicent was ready to marry Mills; and tonight Bruce did not doubt his own love for her—if only he might touch her hand that lay so near and tell her! In the calm night he felt again the acute loneliness that had so beset him in his year-long pilgrimage in search of peace; and he had found at the end a love that was not peace. After the verdict of the judges of the memorial plans was given it would be best for him to leave—go to New York perhaps and try his fortune there, and forget these months that had been so packed with experience.

"We're likely to stay on here indefinitely," Millicent was saying. "I'd rather go away in the winter; the summer is really a joy. A lot of the people we know are staying at home. Connie and Shep are not going away, and Dale says she's not going to budge. And Helen Torrence keeps putting off half a dozen flights she's threatened to take. And Bud and Maybelle seem content. So why run away from friends?"

"No reason, of course. The corn requires heat and why should we be superior to the corn?"

"I had a letter from Leila today. She says she's perishing to come home!"

"I'll wager she is!" laughed Bruce. "What's going to happen when she comes?"

He picked up his hat and they were slowly crossing the lawn toward the gate.

"You mean Freddie Thomas."

"I suppose I do mean Fred! But I didn't mean to pump you. It's Leila's business."

"I'll be surprised if a few months' travel doesn't change Leila. She and Freddy had an awful crush on each other when she left. If she's still of the same mind—well, her father may find the trip wasn't so beneficial!"

From her tone Bruce judged that Millicent was not greatly concerned about Leila. She went through the gates with him to his car at the curb.

"Whatever it is you sent shooting through the night—here's good luck to it!" she said as he climbed into his machine. "Do you suppose that's the train?"

She raised her hand and bent her head to listen. The rumble of a heavy train and the faint clang of a locomotive bell could be heard beyond the quiet residential neighborhood. He was pleased that she had remembered, sorry now that he had not told her what it was that he had committed to the mails. She snapped her fingers, exclaiming:

"I've sent a wish with it, whether it's to your true love or whatever it is!"

"It wasn't a love letter," he called after her as she paused under the gate lamps to wave her hand.

CHAPTER TWENTY

I

Franklin Mills landed in New York feeling that his excursion abroad had been well worth while. Leila had been the cheeriest of companions and Mills felt that he knew her much better than he had ever known her before. They had stopped in Paris and he had cheerfully indulged her extravagance in raiment. Throughout the trip nothing marred their intercourse. Mills's pride and vanity were touched by the admiring eyes that followed them. In countries where wine and spirits were everywhere visible Leila betrayed no inclination to drink, even when he urged some rare vintage upon her. The child had character; he detected in her the mental and physical energy, the shrewdness, the ability to reason, that were a distinguishing feature of the Mills tradition. Shep hadn't the swift, penetrating insight of Leila. Leila caught with a glance of the eye distinct impressions which Shep would have missed even with laborious examination. Shep, nevertheless, was a fine boy; reluctant as he was to acknowledge an error even to himself, Mills, mellowed by distance, thought perhaps it had been a mistake to forbid Shep to study medicine; and yet he had tried to do the right thing by Shep. It was important for the only son of the house of Mills to know the worth of property.

The only son.... When Mills thought of Shep and Leila he thought, too, of Storrs—Bruce Storrs with his undeniable resemblance to Franklin Mills III. There were times when by some reawakening of old memories through contact with new scenes—in Venice, at Sorrento, in motoring into Scotland from the English lake country—in all places that invited to retrospective contemplation he lived over again those months he had spent in Laconia.

Strangely, that period revived with intense vividness. Released from the routine of his common life, he indulged his memories, estimating their value, fixing their place in his life. That episode seemed the most important of all; he had loved that woman. He had been a blackguard and a scoundrel; there was no escaping that, but he could not despise himself. Sometimes

Leila, noting his deep preoccupation on long motor drives, would tease him to tell her what he was thinking about and he was hard put to satisfy her that he hadn't a care in the world. Once, trying to ease an attack of homesickness, she led him into speculation as to what their home-folks were doing—Shep and Connie, Millicent, and in the same connection she mentioned Bruce.

"What an awful nice chap he is, Dada. He's a prince. You'd know him for a thoroughbred anywhere. Arthur Carroll says his people were just nice country town folks—father a lawyer, I think Arthur said. The Freemans back him strong, and they're not people you can fool much."

"Mr. Storrs is a gentleman," said Mills. "And a young man of fine gifts. I've had several talks with him about his work and ambitions. He'll make his mark."

"He's good to look at! Millicent says there's a Greek-god look about him."

"Millicent likes him?" asked Mills with an effort at indifference which did not wholly escape Leila's vigilant eye.

"Oh, I don't think it's more than that. You never can tell about Millie."

This was in Edinburgh, shortly before they sailed for home. All things considered the trip abroad had been a success. Leila had not to the best of his knowledge communicated with Thomas—she had made a point of showing him the letters she received and giving him her own letters to mail. Very likely, Mills thought, she had forgotten all about her undesirable suitor, and as a result of the change of scene and the new amity established between them, would fulfill her destiny by marrying Carroll.

II

The town house had been opened for their return, this being a special concession to Leila, who disliked Deer Trail. Mills yielded graciously, though he enjoyed Deer Trail more than any other of his possessions; but there was truth in her complaint that when he was in town all day, as frequently happened, it was unbearably lonely unless she fortified herself constantly with guests.

Mills found all his business interests prospering. Though Carroll was no longer in the office in the First National Building, the former secretary still performed the more important of his old functions in his rôle of vice-president of the trust company. Mills was not, however, to sink into his old comfortable routine without experiencing a few annoyances and disturbances. His sister, Mrs. Granville Thornberry, a childless widow, who had taken a hand in Leila's upbringing after Mrs. Mills's death—an experience that had left wounds on both sides that had never healed—Mrs. Thornberry had lingered in town to see him. She had become involved in a law suit by ignoring Mills's advice, and now cheerfully cast upon him the burden of extricating her from her predicament. The joy of reminding her that she would have avoided vexatious and expensive litigation if she had heeded his counsel hardly mitigated his irritation. But for his sense of the family dignity he would have declined to have anything to do with the case.

Carroll had been present at their interview, held in Mills's office, and when he left Mrs. Thornberry lingered. She was tall and slender, quick and incisive of speech. She absorbed all the local gossip and in spite of her wealth and status as a Mills was a good deal feared for her sharp tongue. It was a hot day and Mills's patience had been sorely tried by her seeming inability to grasp the legal questions raised in the law suit.

"Well, Alice," he said, with a glance at his desk clock. "Is there anything else?"

"Yes, Frank; there's a matter I feel it my duty to speak of. You know that I never like to interfere in your affairs. After the trouble we had about Leila I thought I'd never mention your children to you again."

"That's very foolish," Mills murmured with a slight frown. He thought she was about to attack Leila and he had no intention of listening to criticism of Leila. Alice had made a mess of Leila's education and he was not interested in anything she might have to say about her. And Alice was richly endowed with that heaven-given wisdom as to the rearing of children which is peculiar to the childless. Mills wished greatly that Alice would go.

"The matter's delicate—very delicate, Frank. I hesitate——"

"Please, Alice!" he interrupted impatiently. "Either you've got something to say or you haven't!"

At the moment she was not his sister, but a woman who had precipitated herself into a law suit by giving an option on a valuable piece of property and then selling it to a third party, which was stupid and he hated stupidity. He thought she was probably going to say that Leila drank too much, but knowing that Leila had been a pattern of sobriety for months he was prepared to rebuke her sharply for bringing him stale gossip.

"It's about Shep—Shep and Connie!" said Mrs. Thornberry. "You know how fond I've always been of Shep."

"Yes—yes," Mills replied, mystified by this opening. "Shep's doing well and I can't see but he and Connie are getting on finely. He's quite surprised me by the way he's taken hold in the trust company."

"Oh, Shep's a dear. But—there's talk——"

"Oh, yes; there's talk!" Mills caught her up. "There's always talk about everyone. I even suppose you and I don't escape!"

"Well, of course there have been rumors, you know, Frank, that you are considering marrying again."

"Oh, they're trying to marry me, are they?" he demanded, in a tone that did not wholly discourage her further confidences.

"I can't imagine your being so silly. But the impression is abroad that you're rather interested in that Harden girl. Ridiculous, of course, at your age! You'd certainly throw your dignity to the winds if you married a girl of Leila's age, whose people are said to be quite common. They say Dr. Harden used to travel over the country selling patent medicine from a wagon at country fairs and places like that."

"I question the story. The Doctor's a very agreeable person, and his wife's a fine woman. We have had very pleasant neighborly relations. And Millicent is an extraordinary girl—mentally the superior of any girl in town. I've been glad of Leila's intimacy with her; it's been for Leila's good."

"Oh, I dare say they're all well enough. Of course the marriage would be a big card for the Hardens. You're a shrewd man, Frank, but it's just a little too obvious—what you've been doing to push those people into our own circle. But the girl's handsome—there's no doubt of that."

"Well, those points are settled, then," her brother remarked, taking up the ivory paper cutter and slapping his palm with it. Alice was never niggardly with her revelations and he consoled himself with the reflection that she had shown her full hand.

"This other matter," Mrs. Thornberry continued immediately, "is rather more serious. I came back from California the week after you sailed and I found a good deal of talk going on about Connie."

"Connie?" Mills repeated and his fingers tightened upon the ivory blade.

"Connie's not behaving herself as a married woman should. She's been indulging in a scandalous flirtation—if that's not too gentle a name for it—with George Whitford."

"Pshaw, Alice! Whitford's always run with Shep's crowd. He's a sort of fireside pet with all the young married women. George is a fine, manly fellow. I don't question that he's been at Shep's a good deal. Shep's always liked him particularly. And Connie's an attractive young woman. Why, George probably makes love to all the women, old and young, he's thrown with for an hour! You're borrowing trouble quite unnecessarily, Alice. It's too bad you have to hear the gossip that's always going around here; you take it much too seriously."

"It's not I who take it seriously; it's common talk! Shep, poor boy, is so innocent and unsuspecting! George hasn't a thing to do but fool at his writing. He and Connie have been seen a trifle too often on long excursions to other towns when Shep, no doubt, thought she was golfing. What I'm telling you is gossip, of course; I couldn't prove anything. But it's possible sometimes that just a word will save trouble. You must acquit me of any wish to be meddlesome. I like Connie; I've always tried to like her for Shep's sake."

She was probably not magnifying the extent to which talk about his son's wife had gone. His old antagonism to Constance, the remembrance of his painful scenes with Shep in his efforts to prevent his marriage, were once more resurgent. Mrs. Thornberry related the episode of the dramatic club play which had, from her story, crystalized and stimulated the tales that had previously been afloat as to Connie's interest in Whitford. Mills promptly seized upon this to dismiss the whole thing. Things had certainly come to a fine pass when participation in amateur theatricals could give rise to scandal; it merely showed the paucity of substantial material.

He was at pains to conceal his chagrin. His pride took refuge behind its fortifications; he would not have his sister, of all persons, suspect that he could be affected by even the mildest insinuation against anyone invested with the sanctity of the Mills name. He told her of having met some old friends of hers in London as he accompanied her to the elevator. But when he regained his room he stood for some time by the window gazing across the town to the blue hills. The patriarchial sense was strong in him; he was the head and master of his house and he would tolerate no scandalous conduct on the part of his daughter-in-law. But he must move cautiously. The Whitfords were an old family and he had known George's father very well. With disagreeable insistence the remembrance of his adventure in Laconia came back to him.

III

Several weeks passed in which Mills exercised a discreet vigilance in observing Shep and Connie. Whitford was in town; Mills met him once and again at Shep's house, but there were others of the younger element present and there was nothing in Whitford's conduct to support Mrs. Thornberry's story. He asked Carroll incidentally about the dramatic club play—as if merely curious as to whether it had been a successful evening, and Carroll's description of Whitford's little drama and of Connie's part in it was void of any hint that it concealed a serious attachment between the chief actors.

The usual social routine of the summer stay-at-homes was progressing in the familiar lazy fashion—country club dances, motor trips, picnics and the like. On his return Mills had called at once upon the Hardens. Millicent's charms had in nowise diminished in his absence. With everything else satisfactorily determined, there would be no reason why he should not marry Millicent. His sister's disapproval did not weigh with him at all. But first he must see Leila married, and he still hoped to have Carroll for a son-in-law. Leila had entered into the summer gaieties with her usual zest, accepting the escort of one and another available young man with a new amiability. One evening at the Faraway Country Club Mills saw her dancing with Thomas; but it was for one dance only, and Thomas seemed to be distributing his attentions impartially. A few nights later when they had dined alone at Deer Trail—Leila had suggested that they go there merely to please him—as they sat on the veranda all his hopes that her infatuation for Thomas had passed were rudely shattered.

"Well, Dada," she began, when he was half through his after-dinner cigar, "it's nice to be back. It's a lot more fun being at home in summer. There is something about the old home town and our own country. I guess I'm a pretty good little American."

"I guess you are," he assented with a chuckle that expressed his entire satisfaction with her. The veranda was swept fitfully by a breeze warm sweet with the breath of ripening corn. It was something to be owner of some part of the earth; it was good to be alive, master of himself, able to direct and guide the lives of others less fortunately endowed than he with wisdom and power.

Leila touched his hand and he clasped and held it on the broad arm of his favorite rocker.

"Dada, what a wonderful time we had on our trip! I was a good little girl—wasn't I? You know I was trying so hard to be good!"

"You were an angel," he exclaimed heartily. "Our trip will always be one of the happiest memories of my life."

At once apprehensive, he hoped these approaches concealed nothing more serious than a request for an increase in her allowance or perhaps a new car.

"I want to speak about Freddy Thomas," she said, freeing her hand and moving her chair the better to command his attention.

"Thomas!" he said as though repeating an unfamiliar name. "I thought you were all done with him."

"Dada," she said very gently, "I love Freddy. All the time I was away I was testing myself—honestly and truly trying to forget him. I didn't hear from him and I didn't send him even a postcard. But now that I'm back it's all just the same. We do love each other; he's the only man in the world that can ever make me happy. Please—don't say no!"

He got up slowly, and walked the length of the veranda and came back to find her leaning against one of the pillars.

"Now, Leila," he began sharply, "we've been all over this, and I thought you realized that a marriage with that man would be a mistake—a grave blunder. He's playing upon your sympathy—telling you, no doubt, what a great mistake he made in his first venture."

"I've seen him only once since I got back and that was the other night at the club," she replied patiently. "Freddy's no cry-baby; you know you couldn't find a single thing against him except the divorce, and that wasn't his fault. He's perfectly willing to answer any questions you want to ask him. Isn't that fair enough?"

"You expect me to treat with him—listen to his nasty scandal! I've told you it won't do! There's never been a divorce in our family—nor in your mother's family! I feel strongly about it. The thing has got too common; it's taken away all the sanctity of marriage! And that I should welcome as a husband for a young girl like you a man who has had another wife—a woman who's still living—keeping his name, I understand—I tell you, Leila, it won't do! It's my duty to protect you from such a thing. I have wanted you to take a high position in this community—such a position as your mother held; and can you imagine yourself doing it as the second wife of a man who's not of our circle, not our kind at all?"

He flung round, took a few quick steps and then returned to the attack.

"I want this matter to be disposed of now. What would our friends think of me if I let you do such a thing? They'd think I'd lost my mind! I tell you it's not in keeping with our position—with your position as my daughter—to let you make a marriage that would change the whole tone of the family. If you'll think a little more about this I believe you'll see just what the step means. I want the best for you. I don't believe your happiness depends on your marrying this man. I may as well tell you bluntly now that I can never reconcile myself to the idea of your marrying him. I've thought it all over in all its aspects. You've never had a care nor a worry in your life. When you marry I want you to start even—with a man who's your equal in the world's eyes."

He had delivered this a little oratorically, with a gesture or two, and one might have thought that he was pleased with his phrases. Leila in her simple summer gown, with one hand at her side, the other thrust into the silk sash at her waist, seemed singularly young as she stood with her back to the pillar. The light from the windows, mingled with the starlight and moonlight playing upon her face, made it possible to watch the effect of his words. The effect, if any, was too obscure for his vision. Her eyes apparently were not seeing him at all; he might as well have addressed himself to one of the veranda chairs for any satisfaction he derived from his speech.

It was on his tongue to pile up additional arguments against the marriage; but this unresisting Leila with her back to the pillar exasperated him. And all those months that they had traveled about together, with never a mention of Thomas; when she had even indulged in mild flirtations with men who became their fellow travelers for a day, she had carried in her heart this determination to marry Thomas. And he, Franklin Mills, had stupidly believed that she was forgetting the man....

He again walked the length of the veranda, and as he retraced his steps she met him by the door.

"Well, Dada, shall we drive in?" she asked, quite as though nothing had happened.

"I suppose we may as well start," he said and looked at his watch to hide his embarrassment rather than to learn the time.

On the way into town she recurred to incidents of their travels and manifested great interest in changes he proposed making in his conservatories to embrace some ideas he had gathered in England; but she did not refer in any way to Thomas. When they reached home she kissed him good-night and went at once to her room.

The house was stifling from the torrid day and Mills wished himself back at the farm. His chief discomfort was not physical, however; Leila had eluded him, taken refuge in the inconsequential and irrelevant in her own peculiar, capricious fashion. It was not in his nature to discuss his affairs or ask counsel, but he wished there were someone he could talk to.... Millicent might help him in his perplexity. He went out on the lawn and looked across the hedge at the Hardens', hearing voices and laughter. The mirth was like a mockery.

IV

On the following day Bruce and Millicent drove to the Faraway club for golf. He was unable to detect any signs indicating that Mills's return had affected Millicent. She spoke of him as she might have spoken of any other neighbor. Bruce wasn't troubled about Mills when he was with Millicent; it was when he was away from her that he was preyed upon by apprehensions. He could never marry her: but Mills should never marry her. This repeated itself in his mind like a child's rigamarole. Their game kept them late and it was after six when they left the club in Bruce's roadster.

Millicent was beside him; their afternoon together had been unusually enjoyable. He had every reason to believe that she preferred his society to that of any other man she knew. He had taken a route into town that was longer than the one usually followed, and in passing through a small village an exclamation from Millicent caused him to stop the car.

"Wasn't that Leila and Fred at the gas station?" she asked. "Let's go back and see."

Leila saluted them with a wave of the hand. Thomas was speaking to the keeper of the station.

"Hello, children!" Leila greeted them. "Pause and be sociable. What have you been up to?"

"Shooting a little golf," Millicent answered. "Why didn't you drop the word that you were going to the club for dinner? You might have had a little company!"

Bruce strolled over to Thomas, who was still conferring with the station keeper. He heard the man answer some question as to the best route to a neighboring town. Thomas seemed a trifle nervous and glanced impatiently toward Leila and Millicent.

"Hello, Bruce," he said cheerfully, "how's everything?"

"Skimming!" said Bruce, and they walked back to the car, where Thomas greeted Millicent exuberantly. Leila leaned out and whispered to Bruce:

"We'll be married in an hour. Don't tell Millie till you get home!"

"Are you kidding?" Bruce demanded.

"Certainly not!"

“But why do it this way?”

“Oh—it’s simpler and a lot more romantic—that’s all! Tell Millie that everything is all right! Don’t look so scared! All right, Freddy, let’s go!”

Their car was quickly under way and Millicent and Bruce resumed their homeward drive.

“Leila didn’t tell me she was going to the club with Freddy,” remarked Millicent pensively.

“One of those spontaneous things,” Bruce replied carelessly.

When they reached the Hardens’ he walked with her to the door.

“That was odd—meeting Leila and Fred,” said Millicent. “Do you think they were really going to the club for supper?”

“They were not going there,” Bruce replied. “They’re on their way to be married.”

“Oh, I’m sorry!” she said and her eyes filled with tears. The privilege of seeing tears in Millicent’s eyes was to Bruce an experience much more important than Leila’s marriage.

“It will be a blow to Mr. Mills,” said Bruce thoughtfully. “Let’s hope he accepts it gracefully.”

Both turned by a common impulse and their eyes rested upon the Mills house beyond the hedge....

The town buzzed for a few days after Leila’s elopement, but in her immediate circle it created no surprise. It was like Leila; she could always be depended upon to do things differently. Mills, receiving the news from Leila by telephone, had himself conveyed the announcement to the newspapers, giving the impression that there had been no objection to the marriage and that the elopement was due to his daughter’s wish to avoid a formal wedding. This had the effect of killing the marriage as material for sensational news. It was not Mills’s way to permit himself to be flashed before his fellow citizens as an outraged and storming father. Old friends who tried to condole with him found their sympathy unwelcome. He personally saw to the packing of the effects Leila telegraphed for to be sent to Pittsburg, where she and her husband, bound for a motor trip through the east, were to pause for a visit with Thomas's parents.

CHAPTER TWENTY-ONE

I

Bruce returned late one afternoon in August from a neighboring town where Freeman had some houses under construction, found the office deserted, and was looking over the accumulation of papers on his desk when a messenger delivered a telegram.

He signed for it and let it lie while he filled his pipe. The potentialities of an unopened telegram are enormous. This message, Bruce reflected, might be from one of Freeman's clients with whom he had been dealing directly; or it might be from a Tech classmate who had written a week earlier that he would be motoring through town and would wire definitely the hour of his arrival. Or it might be the verdict of the jury of architects who were to pass on the plans for the Laconia memorial—an honorable mention at best. The decision had been delayed and he had been trying to forget about it. He turned the envelope over—assured himself that it didn't matter greatly whether he received the award or not; then, unable to prolong the agony, he tore it open and read:

> It affords the committee great pleasure to inform you that your plans submitted for the Laconia memorial have been accepted. You may regard our delay in reaching the decision as complimentary, for the high merit of some half dozen of the plans proposed made it extremely difficult to reach a conclusion. We suggest that you visit Laconia as soon as possible to make the acquaintance of the citizens' committee with whom you will now take up the matter of construction. With our warm cordial congratulations and all good wishes....

He flung his pipe on the floor with a bang, snatched the telephone and called Freeman's house. Dale answered, gave a chirrup of delight and ran to carry the news to Bill on the tennis court. Bruce decided that Henderson should know next, and had called the number when Bud strolled into the room.

"Looking for me—most remarkable! I was on this floor looking for a poor nut who needs a little stimulus as to the merits of the world-famous Plantag!"

"Fool!" shouted Bruce, glaring at him. "Don't speak to me of Plantagenets. Read that telegram; read it and fall upon your knees! I've won a prize, I tell you! You called me a chicken-coop builder, did you? You said I'd better settle down to building low-priced bungalows—— Oh, yes, you did!"

He was a boy again, lording it over his chum. He danced about, tapping Bud on the head and shoulders as if teasing him for a fight. Bud finally managed to read the message Bruce had thrust into his hands, and emitted a yell. They fell to pummeling each other joyfully until Bud sank exhausted into a chair.

"Great Jupiter!" Bud panted. "So this is what you were up to all spring! We'll have a celebration! My dear boy, don't bother about anything—I'll arrange it all!"

He busied himself at the telephone while Bruce received a newspaper reporter who had been sent to interview him. A bunch of telegrams arrived from Laconia—salutations of old friends, a congratulatory message from the memorial committee asking when they might expect him. The members of the committee were all men and women he had known from childhood, and his heart grew big at the pride they showed in him. In the reception room he had difficulty in composing himself sufficiently to answer the reporter's questions with the composure the occasion demanded....

"Small and select—that's my idea!" said Bud in revealing his plans for the celebration. "We're going to pull it at Shep Mills's—Shep won't listen to anything else! And the Freemans will be there, and Millie, and Helen Torrence, and Maybelle's beating it from the country club to be sure she doesn't miss anything. Thank God! something's happened to give me an excuse for acquiring a large, juicy bun."

"Oh, thunder! You're going to make an ass of me! I don't want any party!"

"No false modesty! We're all set. I'll skip around to the Club and nail Carroll and Whitford and any of the boys who are there. I'll bet your plans are rotten, but we'll pretend they're mar-ve-li-ous! You'll probably bluff your way through life just on your figure!"

"But there's no reason why the Shep Millses should be burdened with your show! Why didn't you ask me about that?"

"Oh, their house is bigger than mine. And Shep stammered his head off demanding that he have the honor. Don't worry, old hoss, you're in the hands of your friends!"

The party overflowed from the house into the grounds, Bud having invited everyone he thought likely to contribute to its gaiety. Many did not know just what it was all about, or thought it was one of Bud's jokes. He had summoned a jazz band and cleared the living-room for dancing.

"Bud was unusually crazy when he telephoned me," said Millicent. "I don't quite know what you've done, but it must be a world-shaking event."

"All of that! The good wishes you sent after the mail train on a certain night did the business. I'd have told you of my adventure, only I was afraid I'd draw a blank."

"I see. You thought of me as only a fair-weather friend. Square yourself by telling me everything."

Their quiet corner of the veranda was soon invaded. Carroll, Whitford, Connie and Mrs. Torrence joined them, declaring that Millicent couldn't be allowed to monopolize the hero of the hour.

"It's only beginner's luck; that's all," Bruce protested. "The pleasantest thing about it is that it's my native burg; that does tickle me!"

"It's altogether splendid," said Carroll. "Having seen you on your native heath, and knowing how the people over there feel about you, I know just how proud you ought to be."

"What's the name of the place—Petronia?" asked Constance.

"Laconia," Carroll corrected her. "You will do well to fix it in your memory now that Bruce is making it famous. I might mention that I have some cousins there—Bruce went over with me not so long ago just to give me a good character."

"How very interesting," Constance murmured.

"Mr. Mills once lived for a time in Laconia," Carroll remarked. "That was years ago. His father had acquired some business interests there and the place aspired to become a large city."

"I don't believe I ever heard Mr. Mills speak of it; I thought he was always rooted here," said Constance.

The party broke up at midnight, and Bruce drove Millicent home through the clear summer night. When he had unlocked the door for her she followed him out upon the steps.

"I'm afraid I haven't said all I'd like to say about your success. It's a big achievement. I want you to know that I realize all that. I'm glad—and proud. Many happy returns of the day!"

She gave him both her hands and this more than her words crowned the day for him. He had never been so happy. He really had hold of life; he could do things, he could do much finer things than the Laconia memorial! On his way to the gate he saw beyond the hedge a shadowy figure moving across the Mills lawn. When he reached the street he glanced back, identified Mills, and on an impulse entered the grounds. Mills was pacing back and forth, his head bowed, his hands thrust into his pockets. He started when he discerned Bruce, who walked up to him quickly.

"Oh—that you, Storrs? Glad to see you! It's a sultry night and I'm staying out as long as possible."

"I stopped to tell you a little piece of news. The Laconia memorial jury has made its report; my plans are accepted."

"How fine! Why—I'm delighted to hear this. I hope everything's as you wanted it."

"Yes, sir; the fund was increased and the thing can be done now without skimping. I put in the fountain—I'm greatly obliged to you for that suggestion. You ought to have the credit for it."

"Oh, no, no!" Mills exclaimed hastily. "You'd probably have thought of it yourself—merely a bit of supplementary decoration. You'll be busy now—supervising the construction?"

"Yes; I want to look after all the details. It will keep me busy for the next year. Carroll is going over to Laconia with me tomorrow."

“Good! It will be quite an event—going back to your old home to receive the laurel! I hope your work will stand for centuries!”

“Thank you, sir; good-night.”

CHAPTER TWENTY-TWO

I

Brief notes from Leila announced the happy course of her honeymoon in the New England hills. She wrote to her father as though there had been nothing extraordinary in her flight. Mills's mortification that his daughter should have married over his protest was ameliorated by the satisfaction derived from dealing magnanimously with her. The Mills dignity required that she have a home in keeping with the family status, and he would provide for this a sum equal to the amount he had given Shep to establish himself. He avoided Shep and Connie—the latter misguidedly bent upon trying to reconcile him to the idea that Leila had not done so badly. He suspected that Connie, in her heart, was laughing at him, rejoicing that Leila had beaten him.

He saw Millicent occasionally; but for all her tact and an evident wish to be kind, he suspected that her friendliness merely expressed her sympathy, and sympathy from any quarter was unbearable. He felt age clutching at him; he questioned whether Millicent could ever care for him; his dream of marrying again had been sheer folly. The summer wore on monotonously. Mills showed himself at the country club occasionally, usually at the behest of some of his old friends, and several times he entertained at Deer Trail.

Shep and Connie were to dine with him in the town house one evening, and when he had dressed he went, as he often did, into Leila's room. He sat down and idly drew the books from a rack on the table. One of them was a slender volume of George Whitford's poems, printed privately and inscribed, "To Leila, from her friend, the author." Mills had not heard of the publication and he turned over the leaves with more curiosity than he usually manifested in volumes of verse. Whitford's lyrics were chiefly in a romantic and sentimental vein. One of them, the longest in the book, was called "The Flower of the World," and above the title Leila had scrawled "Connie."

The lines were an ardent tribute to a lady whom the poet declared to be his soul's ideal. Certain phrases underscored by Leila's impious pencil were, when taken collectively, a very fair description of Constance. Mills carried the book to the library for a more deliberate perusal. If Leila knew that Constance was the subject of the verses, others must know it. What his sister had said about Whitford's devotion to Constance was corroborated by the verses; and there had been that joint appearance of Constance and Whitford in the dramatic club play—another damning circumstance. Mills's ire was aroused. He was standing in the middle of the room searching for other passages that might be interpreted as the author's tribute to Constance when Shep entered.

"Good evening, father," he said. "We're a little early—I thought we might take a minute to speak of those B. and F. bonds. You know——"

He paused as his father, without preliminary greeting, advanced toward him with an angry gleam in his eyes.

"Look at that! Have you seen this thing?"

"Why, yes, I've seen it," Shepherd answered, glancing at the page. "It's a little book of George's; he gave copies to all his friends—said nobody would ever buy it!"

"Gave copies to all his friends, did he? Do you see what Leila's written here and those marked lines? Do you realize what it means—that it's written to your wife?"

"That's ridiculous, father," Shep stammered. "It's not written to Connie any more than to any other young woman—a sort of ideal of George's, I suppose. Connie's name written there is just a piece of Leila's nonsense."

"How many people do you suppose thought the same thing? Don't you know that there's been a good deal of unpleasant talk about Connie and Whitford? There was that play they appeared in—written by Whitford! I've heard about that! It caused a lot of talk, and you've stood by, blind and deaf, and haven't done a thing to stop it!"

"I can't have you make such statements about Connie! There was nothing wrong with that play—absolutely nothing! It was one of the finest things the club ever had. As for George having Connie in mind when he wrote that poem—why, that's ridiculous! George is my friend as much as Connie's. Why, I haven't a better friend in the world than George Whitford!"

"You're blind; you're stupid!" Mills stormed. "How many people do you suppose have laughed over that—laughed at you as a fool to let a man make love to your wife in that open fashion? I tell you the thing's got to stop!"

"But, father," said Shep, lowering his voice, "you wouldn't insult Connie. She's downstairs and might easily hear you. You know, father, Connie isn't exactly well! Connie's going—Connie's going—to have a baby! We're very, very happy—about it——"

Shep, stammering as he blurted this out, had endeavored to invest the announcement with the dignity it demanded.

"So there's a child coming!" There was no mistaking the sneer in Mills's voice. "Your wife has a lover and she is to have a child!"

"You shan't say such a thing!" cried Shep, his voice tremulous with wrath and horror. "You're crazy! It's unworthy of you!"

"Oh, I'm sane enough. You ought to have seen this and stopped it long ago. Now that you see it, I'd like to know what you're going to do about it!"

"But I don't see it! There's nothing to see! I tell you I'll not listen to such an infamous charge against Connie!"

"I'll say what I please about Connie!" Mills shouted. "You children—you and Leila—what have I got from you but disappointment and shame? Leila runs away and marries a scoundrel out of the divorce court and now your wife—a woman I tried to save you from—has smirched us all with dishonor. I didn't want you to marry her; I begged you not to do it. But I yielded in the hope of making you happy. I wanted you and Leila to take the place you're entitled to in this town. Everything was done for you! Look up there," he went on hoarsely, pointing to the portraits above the book shelves, "look at those men and women—your forebears—people who laid the foundations of this town, and they look down on you and what do they see? Failure! Disgrace! Nothing but failure! And you stand here and pretend—pretend——"

Mills's arm fell to his side and the sentence died on his lips. Constance stood in the door; there were angry tears in her eyes and her face was white as she advanced a little way into the room and paused before Mills.

"I did not know how foul—how base you could be! You needn't fear him, Shep! Only a coward would have bawled such a thing for the servants to hear—possibly the neighbors. You've called upon your ancestors, Mr. Mills, to witness your shame and disgrace at having admitted me into your sacred family circle! Shep, have you ever noticed the resemblance—it's really quite remarkable—of young Mr. Storrs to your grandfather Mills? It's most curious—rather impressive, in fact!"

She was gazing at the portrait of Franklin Mills III, with a contemptuous smile on her lips.

"Connie, *Connie*——" Shep faltered.

"Storrs! What do you mean by that?" demanded Mills. His mouth hung open; with his head thrust forward he gazed at the portrait as if he had never seen it before.

"Nothing, of course," she went on slowly, giving every effect to her words. "But when you spent some time in that town with the singular name—Laconia, wasn't it?—you were young and probably quite fascinating—Storrs came from there—an interesting—a wholly admirable young man!"

"Connie—I don't get what you're driving at!" Shep exclaimed, his eyes fastened upon his grandfather's portrait.

"Constance is merely trying to be insolent," Mills said, but his hand shook as he took a cigarette from a box and lighted it. When he looked up he was disconcerted to find Shep regarding him with a blank stare. Constance, already at the door, said quietly:

"Come, Shep. I think we must be going."

The silence of the house was broken in a moment by the closing of the front door.

II

Shep and Constance drove in silence the few blocks that lay between Mills's house and their own. Constance explained their return to the maid by saying that she hadn't felt well and ordered a cold supper served in the breakfast room. Shep strolled aimlessly about while she went upstairs and reappeared in a house gown. When they had eaten they went into the living-room, where she turned the leaves of a book while he pretended to read the evening newspaper. After a time she walked over to him and touched his arm, let her hand rest lightly on his head.

"Yes, Connie," he said.

"There's something I want to say to you, Shep."

"Yes, Connie."

He got up and she slipped into his chair.

"It's a lie, Shep. What your father said is a lie!"

"Yes; of course," he said, but he did not look at her.

"You've got to believe me; I'll die if you don't tell me you believe in me!" and her voice broke in a sob.

He walked away from her, then went back, staring at her dully.

"I've been foolish, Shep. George and I have been good friends; we've enjoyed talking books and music. I like the things he likes, but that's all. You've got to believe me, Shep; you've got to believe me!"

There was deep passion in the reiterated appeal.

When he did not reply she rose, clasped his cheeks in her hands so that he could not avoid her eyes.

"Look at me, Shep. I swear before God I am telling you the truth!"

"Yes, Connie." He freed himself, walked to the end of the room, went back to her, regarding her intently. "Connie—what did you mean by what you said to father about Bruce Storrs?"

"Oh, nothing! Your aunt Alice spoke of the resemblance one night at the country club, where she saw Bruce with Millicent. It's rather striking when you think of it. And then at Bruce's jollification the other night Arthur said your father once spent some time at Laconia. I thought possibly he had relatives there."

"No; never, I think."

"That's what your aunt Alice said; but the portrait does suggest Bruce Storrs."

"Or a hundred other men," Shep replied with a shrug. "You must be tired, Connie—you'd better go to bed."

"I don't believe we've quite finished, Shep. I can't leave you like this! Your father is a beast! A low, foul beast!"

"I suppose he is," he said indifferently.

"Is that all you have to say to me—Shep?"

She regarded him with growing terror in her eyes. He had said he believed her, but it was in a tone of unbelief.

"I suppose a wife has a right to the protection of her husband," she said challengingly.

"You heard what I said to father, didn't you? I told him it was a lie. I'll never enter his house again. That ought to satisfy you," he said with an air of dismissing the matter finally.

"And this is all you have to say, Shep?"

"It's enough, isn't it? I don't care to discuss the matter further."

"Then this is the end—is that what you mean?"

"No," he replied in a curious, strained tone. "It's foolish to say what the end of anything is going to be."

She looked at him a moment pleadingly and with a gesture of helplessness started toward the door. He opened it for her, followed her into the hall, pressed the buttons that lighted the rooms above, and returned to the living-room....

III

Their routine continued much as it had been for the past two years, but to her tortured senses there was something ominous now in the brevity of their contacts. Shep often remained away late and on his return crept softly upstairs to his room without speaking to her, though she left her light burning brightly.

Constance kept to her room, she hadn't been well, and the doctor told her to stay in bed for a few days. For several nights she heard Shep moving about his room, and the maid told her that he had been going over his clothing and was sending a box of old suits to some charitable institution. A few days later he went into her room as she was having breakfast in bed. She asked him to shift the tray for her, more for something to say than because the service was necessary, and inquired if he were feeling well, but without dispelling the hard glitter that had become fixed in his eyes.

"Do you know when Leila's coming home?" he inquired from the foot of the bed.

"No; I haven't heard. I've seen no one; the doctor told me to keep quiet."

"Yes; I suppose you have to do that," he said without emotion. He went out listlessly and as he passed her she put out her hand, touched his sleeve; but he gave no sign that he was aware of the appeal the gesture implied....

It was on a Saturday morning that he went in through his dressing room, bade her good morning in much his old manner and rang for her coffee. He had breakfasted, he said, and merely wanted to be sure that she was comfortable.

"Thank you, Shep. I'm all right. I've been troubled about you, dear—much more than about myself. But you look quite fit this morning."

"Feeling fine," he said. "This is a half day at the office and I want to get on the job early. I'm dated up for a foursome this afternoon with George, Bruce and Carroll; so I won't be home till after the game. You won't mind?"

"Why, I'm delighted to have you go, Shep!"

"I always do the best I can, Connie," he went on musingly. "I probably make a lot of mistakes. I don't believe God intended me for heavy work; if he had he'd have made me bigger."

"How foolish, Shep. You're doing wonderfully. Isn't everything going smoothly at the office?"

"Just fine! I haven't a thing to complain of!"

"Is everything all right now?" she asked, encouraged to hope for some assurance of his faith in her.

"What isn't all right will be—there's always that!" he replied with a laugh.

He lingered beside the bed and took her hand, bent over and kissed her, let his cheek rest against hers in an old way of his.

"Good-bye," he said from the door, and then with a smile—Shep's familiar, wistful little smile—he left her.

IV

Shep and Whitford won the foursome against Bruce and Carroll, a result due to Whitford's superior drives and Carroll's bad putting. They were all in high humor when they returned to the clubhouse, chaffing one another about their skill as they dressed. Shep made a tour of the verandas, greeting his friends, answering questions as to Connie's health. The four men were going in at once and Shep, who had driven Carroll out, suggested that he and Bruce change partners for the drive home.

"There are a few little points about the game I want to discuss with George," he explained as they walked toward the parking sheds.

"All right," Bruce assented cheerfully. "You birds needn't be so set up; next week Carroll and I will give you the trimming of your young lives!"

"Ah, the next time!" Shep replied ironically, and drove away with Whitford beside him....

"Shep's coming on; he's matured a lot since he went into the trust company," remarked Carroll, as he and Bruce followed Shep's car.

"Good stuff in him," said Bruce. "One of those natures that develops slowly. I never saw him quite as gay as he was this afternoon."

"He was always a shy boy, but he's coming out of that. I think his father was wise in taking him out of the battery plant."

"No doubt," Bruce agreed, his attention fixed on Shep's car.

Shep had set a pace that Bruce was finding it difficult to maintain. Carroll presently commented upon the wild flight of the car ahead, which was cutting the turns in the road with reckless abandon, leaving a gray cloud behind.

"The honor of my car is at stake!" said Bruce grimly, closing his windshield against the dust.

"By George! If Shep wasn't so abstemious you'd think he'd mixed alcohol with his gas," Carroll replied. "What the devil's got into him!"

"Maybe he wants a race," Bruce answered uneasily, remembering Shep's wild drive the night of their talk on the river. "There's a bad turn at the creek just ahead—he can't make it at that speed!"

Bruce stopped, thinking Shep might check his flight if he found he wasn't pursued; but the car sped steadily on.

"Shep's gone nutty or he's trying to scare George," said Carroll. "Go ahead!"

Bruce started his car at full speed, expecting that at any minute Shep would stop and explain that it was all a joke of some kind. The flying car was again in sight, careening crazily as it struck depressions in the roadbed.

"Oh, God!" cried Carroll, half-rising in his seat. Shep had passed a lumbering truck by a hair's breadth, and still no abatement in his speed. Bruce heard a howl of rage as he swung his own car past the truck. A danger sign at the roadside gave warning of the short curve that led upward to the bridge, and Bruce clapped on his brakes. Carroll, on the running board, peering ahead through the dust, yelled, and as Bruce leaped out a crash ahead announced disaster. A second sound, the sound of a heavy body falling, greeted the two men as they ran toward the scene....

Shep's car had battered through the wooden fence that protected the road where it curved into the wooden bridge and had plunged into the narrow ravine. Bruce and Carroll flung themselves down the steep bank and into the stream. Shep's head lay across his arms on the wheel; Whitford evidently had tried to leap out before the car struck. His body, half out of the door, had been crushed against the fence, but clung in its place through the car's flight over the embankment.

V

To the world Franklin Mills showed what passed for a noble fortitude and a superb resignation in Shep's death. Carroll had carried the news to him; and Carroll satisfied the curiosity of no one as to what Mills had said or how he had met the blow. Carroll himself did not know what passed through Franklin Mills' mind. Mills had asked without emotion whether the necessary things had been done, and was satisfied that Carroll had taken care of everything. Mills received the old friends who called, among them Lindley. It was a proper thing to see the minister in such circumstances. The rector of St. Barnabas went away puzzled. He had never understood Mills, and now his rich parishioner was more of an enigma than ever.

A handful of friends chosen by Constance and Mills heard the reading of the burial office in the living-room of Shep's house. Constance remained in her room; and Mills saw her first when they met in the hall to drive together to the cemetery, an arrangement that she herself had suggested. No sound came from her as she stood between Mills and Leila at the grave as the last words were said. A little way off stood the bearers, young men who had been boyhood friends of Shep, and one or two of his associates from the trust company. When the grave was filled Constance waited, watching the placing of the flowers, laying her wreath of roses with her own hands.

She took Mills's arm and they returned to their car. No word was spoken as it traversed the familiar streets. The curtains were drawn; Mills stared fixedly at the chauffeur's back; the woman beside him made no sign. Nothing, as he thought of it, had been omitted; his son had been buried with the proper rites of the church. There had been no bungling, no hysterical display of grief; no crowd of the morbidly curious. When they reached Shep's house he followed Constance in. There were women there waiting to care for her, but she sent them away and went into the reception parlor. The scent of flowers still filled the rooms, but the house had assumed its normal orderly aspect. Constance threw back her veil, and Mills saw for the first time her face with its marks of suffering, her sorrowing eyes.

"Had you something to say to me?" she asked quietly.

"If you don't mind——" he answered. "I couldn't come to you before—but now—I should like you to know——"

As he paused she began to speak slowly, as if reciting something she had committed to memory.

"We have gone through this together, for reasons clear to both of us. There is nothing you can say to me. But one or two things I must say to you. You killed him. Your contempt for him as a weaker man than you, as a gentle and sweet soul you could never comprehend; your wish to manage him, to thwart him in things he wanted to do, your wish to mold him and set him in your own little groove—these are the things that destroyed him. You shattered his faith in me—that is the crudest thing of all, for he loved me. So strong was your power over him and so great was his fear of you that he believed you. In spite of himself he believed you when you charged me with unfaithfulness. You drove him mad," she went on monotonously; "he died a madman—died horribly, carrying an innocent man down with him. The child Shep wanted so much—that he would have loved so dearly—is his. You need have no fear as to that. That is all I have to say, Mr. Mills."

She left him noiselessly, leaving behind her a quiet that terrified and numbed him. He found himself groping his way through the hall, where someone spoke to him. The words were unintelligible, though the voice was of someone who meant to be kind. He walked to his car, carrying his hat as if he were unequal to the effort of lifting it to his head. The chauffeur opened the door, and as he got in Mills stumbled and sank upon the seat.

When he reached home he wandered aimlessly about the rooms, oppressed by the intolerable quiet. One and another of the servants furtively peered at him from discreet distances; the man who had cared for his personal needs for many years showed himself in the hope of being called upon for some service.

"Is that you, Briggs?" asked Mills. "Please call the farm and say that I'm coming out. Yes—I'll have dinner there. I may stay a day or two. You may pack a bag for me—the usual things. Order the car when you're ready."

He resumed his listless wandering, found himself in Leila's old room, and again in the room that had been Shep's. It puzzled him to find that the inspection of these rooms brought him no sensations. He felt no inclination to cry out against the fate that had wrought this emptiness, laid this burden of silence upon his house. Leila had gone; and he had seen them put Shep into the ground.

"You killed him." This was what that woman in black had said. She had said other things, but these were the words that repeated themselves in his

memory like a muffled drum-beat. On the drive to the farm he did not escape from the insistent reiteration. He was mystified, bewildered. No one had ever spoken to him like that; no one had ever before accused him of a monstrous crime or addressed him as if he were a contemptible and odious thing. And yet he was Franklin Mills. This was the astounding thing,—that Franklin Mills should have listened to such words and been unable to deny them....

At the farm he paused on the veranda, turned his face westward where the light still lingered in pale tints of gold and scarlet. He remained staring across the level fields, hearing the murmur of the wind in the maples, the rustle of dead leaves in the grass, until the chauffeur spoke to him, took his arm and led him into the house.

CHAPTER TWENTY-THREE

I

Carroll and Bruce dined at the University Club on an evening early in October. The tragic end of Shepherd Mills and George Whitford had brought them into a closer intimacy and they were much together. The responsibility of protecting Shep's memory had fallen upon them; and they had been fairly successful in establishing in local history a record of the tragedy as an accident. Only a very few knew or suspected the truth.

"Have you anything on this evening?" asked Carroll as they were leaving the table.

"Not a blessed thing," Bruce replied.

"Mr. Mills, you know, or rather you don't know, is at Deer Trail. The newspaper story that he had gone south for the winter wasn't true. He's been ill—frightfully ill; but he's better now. I was out there today; he asked about you. I think he'd like to see you. You needn't dread it; he's talked very little about Shep's death."

"If you really think he wants to see me," Bruce replied dubiously.

"From the way he mentioned you I'm sure it would please him."

"Very well; will you go along?"

"No; I think he'd like it better if you went alone. He has seen no one but Leila, the doctor and me; he's probably anxious to see a new face. I'll telephone you're coming."

As Bruce entered Mills's room a white-frocked nurse quietly withdrew. The maid who had shown him up drew a chair beside the bed and left them. He was alone with Mills, trying to adjust himself to the change in him, the pallor of the face against the pillow, the thin cheeks, the hair white now where it had only been touched with gray.

"This is very kind of you! I'm poor company; but I hoped you wouldn't mind running out."

"I thought you were away. Carroll just told me you were here."

"No; I've been here sometime—so long, in fact, that I feel quite out of the world."

"Mrs. Thomas is at home—I've seen her several times."

"Yes, Leila's very good to me; runs out every day or two. She's full of importance over having her own establishment."

Bruce spoke of his own affairs; told of the progress that had been made with the Laconia memorial before the weather became unfavorable. The foundations were in and the materials were being prepared; the work would go forward rapidly with the coming of spring.

"I can appreciate your feeling about it—your own idea taking form. I've thought of it a good deal. Indeed, I've thought of you a great deal since I've been here."

"If I'd known you were here and cared to see me I should have come out," said Bruce quite honestly.

While Mills bore the marks of suffering and had plainly undergone a serious illness, his voice had something of its old resonance and his eyes were clear and alert. He spoke of Shep, with a poignant tenderness, but left no opening for sympathy. His grief was his own; not a thing to be exposed to another or traded upon. Bruce marveled at him. The man, even in his weakness, challenged admiration. The rain had begun to patter on the sill of an open window and Bruce went to close it. When he returned to the bed Mills asked for an additional pillow that he might sit up more comfortably, and Bruce adjusted it for him. He was silent for a moment; his fingers played with the edge of the coverlet; he appeared to be thinking intently.

"There are things, Storrs," he remarked presently, "that are not helped by discussion. That night I had you to dine with me we both played about a certain fact without meeting it. I am prepared to meet it now. You are my son. I don't know that there's anything further to be said about it."

"Nothing," Bruce answered.

"If you were not what you are I should never have said this to you. I was in love with your mother and she loved me. It was all wrong and the wrong was mine. And in various ways I have paid the penalty." He passed his hand slowly over his eyes and went on. "It may be impertinent, but there's one thing I'd like to ask. What moved you to establish yourself here?"

"There was only one reason. My mother was the noblest woman that ever lived! She loved you till she died. She would never have told me of you but for a feeling that she wanted me to be near you—to help in case you were in need. That was all."

"That was all?" Mills repeated, and for the first time he betrayed emotion. He lay very still. Slowly his hand moved along the coverlet to the edge of the bed until Bruce took it in his own. "You and I have been blessed in our lives; we have known the love of a great woman. That was like her," he ended softly; "that was Marian."

The nurse came in to see if he needed anything, and he dismissed her for the night. He went on talking in quiet, level tones—of his early years, of the changing world, Bruce encouraging him by an occasional question but heeding little what he said. If Mills had whined, begged forgiveness or offered reparation, Bruce would have hated him. But Mills was not an ordinary man. No ordinary man would have made the admission he had made, or, making it, would have implored silence, exacted promises....

"Millicent—you see her, I suppose?" Mills asked after a time.

"Yes; I see her quite often."

"I had hoped you did. In fact Leila told me that Millie and you are good friends. She said a little more—Leila's a discerning person and she said she thought there was something a little more than friendship. Please let me finish! You've thought that there were reasons why you could never ask Millicent to marry you. I'll take the responsibility of that. I'll tell her the story myself—if need be. I leave that to your own decision."

"No," said Bruce. "I shall tell her myself."

Instead of wearying Mills, the talk seemingly acted as a stimulus. Bruce's amazement grew. It was incomprehensible that here lay the Franklin Mills of his distrust, his jealousy, his hatred.

"Millicent used to trouble me a good deal with some of her ideas," said Mills.

"She's troubled a good many of us," Bruce agreed with a smile. "But sometimes I think I catch a faint gleam."

"I'm sure you do! You two are of a generation that looks for God in those far horizons she talks about. The idea amused me at first. But I see now that here is the new religion—the religion of youth—that expresses itself truly in beautiful things—in life, in conduct, in unselfishness. The spirit of youth reveals itself in beautiful things—and calls them God. Shep felt all that, tried in his own way to make me see—but I couldn't understand him. I— there are things I want to do—for Shep. We'll talk of that later.... Every mistake I've made, every wrong I've done in this world has been due to selfishness—I've been saying that to myself every day since I've been here. I've found peace in it. There's no one in the world who has a better right to hear this from me than you. And this is no death-bed repentance; I'm not going to die yet a while. It's rather beaten in on me, Bruce"—it was the first time he had so addressed him—"that we can't just live for ourselves! No! Not if we would find happiness. There comes a time when every man needs God. The wise thing is so to live that when the need comes we shan't find him a stranger!"

The hour grew late, and the wind and rain made a continual clatter about the house. When Bruce rose to go Mills protested.

"There's plenty of space here—a room next to mine is ready for a guest. You'll find everything you want. We seem to meet in storms! Please spend the night here."

And so it came about that for the first time Bruce slept in his father's house.

II

Bruce and Millicent were married the next June. A few friends gathered in the garden late on a golden afternoon—Leila and Thomas, the Freemans, the Hendersons, a few relatives of the Hardens from their old home, and Carroll and Bruce's cousin from Laconia. The marriage service was read by Dr. Lindley and the music was provided by a choir of robins in the elms and maples. Franklin Mills was not present; but before Bruce and Millicent

drove to the station they passed through the gate in the boundary hedge—
Leila had arranged this—and received his good wishes.

The fourth of July had been set as the time for the dedication of the
memorial. The event brought together a great company of dignitaries, and
the governor of the state and the Secretary of War were the speakers. Mills
had driven over with Leila and Thomas, and he sat with them, Millicent
beside him.

Bruce hovered on the edges of the crowd, listening to comments on his
work, marveling himself that it was so good. The chairman of the local
committee sent for him at the conclusion of the ceremonies to introduce
him to the distinguished visitors. When the throng had dispersed, Millicent,
with Carroll and Leila, paused by the fountain to wait until Bruce was free.

"This is what you get, Millie, for having a famous husband," Leila
remarked. "He's probably signing a contract for another monument!"

"There he is!" exclaimed Carroll, pointing up the slope.

Bruce and Mills were slowly pacing one of the colonnades. Beyond it lay
the woodland that more than met Bruce's expectations as a background for
the memorial. They were talking earnestly, wholly unaware that they were
observed. As they turned once more to retrace their steps Mills,
unconsciously it seemed, laid his arm across Bruce's shoulders; and
Millicent, seeing and understanding, turned away to hide her tears.

THE END